"[A] VERY COMPELLING DRAMA . . .

What makes Carcaterra's portrait of Vestieri so effective is not only the 'adventures' Vestieri experiences in a career so cold and calculating, but also the author's psychological fathoming of the kind of character that turns to a life of organized crime."

—*Booklist*

"If you thought that the final word had been spoken about the rise of the Mafia and organized crime, Lorenzo Carcaterra's new novel, *Gangster*, will change your mind. . . . This book is an excellent retelling of the Godfather story from a fresh viewpoint."

—*The Roanoke Times*

"Even better [than] . . . *Apaches* and *Sleepers* . . . There is a richness of detail, both physical and psychological, in Carcaterra's description that never gets in the way of the fast-moving plot, but which lends a depth to the novel that brings it closer to literature than standard bestseller fare."

—*Winston-Salem Journal*

"[A] tantalizing coming-of-age story . . . As he did in *Sleepers* and *Apaches*, Carcaterra shows dexterity in humanizing the denizens of the urban underbelly. Through a fine characterization of the enigmatic Vestieri, he provides a stirring perspective on the ways of mobsters and their history."

—*Publishers Weekly*

By Lorenzo Carcaterra

A SAFE PLACE: *The True Story
of a Father, a Son, a Murder*
SLEEPERS
APACHES
GANGSTER

GANGSTER

LORENZO CARCATERRA

FAWCETT BOOKS • NEW YORK

For Susan

A Fawcett Book
Published by The Ballantine Publishing Group
Copyright © 2001 by Lorenzo Carcaterra
Excerpt from *Street Boys* copyright © 2002 by Lorenzo Carcaterra

This book contains an excerpt from the forthcoming hardcover edition of *Street Boys* by Lorenzo Carcaterra. This excerpt has been set for this edition only and may not reflect the final content of the forthcoming edition.

www.ballantinebooks.com

ISBN 0-345-42529-4

Manufactured in the United States of America

First Hardcover Edition: February 2001

First Mass Market Edition: August 2002

10   9   8   7   6   5   4   3   2   1

Acknowledgments

A BOOK IS guided by many hands on its voyage to completion. I owe each set my gratitude. Among them:

Peter Gethers who once again proved to be the best editor any writer could be fortunate enough to have as a partner. His sharp editorial eye helped shape *Gangster* through its many drafts. We've now been together for ten years and four books and it's been pure pleasure.

Thanks to Gina Centrello for her kindness and friendship. I owe her a case of Jolly Ranchers. To the rest of the Ballantine crew—Shauna Toh, Kim Hovey, Ann Weinerman and Amy Scheibe (for forgetting the last time)—a tip of the cap for putting up with my many calls and questions. To Owen Laster and Joni Evans for convincing me to switch gears and write the book I needed to write. To Rob Carlson for coming through in the clutch and to Lou Pitt for walking into my life and helping to steer clear the boat. As always a hug and a big thank you to Jake Bloom. And to Robert Offer for the compassion and hard work. To Susan Lyne for her constant support and to Joe Roth for his strong belief in the words. My story could not rest in better hands.

To my tight circle of friends—Dr. George Lombardi, Hank Gallo, Mr. G., Dr. Rock, Captain Joe, Vincent and Ida Cerbone, Anthony Cerbone, Steve Allie, Liz W., Adriana T., Terrie W., Sonny G., Bill Diehl, Laurie P., Peter Giuliano,

Bruno and Lynn, Timmy V. and Bobby G.—a warm thanks. To Big Jack Sanders: You will always have a place in our hearts. To my family in Italy—especially the four queens— my mom and Zias Anna, Nunzia and Francesca—*un caro abbraccio*. And to Uncle Robert and Aunt Jane Toepfer, thank you for so warmly letting me into your family. And to Caroline Shea and Dustin Fleischman—welcome to the gang.

Finally, to my wife, Susan—thanks for twenty-two years of love and patience. The trip wouldn't have been as much fun without you. To my son, Nick, for bringing light and a smile to each and every day. And to Kate, a special angel filled with love and kindness now off on a journey of her own.

I embrace you all.

PREFACE

Three may keep a secret, if two of
them are dead.
—Benjamin Franklin

Summer, 1996

I HAD COME to watch him die.

His head sank into the center of the pillow, his face an ominous yellow, paper-thin eyelids closed. IV lines and a heart monitor were wired to his frail body, the veins on each arm were a thick purple. A thin blue sheet covered his chest; long hands, more bone than skin, rested flat across its top. He took in slow breaths, gurgles working their way from throat to nose, the rank odor of death floating through the room like seaside fog.

I pushed an ugly metal chair against the side of a cold radiator and sat down, my back to the dark city sky. It was late, well past visiting hours, but the duty nurses let me stay, waving aside the rules for the dying man in room 617B, adopting the indifferent manner he had used to ignore society's demands for the bulk of his life. They walked in at regular intervals, easing their way past the two guards who sat erect just outside the door, their starched whites stretched by slightly expanding waistlines. They checked his blood pressure, monitored the IVs and pumped in extra doses of painkiller with thin needles hidden in the front pockets of their uniforms.

He had been in the hospital for four weeks and a priest had twice been called to administer last rites.

"If he pulls through and you need me again, just call the

parish," the priest said in a raspy voice that sounded more than eager to do God's work. "It's just down the street."

"You've been here twice," I said as gently as I could. "That's more than enough."

"He needs to die in a state of grace." The priest looked across the bed, his liver-patched fingers shaking as they folded a purple vestment. "He would want that."

"No," I told him, my eyes fixed on the dying man. "I don't think he would."

• • •

I WENT TO the hospital every night, leaving work just after six, dropping by my apartment to shower and change before walking the ten blocks north, stopping only to pick up a large salad and two cups of coffee at a Greek diner across from the emergency room. I sat by his bed, the light from the soundless television above us flickering across our faces, the city sounds from the streets below merging with the beeps and buzzes of the monitors attached to his body. Some nights I would feel tears streak down my cheeks, as I saw the life depart from his once strong frame. Other nights would bring waves of anger, tense reminders of the evils he had heaped on those who dared to defy him.

As far as I knew, I was the only one who cared whether he lived or died. He lay in that bed suffering from one of fate's cruelest blows: he had outlived both his enemies and his friends. His children would visit on occasion, concerned more about a future cash windfall than his final days. Each eyed me with distrust, suspicious of my bond with their father, envious of our time together, wondering why he had chosen me to share his secrets. There were two daughters and a son, all grown and with their own families. They had been raised without the burden of financial worry, but their father's steady hand and love had long ago been supplanted by suburban comfort, private school educations, trips to Europe and hefty allowances. There were few shared memories to unite them now and there was little else for them to do during these last moments than sit, stare and leave as quietly as they had entered.

We exchanged nods and glances, never words, our common ground asleep in the bed that separated us. It was a space that seemed as wide and cold as a river, for we had each been exposed to completely different variations of the same man. I wondered what it would be like to be them, to know what they knew and feel what they were feeling. They were afraid to touch or hug him, incapable of shedding a tear at his impending death. It seemed a harsh way to wade through life and the strain of it showed on their faces as they sat still as stones around a father they were never given the opportunity to love.

For them, his death could not come fast enough.

• • •

IT WAS TOWARD the end of the fourth week. I was walking down the hospital corridor, a hot cup of coffee in my right hand, the now-familiar sounds of the floor blending like white noise into the night. Behind me, I heard the elevator bell ring. I turned and saw David, the old man's son, rush out, his neck and shoulders wet from a heavy rain outside.

"I figured you'd still be here," he said in a soft, pale voice, poles apart from his father's deep tones. He was forty-two and a junior partner in a downtown accounting firm, having done all he could to distance his name from that of the man down the hall. He was several inches shorter and twenty pounds heavier than his father had been at the same age, and he always seemed to have a cold.

I sipped my coffee and nodded.

"My sisters and I were talking about it this afternoon," he said, standing close enough for me to smell the Geoffrey Beene cologne lingering on his face.

"Talking about what?"

"About whether we should even bother coming." He looked over his shoulders, making sure none of the nurses overheard.

I shrugged. "Do what makes you comfortable."

"I mean, look, who's kidding who? It's not like he'd even want us around. If he could talk, he'd tell us to get the hell out of his sight. With you it's . . . well, it's different. It's always been different. There's no reason for it to change now."

"You don't need to clear anything with me," I said. "The way he is now, he won't know who's here or who's not."

"He knows *you're* here," David said, his voice taking a step toward hard.

"I'll have somebody call you when he's dead," I told him and turned away.

"You're just like him," David said, as I made my way back to his father's room. "Maybe that's why he cared for you like he did. You're both heartless bastards."

• • •

IT WAS NEARING eleven on a muggy New York night, the Yankees game from Anaheim just beginning, when the door to room 617B eased open. I looked away from the TV expecting a nurse. Instead, I watched a well-dressed older woman walk quietly toward the bed. She looked to be in her late sixties, with thick gray hair combed straight back in an old-fashioned twist. There was a soft glow to her face, lines and wrinkles defiantly held in check. She had sharp dark eyes, red polish spread over manicured nails and a two-piece navy pantsuit under a blue topcoat. She removed the coat, gently folding it and resting it at the foot of the bed.

"Is there a chair for me?" she asked, her eyes firmly on the man in the bed.

I got up and slid mine toward her, watching her walk over to the old man, lean down and kiss his forehead. Her hands stroked his fingers as she lowered her head and whispered unheard words into his ear. I had never seen her before and didn't know her name. I did know, from the ease of her movements, that she cared for him.

She turned from the old man and, for the first time since she entered the room, looked up at me, her eyes clouded.

"You must be Gabe," she said. "He always talked about you. From when you were a little boy."

"I had the idea he didn't like to talk at all," I said, strangely comfortable in her company.

"That's true." A slight smile creased her face. "About most things and with most people." The smile on her face grew wider. "I'm Mary," she said now. "At least I'm Mary to everyone but him."

"And what does he call you?" I returned the smile. It was impossible not to return that smile.

A hint of a younger woman crept into her voice. "Skipper."

"Why?"

"The first time I met him, my father took us out on his boat. Once we were out of the harbor I took the wheel, so the two of them would be free to talk. But he never heard a word my father said. All he did was look over at this kid manning a forty-three-foot boat. He figured none of us would make it back to land."

"He was born on a boat," I said, leaning forward against the bed railing. "He didn't care much for that trip either."

She nodded and went on. "I'd handled the boat many times for my father. I was practically raised on the water. But when I saw him look at me and could see how nervous he was, I decided to have a little fun. So, now and then, I'd give him a frightened look or act as if I didn't know what to do, which made him even more nervous."

"He ever catch on?"

"Twenty minutes into the trip he figured out I was very lucky or very good, and that either way was enough for us to make it back. The next time he caught my eye, he winked. That's all it took. For Skipper to be born and for me to fall in love."

"You were in *love* with him?" I immediately regretted my surprised tone.

"From that day to this," she said, turning once again to the man on the bed. "Nothing's changed but time."

"I'm sorry. I didn't mean for that to sound the way it did."

"No need to be sorry," she told me.

"It's just that I thought I knew everything there is to know about him. All the places and all the people."

"You know the parts he told you," Mary said, shoulders pulled back in perfect posture. "The parts you heard and the parts you lived through."

"What don't I know?" I looked into Mary's eyes, searching for the face of the brash young girl to whom the man in the bed had handed his heart. Despite her calm exterior, there was the scent of a woman at ease with the rules of danger. She had appeared like mist, invisible and unknowing to me until these past few moments, yet fully equipped with secrets I had believed would soon be lost forever.

"There are a few missing parts," Mary said. "They might help you understand everything that happened. I suppose he would have told you, eventually. Now, it's left to me. That is, if you're ready."

"I can't imagine it can be any worse than the parts he already put me through," I said.

Mary studied my face, her manner poised and peaceful. She then glanced at the old man in the bed and folded her arms across her waist. "You may want to get yourself some more coffee," she said.

Behind us, up on the silent screen, the Yankees had taken a one-run lead against the Angels on a Tino Martinez home run.

Next to me, an old man, once strong, fearless and feared, inched closer to his destiny.

Across from me, a woman I had known for less than fifteen minutes was, with the sheer power of her words, about to shift the course of my life.

BOOK ONE

Land of the Free

The greatest of evils and the worst
of crimes is poverty.
—George Bernard Shaw

1

Summary, 1906

He hated dredging up memories.

They did not stir in him a taste for nostalgia or loves lost. He saw in them only one purpose—to harden the shell he had chiseled with care, the one that hid all that could be deemed vulnerable and kept entombed the signs of humanity. When he talked to me about his early years, it was with the voice of a stranger, as if what had been had touched the life of another, one a safe distance removed from the fray. In the telling, his eyes never strayed beyond my face and his voice retained its deep pitch, no matter the emotional import of what was recalled.

I was ten when I first heard the story of his ocean crossing, and as I sat in the hospital room listening to Mary's account of the tale, the early moments of the dying man's life came exploding back, as real, as hard and as fresh as a wave.

His ship was three days out of Naples when the storm hit.

Four levels below the deck, walled-in against an overworked engine, six hundred men, women and children were crammed into a space designed for two hundred. The stench of waste mingled with that of burning oil and spouting steam. The cargo hold, normally a dry haven for luggage and sealed goods, was now little more than a moaning assembly of humanity. Families sat in small circles, huddled under tattered coverlets of soiled sheets and clothes. Infants wailed against the pangs of hunger and the nibbling of rats. The elderly chewed tobacco leaves instead of food, black spittle coarsing down their chins. Women, young and old, sang Neapolitan ballads to lift deadened spirits and prayed daily to a stern God for a quick end to a dark journey.

They boarded the ship under a blanket of darkness, paying twenty-five thousand lira—nearly five hundred dollars— per head to a local broker, Giorgio Salvecci, an overweight landlord who kept a tan overcoat draped over his shoulders regardless of season. Salvecci shipped *skins*—Italian immigrants—across the Atlantic Ocean and into the harbors of New York, Boston and Baltimore. At the turn of the century, during the height of the Italian migration to American soil, Salvecci and his crew of thugs sent fifteen hundred transports a week off to an uncertain future. They were openly indifferent to their customers' ultimate fates; their part of the bargain ended with the payment of under-the-table cash. In return for a few thousand extra lira, Salvecci could also be counted on to supply false documents that would be rubber-stamped at Ellis Island and other points of entry, allowing the less-than-desirable access to the Golden Land.

Convicts, thieves, con men and murderers: all, eventually, made their way to Salvecci. He was their last hope, all that separated them from a long stretch behind the hard bars of an Italian prison.

The ships commissioned by Salvecci to cross the Atlantic were beaten and worn-down cruisers that had seen far better years and far more magnificent voyages. What once had been the pride of a vibrant fleet had been reduced through neglect into ocean-chugging pimps, rushing loads of human hope and misery toward a mysterious new country. The ships had majestic names culled from a more glorious past to cart along with their deteriorating bodies—*Il Leonardo, La Vittoria Colonna, La Regina Isabella, Il Marco Polo*. They had once carried the gold of Venetian merchants across the angry seas of the Adriatic. Now, weighed down with age, they swam slowly over the Atlantic.

The passengers were fed once a day, in the late afternoon, by a large, muscular man covered from forehead to ankles in tattoos. His name was Italo and he came from a northern mountain region known more for rugged terrain than culinary expertise. It would take Italo a dozen trips to fill the bowls of the hungry, as he lumbered down narrow steel steps, carrying a large pot filled with hot stew. He dipped the bowls into the scalding liquid and scampered away, leaving them to devour what he knew to be a meal unfit for animals. On occasion, he would throw large chunks of old bread into the hole and watch dirty hands dive for the delicacy.

Passengers built small fires around which they'd circle, using old wood and clothes in an attempt to stay warm and keep their children safe. It was an eight-day journey of pain, but one that each person on that stifling deck desperately needed to complete. They were leaving behind a land of dry soil and little promise for a place where, they were told, every one of their dreams would come true. That is what they needed to believe, what would give them the courage to go on as around them grandfathers died in silence and infants wailed their last breaths.

The dream of America was more than enough to make Paolino Vestieri want to live. Vestieri was a thirty-six-year-old shepherd from Salerno who had seen a thriving flock of three hundred reduced to a half-dozen, victims of hunger, thieves and sickness. He had an eight-year-old son, Carlo, and a wife, Francesca, eight months pregnant with their second child. Despite the daily difficulties, Paolino had no plans to leave Italy. But then, in the late winter of 1906, his father, Giacomo, was ambushed by a band of camorristas—the Neapolitan Mafia. Ignoring his pleas for more time to pay off a long-standing debt, they stripped him nude, hung him from an olive tree and sliced open his stomach. It would be three days before Paolino got word about his father and was able to find his body, and by then the crows and maggots had had their fill. When he returned home, he found Carlo missing and his wife screaming in ways he had never heard a woman cry before.

"They took Carlo!" she shrieked. "They took my son!"

"Who took him?" Paolino asked, grabbing his wife.

"The camorra," Francesca managed to shout between screams. "They took my boy. They took him for the money your father owed. The money we cannot pay."

"Stop your crying," Paolino said, removing his hands from his wife and heading for the bedroom to get his *lupara*. "I will get Carlo."

Francesca fell to her knees, still crying, head cradled in her hands. "I want my son," she moaned. "I want my son. If they want revenge, tell them to take it from your father. Not from my boy."

"They have already taken it from my father," Paolino said, checking the *lupara* for shells as he walked past his wife and out the door.

· · ·

PAOLINO STOOD IN the center of the small dining room, his eyes on his son and the man standing above him, smoking a thin cigar. The man inched the cigar from his mouth, curls of smoke clouding his thick, tanned face. He patted the top of Carlo's head.

"He's a good boy," the man said, smiling. "Very quiet. No trouble to us. He's almost a part of the family already."

"I will get you your money, Gaspare," Paolino said, the *lupara* hanging over his shoulder, partly hidden by the sleeve of his shepherd's coat. "I give you my word. Now, please. Let me have my son."

"Your father gave his word, too," Gaspare said. "Many times. And I am still left with nothing. Besides, the boy will know a better life with us. We can give much more than you. And with your father out of the way, you will no longer have to live in debt. At least to us."

Paolino looked down at his son and remembered the early mornings when he would lift him onto his shoulders and carry him down the slopes of the olive groves toward his flock. His head was filled with the happy sounds of a boy's laughter, as he urged his father to go faster and catch up to the grazing sheep. That brief and blissful memory was quickly replaced by the image of a grown Carlo, now a hardened member of the camorra, glowering at him from the top of that very same olive grove, standing tall and silent as men with guns raced to fill their pockets with the wages of the working poor. Paolino Vestieri knew he must never allow the son he loved so much to grow up to be such a man.

He stepped closer to Gaspare and his son, ignoring the two men standing on either side of the room. "One way or another," Paolino said, "my son will come with me."

"You talk like a brave man." Gaspare put the cigar back in his mouth, his voice turned harder. "But your actions will show where your courage takes you."

"Let me have my son," Paolino said, feeling the sweat race down his neck and back.

"I have no more to say to you." Gaspare dismissed Paolino with a wave. "Tend to your flock, shepherd. Let me worry about the boy."

Paolino fell to his knees and swung the *lupara* from his back to his hands. But he did not aim it at the criminal Gaspare. The gun was aimed directly at his son's chest. The two men in the corner pulled their own handguns and aimed it at Paolino. Gaspare backed away from the boy, his smoldering cigar now cupped in his right hand. Carlo stared at his father, his lower lip quivering.

"You would kill your own blood?" Gaspare asked. "Your only son?"

"Better for him to be dead than to live with you," Paolino said.

"You don't have the heart for such a move," Gaspare said. "I don't even know if I do."

"Then save him and let him come home with me."

Gaspare stared at Paolino for several minutes, glaring into his eyes, taking slow puffs off the cigar.

"No," he said, shaking his head slowly.

Paolino turned away from Gaspare and looked at his son. It was as if the two of them were now alone. The hard gaze of the boy's eyes told his father all that he felt he needed to know. It would not take the camorra long to steal the young boy's spirit and turn it against those he loved. They would seduce him with romanticized images of power and wealth, easily lure the child in with vivid portraits of a life much more alluring and appealing than that of a shepherd's son. It would be a corrupt life, one without scruples or morals or decency. They had not had enough time to completely tear the boy away from him, not yet, but Paolino could see that such a path had already been paved. The boy would be a thief, a criminal and, one day, a murderer.

"I love you, Carlo," Paolino said and squeezed the trigger.

He watched as the bullet's impact sent his son hard against the stone fireplace. Carlo crumpled to the ground, his face inches from the sparks of the crackling wood, his eyes half-open, dead from his father's hand.

"Now he belongs to no one," Paolino said.

He tossed aside the *lupara* and walked toward the fireplace. He bent down, picked his son up in his arms, turned and left.

•   •   •

I KNEW THIS part of the story well. Its emotional impact had been used by many of the old man's supporters to explain the harshness of his ways. A brother he would never know had been killed by a father he would never understand in a land he chose never to visit. No one could be expected to carry those wounds without scars. As I listened to Mary tell her tale well into the quiet of the night, I wondered how different it all might have been had Paolino Vestieri simply turned his back and not given in to his most primitive urge, not surrendered to the fear of having a son raised in "time-honored ways." I wondered still if the old man had found his brother's death the least bit ironic given the path of his own life. For there was never a doubt that Carlo's murder was the seed that fostered the old man's destiny.

• • •

PAOLINO VESTIERI BURIED his father and son on a hill overlooking the Bay of Naples. They would rest there, protected from the hot summer sun and chilly winds of fall by the same two large pine trees Paolino had once climbed as a boy. As the gravediggers shoveled dirt over the caskets, Paolino looked across the serene landscape and knew he was seeing it for the last time. Gaspare had reported Carlo's murder to the local constable, making Paolino Vestieri something he never dreamed he would be—a wanted man.

He quickly and quietly sold his land, his winter clothes and what remained of his flock to a local merchant. The sum he collected was just enough to cover passage for himself and his wife aboard *La Santa Maria*, scheduled to depart Naples on the night of February 17, 1906. The doctor had warned Paolino that it would be best to delay the voyage until spring, after his wife had given birth.

"Each day we stay is a risk," Paolino told him. "We must leave now."

"It is not a way for a woman to bring in a new life," the doctor said.

"There is no life here," Paolino replied. "New or old."

"Give your wife and child a chance," the doctor pleaded.

"Taking them away *is* their chance," Paolino said.

• • •

HIS WIFE, FRANCESCA, sat against a grease-stained wall, her face half-hidden by thick strands of brown hair. She rubbed her inflated stomach, her eyes squeezed shut, hoping to will away the constant pain. She was a farmer's daughter, an only child raised like a son, toiling on ungiving land from first light of sun to last. Hardship was as familiar to her as the fresh tomatoes from her mother's gardens. Yet nothing she had endured would be enough to harden her for the days ahead.

She had spoken her first words to Paolino at a town gathering to celebrate the final days of the harvest. She was sixteen then, her body as much woman as it was girl, her warm smile quick and easy enough to draw glances from a selection of interested young men. Her relaxed manner convinced even the most hesitant to approach and ask for a brief dance or extend an offer for a cup of homemade wine. She had seen Paolino in the town square on a number of occasions—picking up lumber with his father, laughing and joking with friends on his way home from school, standing in silent prayer in the back of the old wooden church. He was rugged and handsome and, at eighteen, his actions were more those of a man than most of the other boys in town.

He didn't ask her to dance nor did he offer a cool drink. He didn't think either would be the proper first approach. Instead, he handed her a white rose plucked from his mother's garden, smiled and walked away. She returned the smile and the warm feeling in the center of her stomach told her that soon she would be a married woman.

"Those early years together were special," Francesca once told her mother, as both women busied themselves preparing another in an endless cycle of large family meals. "I imagine they always are when two young people are in love. And when Carlo came along, he helped make our life together even better. Then it all ended. A life filled with sun was thrown into a dungeon. And from such a place no exit can be found."

Paolino tried many times to explain his terrible action to his wife, but it was something she would never allow herself to understand. He truly believed that the life of a camorrista was far worse than an early death. He was prepared to go through life knowing he had murdered his own child than to see that boy grow up into one who preyed on those too fearful to return the fight.

"You think it better to be a starving shepherd?" Francesca asked him.

"His life would have been one stained by other people's blood," Paolino said.

"But now it is you who is marked with an even deeper stain," Francesca said, staring at him with a cold, empty hatred. "Such a stain can never be erased. Not in God's eyes. Not in the camorra's. And never in mine."

Paolino knelt before her and pointed to her bulging stomach. "We have another child," he whispered. "We must do all that is possible to raise this one in the right way in the right place. Far from here. Far from these people."

"*We* are these people." Francesca fought back the tears she had shed each day since the rainy morning when she had laid her son to rest. "That cannot be changed, no matter how far away we run. *We* are this place. And *we* are these people."

"I'm not," Paolino said, standing.

"But my next child will be," she said with a chill.

.   .   .

A THIN LINE of oil had made its way down from the engine room. It circled around one of the many small fires built from damp wood and rags, attempts by the passengers to allow shreds of light into their dark world. The oil licked at the edges of the fire, coming to rest just beneath a rusty kettle boiling dark brown water. The fire embraced the oil, causing sparks and flames to widen and spread and rush down the sides of the room like an agitated snake.

The boat rocked from the strength of the storm, heel to hull slapped by vicious waves. The stifling heat mixed uncomfortably with the cold blasts of air and ocean water that shot through cracks in the galley walls. The ship's engines cranked wearily away, trying to keep pace with the storm, sprays of heat and moisture blasting into the crowded hold. A half dozen oil lines were now flowing out of the battered engine room, sliding past feet and rodents, inching close to the heat of a dozen small fires.

They heard the screams before they smelled the smoke and then the panic took control.

Soon, heat and flames were at full attack, sending people running in a mass for the one door leading out of the cargo hold. They climbed over one another, forsaking friendships and family for the sake of one clean breath. The rush to escape left no room for the weak and the elderly who were so easily cast aside. The fires spread quickly and plumes of dark gray smoke covered the hold like mounds of old wool. A young woman, the shorn ends of her dress swallowed by fire, stood with her arms held out and her head tilted back, welcoming the rush of the heat and the call to death. A child was left alone against a wet wall, his small hands covering his ears, his eyes shut, willing himself to another, safer place. An old man sat on a crate in the center of the hold, a hand-rolled cigarette in his mouth, a picture of peace in a place gone mad with fear.

"This cannot be God's will," a lone woman wailed, her body crushed by the rush of bodies. "We have done nothing to deserve this much hatred."

"Look around you," a man shouted back at her. "And tell me how you can still believe that there is a God."

"I will believe in Him till the day I die," the woman insisted, her body weak, her eyes defiant.

"That day has already begun," the man said and squeezed past her, hoping to make it out of the inferno.

• • •

PAOLINO VESTIERI STOOD and watched the rush of flames inch their way to the engine room. He knew it was now down to a question of minutes. He looked at Francesca, overcome by the smoke, white strands of spittle dotting her lips and sweat streaking her brow. He reached over and stroked her face, rubbing his dirty fingers across soft cheeks, and kissed her gently on the lips.

"Ti amo, cara," he said to the woman he loved.

Filomena, the midwife, a scarred old woman in a worn

black dress and tattered shawl, leaned her bulk forward and pressed against Francesca's stomach. Francesca moved her legs farther apart, her feet resting against the back of an old man. She pulled her head up and held her eyes shut, waiting for the pain in her stomach to pass. The screams and cries around her seemed to exist in a faraway place, the smoke that seared her lungs arrived from a territory untouched by madness and ruin. The sharp pangs had been coming at a steady rate for the last hour, knifelike stabs that forced her to dig her nails into the splintered floorboards, covering her fingers in blood.

She opened her eyes and looked up at the midwife.

"Is there enough time?" she asked.

"Only the angels know," Filomena said.

She rubbed and massaged Francesca's legs and thighs with rough, thick hands, inching the baby along, one painful movement at a time.

"What do you need me to do?" Paolino asked, standing over the midwife's shoulders.

Filomena turned her head, arching one heavy eye up toward Paolino, staring at him for several moments. "Do you love this woman?" she asked.

"Very much," Paolino said, avoiding eye contact.

"Then stay behind me and look nowhere but into your wife's eyes." Filomena then turned back to Francesca, leaned closer to her and shouted above the din around them. "It is time now, little one," she said, the smoke from the fire enveloping both of them, its force thick enough to hold. "Take full breaths if you can and push with all your strength. The rest you will leave to me."

Francesca Conti Vestieri nodded and looked around her one last time as she said a silent prayer, wishing that out of all this debris, filth, fire and danger a healthy child would be born. She looked above the midwife at her husband. "Promise me one thing," she said.

"What?" He reached over Filomena, grabbing both of his wife's hands, holding them tight, the blood from her cuts rubbing against the soot and scabs on his skin. He stared into her eyes and through her pain and the heat, the anger and the fear around them, could still taste her fierce hatred.

"You will build a good life in this new country for this child," Francesca said. "Promise me that."

"I promise," Paolino said.

"Promise me!" Francesca shrieked.

Paolino leaned in closer to his wife, his lips brushing against the side of her cheek.

"I promise you," he whispered. "As your husband and as a man."

Francesca nodded, her head and body damp with sweat and blood, her torso cramped.

Paolino stepped away from her, his eyes burning with tears, smoke charring his nostrils and filling his lungs. He looked around, saw bundles of people climbing above one another, reaching for a sky they could not see. The hold was a cauldron of flames, strewn bodies, water bursting through galley holes, cries for help and shouts of despair all blended as one. The hull of the ship was tilted to the right, its aged body tired of the fight, eager to surrender to an ocean that knew no mercy.

The youthful promises of what had once been Paolino Vestieri's dreams of a simple life were now reduced to charred rubble and warm ashes.

·   ·   ·

FILOMENA WAS CRUNCHED down, her elbows sliding on the floor, her hands buried inside Francesca's legs, feeling for signs of a new life. A full fire was burning just behind her, but the old woman ignored all but the task of her chosen profession.

"I see the head," Filomena shouted above the crowd noise, lifting her own head ever so briefly. With a full dose of her strength she tore at the lower rungs of her dress, not stopping until her hands were crammed with cloth. Filomena wiped the blood from the sides of Francesca's legs with the remains of her torn dress, smiling down at the drained young woman.

Francesca bit down on her lower lip, cutting into the skin. "How much longer, signora?" she asked through blood and clenched teeth.

"That is up to you," Filomena said. Crumpled bodies, victims of the crush and the smoke, surrounded them. The tilt of the ship was forcing them to grip even deeper into the wet, soiled boards.

"Push, my child," Filomena whispered. "With all that's left of your strength."

Francesca arched her head back and let out a scream loud enough to echo off the sweaty walls of the cargo hold. Her breath came in spurts and her eyes bulged from the pain. The midwife looked down between Francesca's legs, her hands gently gripping the top of the baby's head, and saw the large well of blood building up around her feet. It was more blood than she had seen in many a birth, and the old woman knew that only the kindness of a grudging God would allow her to walk from this with two lives intact. There was no feeling of time in the cramped hold, each moment gripping its own eternity, each second packed with a lifetime of dark memories. The fire strolled among a people accustomed to life and death entering their world without invitation. They all knew, each and every person in that room, what it meant to be touched by the cold hands of the unwelcome.

• • •

THE WAVE CRASHED hard, bending the side of the wall closest to Filomena and Francesca. The bolt sent them, along with Paolino, veering down the slope of the floor. Their backs touched flames, their hands cast aside the dead. Filomena ended up facedown, her head cut by a sharp piece of rusty iron. Blood rushed down the sides of her neck.

"Let me help you," Paolino said, tugging at the old woman's shoulders.

"Forget me," she said in a groggy voice. "Get to the child.

The infant is who needs you now. The only one you can help."
She reached up and grabbed Paolino's shirt and forced his
face down closer to hers. "The *only* one," she said.

Paolino turned to look at his wife, resting in a heap against
the cold metal of an oil-slicked wall.

"You're wrong," Paolino said in a voice that was filled
more with fear than conviction. "She will live. They will *both*
live."

"You don't have the time," Filomena said, thick plumes of
smoke rushing by her face. "You must go and save what can
be saved."

Paolino rested the midwife's head on the floor and covered
it with a patch of cloth torn from her dress. He crawled over to
his wife, the smoke engulfing him, the flames spouting in all
directions. He pulled at his wife's back until she rolled over
with a thud, splashing his face and chest with thick streams
of dark blood. Paolino looked down at his wife's legs and
rubbed his hands against the waist of his shirt, his eyes
searching for the face of his child among the ruin of her body.
He pulled a rag from his back pocket, cleared some of the
blood and sweat from his wife and then reached down to hold
the baby's head. His right hand gripped its soft top and for
several long seconds he was afraid to do more than hold it. He
looked up and saw his wife's beautiful face, now smeared
with grease and dirt, her cheeks glowing red, her lips tinged a
dangerous shade of blue. He spotted the flutter in her eyes and
wanted to reach up, hold her and tell her how much he loved
her. Tell her how sorry he was for all the pain he had caused.

But he said nothing. Instead, Paolino lowered his head and
once again began tugging at his child, trying to ease the baby
from the safety of a mother's womb. The head was hanging
silent and low as Paolino pulled the shoulders out and then
watched as the rest of the body quickly slid forward. He ignored the screams and shouts around him. He closed his eyes
to the explosions that now rocked the hold and the angry
waves that lashed at the outside of the boat. He ignored the in-

ferno surrounding him as well as the cold ocean waiting to swallow up anyone foolish enough to escape.

He held the umbilical cord in the palm of his right hand, the final connection between mother and baby, and looked around for a sharp object with which to cut it. He stripped a wooden shank off one of the floor panels and began to cut frantically at the cord, desperate to break the baby free. With a final frenzied tug, he cut it clean away and lifted the child from Francesca's body. Holding him at eye level, Paolino slapped him twice on the back with the flat of his palm. He waited for what seemed to be nothing short of a lifetime for a sign of life.

He smiled when he heard the baby's cry rise high above the screams and shouts, roar past the moans of approaching death. His son now cradled to his chest, Paolino brought him close to Francesca's face.

"Look, *amore*," Paolino whispered. "Look at your son."

Francesca looked at her baby through smoke-ravaged eyes and managed a weak smile.

"E un bello bambino," she whispered, gently stroking the infant's forehead. She then closed her eyes for the final time, her hand slipping off her husband's leg down to the floor.

Paolino Vestieri stood, cradling his minutes-old son in his arms, his feet resting against his wife's body, and looked around the hold. He saw the fire now raging out of control. Bodies rested in rows on the floor, many surrounded by the elderly, sitting quietly, resigned to their fate. Mothers rocked back and forth on their knees holding their dead while fathers blindly tossed their children toward the apparent safety of the crammed stairwell. The strength of the fire had reached the engine room, flames wrapping themselves around old pipes, churning pistons and rusty crankcases. The ocean continued its assault, intent on toppling the old ship and bringing her to rest.

For such a young man, Vestieri had seen more than his fair share of death. He had killed a son and buried him in the dry soil of his native land, alongside the violated body of his own father. He had watched his wife die bringing new life into a world she had grown to despise. And now he stood, staring at an out-of-control fire that would so easily welcome him and his child. Vestieri lowered his head, held his child closer to his side and disappeared into the thick smoke of a sinking ship.

There were 627 passengers aboard *La Santa Maria*, even though the official log registered only 176 names. Eighty-one of them survived the ice storm and the engine fire on that frigid February night in the middle of the Atlantic Ocean.

Paolino Vestieri was one.

His son, Angelo Vestieri, was another.

• • •

I LOOKED AWAY from Mary and stared down at the old man in his bed. He had always told me that destiny was nothing more than a lie believed by foolish men. "You choose your path," he said. "You decide the curves of your life." But I couldn't help wondering if he had been wrong. That maybe a life such as his, that began stained by the darkness of death, had already been placed on a preordained track. Such a start could place a hole in a man's heart that no amount of time could repair. It would split his spirit in ways that might chisel it away from basic decency and harden his views and judgments. It could easily help turn him into the man Angelo Vestieri grew to become.

Mary's eyes caught mine and she nodded, our thoughts seemingly cross-linked. "It seems like he was doomed from the start," I said to her.

"That's one way to think of it, I suppose," she said, pouring herself some water from a plastic pitcher.

"What's another?" I asked.

"That his life turned out exactly the way he wanted it to," she said. "As if he planned it himself from the very start."

2

HE WAS RAISED amid rows of tenements crammed against one another like dusty sets of dominos, with as many as three families jammed inside each weary apartment. In the winter, the thin windowpanes cracked from ice caked on their sills, while children slept huddled against the arms of their mothers, shorn blankets their only layers of protection against the brutality of cold city mornings. The summers brought with them a heat so muscular that the walls would sag and the white apartment paint would chip and crack. Turn-of-the-century lower Manhattan was a place where no child was meant to be raised, especially one as poorly suited for its elements as Angelo Vestieri.

As an infant, Angelo was dependent on the young mothers of the neighborhood for the excess milk from their breasts, the risk of serious infection ignored in return for a nourishing meal. He lived minus the warmth of a mother's embrace, in the company of a father who had grown to fear displays of emotion. It was an infancy that helped ease him into the comfortable stance of a loner, needing and seeking the affection of no one. Such beginnings are a common trait among gangsters, who are adept at turning external deprivation into inner strength. I met many men in the gangster life in my years around the old man, and never found one who could be described as chatty. I was known and liked by many of them, and yet knew I would never earn their trust. To trust someone is to take a risk. Gangsters survive by minimizing risk.

● ● ●

YOUNG ANGELO SUFFERED from a variety of illnesses, but poverty meant he would not be soothed by proper medical care. He was plagued by a constant cough, the result, the neighborhood doctor claimed, of breathing in excessive amounts of smoke at birth. His weakened lungs left him vulnerable, his immune system under steady attack from the jet stream of contagious diseases that thrived in the overcrowded tenements lining Twenty-eighth Street along Broadway. Angelo spent large chunks of those early years in a small bed in the back of the three-room railroad apartment his father rented for two dollars a week. There, under an assortment of quilts and jackets, he coughed, shivered and wheezed through long days and empty nights. He never complained, always kept to himself, had great difficulty learning English and was very conscious of the chopped-up manner in which he spoke the language of his new country. Again, the severity of such a shuttered existence would serve Angelo well in his later years, when the ability to be isolated and silent for long periods of time would be perceived as a sign of strength.

Angelo was always lost in waves of thought and most at ease when left alone in a world of his own design. It was only on rare occasions that he would venture out and join other boys his age to play the neighborhood street games on which they thrived—stickball, using shaved-down broom handles; Johnny-on-the-pony; ring-a-levio; stoop ball; penny pitching. "I was a bad fit from day one," he once told me. "It just wasn't important to me to be accepted. What those kids thought about me, what they believed to be true, meant nothing. I was a stranger to them and that was the way I wanted it. It was all I had in my favor back then."

Angelo was in and out of the poverty wards of the area hospitals, constantly forced to fight the effects of the ocean crossing and the flames that had seared his lungs. Three times during those early years he was pronounced days away from death, and each time he recovered. "For no other reason than to prove them wrong," Mary said with a slight smile.

Paolino would stop by the ward every morning before work and every night prior to the start of his second job. In the evening, he would bring along his son's favorite meal, hot lentil soup poured over thick slices of Italian bread, and there, faces lit by the soft light of a nightstand lamp, father and son were warmed by good food and each other's company.

"Where do the ships you work on come from, Papa?" Angelo asked, his mouth crammed with a large chunk of bread.

"Any place in the world you can think of," Paolino said, holding a spoon close to his son's lips. "They arrive every day from Italy, Germany, France, even some countries I've never heard of before. All filled with food and goods from their land. The ships are so heavy that sometimes they barely make it into the harbor."

"Where does all the food go?" Angelo asked, his mind alive with images of long lines of hulking cargo ships slowly slipping into port.

"All across the country," Paolino said. "Stores, restaurants, shops. It is a large country we are now part of, Angelo. There is plenty of food and work for everyone who wants it."

"Even for us, Papa?" Angelo said, scooping out the last of the lentils from the bowl his father held cupped in his hands.

"This country is filled with people like us," Paolino said, wiping at his son's chin with the folded edge of a cloth napkin. "It is a special place for a boy like you. It can grant any wish and take you to places that go beyond any dream."

"Will I be able to work on the big ships when I'm bigger?" Angelo asked. "Like you do, Papa?"

"Even better, little Angelo," Paolino said with a wide smile. "One day, you can even own one of the big ships. Be a rich man. Sit back and let others work for you."

Angelo rested his head against the soft pillow, looked over at his father and smiled. "That would be nice, Papa," Angelo said. "For both of us."

Paolino rested the bowl against the side of his chair and leaned over and held the sickly boy in his massive arms, rocking him gently until his eyes closed from the weight of illness and a healthy meal.

• • •

AFTER ONE FOUR-MONTH hospital stay, Paolino decided to move Angelo into the downtown apartment and care of Paolino's great-aunt, Josephina, a widow who lived across the hall from the lonely duo. Josephina was a hefty woman, with thick, flabby arms and legs mapped from foot to upper thigh by ridges of swollen veins. She had dark olive eyes hidden under massive curls of black hair tinged with gray, and a quick and easy smile. She was a formidable-looking woman, with a quick-to-surface temper and a ragged scar streaming down both sides of her chin, the result of a decades-old dog bite. But she loved and cared for Angelo and sought to give him the mother's attention the boy clearly lacked though never outwardly craved. She embraced the boy, welcoming him under the shade of her large wings not as a son but as a student. "She didn't believe in the evils of the camorra or the mafia, which put her at odds with Angelo's father," Mary said. "But how could she believe otherwise? She was the proud wife of a slain crime boss. She respected and held to the traditions of their ways. And she passed those ways down to Angelo."

Josephina would sit him up in bed, his back against her side, a heavy hand gently stroking his thick hair, and tell him stories about the land where his bloodlines rested. "It all began because of the French," she told him one morning, both of them sharing a cup of hot chicken broth. "That's what the word *mafia* means—Morte Alla Francese in Italia. Death to the French in Italy."

"Perche?" Angelo would ask, in his half-English, half-Italian way of speaking. "Why dead?"

"Centuries ago, they came in and took land that did not belong to them," Josephina said. "It belonged to us, to the

Italians. The police, they did nothing, out of fear. The politicians did nothing, because that is what they were paid to do. That left it up to the men of the towns to form a group that only they could trust."

"Did they win?" Angelo asked. "Did they get their land back?"

"Much blood was spilled, but yes, they won their fight," Josephina said. "And no one ever touched their land again."

"Was your husband in the group?" Angelo asked, reacting to the story as most children would to a favorite fairy tale.

"Yes," Josephina said. "He was *capo* of the town where we lived and where he died."

"Papa says that it was to get me and Mama away from men like Uncle Tomasso that we came to America," Angelo said.

"Your father is weak," Josephina hissed in a dismissive tone. "He will never be more than what he is, a piece of furniture moved about by other people."

"I am weak, too," Angelo said, sad eyes peering up at Josephina.

"That will change," Josephina said, a large hand reaching out and caressing the boy's face.

． ． ．

ALL THE GANGSTERS I have known are superstitious, and it stems from childhood days spent with women such as Josephina, who spoon-fed them hand-me-down tales that have no weight in a modern world yet have lingered for centuries. Their everyday fears go miles beyond the simple black cats and open ladder phobias most people demonstrate and are driven by dreams, numbers and suspicion.

"Do you know his biggest fear, courtesy of Aunt Josephina?" Mary asked, shaking her head in disbelief.

"Maybe I do," I said. "If you came into a room with your jacket buttoned it meant you were planning to kill him."

"That was a good one," Mary said. "But the one I got the biggest kick from was that he would never sit at a table or even be seen with a woman who had red hair."

"Why not?"

"It was the color of the devil," Mary said. "And Josephina believed that they had the power to turn the hearts of the most loyal of men."

"Do you think he really believed all that?" I asked.

"I hope to God he did," Mary said, the smile gone from her face. "He had more than one man murdered because of them."

. . .

ON SUMMER AFTERNOONS, Angelo would sit on the middle step of his tenement stoop, staring at the faces in the crowds that squeezed their way past. The street was congested with human and horse-drawn traffic, and thick piles of manure and litter lined both ends of the sidewalk. Across the street from Angelo's building was a dilapidated saloon with an unhinged front door, chipped walls and an uptown name.

It was called the Café Maryland.

Inside its dark, beer- and bloodstained interior, local gangs met to plot their murders and burglaries, map out hijacking routes and collect on their cash loan-outs. In the summer of 1910, three men were shot and killed after a long and loud argument over a woman whose company many of the bar patrons had already shared. The morgue attendants pulled their black van up to the front door soon after the final shots had been fired, scooped up the bodies and vanished back into the darkness, shrugging their shoulders and laughing after another night of battle between "the dagos and the micks."

Angelo was warned by his father never to step near the Maryland. "The people in that bar and the people we escaped from are one and the same," Paolino said. "There is no difference." Paolino ached to spend more time with his son, but the need to work two jobs that barely brought in enough money put an end to such fatherly desires. He worked three full day and night shifts at the midtown piers, helping unload the ships that flooded in and out of the packed harbor. For that, Paolino earned seven dollars a week, but he had to kick back half of that to Chick Tricker's enforcers, who guaranteed the work in return for the payoff.

In the first decades of the twentieth century, Chick Tricker ran Manhattan's Lower West Side. Tricker was a saloon keeper who found hiring out thugs as collectors an easy route to a more lucrative lifestyle. So while an army of hard-working men headed home each night to soak aching muscles, wondering aloud if an honest life was worth living, Tricker stood behind the wood of his bar, a bottle of his finest to his right, and counted his haul, at peace with his place in the American Dream.

Paolino's remaining nights were spent in a little West Twelfth Street slaughterhouse killing, skinning and slicing pigs and sheep for morning delivery to the area meat markets. Not lost on him was the irony that whereas in Italy he once tended to the needs of a flock, he was now here, in America, slicing open their throats. With this job, he was allowed to keep all the money he earned, working straight twelve-hour shifts in near-darkness and unsanitary conditions bordering on the criminal. In addition to his six-dollar salary, Paolino was given two lambs' heads a week, which Josephina would marinate in red wine vinegar and crushed garlic and then roast over a tin wine barrel. Those Sunday afternoon meals were as close to heaven as Paolino Vestieri was meant to find on this earth.

The long hours he worked and the small sums of money such jobs produced left Paolino not just broke but broken. And it made a hard impression on young Angelo. "I watched him come home at night and I'd pretend to be asleep," he told me, tending with care and patience the long rows of olive trees that took up three acres of his Long Island estate. "He looked so beaten, so powerless. He'd sit on the edge of his bed and hang his head, too tired to even take his clothes off. At first I felt so sorry for him. But with time sorrow turned to pity. I knew I could never lead his life. Even death would be a better option."

Paolino didn't have much social life. He had a few male

friends who, on occasion, would get together for brisk games of *briscola* or *sette bello*. On summer days, he sometimes walked alone at the edge of the West Side piers, the harsh glare of the sun turning the Hudson into a long sheet of blue glass, and thought about his second son. Was such a cold country the place for a frail boy to find and make his way? Would he have the courage to deal with the challenges his father envisioned him facing? And would he amount to more than what Paolino saw in himself—a man of simple dreams living a life of wasted wishes.

On rare occasions, Paolino pictured himself married again, a woman at home to supply warmth and comfort and a smiling face to a tired man. Despite his weak financial status, Paolino was still considered a worthy catch among the middle-aged widows and old maids of the neighborhood. But those visions were fleeting, leaving in their wake only the warm memory of Francesca secure at his side. His mood was laced with sadness as he wandered on his walks, wondering whether there had been any point in his leaving Italy. There was, after all, little difference between paying tribute money to the camorra of his homeland or to the Irish thugs of New York.

As he walked home, Paolino almost always thought of Carlo, the son he had murdered. His guilt had grown in the years since the shooting, and it brought along with it the burden of doubt. He was no longer convinced that his action had been the right one, his time in America stripping him of the moral high ground he had easily walked for so many years. He would close his eyes and try to erase the image of the bleeding boy lying dead in the hot, airless room. But he could not. That picture was forever seared into his memory. The void in the center of his stomach told him he would need to live the rest of his life in step with an irrepealable wrong. And for a man like Paolino Vestieri, struggling to make ends meet in a new land, the lethal combination of doubt and guilt could simply prove too powerful to overcome.

. . .

ANGELO WAS SEVEN when he was drawn into his first street fight. He went up against a ten-year-old named Pudge Nichols, a school yard tough who spotted easy pickings in the nervous-looking boy with the stammer. The added fact that he was an Italian with a limited English vocabulary made it all the more enjoyable for the burly Pudge. Within seconds, Nichols towered above Angelo, his right hand open and held out, his left balled into a tight fist.

"Let's see it, wop," Nichols said.

"See what?" Angelo managed to stammer.

"Your money," Nichols said.

"I no have money," Angelo said.

"You gonna live in this place, you gotta learn the rules," Nichols said with a tone of disdain. "Rule one is when you see me you come across with money. It ain't a hard rule to remember. Even for a moron."

"I no have money," Angelo said, straining over each word.

Pudge Nichols opened his left hand and slapped Angelo across the face. The sting of the blow brought tears to Angelo's right eye and a shiver to his body.

"I no have money," Angelo said, tugging at the empty pockets of his gray shorts. "You see? No money."

Pudge smiled and rested a beefy hand on Angelo's shoulder, squeezing hard. Angelo stiffened but didn't move.

"Okay," Pudge said. "You got no money. Then give me something else."

"What?" Angelo asked.

Pudge looked at Angelo, the red welt on his face, the tears running down his cheeks, the fear in his eyes and he snorted out a laugh. "Your clothes," Pudge said.

Angelo stared at Pudge, at first not understanding the request and then, once he did, he slowly shook his head. "No," he said in a voice that hid his fright.

"You can't say no," Pudge said. "You're too stupid to even know what no means."

"No my clothes," Angelo said.

"I take home your clothes or you take home a beating."

"You no take nothing from me," Angelo said.

Pudge immediately landed three blows, swinging from a crunched-down stance. The first two glanced off Angelo's right arm. The third one caught the side of his neck and sent him to the pavement. He landed on his hands and knees and Pudge twice kicked him in the back, forcing all the air out of the damaged lungs.

"You gonna let yourself end up dead for these shitty clothes?" Pudge demanded, barely out of breath.

"You no have my clothes," Angelo said, barely able to get the words out, then he crawled toward a street sign, stretching to reach its base and hoist himself to his feet. Pudge grabbed the back of his hair, stopping him in mid-crawl. He began to punch methodically, landing hard right-hand shots to Angelo's head, holding the back of the boy's hair with his left. Blood from Angelo's mouth and nose splashed across Pudge's white T-shirt and freckled face. A circle of locals had, by now, stopped to watch the fight, a few muttering under-the-breath condemnations of the one-sided match. But no one made a move to stop it.

Pudge let go of Angelo's hair and watched the boy crumple to the ground, his head dangling over the edge of the sidewalk. Pudge bent down and pulled off one of Angelo's shoes.

"Your clothes are too bloody to do me any good," Pudge said disgustedly. "But the shoes are okay. This way, I don't walk away empty."

"You take that boy's shoes and it'll cost you your life."

The voice came from behind Pudge. It was the throaty, sexy voice of a woman. Pudge looked at the group in front of him and saw their expressions change from disapproval to fear. He stood, turned and stared at Ida the Goose.

Ida Bernadine Edwards was the most beautiful woman on the West Side. She was also one of the toughest, carrying two loaded guns at all times. The queen of the Café Maryland, Ida had been a mistress to many of the area's gang leaders. She was in charge of her own crew of thieves, and if the corruption-riddled New York City Police Department had been inclined to investigate tenement and bar murders, it could have pinned Ida the Goose's name next to at least six.

"Don't even think about a run," Ida told Pudge, who was about to bolt down the street. "I can shoot you in the back just as easy as in the chest."

"I ain't gonna run," Pudge said, meekly shaking his head.

"Help that boy to his feet," Ida ordered. "Then bring him into the Café. There's a back room with a long table over near the kitchen. Put him on that. And wait there with him till I get back."

"Where you goin'?" Pudge asked, his eyes growing wider as Ida the Goose walked toward him.

"The boy needs a doctor." Ida stared down at him with a set of ocean-blue eyes. "Come the end of the day, you might, too. It seems like a good idea for me to go find one. You got any other questions for me?"

"No," Pudge said.

"Then get out of my way," Ida said. "And go do what I told you."

Ida the Goose lifted the front lip of her long brown skirt and moved past Pudge, ignoring the small crowd, heading up toward Broadway and an alcoholic doctor who owed her money and a favor.

．　．　．

GANGSTERS, IF THEY are shaped by anyone at all, are chiseled by the women in their early lives. Angelo's childhood models were Josephina and Ida the Goose, two women whose guidance and nurturing were bound to lead him down but one path. "He didn't have a family of his own, other than his father," Mary said. "So he made one from the people he met. Josephina became his grandmother, Pudge his brother and Ida replaced the mother he lost at birth. He listened to them, trusted them and, most important, he learned from them."

He was an eager student hoping to survive the indifferent

streets of a harsh city. He was also a child who silently longed
for affection and who found it in the company of the unlike-
liest of trios. In another place, living among the honest and
hardworking, Angelo Vestieri might well have grown up to
live a life of simplicity and little consequence. But his road
was paved with more dangerous material.

We can ignore, even fight, our destiny, but ultimately we
must yield. It was true for Angelo. It was true for me.

• • •

IDA THE GOOSE took in the wounded boy and cared for him.
She directed the doctor to mend his wounds and warned
Josephina to keep Angelo away from his father long enough
for the visible bruises to heal.

"Why do you do this for him?" Josephina asked Ida,
staring at her as both women drank from glasses filled with
dark Irish whiskey.

"I got a weak spot for strays," Ida said, downing the last of
her drink. "Found a kitten about two years ago in the alley behind the Café. She was pretty beat up, near dead, far as I could
tell. Now, she's tough and hard enough to kill three cornered
rats."

"And you think you will take Angelo and make him tough
and hard?" Josephina said. "Like that cat?"

"No," Ida said. "I'll just try to teach him enough to keep
him from gettin' killed."

"He looks and acts weak," Josephina said. "But inside, he
has much strength."

"He better," Ida the Goose said.

Josephina stared at Ida for several moments. She then
nodded and smiled and refilled their whiskey glasses.

• • •

IT WAS CLOSE to sunrise, light creaking through the windows
of the Café Maryland. Angelo walked quietly down the
center of the room, the smell of stale smoke and old drink
fouling the air. He was wearing a robe two sizes too large over

his pajamas and work shoes in the place of slippers. His face was still bruised and sore, one eye half-shut, and his back and chest hurt to the touch. Angelo pushed aside a chair and opened the door to Ida's back room. It was his first time in here and he marveled at how clean and well-kept it all looked, the furniture neat and polished, the framed photos on the walls orderly and dust-free. He stepped deep into the room and stood in front of Ida's bed, staring down at her sleeping form, her back to him, her face resting on a pillow curled against a brown wall. Angelo sat on the floor, his robe wrapped around him like a quilt, and leaned his head against the side of the bed. He reached a hand up and rested it on top of Ida's rich, curly hair, his fingers buried inside the thick strands. His eyes were open and brimming with tears as he listened to her steady flow of breath. He leaned in closer and placed his head against the small of Ida's back and closed his eyes, at peace in the silent room. *"Grazie tanto, signora,"* Angelo whispered to Ida seconds before he dozed off. "Thank you so much."

Ida's eyes were open, staring at the dark wall inches from her face. She waited until the boy was sound asleep, turned slowly and lifted him up onto the bed, covering him with her blanket. She stared at his wounded face and rubbed a warm hand against his hard bruises. Ida kissed Angelo on the forehead and then rested her head back down on her pillow. She closed her eyes and surrendered to sleep, her arms gently wrapped around the frail boy she had rescued.

. . .

TWO WEEKS LATER, on a rain-swept Sunday morning, Ida the Goose called Pudge Nichols into the Café Maryland.

"I ain't punched anybody since I did the wop," Pudge said, standing in the Café's doorway, a gimme cap clutched in his hands. "I swear."

"It's a start," Ida said, glancing at him above the rim of a large white coffee mug.

Ida was standing behind the bar, a spit-shined black boot

curved onto the metal pipe that ran along its base. Even in the semidarkness of the large room, her eyes shone. Her dark hair was pinned up, long strands inching their way down toward a luminous face. Ida slipped a hand-rolled cigarette into the corner of her mouth, slid a long wooden match down several inches of the bar until it sparked and then put the lit end up against the raw tobacco. She waved Pudge closer, smoke drifting out of her nostrils. The boy walked toward her, hesitant, his eyes scanning the Café.

"I'm all the company you're gonna get," Ida said. "Got a little wild in here last night. Everybody's out sleepin' it off."

"What do you want?" Pudge asked, reaching the bar and staring up at Ida with nervous eyes.

"It might be a good idea for you to relax a little," Ida said. "I'm not in the business of hurting kids. Not unless I got good reason."

Ida reached under the bar and came up with a fresh cup of coffee, which she pushed across the wood. Pudge eased his way onto a stool and put his hands around the cup. He took a long sip and looked around the Café. "It true what they say about this place?" he asked. "About all the people been killed in here?"

"I don't see your old man around anymore," Ida said, ignoring his questions and coming back with one of her own. "He doin' a stretch or a split?"

"He left just before Christmas," Pudge said with a shrug. "I don't mind. Don't get yelled at as much and my mom is too drunk to spend her nights whackin' me around."

"So long as you're happy," Ida said, blowing a lungful of smoke up toward the ceiling.

Pudge leaned forward against the bar, the cup cradled in both hands. "So why am I here?" he asked.

"It's about that boy you did a number on," Ida said.

"The wop?" Pudge said.

Ida nodded and handed Pudge what was left of her cigarette. He put down his cup, reached for it, brought it to his mouth and took a long pull.

"What about him?" Pudge asked, trying not to react to the warm burn of the tobacco on his lungs.

"I want you to take care of him," Ida said. "Make sure nobody else does to him what you did."

"I don't get it. What's this really about?" Pudge asked, tossing aside the cigarette.

"It's about what I want," Ida said. "And it's about what you're going to do, which is keep him safe."

"And what if I don't?" Pudge asked.

"I might forget about it," Ida said. "Or I might go out and find somebody with nothin' much else to do but beat the shit outta *you*."

"This is nuts!" Pudge said, raising his voice and slamming his hands against the cool wood of the bar. "The kid's a loser. You see him walk, you wanna belt him, just for kicks."

"And that's where you come in," Ida said. "Pass the word around. They mess with him, it's like messin' with you. You got a strong enough rep that the rest of the street kids'll back off."

"How long you want this to go on?"

"Till I say otherwise," Ida said. "You gave him a pretty solid workover. I don't want to see that happen again. From here on, that kid cuts himself, somebody else is gonna bleed. Even if that somebody has to be you."

"What do you get outta this?" Pudge stepped down from the stool, his frown showing that he was resigned to his fate.

"There's nothing to get," Ida said, smiling and walking down the length of the bar. "Maybe we just do this one on the arm."

Pudge watched her leave and shook his head. "Bodywatchin' a wop," he mumbled. "I'm better off being found dead."

"I can make that happen," Ida the Goose said, over her shoulder. "If that's your choice."

Pudge Nichols didn't respond. He just turned and ran out of the Café Maryland.

GANGSTERS HAVE FEW friends. It is the nature of the life. There is a story Angelo always liked to tell me when I was younger, one he never tired of repeating, and which, to him, summarized the gangster ethic. "A father puts his son on a ledge, fifteen feet from the ground," Angelo would say. "Kid's about six. The father then tells the kid to jump. The kid shakes his head, afraid to make the move. The father tells him not to worry, Daddy's here and Daddy will catch you. The kid swallows hard, clenches his hands and makes the jump. The father moves out of the way and lets the kid land on the ground, cuts, bruises, scrapes, what have you. The father bends over and points a finger in the face of his crying boy. And then he tells him, 'Remember one thing. In this life, never trust *anybody*.' "

It is rare in the gangster life to find someone to confide in. It is even rarer to find a friend. The majority of alliances are forged out of territorial expedience and adhere strictly to business policies. Those friendships last for as long as there is profit to be made. "You wash my back and I wash yours," Angelo would say. "Until the time comes to shoot you in the back."

With Pudge Nichols, friendship came out in its most natural colors. It grew out of hatred and evolved into a bond chain-linked to loyalty and mutual respect. Pudge and Angelo fed off each other's strengths, protected their weaknesses and allowed no one to infiltrate their well-constructed wall of trust. Within the confines of their brutal world, the two lived as one. "They were so unalike in both manner and personality," Mary said. "But they grew to truly love each other. In fact, I don't believe there was anyone in this world Angelo ever loved more than Pudge. And even in that love, as pure as it was, there was risk."

• • •

ANGELO AND PUDGE walked with their heads down against a bitter, icy wind. It came whipping off the East River with a series of angry howls, lashing at their worn winter clothes.

"Let's duck inside the Maryland," Pudge said, shoving his hands into the rear pockets of tattered knickers. "Just until I get the feeling back in my toes."

"We be late for school," Angelo said in his stilted English. "Teacher get angry."

"That makes two good reasons to do it," Pudge said.

"We no go all this week," Angelo said. "The teacher soon will call my papa."

"Ida needs us to move beer outta the basement," Pudge said. "That pays. School don't."

Pudge had followed Ida's instructions religiously and stood by Angelo, ensuring no harm would come to the boy at the hands of any other neighborhood toughs. He felt the best way to ensure Angelo's safety was to be seen constantly at his side, in full view of all the hungry eyes searching the city streets for targets and scores. The fact that Angelo was Italian made Pudge's task even more daunting. Back then, Italians were seen as little more than thieves, moving by the thousands into what had once been Irish strongholds and stealing all the low-paying jobs. Street fights between the two groups occurred daily and any truce that was forged always proved fleeting.

By the winter of 1913, as the bitter taste of World War I depressed the country's spirit, New York City's streets had become ethnic battle zones. It was the age of the Gangs, a crime-controlled period in which more than one hundred fifty rampaging squads ruled over the citizenry by the sheer force of their hard fists. The borough-wide municipal police department was understaffed, poorly trained and alarmingly corrupt. Random slayings occurred daily throughout the city, with overpopulated lower Manhattan leading the case files. Daylight muggings and holdups were so commonplace, they hardly merited a passing spectator's glance let alone a mention in the next morning's newspapers. Well-equipped and organized teams of home invaders cleared apartments of their dwellers' meager possessions, transforming hot swag into instant cash through an intricate network of well-positioned fences.

Prostitution was rampant, feeding off the frustrated desires of hardscrabbling immigrants looking to ease their plights by seeking comfort in unknown arms. A pimp or madam with a dependable stable of attractive women could clear a $400 profit per week—the equivalent of the police commissioner's annual salary. The majority of the working prostitutes were runaways, fleeing the dense poverty of other climes, though a small handful were either widows left without any income or wives of men unable to find work of their own.

Saloons and bars dotted the downtown landscape and most were filled to capacity six nights a week, pouring out watered-down beer, bathtub gin and week-old whiskey to tired faces and eager hands. Most mornings, the streets were lined with men dozing against doorways or stooped under parked stalls, their financial and family troubles reduced to foggy memories.

But by far the biggest vice confronting the immigrants and the one that encouraged addiction on a daily basis was gambling. The passion for betting on a daily number was common ground between Italian and Irish immigrants in turn-of-the-century New York, and an army of street hustlers and gangsters was eager to profit from this passion. Hundreds dealt in the fast and deadly numbers game. Many became rich. More than a few died in the attempt.

No one was better at it than a thin, dapper man with a soft voice and an easy smile.

His name was Angus McQueen.

On the street he came to be known as Angus the Killer, and he rose to criminal prominence after spending his formative years as a high-ranking member of the Gophers, one of the more powerful Manhattan gangs. They ruled through the strength of their number, counting as many as five hundred members at their peak. The area running from Seventh Avenue down to the Hudson River, covering Twenty-third to Forty-second Streets, formed the heart of Gopher territory.

Their gentle name belied their barbarous natures. The gang was called Gophers because their hideouts and stash drops were located in tenement basements. They were often at war with rival gangs, most notably the sinister Five Points and the vicious Eastmans. It seemed as if each week brought news of the death or clubbing of at least one member of one of the squads.

Beyond their ease with cracking heads and maiming bodies, a few of the more notable gang leaders displayed a unique flair for business. One-Lung Curran, a Gopher waterfront boss, earned a small fortune by converting stolen policemen's winter coats into ladies' wear, causing a fashion sensation during two Garment District seasons. Curran suffered from a chronic tubercular condition and ran his business from a Bellevue Hospital bed, turning a third-floor ward into a workable sales office.

Buck O'Brien, a Hell's Kitchen Gopher boss, invested his illegal profits in the stock market. His portfolio was helped by insider tips he received from Wall Street high-rollers he supplied with free women and drink.

Neither man had the foresight of Angus McQueen, who saw a future in which the rows of low-rent bars would be replaced by upper-tier nightclubs featuring top-of-the-line talent and stiff cover charges. In time, McQueen would own percentages in three dozen such places, including Harlem's famed Cotton Club.

These were the robber barons of lower Manhattan. Violent visionaries backed by gangs and guns who rode through town on the backs of poverty. There was a Gold Rush in illegal trade to be mined, and they took full advantage of the opportunity. Where many only saw teeming streets filled with disease and the destitute, Curran, McQueen and the others who followed in their wake saw thick pockets of riches, as the eager hands of the poor were quick to spend what little money they had on gambling, women and drink. And best of all, there was no one there to stop them. "He used to say it was like living in the Wild West," Mary said. "The black hats made the rules and the white hats followed them. If you were weak, you were doomed."

"They could have moved," I said. "Tried to make it in another place, another city."

"Where would they go?" Mary asked me, her eyes sad but firm. "And where could they go that would be so different?"

• • •

ANGUS MCQUEEN OWNED the street where Angelo Vestieri and Pudge Nichols lived. He was a scrawny man who didn't need to be seen in order to have his presence felt. Angus never raised his voice and always kept his word. His parents moved out of a run-down flat in East London and brought him to America when he was eleven. By then, McQueen had more than his fill of poverty and was determined to live his days soaking in the pleasures of wealth. And in the America he found, Angus learned that the fastest way to fulfill that childhood quest was with a loaded gun.

He killed his first man when he was seventeen and became a Gopher boss a year later. By the time he was twenty-three, McQueen's murder count had risen to seven. He kept a thick lead pipe wrapped in newspaper in his back pocket, a set of brass knuckles next to his wallet, a blackjack hanging from a leather strap around his neck, and a holstered gun close to his heart. He never held a formal job and loved seeing his name and criminal exploits written up in the papers. Angus McQueen was the first Manhattan gangster to attain mythic status among his peers. It was a position he loved having and he did all he could to maintain his lofty perch. Killing for it was the least of his concerns.

While Angus grew richer, Paolino Vestieri turned more despondent. The harder he worked, the less he seemed to earn. His living conditions did not improve and he began to drink more than his usual amount. He felt Angelo drifting away, lured by the streets and influenced heavily by the trio of Ida the Goose, Pudge Nichols and his own aunt, Josephina. He did not blame the boy. In their company, he was at least offered some promise of hope, a glimmer of an escape. Sitting next to his father, even a boy as young and innocent as Angelo could smell the fear.

Paolino cut a fresh piece of cheese and held it out for his son. The boy took it, split it in half and put a chunk in his mouth. He lifted the small cup of water mixed with a few drops of red wine at his feet and drank it down.

"How much time they give you to eat, Papa?" Angelo asked.

"Twenty minutes," Paolino said. "Sometimes more if the ships are close to loaded."

They sat on two crates, their backs to a redbrick wall, the crowded pier spread out in front of them. The food rested on white handkerchiefs by their feet, the hot midday sun warmed their faces. "What is in the ships?" Angelo asked.

"Different kinds of fruit, some days rice," Paolino said, finishing the last bite of cheese. "Cured meats when the weather is cold. They always come in full and they always go away empty."

"Do you get to keep any of what's on the ship, Papa?" Angelo asked.

"He's lucky he gets to keep his job."

The voice came from behind Angelo and he saw the giant shadow lurking over him, obscuring the sun. Angelo and Paolino turned together and stared up at the man. Angelo cast a quick glance toward his father and saw a look of fright cross his face.

"Hate to put a break to the family picnic," the man said. "But there's work waitin' to be done."

The man was tall and muscular, with a full head of dark hair and eyebrows thick as hedges. He squinted when he talked, more out of habit than avoidance of the sun. He held an unlit cigar in one hand and had a grappling hook hanging off his shoulder.

"I have ten more minutes," Paolino said.

"You have what I say you have," the man said. "Now get up off your ass and move."

Paolino looked at Angelo, his face a mask of embarrassment, forced a smile and stood up. "Stay and eat your fruit," he said to the boy. "I see you tonight when I finish."

He leaned over and kissed Angelo, holding the boy close to him for a few seconds. "C'mon, c'mon," the man behind them said. "It ain't like you're off to fight a war. Put a step in it."

Paolino grabbed his handkerchief from the ground, rubbed the top of Angelo's head, then started a slow walk toward the open doors of the pier. The man jammed the cigar into his mouth and took a short run toward Paolino. He stopped and reared up his leg, the bulk of his heavy work boot landing square in the center of Paolino's back. "When I say move, I mean move," the man snarled. "That don't fit right with you, then you can take your ass to another pier."

Angelo stood, his fists closed, his eyes lit with rage, but said nothing. He watched his father face the man and then look back over at him. Paolino's face was pale and empty, a man resigned to his plight. Angelo's was beet red and trembling, angry over his inability to do anything but watch his father be bullied.

They both watched Paolino disappear into the mouth of the pier. The man shoved Angelo with an open palm. "Clean up this mess," he said. "And get the hell out of here."

Angelo glared up at him. "What is your name?" he said.

"Forget my name," the man said. "We ain't ever gonna be friends. Now clean up the mess and get the hell outta here."

"What is your name?" Angelo asked again, taking two short steps closer to the man.

"You're gonna get yourself hurt, kid," the man said, his words clipped and angry. "Now do what I told you before it's too late."

"I want to know your name," Angelo said.

The man lifted his hand and smacked Angelo hard across his face, leaving finger marks in his wake. He grabbed the boy by the shirt collar and lifted him off his feet, their faces separated by inches. "My name's Carl," the man snarled.

"Carl Banyon. And in case you ever start to forget it, this will help you remember."

Banyon pulled a straight razor from his back pocket and snapped it open. He saw Angelo's eyes widen at the sight of the blade and he smiled. "You can cry if you want," Banyon said. "I won't care."

Angelo saw the blur of the razor and felt its sting. The warmth of his own blood soon flowed down the side of his face, pouring out of the four-inch gash Banyon had opened just above his right eye.

Angelo turned and grabbed his handkerchief from the ground and put it up to his face. He heard Banyon's heavy footsteps walk off in the distance. He felt dizzy and nauseous from the loss of blood. He heard men walk past him, speaking a hard English he didn't understand, and knew none of them would stop to help. They were either too afraid of Banyon or too indifferent to his plight. He stayed there and stared up at the sky, unable to cry, not wanting to move. In the distance, he heard the horns and whistles of a large ship pulling out of the harbor, heading for a country far removed from the one his father had chosen as the place to build a better life.

• • •

JOSEPHINA COMBED BACK Angelo's black strands of hair with a wet comb. She was careful not to go near the blood-spotted bandage that covered the gash above his right eye. It took a dozen stitches to seal the zigzag wound and a full day to convince Paolino that revenge against Carl Banyon was not for him to take.

"He should die for what he did to my boy," Paolino said.

"And then what will happen?" Josephina said. "You end up in prison and Angelo loses his father."

"At least then he would have a father he could respect," Paolino said.

"You are to do nothing," Josephina said. "In time, revenge will be had. Only it will not be dealt from your hand."

"If not me, then who?" Paolino asked.

Josephina turned away and did not answer.

• • •

"WHO IS THIS man Ida wants me to meet?" Angelo asked, the starch of the tight white shirt chafing against his neck.

"He is a boss," Josephina said. "He has the power to help you."

"Help me do what?"

"To not be like your father," Josephina said. "Paolino is a weak man. And this is a country that gets strong off its weak. A man like McQueen will teach you the things you need to know."

"Papa teaches me things I need to know," Angelo said. "Things he says will help turn me into a good man."

"You will be a good man, Angelo," Josephina said. "But one who lives his own life in his own way. Not someone who must work until his body can no longer stand."

"Will this man love me the way Papa does?" Angelo asked.

"You don't turn to a man like McQueen for love," Josephina said. "But he will teach you about loyalty and such lessons bring with them a much heavier burden. Love enters and leaves when it wishes. Loyalty stays forever. And for you that means until the day McQueen dies or is no longer a boss."

"And then?"

"And then we will see how well you have learned your lessons," Josephina said.

• • •

GANGSTERS ALL THIRST for power and will do all they can to achieve and keep it. That is their real code, the only one they truly adhere to. Loyalty, faith, friendship are all tools used to keep control of the power. The need to grasp at the power is planted in them during their childhood years when, surrounded by poverty, they seek out the one who has risen above it all. In poor neighborhoods, especially in the early years of the twentieth century, the one who rose the highest and accumulated the greatest power was almost always a criminal. "There was no romance to the notion of being a gangster," Mary said. "Angelo would be the first to tell you that. It was just a refusal on his part to live his life at the mercy of men like Carl Banyon. Watching his father get kicked and be treated in such a heartless manner hurt Angelo much more than that cut from the razor. That was the deeper wound. The cut was merely a reminder of what he had seen. And what he needed to never forget."

· · ·

PUDGE TOSSED THE rubber ball against the side of the dark brick wall and caught it with one hand. Angelo sat off to the side, his back wedged between the rear entryway into the tenement building, his arms wrapped around his legs. Pudge bounced the ball on the cracked concrete, the shade from the heavy strands of laundry hanging off the thick clothesline boxing him into the cool shadows. "I never set out to be your friend," Pudge said to Angelo. "I only did it so Ida wouldn't have done to me what I did to you."

"I know, Pudge," Angelo said. "Maybe soon she will let you out of it."

Pudge shrugged and walked over toward Angelo, still bouncing the ball by his side. "I don't think so," he said. "I'm probably stuck with you for a while."

"I'm sorry, then," Angelo said, looking up at him.

"I was too, at the start," Pudge said. "But to tell you the truth, you haven't been as big a pain in the ass as I figured you'd be."

Angelo smiled. "It has been good to have a friend," he said.

"When we go in to meet this guy McQueen, we're going to have to be more than that," Pudge said. "If he's going to take us on, he's taking us as a team. And that's what it's gotta be, you and me, together. Won't work any other way."

"You can't always look out for me," Angelo said. "And I cannot protect you the way you protect me."

"It's worked so far," Pudge said. "Let's give it some more time. See how it plays out." He sat down across from Angelo, squeezing in on the other end of the entryway. "Maybe you'll turn out to be tougher than all of us."

"I'm too scared to be tough," Angelo said. "But I promise to always be your friend. And I will never betray you."

Pudge stared over at Angelo and nodded. "Same goes for me," he said. "And for the kind of work we're about to get into, that might be all that we need."

• • •

ANGELO AND PUDGE stood silent and at attention, watching as Angus McQueen finished a game of solitaire. He had small hands, nails neat and trimmed, and he flipped the cards over gently onto the top of the polished wood table. There was a smoldering cigarette tilted into an ashtray on his right and an empty cup of coffee to his left. He spoke without lifting his eyes from the cards.

"Ida tells me I should put you two boys to work," Angus said, studying the jack of spades in his hand. "You agree with her?"

Pudge looked at Angelo, nodded, then turned back to McQueen. "Yes," Pudge said. "We're ready to work."

"At what?" McQueen asked.

"We're up to doin' anything," Pudge said.

McQueen picked up his cigarette and took a long pull on the wet tobacco. He looked up at the two boys, his eyes squinting from the swirling lines of smoke. "Anything?" he said. "That covers a lot of territory."

"I'm not afraid," Pudge said. "If that's what you're thinkin'."

"Well, I know you're not afraid of me," McQueen said, a small smile creeping across his face. He rested the cards facedown on the table and stubbed out the tip of the cigarette. "Let me take some time and think on it," he said, pushing his chair back. "See what I can find. It'll be runner's work at first. Nothing big and nothing that pays great."

"We ain't picky," Pudge said.

"You can't afford to be," McQueen answered.

He walked around the table and stood next to Angelo, resting a hand on the thin boy's shoulder. "I heard about your run-in with Banyon," he said. "I hope it hurt."

Angelo looked up at McQueen and nodded. "Yes," he said. "It hurt."

"Good," McQueen said. "That means you made yourself an enemy. And if you're going to work for me you're going to have plenty of enemies."

"And don't count on having too many friends either," Ida the Goose said.

"You only need yourself one of those," Angus McQueen said, reaching into his vest and pulling out a fresh cigarette. "A hundred enemies and one friend will make you a rich man in business. *Any* business."

Pudge shrugged and pointed a thumb at Angelo. "I got me no problems there," Pudge said. "So long as I'm with him, I'll have more than my share of people who hate me."

Angus McQueen lifted his head back and laughed. "You're a lucky lad, then," he said. "You haven't even started and already you're a step ahead."

"Might even die a rich man," Ida the Goose said, smiling. "You play it right."

Angelo glanced at Pudge. "I will not let you die," he said through lips that barely moved.

"Thanks," Pudge said. "I'll sleep better now."

Ida the Goose and Angus McQueen exchanged a nod and a smile.

* * *

PAOLINO STOOD KNEE-DEEP in the clear waters of City Island Bay, his pants rolled up to his thighs and his hands sifting through the bottom's soft sand. He looked up at Angelo sitting on the center plank of a rowboat and smiled. The boy, a half-filled bushel of clams resting between his legs, smiled back. The hot morning sun beat down on both of them.

"How many do we have so far?" Paolino yelled across the short distance separating them.

"About fifty," Angelo called back. "Maybe more."

Paolino squinted up at the sun, its warm rays turning the pall of his white skin a bright shade of red. "Three more hours," he said. "By then, the basket will be full."

"Are all these clams for us?" Angelo asked, his white T-shirt bunched up and hanging around his neck.

"As many as we can eat," Paolino said. "The rest we give to the people in our building."

"Do you want your drink, Papa?" Angelo asked, reaching for a bottle of red wine wrapped in cloth.

Paolino rinsed his hands in the clear water and walked toward Angelo. The two of them had left lower Manhattan in the middle of the night and hitched a ride on a friend's milk wagon heading up to the Bronx to make its deliveries. They slept for most of the five-hour trip and stared out at the passing scenery during the rest of it. A gulf was developing between the boy and his father and Paolino felt powerless to prevent its expansion. The hours he spent with his now-eight-year-old son were too few to matter, stolen minutes jammed in between work and sleep. It was one more fault he could lay at the doorstep of his new homeland.

Paolino had cursed Italy for the ease with which it submitted to the dark hands of organized crime. But now, here in New York, he saw greater dangers. The streets of lower Manhattan sucked up boys like his Angelo and thrust them into a sinister realm where their torn pockets would be lined with wads of easy money. At such a young age Angelo had already glimpsed an escape route from the cramped confines of his dead-end tenement life.

Paolino flipped his shirt over the side of the boat. The sun and sparkle of the water reminded him of an earlier time, when his days were marked by long walks across green hills and fresh meadows and along tree-lined roads, herding his flock, his own future as clear to him as the overhead sky. That short period seemed galaxies removed from where he now stood. He felt as if he were in the middle of someone else's life, cruising by, honing in on the memories of a stranger.

"I do not remember the last time I was out in the sun," Paolino said. "It feels good."

"How much longer will we stay?" Angelo asked. His English was improving daily, deterred only by his occasional stutter and living among New York Italians, who found it much easier to speak in their own tongue than to add the demands of a new one to their burdens.

"Milk wagon will be by to pick us up at four," Paolino said, taking the wine bottle from his son. As he swallowed the homemade brew, Paolino stared at the boy's face, the youthful features so much a carbon copy of his wife's that it made him wince. "Why? You have someplace to go?" he asked, wiping his chin and handing Angelo back the bottle.

"Pudge needs me," Angelo said.

"He needs you to do what?" Paolino asked.

"I don't know," Angelo said.

"Listen to me, Angelo," Paolino said, a wet hand resting on top of the boy's knee. "I know it is hard for you now. The way we live is not the best. But it will be better. Hard work will make it better. That is the only way I know and the only way I want to teach you."

"Angus McQueen does not work hard," Angelo said. "And he lives better."

"Angus McQueen is a criminal," Paolino hissed, hatred for the man and his methods coloring his eyes. "He's not good enough to work. He lives off *my* work. *My* sweat. He will show you a life that is wrong. A life filled with poison."

"He show me how to play cards," Angelo said.

"You are young still," Paolino said. "When you are older, he will show you more than card games."

"Are you afraid of him?" Angelo asked.

"I am afraid for *you*," Paolino said. "I know what harm these people bring. I saw it in Italy with my own eyes. I do not wish to see it happen here. Not again."

"Is that why you came to this country?" Angelo asked, staring at the bushel of clams.

"I came for you," Paolino said. "I wanted a better life for you than what we had in Italy. I cannot do that if you choose these other people over me."

"They are my friends," Angelo said, lifting his eyes to Paolino.

"But they are my enemies," Paolino said. "If you stay with them, become a part of them, you cannot ever be a part of me."

Angelo looked away, his eyes scanning the bay, his face soft and warm. "I love you, Papa," he whispered. "But I do not want to be like you."

Paolino stared at his son's profile and fought back the urge to cry. He had always thought of Angelo as weak, ill-suited for the demands of a harsh country. He knew now that he was wrong. Behind his son's frail body there was hidden a hard core, one that would absorb all that it needed to survive.

"You will not be like me, Angelo," Paolino said, stroking the boy's head with a wet hand. "You are too strong. There will be many fears to be faced in your life, but that will not be one of them."

Angelo turned back to look at his father, the blazing sun directly above his head. "You rest, Papa," he said. "I will finish the clams."

Angelo jumped into the water, took a few strides closer to land and spent the rest of the afternoon in the hunt for buried clams.

•   •   •

JOSEPHINA AND ANGELO walked down the crowded street, the old woman's right hand at rest under the boy's left elbow. It was late afternoon on a summer's day and the streets were crammed with men coming home from jobs and women rushing to steamy apartments to begin preparing the evening meal. Angelo clutched a small paper bag filled with vine-ripe tomatoes and red onions to his chest. He and Pudge were working as part-time runners for Angus McQueen, making twice-weekly pickups and money drops in the back rooms of bars and diners. Angelo was paid two dollars a week and the weight of the money felt good in his pocket. It was his first taste of illegal money and he loved it.

"Money is the only reason anybody ever becomes a gangster," Pudge would often say, usually after a big meal. "Everything else follows that. The money is the bait that draws you in. You don't believe me, then name one gangster worth his weight in vinegar who started out in life anything *but* dirt poor. The cars, the broads, the fancy digs, that all comes later, but it's the bite of cash that gets you hooked. Then, by the time you got enough socked away that you want out of the life, there's nowhere for you to go. Being a gangster is all you know and all you can be. And it's how you're gonna die. All of it off of that first dollar you made back when you were a kid."

"I would like to buy you something," Angelo said, looking up at Josephina. "A gift."

"What is there that I need?" the old woman said with a shrug. "We have our food for tonight and fresh milk for the morning. Save your money. Don't make it fly away as soon as it lands in your hands."

Angelo looked at the passing stands, their wooden crates packed full with watered-down fresh fruit and vegetables, rows of fish and meat resting on huge slabs of ice next to them. As they turned a corner, he spotted a small man in a wool sweater, roasting chestnuts over the lid of an open barrel. "Wait here," he said to Josephina, giving her the tomatoes and onions to hold. She stood and smiled, watching as the vendor handed Angelo a paper bag filled with roasted chestnuts. He paid the vendor, walked back and handed her the bag. "I know you like them," he said.

Josephina took the bag from Angelo and nodded, touched by the gesture of a boy she had grown to love. "I used to roast them for my husband," she said, staring straight ahead. "We would eat them in the evening along with one or two glasses of wine. It was our time together. I always liked the way it made the house smell. Now, when I walk past one of those carts, the smell of the roast reminds me of my husband and those nights."

"I did not buy them to make you sad," Angelo said.

"I am not sad, my little one," Josephina said. "Those are my happy memories and they help me to forget that I live in such a place."

"Papa always says that our life here will soon get better," Angelo said. "For him and for all of us."

"It will get better for some," Josephina said. "But your papa will not be one of them. He is a dreamer who does not know how to bring his dreams to life."

"He is mad with me since I began my work for Angus," Angelo said. "He says the money I get from him is blood money."

Josephina stopped and turned to face Angelo. "*All* money is blood money," she said. "Remember that like you remember your name."

"I want to give him the money to help pay the bills," Angelo said. "But he won't take it."

"He will never take it," Josephina said. "He has his code and, in time, you will have yours."

"But I want to help," Angelo said.

"The best way to do that is to help yourself," Josephina said. "Learn all you can about this world and go out and find your place in it."

"Why?" Angelo shrugged. "They hate us in this world."

"Time will change all that," Josephina said. "Some day soon, the door will open for the few who are ready. Make sure you are one of them."

"And I will take you with me," Angelo said, resting his head against the old woman's large arm.

"That would make me very happy, little one," Josephina said with a wry smile, pausing at the base of the tenement stoop. "But the future arrives without invitation and we never know what burdens or pleasures it brings."

"Pudge is coming for supper," Angelo said, helping Josephina walk up the steps. "Is that okay?"

"Only if he comes with an empty stomach," Josephina said. "Tomato and onion salad, fresh bread, lots of wine and, thanks to you, roasted chestnuts. He must be ready to eat nothing less than a feast."

"Pudge loves to eat," Angelo said. "Ida said the only time he doesn't have food in his mouth is when he sleeps."

"Then tonight, your friend Pudge will be a very happy young man," Josephina said.

. . .

IN THE LATE fall of 1914, poor living conditions and old age caught up to Josephina. She was felled by a string of illnesses—a monthlong battle with the flu damaged her lungs, a kidney infection left her weak and vulnerable and the shooting pain in her lower back could no longer be attributed to excess weight. For the first time in her life, Josephina was bedridden and dependent on others.

The medication she was given made her drowsy and, at times, delirious. As Angelo watched a parade of doctors march in and out of the apartment, he kept a steady vigil. He tried to cheer the old woman by repeating the bawdy jokes of southern Italy she had so often told him. He held her hand when the pain grew strong and watched silently as she struggled to regain her breath. To help ease her through the day, Angelo would ask her about her life in Italy and only then, as the memories slowly began to take root, would he see the color return to her face.

"Do you miss it?" Angelo asked.

"It is my home," Josephina said. "America will never be that for me. It is just a place to live. Nothing more."

"Why did you leave?" he asked, handing her a hot cup of water boiled with lemon skins.

"My husband was murdered," she said, staring at the boy with hard eyes. "He was a respected man, but to someone younger and looking to make an impression that respect meant nothing. He was shot in the back and left to die."

"What happened to the man who shot him?"

"It was not my place to ask," she said. "I needed to bury a husband."

"What was he like, your husband?" Angelo asked, taking the cup from her and placing it on a shaky end table.

"To me, he was kind and gentle," Josephina said. "To others, he was what his work called for him to be."

"Was he a boss like Angus?"

"Yes," Josephina said, nodding, her face cringing at the bolts of pain winding their way through her body.

"Papa said he was a killer," Angelo said, reaching for a wet cloth and resting it across Josephina's forehead.

"He killed only men," Josephina said, forcing herself to sit up, her right hand gripping Angelo's arm. "He would never do harm to a child. *Any* child. Especially one that was his own. Such work is best left to those with the stomach for it."

Angelo pulled his arm away from Josephina's grip and stood against the side of the bed. The blinds were drawn, but the heat of the hot afternoon sun still burned through. "What do you mean?" he asked, his voice steady, the wheeze coming up from his throat the only betrayal to his nervousness.

Josephina took a deep breath, the air rattling around her lungs like crushed chains. She picked up the cup and drank the last of the lemon water. She looked at Angelo, the soft tears of a hard woman in her eyes. "I cannot turn a son against his father," she said. "No matter the sin."

"He is my father," Angelo said. "I will not turn away from him."

"You are being shown another way by a harder set of hands," she said. "And there is no place for your father in such company."

"I will make a place for him," Angelo said, his soft eyes staring deep into Josephina's weary face.

The old woman smiled and nodded, wiping her damp upper lip with a crumpled handkerchief. "And what of Angus and Ida and Pudge?" she asked. "Will you always make a place for them?"

Angelo hesitated and then nodded. "Yes," he said.

"You cannot have both, my little one," Josephina said. "One day soon, you will have to choose between them. Such a choice will clear the path for the life you will lead as a man."

"I cannot turn away from my father," Angelo said. "He has given up all he has for me."

"And will you give up all that you may one day have for him?" the old woman asked. "Would you do that for your father?"

"Yes," Angelo said.

"Then you must know," she said. "And it must come from my lips since I am the only one who holds the truth. After my death it will be buried alongside me."

"Tell me, then," Angelo said. "Please."

"You had an older brother," she said. "Back in Italy. His name was Carlo and he died when he was eight years old. About the same age as you are now."

"How did he die?" Angelo asked, removing the wet cloth from Josephina's forehead.

"He was shot," she said, the words leaving her mouth as if they were each embraced by a bubble. "Killed by a man he trusted and loved."

"What man?" Angelo asked, standing erect, bracing for the answer.

"Your father," Josephina said. "Paolino murdered his own blood to keep him away from a life with the men of the camorra."

"Men like your husband?" Angelo asked.

"Yes," Josephina said.

Angelo lowered his head and turned away from the bed. Josephina reached out, grabbed his hand and held him in place. "You must not let him know," Josephina said. "Do not show him your true face until the time is right."

"When will that be?" Angelo asked.

"When you have made your choice," Josephina said. "Until then, say and do nothing."

"He will see it in my eyes," Angelo said.

"He is a broken man," Josephina said, her head back on her pillow. "And broken men are blind to what they should see."

"Why did you tell me?"

"You must never be the man he is," Josephina said, her words spoken in softer tones. "You need to be strong where he is weak. You must stand up to your enemies and not run from them. You can never hide, Angelo. But you can always fight."

"Is that why Papa tells me to stay away from Ida?" Angelo asked, the slants of the sun bringing sparkle to his eyes.

"He fears her," Josephina said. "The Englishman, McQueen, too. But you will let them be the ones to show you the way out. Don't worry, little one. You will live to meet your destiny."

"What will happen to Papa?" Angelo asked.

"He, too, will meet his destiny," Josephina said.

Angelo walked away from the bed. He drew open the shades and stared out across the rows of tenement rooftops, his arms folded against the pain in his chest, his mind crammed with clouded images of a mother he would never know and a brother he never met.

And of a father he would one day have to confront. All of it fueled by a feeling new to his soul—hate.

• • •

TO UNDERSTAND A gangster's true motives always look to revenge. It is the engine that sustains and drives him forward, augmenting an insatiable quest for power. The thirst for revenge can be found boiling below the hard surface, coiled and waiting silently to strike. It is the calling card of all the great gangsters—the hunt for the get-even. "Revenge is something we all want," Pudge said. "But there's nothing that gives you a better taste of that than being a gangster. Who knows? Angelo would have turned to it anyway, seeing as how he didn't have all that many choices. But the day he found out about his brother, the day he learned the truth about his father, it was on that day, Angelo Vestieri became a gangster. The old woman had done the job she set out to do. She blew up the bridge connecting Angelo to his father and set him free to be one of us."

．　．　．

TWO WEEKS AFTER he had learned about his past, Angelo Vestieri was on his knees, holding Josephina's hands, his head bowed, listening as she took her final breaths. The boy fought back tears with stubborn determination, not wanting to show weakness in front of a woman who had taught him that it was a trait to be feared more than any illness.

"I am glad you are with me," Josephina said, her voice a whisper.

"I don't want you to die," Angelo said, his head still down, resting on the old woman's sunken chest.

"It is my time," Josephina said.

"I will never forget you," Angelo whispered.

"Never forget my words," Josephina said.

Angelo lifted his head and stared at Josephina and nodded.

The room was dark and still, the blinds moving to the cool breeze of a late-night wind. Angelo stayed there, holding tight to the old woman, his eyes closed, his hands gently stroking her face. Her body keeping him warm for a final time.

3

Summer, 1918

ANGELO AND PUDGE reached the top rung of the factory's rear
fire escape and looked down at the alley four stories below. A
heavy rain had soaked their pants and shirts and their palms
were brown from gripping the rusty handrails on the way up.

"As if getting here wasn't enough of a bitch," Pudge, now
fifteen and treading the road between man and boy, said,
peering into the darkness. "Going down's gonna be twice as
hard. We gotta find a way out through the front."

"Spider's in the alley," twelve-year-old Angelo said. "And
he's not going to wait long."

"We'll go from the front to the back," Pudge said. "I don't
see a big problem."

"It's not part of the plan," Angelo said, gazing into the factory through the panes of a locked window.

"The *rain* wasn't part of the plan," Pudge said. "But here it
is and now we gotta make it work for us."

"Let's get inside and do what we came to do," Angelo said
as he yanked a small lead pipe from his back pocket. "We
finish up and then figure which way out is the best."

Pudge cast his eyes down, watching sheets of rain disappear into a void. "I liked it better when you didn't talk so
much," he said, watching Angelo smash a pane of glass with a
swing of the pipe.

Angelo eased his hand past the shards of glass and un-latched the lock. "Me too," he said.

"There's gotta be over a hundred crates here," Pudge said, walking past wooden boxes packed from floor to ceiling, a lit candle in his right hand. "How are we supposed to know which ones got pocket watches in 'em?"

"Look for the ones with the blue stamps on the sides," Angelo said. He was on the other end of the massive warehouse floor, his voice echoing across the large room, his shadow a string of eerie shapes moving to the flicker of the candle. "And they'll have French words written on 'em."

"I can't read French," Pudge shouted.

"Then pull down the crates not written in English," Angelo said. "Even if they don't have watches, there should be something inside worth money."

"Now you gotta speak more than one language to pull a heist," Pudge muttered as he hoisted himself up a side of stacked crates, trying to read the labels in the dark.

The two worked the room in silence, going about their task like two trained professionals, which is what they had become in the five years they'd spent under the guidance of Angus McQueen and Ida the Goose. McQueen broke them into his ranks at a slow pace. He spent months working with both on the art of the con, giving verbal lessons deep into the night about the multitude of ways to turn an honest man's cash into a hardened one's profit. McQueen chose selected members of his *lift* team, pickpockets who prowled the financial district, to teach the boys the best way to pull a thick wallet from a well-cut pair of trousers. Once they mastered that, he let them work on midnight hijack runs, hiding them in the shadows until the signal was given to come in and help shift the stolen cargo from one packed wagon onto another.

Both Angelo and Pudge had left school after the third grade, their formal education officially replaced by the more regimented demands of daily gangster lessons. Angelo improved his reading skills by following the crime stories written up in the New York tabloids. Pudge spent his leisure time working in the Maryland, helping Ida keep the place clear of unwanted guests. "Those were their innocent years," Mary said to me, as we walked down the well-lit hospital corridor. "I know it may sound strange to say, given what they were doing and what they were being taught, but it was a good time for the both of them. Maybe their happiest time."

· · ·

ON ANGELO VESTIERI'S twelfth birthday, McQueen and Ida handed him a large box wrapped in brown paper and topped by a thick blue ribbon. Angelo took the package and held it firmly to his chest, looking up at the smiles spread across the faces of both Ida and Angus. Pudge stood behind him beaming.

"Happy birthday there, kiddo," Angus said.

"You earned this one," Ida the Goose said as she leaned down and kissed Angelo on the cheek.

"Whatever you do, don't use it on me," Pudge said, giving Angelo a playful nudge in the ribs.

Angelo lifted the ribbon from the package and rested it on the bar. He undid the wrapping paper, letting it fall to the floor. He ran his fingers across the soft surface of a red velvet box and smiled as he opened the lid. Inside was a small-caliber revolver, surrounded by a circle of a dozen bullets.

"Thank you so much," Angelo said in a voice still many miles from manhood. "I will never forget you did this for me."

Angus McQueen curled an arm around Angelo's shoulders. "Use it in the best of health," he said.

· · ·

PUDGE TOSSED THE crate to the floor and watched it crack open. Half a dozen pocket watches slid toward his feet. "Over here," he shouted, scanning the crates above his head. "They're stacked about eight deep in the corner."

"This is going to take time," Angelo said, now standing next to Pudge, watching as he stuffed the watches back into the open crate.

"All night, from the looks of it," Pudge said. "And that's even if we bring Spider up from the cart to help."

"Leave him where he is," Angelo said. "We hold to Angus's plan. No changes."

"Angus couldn't have been thinkin' we'd find us eight full crates," Pudge said. "If he was, he woulda sent out a bigger crew. The time it's gonna take to pull all these ain't worth the gamble. There's gotta be a guard *someplace* in this building and he's gonna hear us and that means he finds us."

Angelo bent down and picked up one end of a crate. "We'll deal with it when he does," he said, looking over at Pudge.

· · ·

ANGELO AND PUDGE had moved the first three of the eight crates into the back of Spider MacKenzie's cart, rain still coming down hard and cool, a touch of relief to a sweltering summer night. They walked back to the warehouse, eased past the jimmied front door, their confidence at full boil.

"This is gonna end up to be some haul," Pudge said, taking the steps two at a time. "We might even get boosted for a job like this one."

"If I remember, *you* wanted to take out only three crates," Angelo said.

"That was just a quiz, like those nuns used to give us," Pudge said. "Wanted to see how you did with some heat on."

"It looks to me like I passed," Angelo said.

"I'll let you know when we finish," Pudge said.

They were on the fourth-floor landing when they saw a shadow from a lantern on the wall. They threw themselves to the ground, their hands gripping the edges of the iron steps.

"Stay low and stay quiet," Pudge whispered. "He might just be doing his rounds."

Angelo glanced down between the landings, the light from the lantern moving back and forth as if on a swing.

"He's coming this way," Angelo said.

Pudge eased down three steps until he was next to Angelo,

close enough to smell the lingering odors of the pan-roasted onion dinner they had shared earlier. "We can break for it easy," Pudge said. "Odds are good he's old and don't give too much of a shit about his job. We leave with what we got."

"We still got five crates left to take," Angelo whispered. "And if he don't care about the job, he won't care about five more crates."

Pudge reached into the back of his waistband and pulled out a brown revolver, holding it against his chest. They waited, quiet and calm, as the guard moved up the steps, flashing his lantern into corners, seeing nothing but shadows and rats. Angelo pressed a hand against his chest, the burning pain in his lungs always kicked into higher gear by tension. He had yet to grow comfortable with confrontation and had still not mastered the calm poise that he felt he needed in order to not only survive but to thrive. He loved the planning and all the work, thought and detail that went into running a heist, but as he looked over at Pudge, primed and ready for action, he knew he was still years removed from pulling a gun and taking a life. What he lacked in the violent end of the gangster trade, however, Angelo more than made up for with a bullet-like quickness of mind. In that sense, he and Pudge were the perfect team, one prone to violence, the other quick to settle a dispute with thought.

The guard was a retired police officer fifteen years into a meager pension. He swung a wooden baton in his right hand and held the lantern in his left. His name was Seamus Connor, father to two and grandfather of three. He was unarmed and had finished half a pint of whiskey before beginning his nightly tour. He turned toward the top rung of steps, his breath heavy, whistling a childhood ballad.

Seamus froze when he saw the two boys sitting with their backs to the steps and their legs spread open, two pistols aimed straight at his chest.

"Does your wife like watches?" the younger of the two asked.

"What kind of watches are we talkin' about now?" Seamus

asked. He rested the baton on the step nearest his feet and wiped at his forehead with the flat of his free hand.

Angelo and Pudge uncocked their guns and shoved them back in their waistbands. Pudge walked down the steps toward Seamus and put a hand on the older man's shoulder.

"The kind you're gonna help us cart out of here," Pudge said.

"The wife loves those," Seamus said.

He walked past Angelo and Pudge, the lantern shoved forward and led the way to the storage area to help finish a night of plunder.

"You think there's anybody left that's not dirty?" Pudge whispered to Angelo.

"I don't know," Angelo said. "But I think the answer is no."

"And what does that tell you?" Pudge asked.

"We die rich," Angelo said.

• • •

PAOLINO VESTIERI STARED at the gun cupped in his hands. He was in Angelo's room, a compact area large enough to hold a small bed and a broken bureau, nestled toward the back of the railroad apartment the two shared. He had found the gun shoved under the bottom of a thin feather mattress. He sat on the edge of the bed, his body trembling with anger. Paolino was well past the point of shedding tears for his son. They seldom spoke, and when they did, the conversation drifted toward argument. Paolino felt overwhelmed and overmatched. The corruption that was a way of life in New York had crept into his home and stained his son and there was little he could do about it. Attacking Angelo with physical or verbal violence only served to firm the boy's resolve. Attempts to reason with him were volleys of wasted words. He was in the midst of a losing fight and it was aging him faster than the long, hard hours of work and the nights of scant sleep. Paolino Vestieri was a beaten man seeking a painless end to a futile battle.

"Put the gun back, Papa."

Paolino had not heard Angelo come in. The boy had the footsteps of a ghost, a worthy trait in his profession. Angelo stood in the entryway, his hands at his sides.

"Where did you get this?" Paolino asked quietly.

"It was a gift," Angelo said. "From a friend."

"A friend does not give a gun as a gift."

Angelo walked into the room and sat down next to his father. "This one does," he said.

"And what will you do with such a gift?"

"It will remind me," Angelo said in a near whisper.

"Of what?" Paolino's eyes searched the boy's face.

"Of what I am without it, Papa."

Paolino tossed the gun to the center of the bed. He thrust out his hands and balled them into fists. "These are all any man needs to get him through life," he said. "They will feed those who depend on him and protect those he loves. A gun can never do that."

"A gun can earn you respect," Angelo said, his eyes on his father's scarred hands.

"No, Angelo," Paolino told him. "It will only earn you an early death."

Angelo lifted his head and stared over at his father, his face a blank mask. "Like it did for my brother," he said.

The words struck Paolino like a hard blow and left him short of breath. He closed his eyes and tried to shed the image of the bullet going through Carlo's body, an image so vivid and real, he felt he could extend his hands and touch his first son's soft, bloody skin. He had fought so hard to bury such pictures from his mind, to leave them behind him as he had with so many other, less painful memories. But now, fueled by Angelo's surprising words, this one had come back from his haunted past and hurled its way vividly into his mind's eye. He could smell the smoke from the hot *lupara*, feel the heat in the small room, see the life drain from his son's angelic face. All of it arriving with a force fierce enough to shake him and send him reeling downward into a dark and empty void.

"You put a bullet into your own son," Angelo said, standing now, hovering over his father. "With your own gun. And it wasn't an act of love. It was the act of a coward."

"That moment follows me to the grave," Paolino said, struggling with the words. "It haunts me every day. There can be no forgiveness."

Angelo leaned past Paolino and grabbed the gun from the bed. He held it against his leg, one finger toying with the trigger. "I live with a father who has killed his own son," Angelo said. "Do you still need to know why I need such a gift?"

"I would never do you harm, Angelo," Paolino said. "There was a reason for my mad act against your brother. And it is not a pain I wish to ever repeat."

"You didn't want to lose him to the camorra," Angelo said. "So you lost him to a bullet."

"And now I have lost you to the Americans," Paolino said. "The price of my sin only grows stronger."

"I am sorry for that, Papa," Angelo said, sadly. "But you have not lost me. I will be there for you if there is ever the need."

"I need a son by my side," Paolino said, tears crowding his eyes. "Not a gangster."

"A son can be both," Angelo said.

"Not for me," Paolino said.

Angelo nodded and slid the gun into the back of his pants and walked out of the apartment, the sound of the door slamming behind him echoing through the empty rooms.

• • •

GANGSTERS AND THEIR fathers seldom get along. It is why, as children, they seek out other role models, neighborhood men to whom they can turn for guidance and attention. But the men they seek serve more as recruiters than as parents, their ultimate goal being to bring one more member into their ranks. Often gangsters are raised in homes without a father, the absence caused by death, prison or abandonment. When his father is around, the budding gangster will compare him to his street mentor in a contest that cannot be won. "Paolino was born scared," Pudge once told me. "He was afraid to stand up for himself in Italy and he was twice as scared over here. The one brave moment in his life came on the day he killed his son. Strange enough, that was a gangster move. The only one he ever made. And it cost him Angelo, his wife and everything else that ever meant anything to him."

•   •   •

ANGUS MCQUEEN SAW an emotional opening in Angelo Vestieri and exploited it from the day the two first met. He fed the boy's need to belong and nurtured him in ways he knew would be irresistible to one so young. McQueen was a good gangster and an expert at exploiting any perceived weakness. He knew that Angelo's silent nature represented a cry for a father figure, someone he could look up to and emulate. The boy would never get that at home. But he could easily get it from Angus McQueen.

In return, McQueen won the loyalty of a young man he had shaped and defined. There are no acts of kindness in the underworld. There are only favors done for a price and payback that is sought with a vengeance. Angelo Vestieri's gangster education was a long-term loan from Angus McQueen. A loan Angelo would one day be expected to repay.

•   •   •

THEY SAT THREE across in the front row of the crowded and smoke-filled arena, Angus comfortably in the middle, between Pudge and Angelo. It was halfway through a ten-bout semipro boxing card and the trio was already seventy-five dollars richer, thanks to Angus's can't-lose wagers.

"How come you always know who's going to win?" Pudge asked.

"I listen to my gut," Angus said with a smile. "Which is easy to do when you know the winner."

"So all the matches are rigged?" Pudge asked.

"Except for the last bout," Angus said. "That's straight-out legit. And only a fool lays his own money on that."

"Does everybody know the fights are fixed?" Angelo asked. He was looking into the ring, watching two middleweights go through their prefight routine.

"Only the ones who need to know," Angus said. "Like us."

"If they're all rigged, then where's the gamble?" Pudge asked.

"The gamble is in the *rig*," Angus said. "Just like anything else we do, before we go in we know where we stand. Never make a bet you can't win and never take a risk unless you know where it's gonna take you."

"What if you can't find out?" Angelo said, ignoring the clutching pain in his lungs caused by the clouds of cigar and cigarette smoke.

"Then make sure the papers spell your name right," Angus said. "Because you'll be a dead man before you'll ever be a rich one."

The bell rang to start the first round. The two fighters circled each other slowly, their fists up, feet firm to the ground, breath coming in snorts through the rubber mouthpieces.

"I like the short guy in the black trunks," Pudge said. "I've seen him fight once before. The guy he was up against beat on him like a rented mule, but he never went down."

"Cheer for him all you want," Angus said. "But your money's working on the tall gent with the tattoo parlor running up his arms. 'Cause that's who's gonna win."

Angelo looked around the arena, at the excited faces of the hardworking men wagering table money they couldn't afford to lose on fights whose outcome was predetermined. They were easy targets for experienced thieves as they sought simple pleasures and a few hours of relief from their sad lives. Even this rare free time was controlled by others, men who never once lost their grip on the reins of power. Angelo found himself staring at the crowd, at these men who seemed to him to be mirror images of his father, Paolino, stubborn souls who believed that the willingness to work hard would earn them the right to live well.

I heard Angelo use the phrase "sucker money" many times in our years together. To a gangster, it refers to everything from a hard-earned weekly paycheck to a bet placed on *any* event where the outcome seems to be in doubt. It is money that quickly rotates from a boss on gangster payroll to a working man and then back to the gangster. It is the sustaining blood of the underworld.

"There are only two ways to go in this life," Angelo once told me. "The sucker's way and our way. And you always have a choice as to which way you take it. Don't let anybody tell you different. You don't fall into it, and it doesn't land in your lap. I chose to be what I am. I didn't want to live in the dark and leave it to others to decide what time I got up, how much money I made or what kind of house I lived in. I picked my way and I never looked back. No regrets."

• • •

THE FIGHT ENDED in the middle of the third round, when the thin boxer with the string of tattoos landed a half-dozen soft blows to his opponent's midsection. The short fighter crumpled to the canvas, gloves flailing, eyes closed, listening as the referee counted ten.

"My mother's hit me a lot harder than that and I didn't get close to being put down," Pudge said.

"You were never told to go down," Angus said. "Now, let's go find Hawk and pick up our winnings. Then we'll take ourselves a walk."

"It's pouring out," Pudge said.

Angus stood up and stared down at the boy. "Water scare you?" he asked, his voice a bit harsh.

"Nothin' scares me," Pudge said.

"Then we'll walk," Angus said, making his way down the aisle and out of the arena.

• • •

THEY STOOD UNDER the awning of a shuttered restaurant, the rain around them beating the streets with an angry rush. Their clothes were soaked through and dripping onto the thin red carpet still lining the entrance. Angus reached into his shirt pocket and pulled out a damp sheet of paper and some tobacco and hand-rolled a cigarette. He lit the wet end and took a deep drag, swallowing most of the smoke.

"This is as good a place as any we'll find tonight," he said.

"To do what?" Pudge asked, casting a concerned glance toward Angelo, who was shivering in his thin jacket and slacks.

"To go over some business," Angus said, trying to protect the cigarette from the wind and rain. "You two been getting by pretty well with the scores I been giving out. Every job comes in clean and with a nice payoff."

"That's a good thing, right?" Pudge said, moving closer to the doorway.

"It's a very good thing," Angus said. "But now it's time to make a good thing even better."

Angelo stared at him as he finished off his cigarette and tossed the remains into a large puddle. He liked Angus McQueen and respected him as a boss. But he also knew, from his many talks with Josephina and Ida the Goose, not to grant him his total trust. So long as he and Pudge maintained their value and kept up their profit flow, they would be held in high regard. The minute they slipped, Angus would toss them aside as casually as he flipped that last cigarette.

"I'm taking over one of the downtown piers," Angus said. "Curran and Eastman are givin' up their end for a small piece of my numbers action. In return, I take my cuts from the workers' checks and whatever swag we can lift off the ships."

"Which pier?" Angelo asked, moving closer to Angus.

"It's one you know pretty well," he said. "Pier sixty-two. The one your old man works on."

"Carl Banyon runs that pier," Angelo said, remembering the name as easily as he remembered the cut above his eye. "You going to keep him on?"

"That's up to you two," Angus said. "Your job is to watch that pier. Make sure the money's flowing in the direction it should be, meaning toward me. Pick up the collection from the workers on payday and bring it down to me at the Maryland."

"My father's, too?"

"Why should I cut him any favors? He's nothing to me. You want to take it out of your end, then that's your business. So long as the cash in my hand is the cash I'm expecting, you'll get no beef."

"When do we start?" Pudge asked.

Angus pulled his pocket watch from his vest and peered down at it in the darkness. "The pier opens in about three hours. Make sure both of you are there. It don't look good if the boss is late on the first day." He put the watch back in its slot and lifted the collar of his tweed coat. "You get any trouble, I'm expectin' you to handle it," he said. "You might still be boys to those that look at you. But you're *my* boys, and that should give you all the edge you'll need."

Angus turned and walked back into the storm, leaving Angelo and Pudge standing under the awning, watching him disappear.

"Looks like we got ourselves a pier to play with," Pudge said.

Angelo looked straight ahead and nodded, his right hand inside the side pocket of his jacket, his fingers wrapped around the hard barrel of a revolver.

• • •

CARL BANYON STOOD in the center of a circle of forty men, a thick wad of chewing tobacco rammed inside the corner of his mouth. The doors to the pier behind them were closed and padlocked. An extra-tonnage cargo ship, *The Tunisia*, was docked by the side, waiting to be loaded with crates of fresh-cut lumber and sent on its way.

"Angus McQueen's taken over this pier," Banyon said to the men. "That don't mean a damn thing to me and it sure as shit don't mean much to any of you. You still wanna work, you still gotta pay. And the person you pay is always gonna be me."

Banyon saw the men's eyes shift away from him and over his shoulder. He turned and saw Angelo and Pudge, dressed in clean dry clothes, walk around scattered puddles and toward the circle. The rain had turned to early morning mist, the heat causing thin lines of steam to rise from the hard ground.

Angelo looked at Banyon and smiled when he saw a hint of recognition in his face. He gave a quick glance to the other men in the circle and stopped when he saw his father, Paolino, standing among them. Pudge was the first to reach the group, his hands inside his pants pockets, a slight smile on his face.

"If you're lookin' for your school, it's up the other street," Banyon said, easing his way into the front of the group, facing down Pudge, spitting a stream of tobacco juice into a puddle inches from his feet.

"McQueen sent us," Pudge said, loud enough for all to hear.

"What's the limey been doing?" Banyon shouted with half a laugh. "Liftin' his crew outta cribs?" He leaned over, poised to spit another line of tobacco, this one aimed even closer to Pudge.

"That's a bad habit to have," Pudge said, opening his jacket to show the gun jammed in his waistband.

Banyon looked first at the gun, then in the boy's eyes. He had been around long enough to know when intentions were real. Whatever fear, if any, Pudge Nichols had was buried deep inside a harsh exterior and far from any man's gaze. Banyon swallowed and took a step back.

"Nothing changes," Angelo said. "Instead of paying you every week, they pay us."

"Is that how McQueen wants it?" Banyon said, walking over to Angelo, his temper at idle, his hands balled into fists of frustration.

"It's how we want it," Angelo said, running a hand over the scar above his eye.

"I ran this pier for almost ten years," Banyon said, a degree of resignation in his voice. "And I ran it good, too. My crews always sent the ships out on time."

"You ran it with your mouth," Angelo said with disdain, looking past Banyon and catching his father's hard gaze. "You just sat back and watched other men sweat out the work. But even that wasn't enough for you."

"I can run it for you the same way," Banyon said, looking from Angelo to Pudge, sweat running down the sides of his face. "Or any other way you like."

"I don't think so," Pudge said, the fingers of his right hand wrapped around the gun barrel jutting out from his pants pocket.

"You work the hole," Angelo said, stepping up closer to Banyon. "With the rest of the men."

"You can't put me in with the dagos," Banyon said, lowering his voice, his eyes shifting from Angelo's face to the hand on Pudge's gun. "They hate my guts. They'll leave me for dead the first chance they get."

"So will we," Angelo said in a harsh and distant voice that lifted him past his tender age.

"Where do you keep the key to the doors?" Pudge asked Banyon.

"In my pocket," Banyon said, patting his shirt softly, the arrogance floating out of his body.

"Then you better open them and let the men get to work," Angelo said. "And you either lead them in or deal with us out here."

"Whichever way you go, make it quick," Pudge said. "That ship needs to be loaded and my guess is it ain't gonna do it alone."

Angelo and Pudge stood their ground and stared hard at a defeated Banyon. The dwarfed dock boss took in a deep breath, wiped the sweat from his face, nodded and turned away, leading the workers toward the pier doors and a full day of work. They followed in a tight group, eager to extract their revenge for a decade's worth of torment.

All except for Paolino, who stood in his place and stared at his son.

"Anything wrong, Papa?" Angelo asked.

"You take money from me now, too?" Paolino asked. "Just like all the rest."

"You can keep your salary, Papa," Angelo said, his voice returning to its normal tones. "Your payoff's covered."

"Covered by who?" Paolino asked. "You?"

"Yes," Angelo said. "By me."

Paolino reached into his pants pocket and pulled out two crumpled dollar bills. He tossed them into a puddle by Angelo's feet.

"I pay my dirty money now!" Paolino said, his voice filled with rage and hatred. "And I pay it to you! My son!"

Paolino turned and walked away from Pudge and Angelo, his head down, his eyes filled with tears.

"I still think we should have tossed Banyon in the drink," Pudge said, turning his back to Paolino and the pier. "Let the rats have their way."

"He belongs to the workers," Angelo said. "They'll do a better job than the rats. Believe me, Banyon won't live long enough to earn a week's salary."

"And what about your pop?" Pudge asked.

Angelo looked at Pudge and shrugged. "He's happy when he's working," he said. "It's what he wants and it's what he'll get."

Angelo clutched his stomach, turned and started a fast walk away from the pier. Pudge, surprised by the sudden move, ran after him.

"Where are you going?" he asked.

"I need to find a place where nobody can see me," Angelo said.

"See you do what?"

"Throw up," Angelo said.

4

Summer, 1923

IT WAS A busy time.

Twenty-four-year-old bond salesman Juan Terry Trippe quit his job to join his friend John Hambleton to start a plane taxi service called Pan American World Airways. The nation's first supermarket opened in San Francisco and Frank C. Mars, a Minnesota candy maker, earned $72,800 in less than a year, with a new bar he called the Milky Way. *Time* published its first issue and more than thirteen million automobiles clogged the roadways. Adolf Hitler and Benito Mussolini began their push to power in Europe. Stateside, workers and executives forked over larger chunks of their money to the government in the form of a federal income tax, led by John D. Rockefeller Jr. who paid $7.4 million under the existing rates.

And in New York City, the gangsters got richer.

It was a period of expansion and upheaval and it all helped to serve the gangster interest. No one law did more for their personal gain than what was first called the Prohibition Enforcement Act and later the Volstead Act, which made the sale of alcoholic beverages anywhere in the United States a crime. The law, which passed on October 20, 1920, served as the midwife to the birth of twentieth-century organized crime. It opened wide the vault and gave the enterprising gangster free reign in dozens of untapped markets, including trucking, distribution and nightclubs—all of which served the public's desire for a nickel glass of beer.

Wherever the opportunity for making money existed, the gangster was quick to marshal his resources.

When race riots erupted across twenty-six cities in 1919, sending urban blacks scurrying deeper into the pockets of poverty, Angus McQueen and his ilk were ready to cash in. They tripled the number of betting parlors in the poorer neighborhoods, charging only a penny a wager on the number of the day. Soon, the gangs were hauling in profits of over ten thousand dollars a week in what was referred to on the streets as "the nigger numbers."

The circuslike trial of Nicola Sacco and Bartolomeo Vanzetti, arrested for a Massachusetts payroll robbery and murder, convinced a silent minority of Italian-Americans that justice could never be had in their adoptive homeland, making them more than receptive to the recruitment overtures of Italian gangsters. In addition to those willing workers, there were 3.5 million more Americans without jobs and, with twenty thousand businesses failing each year, the prospects would only grow higher. The gangsters were again quick to capitalize on such an availability of cheap labor, offering tax-free solid wages in return for a pulled gun or a late-night heist.

In 1922, the *New York Daily Mirror* began publication and, along with the still-infant *New York Daily News* and a cluster of other tabloids, devoted full, detailed coverage to the better-known hoodlums, turning many of them into recognizable names and faces, helping to fuel the public image of the gangster as celebrity.

"I can't think of any other time in history where it would have been better for us to get our start," Pudge once told me. "It was almost as if the people wanted us to come in, set up shop and take over the place. Anywhere you turned, things broke our way. Prohibition, the Depression, the trouble over in Europe, what have you. You name it and we figured a way to turn misery into money. We went to bed poor and we woke up rich. In those times, nobody could make something like that happen faster than a hood."

•   •   •

ANGELO VESTIERI AND Pudge Nichols strolled side by side down a West Side street, each munching on a roast beef sandwich.

"You want to get some coffee first?" Pudge asked. "We got time."

Angelo shook his head no. "Let's get it over with," he said.

Angelo, now seventeen, had grown tall and angular during his years working for Angus McQueen. His tan face was highlighted by a pair of dark, fiery eyes and ivory cheekbones; his thick hair was combed straight back, twin curls always hanging off his forehead. He seldom smiled and buried his alert nature behind a well-honed cloak of indifference. He wore his shirts and sweaters several sizes larger, hoping to disguise a slender frame. While it allowed him to appear bulkier, the habit gave him a perpetually disheveled look.

Pudge, at twenty, still had a boyish face. He was quick to smile and easy to irritate, and the freckles that once dotted his cheeks had given way to the shaving stubble of a man. His upper body was rock hard, with Popeye forearms and biceps that had earned him his fair share of arm wrestling victories. He favored thick sweaters or thin T-shirts, depending on the day's weather, and his curly blond hair was always windtossed. He walked with the confident strides of the street thug—chest tilted back, arms locked and bent at the elbow, each step taken with attitude and purpose.

"What do you know about this guy?" Angelo asked, tossing the last bite of sandwich into his mouth.

"Just what Angus told me," Pudge said. "Plus a little I picked up on the street. His name's Gavin Rainey, but he answers to Gapper, at least down at the piers he does. Word is he's as ugly as he is nasty."

"I heard that name before," Angelo said. "He's got a small crew working over by the tunnels."

"One and the same," Pudge said. "They pull small-time stuff for the most part. Vendor shakedowns, low-end lifts, two-percent street vig, that kinda action."

"Breaking into one of our clubs doesn't fall under that," Angelo said.

"You go to all the trouble of breaking into a joint, you'd think they would come away with a bigger haul," Pudge said, crossing the street against the oncoming traffic, pulling Angelo along with him.

"What did they leave with?"

"Five hundred in cash and some coats and jackets," Pudge said with a dismissive shrug. "On top of that, they did a number on the bar. I think that pissed off Angus more than the break-in."

"The club's only been open for three weeks," Angelo said. "And business has been slow to come in."

"Probably why the fool picked it. He went in expecting a small haul, figuring we'd just shrug it off."

Angelo came to a stop and turned to face Pudge. "He figured wrong," Angelo said.

•   •   •

ONE HOUR LATER the dark Ford sedan pulled up curbside with Spider MacKenzie behind the wheel. He looked over at Angelo and Pudge, picked up his fedora and got out of the car.

"What'd you do, stop off in Jersey for a steak?" Pudge asked, irritated over the wait.

"Traffic," MacKenzie said.

Timothy "Spider" MacKenzie was in his late twenties, well-groomed, well-mannered and fiercely devoted to Angus McQueen. He never spoke unless it was absolutely necessary, treating the utterance of each word as if it were hard labor. He had been with McQueen since the early Gopher days, graduating from street runner to bodyguard and driver in less than a decade. He was also the gang's chief enforcer, using club, brass knuckles or gun to silence any victim.

"You figure on him being up there alone?" Pudge asked.

"He's a heavy boozer," Spider explained. "I expect he's just sleepin' one off."

Angelo started toward the tenement across the avenue. "It doesn't matter if he's alone or with a crowd, we still have to go in."

Pudge watched Angelo walk away. They had grown inseparable in the years since Ida the Goose had forged their alliance. In that time, Angelo had listened and learned well the lessons taught by those preparing him for a gangster's life. He already possessed many of the attributes needed for success—he was fearless, never shied away from a duty and was prepared for even the best plan to go awry. He had an eagerness for battle matched only by a reluctance to use force. Angelo had an innate ability to turn a foe into a friend with a well-timed phrase or a fair cut of a new deal. It was that trait, more than any other, that would enable him to survive longer than most gangsters. Pudge was always quick to pull a trigger. But Angelo knew, in the long run, that was the wrong approach. A gangster's survival depended not on the destruction of his enemies but on the strength of his allies. The ability to keep a business partnership thriving was what ultimately kept a successful gangster alive. In that, Angelo Vestieri needed lessons from no one.

•   •   •

GAVIN RAINEY SAT upright in a hard-back wooden chair and waited to die.

He was a tall man with thin strands of hair across a freckled face. Beads of sweat broke from his head and ran into his eyes. He looked decades younger than Angelo and Pudge had imagined he would and nowhere near as vicious as his street reputation. The hard-guy demeanor deserted him the minute he saw the three men enter the foyer of his cold-water walk-up. Without a word, Spider MacKenzie grabbed Rainey with both hands, dragged him up two flights of stairs and tossed him inside his well-furnished, two-bedroom apartment.

"You can pull me outta this one," Rainey pleaded. "Alls you need do is cover my owe-back to McQueen."

"It's not so much what you took and what you did," Pudge said. "It's how it looks to have you get away with it."

Spider MacKenzie pulled a revolver from inside his jacket, walked over and shoved the barrel against Rainey's temple. He cocked the trigger and looked up at Angelo and Pudge for a signal.

"I'll give McQueen half my weekly haul," Rainey said, the sweat pouring down now in thin streams. "To make it up to him, so he don't lose face."

"How much is your haul?" Angelo asked.

"I clear about seven hundred a week. That's after I pay off my crew."

"If you bring McQueen that seven hundred a week, you'll make it through the day without a bullet in your head," Angelo said.

"*All* of it?" Rainey asked, looking over at Angelo. "I'm not about to give up my whole take."

"Guy's got a gun to his head and he's still lookin' to work out a deal." Pudge shook his head. "You gotta admire the balls."

"Angus said to take him out," Spider said, pushing the gun against the Gapper's temple. "Not to make him a partner."

"You can't make a profit off the dead," Angelo answered. He was standing at the far end of the room, hands inside his pants pocket, his back to an open window, staring at Gapper. "Can you?"

Gapper swallowed hard, blinking his eyes to break the beads of sweat off his lids. "That leaves me with zero," Rainey said, looking up at MacKenzie and seeing eyes eager to pull a trigger.

"It also leaves you alive," Angelo told him.

"And you don't hit any more of our spots," Pudge added. "Go and make your money off somebody else's nickel."

"McQueen's not gonna like this," Spider said, looking at both Angelo and Pudge.

"He's going to like it plenty when he starts counting that money every week," Angelo said.

"So, what's it gonna be?" Pudge asked Rainey. "Are we in business or do I need to have flowers delivered to the undertaker?"

Rainey closed his eyes and took in a deep breath. His shirt was stained through with sweat and his thick hair was matted down against his forehead. He opened his eyes and nodded. "You guys ain't nothin' but a bunch of crooks," he said. "I just want you to know that."

"Thank you," Angelo said.

• • •

IDA THE GOOSE stood behind the bar of the Café Maryland, filling a whiskey glass to the rim and lighting a smoke. She looked at Angelo, sitting across from her, eating a thick slice of cherry pie. "You want some coffee with that?" she asked.

"Some milk, maybe," Angelo said, the side of his mouth stuffed with remnants of pie.

Ida leaned under the counter and pulled out a half-filled milk bottle from the ice box with one hand and an empty glass with the other. She poured the contents of the bottle into the glass and slid it across to Angelo.

"Every gangster I know starts off drinking milk because he likes it," she said, smiling and pointing to the glass. "Then, when they get older, they drink it because they have no choice."

"Why's that?" Angelo asked.

"Stomach problems," Ida said. "Comes from years of keeping everything bottled up inside, never showing what you really feel, acting like we're not scared at all. When the truth is all we want to do is run and hide under a safe spot until the shooting's all done."

"Angus says you can always spot a gangster who did jail

time," Angelo said. "He has a glass of milk with his meals and his drinks. Hides the ulcer he got doing the stretch."

"It ain't the healthiest line of work around, that's for damn sure," Ida said. "Which is why I think it's time for me to get out."

"And do what?" Angelo said, stunned. "This place and the people in it is what you know. What you care about. Me included."

"You have to have a feel for this business," Ida said. "You have to sense when the time's right to get in and when it's best to yank up stakes. That time for me is now."

"What will you do?" Angelo asked.

"I made a lot of money working in here." She looked over the Café with an owner's pride. "And I managed to save a lot of it. Now's as good a time as any to put the money to some use."

"You know, I don't even have a picture of my mother," Angelo said. "It was like she was never even alive. Josephina helped with that a little, but she died while I was still a kid. You're as much a mother to me as anybody."

Ida the Goose stared down at her glass of scotch and smiled. "I can still be that for you," she said in a near-whisper. "Only it won't be out of here. Be out in the country somewhere, in a place where you can take a deep breath and not spit out smoke."

"You have a place picked out already?" Angelo asked.

Ida looked up and nodded. "Roscoe, New York," she said. "About a hundred and fifty miles from here. My grandfather died a couple of years back, left me a small house and five acres of trees. All I need to do is buy a car, some furniture and throw the rest of my cash in a local bank."

"What about the Café?" Angelo said. "You gonna sell it or shut it down?"

"Neither one," Ida said. "I'm giving it to you and Pudge to run. As long as the business holds up, she's good for a clear two hundred a week. Send about fifty of that up my way and keep the rest for yourselves."

"We don't know anything about running a place," Angelo said.

"Then you'll learn," Ida said. "Or you go out and hire somebody who does know and you make sure he doesn't steal more than his share from out of the till."

"When do you go?" he asked, watching her take his empty glass and plate and drop it in the slop sink.

"In about a month," she said. "Maybe a little less than that. I don't have all that much to pack and I just said good-bye to one of the only three that matter to me."

"I didn't know that was a good-bye I just heard," Angelo said.

Ida the Goose cupped one hand around Angelo's face and stared into his eyes. "I did my best for you," she said. "I told you close to all I know about the business you're gonna be in and what I forgot wouldn't be of much help to you anyway. From here on out it's up to you and Pudge, and you got no breathing room for mistakes."

Angelo held Ida's hand close to his face. He turned and kissed her palm, then stood up to leave. "Thank you," he said in a low voice.

"For what?" Ida said with a shrug and a sad smile. "For helping turn you into a gangster? If you're as smart as I think, you'll end up hating me for it one day."

"That's a day that'll never come," Angelo said as he turned and walked out of the Café. Ida the Goose poured herself a fresh scotch and watched him go.

• • •

ANGELO SAT AT the head of the small kitchen table, dabbing the edge of a thick slice of Italian bread into a bowl of lentils and sausage. His elbow brushed against a jelly jar filled with red wine made by a neighborhood priest. He looked up when his father walked into the room, holding a weathered brown valise in his right hand, a thin blue jacket draped over his left arm. Paolino dropped the valise to the wooden floor.

"I am leaving," he said to his son. "For good. There is no need for us to keep living our lives in this way."

"It must be something in the air," Angelo said. "Everybody's looking to get out of town."

"This is no joke. I am leaving and never coming back."

Angelo took a long sip of the wine and nodded. "Do you want me to stop you or go with you?" he asked.

"Not one or the other," Paolino said. "You are not a part of me anymore. You belong to them now. The ones who have taught you so well how to hate."

"They taught me what I needed to learn," Angelo said.

"You did not need to learn to steal," Paolino said, "or take money that others worked to earn, force them to pay money they do not have. You are in the company of criminals now and it is where you belong."

"And where would you want me to belong, Papa?" Angelo asked, pushing his chair back from the edge of the table. "With you?"

"That was once my greatest wish," Paolino said. "But it, too, has disappeared, along with all my other dreams."

"And what is left, Papa?"

"Only what you see before you," Paolino said. "And that is not a place for my son to be. Gangster or not."

Paolino stared at his son through the eyes of a defeated man. He picked up his valise, turned and opened the apartment door. Angelo moved away from the table, the wine jar in his hand, and watched his father walk out of his life. Angelo looked away and leaned against the side of the open kitchen window. His eyes scanned backyard alleys, tar rooftops and clotheslines weighed down with fresh-washed sheets. He put a hand up to his face and let the tears flow through his fingers, his body heaving with the pain he had taught himself so well to hide.

"Adio, Papa," Angelo whispered. *"Adio."*

5

Spring, 1924

ANGELO VESTIERI SHIFTED the gears on his new Chrysler motorcar, smiling as the high-compression engine moved with factory-efficient ease from one cylinder to another. Pudge Nichols sat next to him in the passenger seat, scanning the front-page stories in the morning paper.

"You believe what this guy's trying to pull?" Pudge asked, folding the paper and tossing it onto the backseat, a look of disgust on his face.

"Who are you talking about now?" Angelo made a sharp right turn onto Broadway from Twenty-third Street, his left foot riding the pedal of the newly designed, four-wheel hydraulic system.

"This Marcus Garvey," Pudge said. "He wants all the colored people to move out of America."

"And go where?" Angelo asked, turning to look at Pudge.

"Lybia . . . Liberia," Pudge shrugged. "Who the hell knows?"

"That's in Africa," Angelo said, his attention back on the crawling traffic. "He wants to have his people move back to Africa."

"And do what? They think there's gonna be more work for them over there than there is over here? You gotta be six drafts into a keg to think that."

"It doesn't sound like that crazy of an idea to me," Angelo

said. "The coloreds haven't exactly been given an easy go of it over here, so maybe a fresh start would be worth a shot."

"Angus would love to hear that kind of news," Pudge laughed. "He's been getting rich off those nigger numbers. If that well went dry, he'd piss blood."

"He would just figure a way to make even more money off somebody else," Angelo said. "It's what he does."

"How come you agreed to the meeting with Jack Wells?" Pudge asked. "He knows we work for McQueen and we haven't been making any noise about going somewhere else."

"He's a smart businessman and a patient one," Angelo explained. "He knows that sooner or later, we're both going to be looking to move up. Maybe he's thinking it's sooner."

"I don't see how us running bootleg for Wells is going to put any more in our pockets than the cut of the action we already get from Angus. And we know we can *trust* Angus."

"Let's listen to what he has to say," Angelo said. "He might be planning to make a move on Angus and he may not think he can do that without the two of us on his side."

"Who's gonna be with him at the meeting?"

Angelo reached into his vest pocket and pulled out a small notebook. He handed it to Pudge, who flipped it open. He read through three red lights and then looked up.

"How bad?" Angelo asked.

"Nothing we can't handle in a squeeze," Pudge said. "Larry Carney's a little bit of a wacko, but he's a solid triggerman. This other guy, McCain, his job is to cover Wells at all times, even take a bullet if he has to, just to keep the boss alive."

"What about Popke?" Angelo asked. "How good is he?"

"Popke likes to be called Big John the Polack," Pudge said. "That alone should tell you how full his cabinet drawers are. But none of them'll say a word to us, unless things go foul. It's not their place or their job to talk."

"And we only talk to Wells," Angelo said. "Let's do it the way Angus taught us. As far as we're concerned, he's the only face in the room."

"Ida always says everything's in the eyes," Pudge said. "We'll know which way he's thinking and which way he's going just by the way his eyes move."

"What if he's not thinking of making us partners?" Angelo said, stopping the car and looking across at Pudge. "What if he's planning to kill us? What do we do then?"

Pudge pointed over Angelo's shoulder to a restaurant and smiled. "It's a little late to be asking that of me now, Ang," he said, "seeing as how we're already here."

• • •

GANGSTERS LIVE FOR the action. The closer to death, the nearer to the heated coil of the moment, the more alive they feel. Most would rather succumb to a barrage of bullets from a roomful of sworn enemies than to the debilitation of old age, dying the death of the feeble. A gangster becomes as addicted to the thrill of battle and the potential to die in the midst of it as he does to the more attractive lures in his path. In his world, the potential for death exists every day. The better gangsters don't shy away from such a dreaded possibility but rather find comfort in its proximity.

"You're born waiting for the bullet," Pudge would say to me. "So when it does come, that second before it hits is not a surprise. You can't survive, let alone be any good in this racket, if the idea of getting killed makes you nervous. You need that extra edge going into the room. The guns on the other end will be looking out for that fear. If they don't see it, they hesitate and maybe that gives you the couple of seconds you need to make it out of there alive. I tell you, kid, if you want to make a killing in this business, you can't ever be afraid to die."

• • •

ANGELO AND PUDGE walked toward the restaurant, their heads up, their manner casual and relaxed. They were a two-man team working as one. They had learned to feed off each other's strengths and hide their weaknesses from all other eyes. Angelo was quiet force where Pudge was all fire. Pudge was a hitter, walking into any situation and expecting nothing less than a showdown and a shoot-out. Angelo would balance his friend's attack mode with a thoughtful sense of diplomacy, looking to convert yet another believer to their side. Their unique style had garnered attention from rival gangs and earned them the respect of a number of underworld bosses. As with any corporate structure, even one as primitive as 1920s organized crime, young talent was always in demand.

So it was as no surprise to either Angelo or Pudge when the call came from Danny Fanelli, a Jack Wells bodyguard, asking them to join their boss for an informal meeting. Wells was a short-tempered and ill-mannered thug who had motored swiftly through the criminal ranks. He held the butcher's cut of all the action coming into and out of the Bronx and was looking with hungry eyes to expand into the other four boroughs, Manhattan in particular. He craved a chance at the nightclub and speakeasy money that Manhattan generated. But making a move into the most sophisticated borough meant taking on Angus McQueen, and Wells was savvy enough to know a blood war would be inevitable as well as risky. For two decades, McQueen had held on to his turf, beating back every threat and challenge. In order to take him down or at least cripple his power base, Wells looked to plant doubt into McQueen's troops, make them think there was a dent in their boss's thick shield. The first step to achieving that goal was to secure Angelo Vestieri and Pudge Nichols to his side.

. . .

"HELLO, MR. WELLS." Angelo stretched across the dark booth in the rear of the empty restaurant to shake hands. "Thanks for asking us to come around."

"Call me Jack." Wells tightened his grip around Angelo's hand.

"Business must not be so good," Pudge said, gazing around

at the empty tables. He glanced at the two gunmen still standing by the front door and the two others behind him, sitting in the corner, sipping coffee. "I hope you don't have a piece of the action."

"Why don't you boys relax," Wells said. "Maybe have a little something to eat."

"What's good here?" Pudge slid into the booth next to Angelo and across from Wells.

"The apple pie's top-shelf," Wells said. "And the milk's farm fresh. It comes from a place I own up in the northeast Bronx."

"I'll try it," Pudge said. "And a glass of milk with a scotch on the side."

Wells nodded, his narrow eyes focusing on Pudge before they moved slowly over to Angelo. "How about you, kid?" he asked. "You want to give the pie a shot?"

"I'm not here to eat, Mr. Wells." Angelo watched one of the men from the back lift the glass lid off the top of an apple pie platter, cut a thick slice and scoop it onto a plate, then walk the plate to the booth, sliding it across the counter to Pudge. "And I'm not much of a talker either. So why don't you tell us what you want us to hear?"

Wells turned to one of the two goons at the back table and pointed down to his empty cup. He waited while one of them ambled over and gave him a hot refill. Wells lifted the cup, took two long gulps, then turned his attention back to Angelo and Pudge.

"I'm gonna make a move on McQueen," Wells said. "By the time I'm through, I'll be holding all his action."

"Why are you telling us?" Angelo asked, his voice free of any emotion.

"I want you both to leave McQueen and come work for me," Wells said. "I'll pay you more and give you each a bigger cut from the clubs. When your boss goes down, you boys will have to work for somebody. Why can't that somebody be me?"

"Angus hasn't given us any reason to leave," Pudge said. "Least none that I ever saw."

Wells smiled and nodded. "You're loyal to him," he said. "I respect that. It goes a long way with a guy like me."

"But you still want us to leave him and join up with you," Angelo said. "Loyal or not."

"Loyal doesn't mean stupid. You have to be smart enough to know when it's the right time to make your move. I'm here to tell you that time is now."

"Thank you for your offer, Mr. Wells," Angelo said.

"Forget the thank you. What's your answer?"

"No." Angelo's face was a barren mask.

"That's a big mistake, kid," Wells said. "Things'll only end bad for you if you leave this meeting and you're not on my side."

"Then things will end bad." Angelo kept his hands folded in front of him.

"What about you?" Wells asked Pudge, tapping him on the arm.

"We came in together," Pudge said, standing. "We go out together."

"That's it, then," Wells said, watching Angelo ease out of the booth and adjust his jacket. "The meeting's over. There's nothing more for us to talk about."

"There are two things you should know," Pudge said, standing over Wells.

"And that's what?" Wells asked, his manner now reduced to a low-boil anger.

"I never did get my drink," Pudge said. "And your apple pie stinks."

Angelo and Pudge walked out of the quiet restaurant, their backs to Wells and his four gunmen.

Behind them, an angry Jack Wells stared down at his empty coffee cup, his two hands balled into fists, violently punching the sides of his red-leather booth.

. . .

ANGELO WAS WALKING across Third Avenue, ignoring the up-town traffic and a light, misty rain, when he first saw Isabella Conforti. She was standing in a doorway next to an open-air fruit stand, an Italian language newspaper folded over her head. She wore a checkered red dress, a handwoven blue sweater and two-inch wood clogs. Her long brown hair only partially obscured a push-button nose, charcoal eyes and a magical smile. She scanned the street, her right foot tapping impatiently against the edge of the concrete entryway.

Angelo stopped in front of the fruit stand, selected two fresh peaches and handed them to the vendor. He watched as the small, muscular young man in a long-sleeved white shirt wrapped the peaches inside a single sheet of newspaper. Angelo handed him a five-dollar bill.

"The change is yours to keep," Angelo said, "*if* you can tell me the name of the girl waiting in the doorway."

The vendor held the five in his right hand and turned to look at the tenement. He came back to Angelo and smiled. "Isabella," he said, sliding the bill into the front pocket of his work pants.

"Do you know her family?" Angelo asked.

"You only asked for her name," the vendor said.

Angelo stepped up closer. "And now I'm asking about her family."

"Her father is a *macellaio*," the vendor said, lowering his head and voice. "You know, how do you say it in English?"

"A butcher," Angelo said.

"That's it, butcher," the vendor said, snapping his fingers and smiling. "He works downtown in the place where they kill the animals."

"What about her mother?" Angelo asked.

"She died, maybe five years ago," the vendor said. "She was sick for a very long time."

"She have anybody else?" Angelo took the peaches from the vendor.

"A brother," the vendor said. "Three, maybe four years younger. Nice boy and a hard worker. I use him sometimes to help clean up the store. Now you know all that I know and you have your peaches."

"What's your name?" Angelo asked, putting out his hand.

"Franco," the vendor said, meeting Angelo's firm grip with one of his own. "Franco Rasti."

"Thank you, Franco," Angelo said. He looked at the wet and gleaming racks of fruits and vegetables. "You have a good business here. I will buy from you again."

"Two peaches for five dollars," Franco said with a wide grin. "At those prices, I will bring the fruit to you."

• • •

"WOULD YOU LIKE a peach, Isabella?" Angelo stood in front of her, the rain getting stronger, slapping at his back and shoulders.

"How do you know my name?" she asked in a voice soft as a cloud.

Up close, Isabella's beauty was even more striking and the look of suspicion etched across her face only added to its allure.

"I paid Franco five dollars for these peaches," Angelo said, ignoring the question. "Have you ever eaten a fruit which cost so much?"

"No." She watched Angelo undo the newspaper wrapping and hand her a peach. "That's because I have never met a man stupid enough to pay such a price."

Angelo smiled as Isabella took the peach from his hand. "The stupid man is the one who keeps you waiting in the rain," he said.

"My father would not like a stranger calling him stupid," Isabella said. "Especially a young stranger who pays so much money for fruit."

"And he would be right," Angelo said. "I apologize. To you and to your father."

Isabella smiled and tilted her head to one side. "It would be easier for me to accept an apology if I knew who it was from."

"The wet fool before you is Angelo Vestieri," he said.

The rain was coming down now in hard sheets, soaking through the back of Angelo's jacket and pants. He lowered his head against its force, but kept his eyes locked on Isabella. He watched as she split the peach in half and pulled the pit from the core. They both smiled when she took a small bite, a pearl of juice hanging off her lower lip.

"And why are you here, Angelo Vestieri?" she asked, her early caution wiped away by the rain and Angelo's warmth.

"I love the rain," Angelo told her. "And I hate for a good piece of fruit to go to waste."

"But when the rain stops and you have eaten your fruit, what will you do then?" Isabella's face gleamed from the splashes of water bouncing off her cheeks and neck and Angelo thought her bright smile could melt a demon's heart.

"I will still be hungry. So I will go and look for a place to eat."

"Why not at home with your family?" Isabella bit off another chunk of the peach.

"I like to eat alone," Angelo said. "In quiet restaurants."

"My father and I are going to my aunt Nunzia's for dinner," Isabella said. "You can come with us if you like."

"I would need to ask your father for permission."

"That's a good idea." Isabella finished the last of the peach and broke out into a schoolgirl's laugh. "That way, you'll have something to say when my stupid father sees you and asks why a young man is standing in the rain talking to his daughter."

"Where is he now?" Angelo asked, the cold wetness seeping through his jacket and shirt onto his skin.

"Right behind you," Isabella said, pointing a finger past Angelo's shoulder.

Angelo turned and faced a middle-aged man about his height, but carrying a hundred pounds more in weight and muscle. He was wearing a black striped shirt, its front turned dark by the rain, and a white bloodstained butcher's smock. Angelo offered him the remaining peach.

"You won't believe what I paid for it," Angelo said.

"Was it worth it?" Giovanni Conforti asked, taking the piece of fruit.

"Every penny," Angelo said.

6

Fall, 1925

THE OVERWEIGHT MAN in the soiled white shirt sat with his back pressed against the thick pillows of the cigar-colored couch. The room was small and sparsely furnished, littered with the remains of half-eaten meals and empty pints of back-door whiskey. Angelo, his hands inside his pants pockets, looked out the open window and stared down at a young couple walking into Charley Sutton's East Side restaurant. Pudge was across the room, his fists resting on his hips, standing directly over the overweight man.

"I was gonna bring you the money," Ralph Barcelli said, his voice a series of heavy rasps. "You know, save you guys a trip over here."

Barcelli was a forty-year-old low-level drug dealer and numbers runner. He earned just enough to feed his hunger for whiskey, horses and underage girls. What he couldn't earn he borrowed at exorbitant street rates, putting himself forever behind the financial eight ball.

"But you didn't," Pudge said. "You made us come and get it."

"I had to go and make a run for Tony Faso," Ralph said, a slight trembling of his lower lip betraying his fear. "If it weren't for that bit of business, I would have done like I said. But I couldn't be in two spots at the same time. You understand my position, right?"

"I don't care where you went before we got here and I don't care where you're going after we leave," Pudge said. "What I care about is seeing the money you owe me *while* I'm here."

"You got no worries on that count," Ralph said, scratching at a patch of gray-tinged stubble. "I got it all wrapped up for you, you know, like a birthday present. It's in the little room in the back."

Angelo looked away from the window. "I'll get it," he said, walking with his head down into the narrow corridor.

"You need for me to do anything, just ask," Ralph said. He was blinking nervously as his sleepy brown eyes followed Angelo, bubbles of perspiration forming in circular patterns on top of his bald head.

"Sit there and shut up ought to cover your end," Pudge said.

• • •

ANGELO OPENED THE door leading into the small back room and took a step back, thrown by the stench of dry urine and the sight of a young girl curled up under a soiled white sheet. Resting next to her, in a corner of the rumpled bed, was a shoe box with a nylon cord tied around it. Streaks of sunlight filtered in on long strings of dust lines through the glass of a closed window, its grimy shade rolled to the top.

Angelo walked into the room, stepped over to the bed and removed the sheet, tossing it to the floor. The girl didn't flinch. She was naked except for a cream-colored blouse covering her rail-thin upper body. She stared up at him with eyes that were as clear as they were distant.

"What's your name?" Angelo asked.

"Lisa," the girl said in a fuller voice than the one he expected.

Angelo placed her at somewhere between fourteen and seventeen, the clear-skinned, soft-glazed brilliance of her years chewed up during the time she spent in the sour embrace of Ralph Barcelli. She was bone-frail, her long brown hair hanging over her shoulders like thin strands of straw. Her sunken cheeks were ash-white.

"How old are you, Lisa?" Angelo asked, briefly distracted by the two empty pints of whiskey on the nightstand.

"How old I am depends on who you are," Lisa said as she propped herself up on one elbow, her small breasts resting flat against her chest.

Angelo pulled a black pocket knife from his vest pocket, snapped it open and held it against his thigh. He sat down on the edge of the bed and cupped one hand across Lisa's face.

"What is he to you?" Angelo asked, tilting his head toward the open door behind him.

"Who do you mean?" Lisa asked, her eyes moving from Angelo's face to the six-inch knife he held in his hand. "Ralph? He's just a friend. He gave me a place to stay when I needed one."

"This place?" Angelo asked.

"I guess it ain't much to the likes of you," Lisa said. "But it's a lot nicer than where I come from and a whole lot better than being on the street."

"Do you have any family?" Angelo asked, removing his hand from the girl's face.

"Family's not what I would call them," Lisa said with a shrug. "And living with Ralph may not be heaven, but it ain't hell neither."

"Where would heaven be for you?" Angelo asked.

Lisa smiled for the first time, the thin rays of sun bouncing off her tobacco-stained teeth. "A place where there's a lot of pretty mountains," she said. Her vacant eyes looked past Angelo, out toward the closed window. "I used to dream about a place like that all the time when I was little. I would see horses running loose and cold water coming down off the rocks. I don't even know if there are places like it anywhere in the world. I just saw it in my dreams."

Angelo lifted the knife, leaned across the bed and reached for the box. With one quick swipe, he sliced open the cord and jammed the blade back into its slot. He tossed aside the lid, reached inside and pulled out a handful of cash. He put the knife back in his vest pocket and began to count the money.

"Jesus Christ!" Lisa said. She sat up and stared down at the money in Angelo's hands. "I never thought Ralph had that kind of money," she said.

"He doesn't," Angelo said, keeping up his silent count.

Angelo patted the bills into a neat pile, pealed off three hundred dollars in tens and tossed them back into the shoe box.

"Get dressed," he said. He stood up, looked down at Lisa and handed her the rest of the money. "Pack all your clothes. Then take this money. Buy yourself a train ticket and go find those mountains."

"What about Ralph?" Lisa barely got the words out. Her mouth had gone dry.

"I'll talk to him," Angelo said.

Lisa jumped off the bed and threw her arms around Angelo, nearly knocking him off balance.

"I want to thank you so much," she whispered into his ear, holding him close.

Angelo lifted her head and looked into her eyes. "Thank me by forgetting you were ever here," he said. "I don't even want it to be a memory."

• • •

"WHAT TOOK SO long?" Pudge asked. He was standing behind Ralph and had one hand on his shoulder. "What'd he do? Bury it?"

Angelo walked over to Pudge and handed him the shoe box. "He's three hundred short," he said.

"What are you saying?" Ralph shouted. He looked from Angelo to Pudge, his mood ricocheting between anger and fright. "I don't know what shit your friend's trying to pull on you, Pudge. But I put that money in the box myself. *All* of it."

Pudge slapped Ralph on the back of the head with the shoe box and then tossed it to the floor. He held the money in his right hand. "*All* of it ain't in my hand," he said. "Giving me half is like giving me nothing."

"Don't scam me on this one, fellas," Ralph pleaded, lines of sweat running down his face. "You wanna take my money, do it another time. Not when I'm this far behind on my payments."

"You're still behind," Angelo said. "Three hundred dollars."

Ralph stood and pointed a trembling finger at Angelo. "You son of a bitch!" he shouted. "You know that money was there. It was either you that took it or that little tramp in my bed."

"Box was closed when I got in the room," Angelo said. "The girl didn't go near it."

"What are you going to do about this, Pudge?" Ralph asked, turning his back on Angelo.

Pudge stared at Angelo for several minutes and then nodded his head. He folded the money and shoved it into the side pocket of his jacket. "I'm going to do you a favor," Pudge said.

"What kind of favor?" Ralph asked, looking from Pudge to Angelo.

"You got another week," Pudge told him. "That should give you plenty of time to get the three hundred you still owe. We'll be back then to pick it up."

"And Lisa leaves exactly the way she is right now," Angelo added. "Any different and I'll hear about it. Then, I'll be back here a lot sooner." He looked at Ralph, who was trembling furiously. "Be smart," Angelo said. "Vote to live."

As they walked out of the drug dealer's foul-smelling room, Pudge turned to his friend and partner. "I don't know what went on in there," he said. "But she's not gonna use the money for what you think she's gonna use it for."

"All I did was give her a chance," Angelo said. "What she does with it is up to her."

"Sometimes I wonder if you're tough enough for this business," Pudge said. "Then sometimes I wonder if you're just so damn tough, you don't care what it is I'm wondering."

• • •

I TOOK A deep breath and smiled over at Mary. As she told me her stories about Angelo's early days, she would make a point of looking at him, occasionally reaching out her hand and resting it on top of the bedspread. It was almost as if he were speaking to me through her. She was his anointed messenger and it was a role she gladly accepted.

"Do you want to go and get something to eat?" I asked. "Or maybe just take a walk? Be nice to get out of this room for a while."

"I don't know if that's such a good idea," Mary said, a sparkle in her eyes. "Angelo always said you liked to eat strange food."

"To him, that means anything that *doesn't* have red sauce over it," I said.

"He told me if someone was ever going to poison his food, he would at the very least die eating something he enjoyed," Mary said. She stood and leaned over, grabbed her coat from the base of the bed and tossed it casually over her shoulders.

"I'll keep it simple," I said, placing a hand against my heart. "I promise. Nothing more foreign than a burger and coffee. At this hour, that's probably all we'll find that's open anyway."

"Sounds safe enough." She threw a quick glance over toward Angelo, his eyes and mind still closed to the outside world, as she led me out of the room.

As we walked together, first down the hospital corridors and then onto the Manhattan streets, I talked to Mary about the resolute eating habits of Angelo and his crew. I found gangsters loyal, first and foremost, to food from their country of origin. In Angelo's case, that was Italy. After that, every-thing was broken down into distinct categories not found in any cookbook. Eating Chinese food was an accepted ritual that started when the Italian mob began to do business with the Triads in the 1930s. The Friday nights of my childhood were spent with Angelo eating Chinese takeout spread across a black table in white containers in the back room of his midtown bar. "Ordering Chinks on Friday night is an American tradition," Pudge, the gangster equivalent of Julia Child, told me. "It's the one thing we do that everybody else does."

Other cuisines presented a greater ethnic dilemma. French food was almost always ruled out. "They don't wash regular and you can't trust people like that with food," Pudge elaborated. Eastern European meals of any kind were not even considered. "Be serious," Pudge would say, "they can't feed themselves over where they come from, how they gonna feed me?" Jewish food was acceptable, especially since much of Angelo and Pudge's business dealings were with gangsters from that background. "You can never go wrong with a bagel and a little cream cheese," Pudge said. "It goes down good with coffee." And soul food, like any other gangster dealings with African-Americans, was handled quietly. "To tell you the truth, as good as their food is, you can only eat that stuff when you're young," Pudge said. "You get older, it gets to be tough on the stomach. That's reason number one why not too many black gangsters live to be old men. It's not the bullets that do them in. It's the short-eye ribs."

• • •

THE BLANKET WAS spread out under the shade of a large, leafy oak tree. It was a breezy day with a warm sun holding off the impending arrival of cold weather. Isabella lifted the lid on the large wicker basket and began to gently pull out its contents. Angelo sat across from her, his arms stretched out behind him, a serene look spread across his face. She caught his look and returned it with a smile. "I made roasted peppers and cheese sandwiches," she said. "And my aunt made her olive salad for you. She says you can't ever eat enough of it."

"She wants me fat," he said, watching as Isabella carefully set out the food, plates and silverware. "She said fat men make better husbands."

Isabella placed two thick sandwiches on Angelo's plate and tilted her head away from the sun's glare. "You'll make a good husband." She widened her smile. "It won't matter what you weigh."

When he spoke, his voice was serious and quiet. He leaned forward and put a hand on Isabella's arm. "Will it matter what I do?" he asked.

Isabella stared at him for several moments, the smile passing from her face and then nodded. "I only know what I see in front of me, Angelo," she said. "And what I see is a good man who is sometimes sadder than he should be."

"I'm never sad when I'm with you," Angelo told her. "These last few months have been happy ones for me. It's just not easy for me to show you or tell you how I feel."

"Why?" Isabella sat inches across from him, her long white skirt spread out around her, the wind pushing her thick hair past her face.

"I see the way you are around your father and the rest of your family," Angelo said, looking away from Isabella and out across the Central Park skyline. "How quick you all are to laugh, hug, kiss, even cry. I wish I could be like that. But I know that I never can. And I'm afraid that might not be enough for you."

"To me, you will always be the handsome boy in the rain who bought me a piece of fruit. That is the Angelo that has touched my heart. I don't need you to be anything more."

"Will you feel the same, even after you know more of who I am?" Angelo asked, close enough to Isabella to smell the sweetness of her skin.

She looked deeply into his eyes and smiled her little girl smile. "There is nothing that can change the way I feel," she said. "Even if you grow fat eating all of my aunt's olive salad."

Angelo smiled and let out a rare laugh. "Then we should eat," he said, the fall sun gently warming them both.

. . .

IDA THE GOOSE had her back to Angelo and Pudge, one foot resting on a tree stump, one hand holding the wooden end of an ax. The sun was coming down off the mountain, washing the wooded valley below and Ida's cabin above in a final blast of strong light. Angelo and Pudge each carried a bucket of fresh beer in one hand and a bottle of scotch shoved under one arm. They had parked their sedan down the hill and walked the steep incline up to Ida's place. It was late on a Saturday afternoon and the drive to Roscoe had taken most of their day. Angelo enjoyed the beauty and the serenity of the surroundings as well as the sense of freedom he felt behind the wheel of a car moving across an open road. Pudge slept for a good portion of the ride, more at home walking a concrete pavement than trekking down a dirt path. They had visited Ida three times since her move upstate six months earlier and each time found her to be as relaxed and as happy as they'd ever seen. "I don't get it," Pudge said to Angelo, as he stared out at the passing rows of trees. "You'd think Ida would go nuts living out here in the woods. You gotta wait for it to rain just to have something new to talk about."

"I like it up here," Angelo said. "It's quiet."

"So are cemeteries," Pudge said. "And I don't want to be found in one of them anytime soon either."

• • •

IDA THE GOOSE lit a cigarette as Angelo and Pudge drew closer. She tilted her head back and blew the smoke toward an unmarked sky. "You boys would make for a pair of terrible hunters," she said, turning her head to glance over their way. "Unless you wanted to be seen and heard by anybody within ten miles."

"We would have crawled our way up," Pudge said. "But we didn't want the beer to spill."

She stomped out her cigarette with the toe of a worn boot and walked up toward the cabin. "I got a beef stew on low boil," she said. "And some fresh cornbread a neighbor gave me. Put the beer next to it and it sounds like a meal to me."

"It doesn't matter what you got," Pudge said, falling

into step behind Ida. "I'm close enough to a faint I'll eat anything."

Angelo lingered a little farther behind, taking in the fresh-air scents and postcard scenery. Though he sorely missed Ida's company and counsel, he appreciated her quest for peace and was happy she had found it in such a place, far removed from the risks and turmoil of a gangster's life. He wondered if he would survive the business long enough to seek and find his own corner of solitude.

• • •

THEY ATTACKED THEIR meal with country hunger, each one finishing two large bowls of stew and a half dozen heavily buttered cubes of cornbread. They ate in silence, at ease with one another, content to let the meal rule over conversation. Pudge tapped into the second pail of beer and Ida had a fresh cigarette poised by her mouth when Angelo spoke his first words since they had sat down at the small dining-room table.

"I'm thinking of getting married," he announced.

Pudge and Ida looked at one another before turning their gaze to Angelo. "You got somebody in mind or is this just a feeling that's taken over?" Ida asked.

"Her name is Isabella," Angelo said.

"The butcher's daughter you walk home from work every day?" Pudge asked, incredulous.

"Yes," Angelo said.

"You in love with her or you just think you are?" Ida asked.

"It's for real," Angelo told them. "I wouldn't have said anything about it if it wasn't."

"That's bad," Pudge said. "She feel the same way about you?"

"Not in so many words," Angelo admitted. "But I can see it in her face."

"That's even worse." Pudge poured himself a fresh mug of beer.

"What kinda work does she think you do?" Ida asked.

"I told her I work for a downtown businessman, but she's

too smart for that to last long. And if she's going to be my wife, she will need to know the truth."

"She doesn't need to know anything," Ida said. "At least not from you. If she's as smart as you say, she'll figure it out on her own. If she hasn't already."

"You sure you wanna go and get married this early?" Pudge asked.

"I'm not like you, Pudge," Angelo said, his voice calm, his beer glass untouched. "I can't go from girl to girl and forget about them the minute they're gone. I wish I could. It would make my life a lot easier. But it's just not the way I am."

"I almost got married once," Ida said with a smile crammed with memories. "I was still young, long before I got hooked up in the rackets. We exchanged rings and even looked at places we might live."

"Did you love him?" Angelo asked.

"I was young enough to think so and old enough where I should have known better," Ida said.

"So you bailed on him?" Pudge said, exchanging his empty glass of beer for Angelo's full one.

"No, it was his call," Ida said, shaking her head. "He swept me away, only it was not the way I had in mind. He went and married someone else. He left my life as fast as he came into it."

"You ever see him again?" Pudge asked.

"Once, years later, he came into the Café," she said. "His marriage had busted up by then. He looked different and so did I, but we recognized each other. We didn't say anything. He ordered his drink, finished it and walked out. I guess it ended the way it was meant to end."

"Any of this cheering you up?" Pudge asked Angelo.

"I don't know what to say to her," Angelo said, his eyes moving slowly from Pudge to Ida. "I have never told anyone I loved them. The few that I do love know it without me having to say anything."

"That only works with people like us," Ida said. "A young

girl needs to hear the words if she's going to believe in the man."

"If you really feel it, it's not going to be a hard thing to do," Pudge said. "Even for somebody who hates to talk as much as you."

"She's a lucky girl," Ida said, raising a glass of whiskey toward Angelo, a lilt of sadness in her voice.

Angelo sat back in his chair and nodded. "I hope that will always be true."

The three stayed together until the beer ran out and the whiskey bottles were empty. Then, their good-byes said under a clear moon, Angelo and Pudge left Ida on her front porch and walked back down the incline toward their car. They drove away from the wooded stillness and back into the dangers of New York nights.

. . .

MARY SETTLED ONTO the circular stool and watched the elderly man behind the counter write down her order. "This is nice," she said. She smiled as I slid the menus back in place between the ketchup bottle and the napkin rack.

"Don't expect too much," I said. "I've been coming here since I was a kid and the food was pretty bad even then."

"No, I meant being with you," she said. "I've always wanted us to spend some time together but I could never quite manage it. I'm only sorry it's happening now, under such sad circumstances."

"Why would you want to spend time with me?" I watched as the counterman slid over two large glasses of Coke with crushed ice.

"Well, Angelo spoke about you so often," she said, pulling the white paper from her straw. "I wanted to see for myself what kind of young man you were."

"Have I let you down yet?"

"No," she said with a bright smile. "But there's still plenty of time."

"What sort of things would he tell you?" I asked.

"Just general information. Being specific is not one of Angelo's strengths. But I know you're married and have two children. I know you have your own business. And I also know you're a terrible actor." She laughed as she said the words.

"I can't believe he told you about that," I said, shaking my head. "I can't believe he would even remember it. That was so many years ago."

"Angelo would put an elephant's memory to shame." Mary moved her arms away from the counter as the old man put down two cheeseburger platters in front of us.

"I was just a kid, about sixteen," I said, reaching for the ketchup. "I had saved some money from a summer job and signed up for an acting class down at HB Studios in the Village. You know, just to see if I was any good at it."

"And were you?"

"I thought so," I said. "And I thought so even more when I got a part in an Off-Off-Broadway play. I got so excited that I asked Angelo and Pudge to come down and see me in it."

Mary put her burger back on the plate and kept a napkin folded and spread across her mouth, trying to bury her laugh. "And?" she asked. "What was their critical reaction?"

"Pudge said it would be best for everybody if he found the writer and the director and shot them both," I said. "And that it would be best for me if I tried another line of work."

"And Angelo?" Mary said, now not even bothering to hide the laugh. "What did he have to say?"

"He said Lee J. Cobb and George C. Scott were great actors." I had to smile at the memory. "And they had two things I didn't have: talent and a middle initial. Then he put on his hat and walked out of the theater. We never talked about it again."

"You stopped going to classes after that?" she asked, placing a hand on top of mine.

"I thought about it and figured he was at least half right," I said. "I could have always added an initial to my name. I just would never have had the talent."

"Are you happy with the way your life's turned out?" Mary asked.

"I have two great kids and a business that pays the bills," I said. "I have a wife who listens to me when I talk and a dog that always seems happy to see me."

"And is that all that you wanted it to be?" Her bright eyes shone like lanterns against my face. I felt as if she knew everything I was feeling and could read any thoughts that passed through my mind.

"What you want your life to be and what it becomes are never the same," I said. "Angelo would be the first to tell you that. It's only about what you end up with or what you settle for. And by the time that happens, it's too late for you to do anything else."

"What would you have changed?" she asked.

"The last twenty years," I said.

7

Spring, 1926

JACK WELLS WAS sitting in the back room of Baker's Bar on the northeast corner of Tremont Avenue in the Bronx, nursing a mug of ice-packed root beer. He watched the nervous man sitting across from him light a cigarette, take a deep drag and blow the smoke up toward the tin ceiling.

"If I get caught on this, it's over for me," the man said, his voice a trembling whisper. "A hothead like Pudge Nichols won't give in to reason. He'll come right at me with a gun in his hand."

"Then make sure you don't get found out," Wells said. He wiped a line of foam from his upper lip with the back of his hand.

"I wouldn't even be doing something like this if I had a better stable of girls working for me," the man said. He had smoked the cigarette down to the butt. "The ones I got couldn't get laid in prison if they were holding a handful of pardons."

"Listen to me, Francis," Wells said, his eyes boring in on his companion, giving his words extra weight. "I may not look like a busy man to you, but I am. So, knowing that, the last thing I need to hear about is how hard a balls-on-his-ass pimp has it. You don't like your life, bitch about it to your mother. Now tell me, can you handle this or not?"

"I think so," Francis said with a slow nod.

"I want to hear a yes or a no," Wells said. "Anything else, I go deaf."

"Yes, Mr. Wells," Francis said. "I'll handle it."

"That's good news," Wells said. "I'll let you and Fish work out the details. What matters most is that you get him inside that room. My crew handles it from there."

"When do I see you again?" Francis asked. He bit down on his lower lip. "You know, so I can pick up the payment."

"You're *never* going to see me again!" Wells jabbed his index finger against the center of Francis's sweaty forehead. "You live through this, you die through this, it makes no difference. I just gave up all the time I got to give to a pimp."

· · ·

CARMELLA DALITO RESTED a gnarled, vein-riddled hand over her mouth and stared across the small table at Pudge Nichols, her dark eyes shining off the shimmer of the candlelight. Angelo stood directly behind Pudge, his arms folded, staring down at the small wooden bowl at rest in the center of the table. The old woman, whose thick rolls of gray hair framed a scarred face, was a *Strega*, an Italian witch, paid to relieve Pudge from the pain of a lingering headache.

"I still think we would have been better off going to see that doctor on Little West Twelfth," Pudge said. He never took his eyes off the old woman, careful to gauge her every move. "Drunk or sober, he might have come up with something to help me."

"This is better than going to a doctor," Angelo said.

"This is starting to creep me out," Pudge said. He ran a finger under the brim of his heavily starched shirt collar. "Maybe I should learn to live with the headaches."

Angelo put a hand on Pudge's shoulder. "Stay calm," he advised.

"You ever get sick, first stop I make is to find a guy with a white coat," Pudge said. "I don't drag you off to see a witch, that's for sure."

"She'll do more than just clear away those headaches,"

Angelo said as he took a step back into the shaded darkness of the small room.

"Let me take a shot at it," Pudge said. "She's gonna put back that missing toe on my foot."

"Even better," Angelo said. "When Carmella's finished, you will know who it is that is giving you those headaches."

Pudge turned away from the old woman and looked up at Angelo. "You serious?" he asked.

Angelo stared back at his friend. "Yes," he said.

Pudge smiled at Carmella and patted her on the hand. "Okay, sweets," he said, a wide smile now on his face. "Give us the works."

Carmella reached behind her, picked up a glass of water and emptied it into the wooden bowl. She lifted a small tin of olive oil from the side of the table and poured the thick yellow liquid into the bowl, watching as it formed a slick on the surface of the water. She yanked a rumpled linen handkerchief from her dress pocket and spread it across the table. In the center of the handkerchief, soaked through with blood, was an eye.

"It's the eye of a goat," Angelo whispered to Pudge. "She will mix it in with the water and oil."

"Then what?" Pudge asked.

"Then I will know who wishes bad for you," Carmella said, speaking for the first time. Her voice was softer than her harsh looks. "And then you will know, too."

She picked up the eye and dropped it gently into the oil and water. She stared down at it, watching as it floated in the stillness of the bowl. She placed the tips of her fingers around the lid and looked up at Pudge.

"Wet your fingers with the water," she told him. "Then, put your hands down flat on the table."

Pudge did as he was instructed. The old woman tilted her head back and closed her eyes, low-moaning a string of Italian phrases. She shook and stammered, her back arched, her fingers spread inside the bowl. She tilted her neck up to the chalk-white ceiling.

Pudge sat there mesmerized by the old woman's physical gyrations. "If she's looking to scare the shit outta me," he said in a low voice, "she's about half the way there."

Carmella leaned over the edge of the table, inches from Pudge's face and clamped down on his wrists with her gnarled hands. She stared into his young eyes, her face a cracked wall of purple veins, white scars and ragged lines. Pudge kept still, anxious to see the end result of the old woman's voodoo quest.

"It is a woman who will cause your blood to flow," the *Strega* said. "She will make you reach out for the comforts of death."

"What's her name?" Pudge asked as he turned briefly and looked over at Angelo.

"She will give you the love of her flesh," Carmella said, ignoring the question, locked into her *Strega* glare. "And you will take it. Your desires will cause you great pain."

"She's not going to give me the name?" Pudge asked Angelo.

"She doesn't know names," Angelo said. "She only knows actions. We figure out the rest."

"This smells like a scam to me," Pudge said. "All she's doing is reeling us in like two saps."

"It's not a scam," Angelo insisted. "I've used her before and she's never been wrong."

"How the hell do you know she's never wrong?" Pudge asked, turning to face Angelo. "Unless these headaches are making me deaf, too, I didn't hear her tell us anything. She didn't give up anybody."

"It's hard for her to narrow it to one woman," Angelo said. "You've got a lot of girlfriends."

"What if we throw a little more money her way?" Pudge said. "Maybe that'll help her see a face in the water bowl."

"No," Angelo said, looking over at the witch. "She's told us all she knows."

Pudge pulled his hands away from the old woman and

stood. "So what now?" he said to Angelo. "I spend the rest of my nights with you?"

"You have to learn to listen as much to what the witch didn't say as to what she did," Angelo said, nodding his thanks to Carmella. "She told us everything we need to know. There's going to be a trap. A cover to get you to a place where you'll feel safe. And the gun that's used will come from someone else's hands."

"Whose?"

"Jack Wells," Angelo said. "He's the one who wants us both dead."

"Why me first?" Pudge asked as he followed Angelo out of the *Strega*'s room.

"He fears you more," Angelo said. He stood in the stairwell as he spoke, his words direct and filled with calm. "You're the dangerous one. Once you're dead, he doesn't think he has anything to fear from me."

"I need some fresh air." Pudge eased past Angelo and walked down the flight of steps.

"How's the headache?" Angelo asked, following him.

"It's gone," Pudge said over his shoulder. "But now my stomach's starting to bother me."

"You want to go back up and see the *Strega* about it?" Angelo asked.

Pudge stopped and turned to look at Angelo. "I'll take a pass," he said. "She gave me enough good news for one day."

• • •

ALL GANGSTERS ARE superstitious. Their phobias travel well beyond the acceptable and venture into arenas rarely visited by those not in the underworld. Jimmy "Two-Gun" Marchetti never passed a church without kneeling and making the sign of the cross and he always began his day with a black coffee and four large cloves of garlic. He believed both habits would keep him safe from harm, which they did until two days before his twenty-seventh birthday, when he was gunned down in an East Side bar.

Most gangsters believe in the healing powers of *Stregas*, prefer cats to dogs because of their alleged spiritual strengths and always follow the same ritual on the day of a prearranged kill. As a group, they are always wary of anyone detecting a pattern to their movements. Yet they routinely eat their meals in the same restaurants, venture down the same streets and treat their daily schedule as if it were chiseled in granite. The pockets of their suits and overcoats are crammed with lucky items—a coin from a first payroll heist, a bullet fragment removed from a leg, a religious figure meant to ward off evil, a ring given by a first gang boss. All are meant as safety valves.

Angelo wore a St. Joseph's medallion around his neck, left to him by Josephina. He was not a religious man, but he believed the strength of the medal helped him ride free of the danger zone. "I put two fingers up to the medal when I went out on a job," he told me. "I can't say for sure it helped, but I figured it was a good thing to have on my side."

Angelo understood that to be good at his work and survive, you needed to be fearless in a business ruled by fear. So gangsters turn to the small things—bracelets, billfolds, same tie worn on the same day, a walk in a cemetery—whatever it might be, to give them that extra edge. "Being superstitious is married to being careful," he told me. "And being careful goes hat in hand toward helping a guy like me stay alive."

.   .   .

ISABELLA QUIETLY CREPT up behind Angelo and placed a hand on his shoulder. He sat facing a window, his back to the door, in the corner of his room above the bar. "I was worried," she said in a soft voice. "You haven't been around the past few days."

"I need time alone," Angelo said.

"Can I help?" She stepped around him, her hand still touching him, and stood staring at a hard face and soft eyes. The room was dark, the only light filtering in through the drawn shades of an open window.

"You have never met my father," Angelo said, looking at

her, finding comfort in her beauty and warmth. "He's a good man but an unlucky one. Thousands of men like him came to this country, worked hard, made a place for themselves and their families. He was unable to do that, no matter how hard he worked, he could never make the next move."

"Many men work hard and stay poor," Isabella said. "There is no crime to it, no shame. It's as true in Italy as it is here."

"I never wanted you to meet him," Angelo said. "I wish I didn't feel that way about him, wish I wasn't so angry and so ashamed."

"Being poor is not something to be ashamed about, Angelo," Isabella said.

"It's not about being poor," Angelo said. "It's about a murder."

Isabella sat down across from Angelo and stared at him, his face blocked by the shadows of the room. "Whose?"

"My father came to America not to seek a fortune or make a new life," Angelo said. "He came here to run from a crime. He came because he had murdered his own child."

Isabella gasped when she heard the words, her hands clasped across her face. "Why? Why would any father commit such an act?"

"A man pulls a trigger for many reasons." Angelo's low voice started to break. "Most of them wrong."

"Your father's gone, Angelo," Isabella said, regaining her calm. "He is the one who must live with what he has done, not you."

Angelo leaned closer and held her hands, gazing deep into her dark eyes. "All that I have learned, everything that my life has prepared me for tells me my brother's death must be avenged. And it can only be avenged by me. But I don't know if I have such courage. He is my father and I love him very much."

"Your father faces his crime every day that he lives. Is that not enough to satisfy vengeance?"

"In some worlds, yes," Angelo said. "But not in mine. My

father lives and my brother lies dead. And the price must be paid."

"Then that would make you just like him," Isabella said. "Do you have the courage to live with that?"

"I'm afraid to know," Angelo said. He stood up, reached out his arms and held Isabella very, very close.

. . .

IF A YOUNG woman such as Isabella were to become a gangster's wife, she would do so on her own terms and be primed to follow the traditional patterns put in place centuries ago in Italy. Most of these women were strong-willed and fully aware of what it was their men did for a living. They were raised to love and respect their husbands and demand the same treatment in return. Mistresses would not be tolerated and her rule of the house and children was never to be questioned. "You had a wife back in those days it was like having yourself a partner," Pudge said. "They weren't blind to what went on, and you could count on them to be loyal from the get-go. Those were marriages that lasted until death, usually his. And if she wore the widow's black and kept her husband's name and her reputation clean, the bosses made sure she was well taken care of for the rest of her years. None of that holds true now. We're as much of a disaster as the rest of the country when it comes to marriage. But back then, when a wife said she loved you, you could chisel it in stone."

. . .

THE JAZZ QUARTET was winding down a slow rendition of "Alexander's Ragtime Band," the large dance floor below them crammed with the young and high-heeled. Angelo held Isabella's hand as they both watched the dancers sway and shimmy to the beat. He caught the glow in her eyes, allowing her to be swallowed by the glitter and romance of a world that whirled along on fast forward.

"What do you think?" Angelo asked, raising his voice to be heard over the music.

Isabella answered his question with one of her own. "Do you spend much of your time here?"

"Mostly for business," he said. "The man I work for owns the club."

Isabella took a sip from a glass of cold water and smiled at him from above the rim. "Is tonight business?"

"No," Angelo said, shaking his head.

"Then you must have something important to ask me. Or else why bring me here?"

Angelo looked over at the crowded Cotton Club dance floor. He studied the faces of the soft-skinned men in their smart-tailored suits and the young women whose eyes gleamed in their presence. Old money mixing easily with the new-found wealth of the illicit. All of them with too much free time and excess amounts of cash. These were the people Angelo would feed off of as he continued his rise through the ranks of the mob. They would buy his whiskey, frequent his clubs and invest in his illegal pursuits. Next to them, Isabella was a vision of freshness and love, a bright light casting a sharp glow across a decadent room. He turned to look back at her, her open face trusting in him only, ignoring all other movements around them.

"I've wanted to ask you for six months," Angelo told her. "I just haven't been able to put the right words together. It's not what I do well."

"And I've been waiting six months for you to ask. Right words or not, my answer will still be the same."

"Is that answer a yes?" Angelo said, staring at Isabella above the glare of the candle in the center of the table.

"Is it so impossible to ask the question?" Her fingers gently stroked the top of Angelo's hand.

"Be my wife, Isabella," Angelo said. "I have been in love with you from the second I handed you that peach."

"That very expensive peach," she laughed.

"I wish to make you happy, Isabella. It is all that matters to me."

"Have you talked to my father yet?" Isabella asked.

"Last Christmas. He's been waiting as long as you have for me to ask you."

"He probably has the wedding all planned out already." She took another sip of water and glanced over her shoulder at the dance floor, dozens of couples dancing to a clarinet-led blues medley. "Do you like to dance?"

"I never have," he said in a shy whisper.

"I never have either," Isabella said. "My father always told me that my first dance would have to be with the man I love and expect to spend the rest of my life with."

Angelo stood and stepped over to Isabella and reached out his hand. "Would you dance with me?" he asked.

"Yes," she said, lifting her head and smiling up at him. She took Angelo's hand and followed him to the dance floor.

They held one another close, finding comfort in each other's grasp, heads at rest on shoulders, feet sliding across the waxed wood floor. The music washed over them like sun-splattered waves, as they both kept their eyes closed and their minds filled with the youthful dreams of a couple enjoying the first taste of love.

• • •

JAMES GARRETT WAS a New York City first-grade detective. He was tall, reed thin and had a rich crop of carrot-red hair. He had been a cop for twelve years and was married to an overweight Catholic schoolteacher who was far too religious for his taste. They had an eight-year-old son who lost the sight in his right eye after a playground accident. Around the station houses he worked Garrett was considered a solid badge. He did his job, cleared his desk of unsolved cases and always found the time to lend a hand to a nervous rookie or an over-worked veteran. Garrett liked being a detective, deriving pleasure from the power he wielded with a flashed badge.

With that power came access and it allowed James Garrett, the forty-one-year-old son of a merchant seaman, a free pass to the good life he could not otherwise afford on a detective's salary. Front-row tables at choice restaurants, prime seats at boxing matches and baseball games, easy entrée to opening night on Broadway and the best medical care available for his ailing son were there for the taking, so Garrett grabbed it all with a fierce hunger. He was much more than a good cop with an impressive arrest record. He was also a dirty cop with a monthly on-the-pad income that tripled his detective's salary.

He was politically savvy and navigated the silent sanctum of the corrupt wing of the New York City Police Department with a politician's discretion. He made it his business to be known and to be in the know, playing his game in the warmth of the murky shadows. He was shaded in safety by captains and deputy police commissioners, ward supervisors and district bosses, all of whom relied on him for their weekly envelopes.

To the average citizen, James Garrett was the very portrait of the cop who cared, his choirboy looks, Boy Scout smile and diligent work habits all the evidence they needed to back up that belief. They could count on him to be there to protect their lives and defend them against the rampant crime taking hold of their streets.

The underworld held a different portrait of James Garrett. To them, he was a bought badge, paid to protect and serve the best interests of Jack Wells.

In addition to his regular payoffs, Garrett had been put in charge of Wells's citywide payroll. This gave him complete access to the black books containing all the names and sums received by the corrupt elite. Most other gangsters would have been leery to give any one cop such enormous clout. They would fear exposing themselves to potential extortion and betrayal. But Jack Wells was never one to worry. He took pride in his chosen role of the rebel gangster and felt that with fear and intimidation he could hold sway over anyone, especially a cop with a stained badge.

· · ·

GARRETT STOOD IN the dark entryway, across from the lights and steady traffic stream outside the Cotton Club. He stamped his feet against the cold, hard concrete step. He lit a cigarette, the glow from the match highlighting a run of freckles dotting the sides of his cheeks and neck. He tossed the match aside, took a deep drag from the unfiltered Camel and stepped out of the darkness. He walked with confidence and ease toward the Cotton Club entrance. He smiled when he saw Angelo step out of the club, crunch a tip into the doorman's palm, exchange a few words and then turn right. He was heading downtown, his arm wrapped around Isabella's shoulders.

Garrett picked up his step and eased in behind them. He watched them walk, content for the moment just to follow, listening as the low murmurs of their voices echoed down the empty street.

"Where are the dago lovers off to now?" Garrett asked. He was close enough to Angelo and Isabella to be partially hidden by their shadows.

Angelo gripped Isabella's shoulder tighter and stopped walking. He looked straight ahead, waiting to see the face behind the voice. Garrett walked around them, one hand in his jacket pocket, the cigarette still dangling from his mouth. "How can you stand being in a place like that?" he said, nodding his head back toward the Cotton Club. "You should have a little more respect for your lady than to bring her to a jig bar."

Angelo stared at Garrett, did a quick check on his clothes and demeanor. He was looking not to put a name to the face but to determine motive. He knew the man blocking his path wasn't a gangster and this wasn't going to be a hit. A shooter never takes the time to talk or risk being seen by any potential witness. That meant the man tossing the cigarette to the ground was nothing more than a messenger, paid to act tough, but not a real threat. He looked too old to be new at verbal shakedowns and too young to be used as a sacrificial setup, a dupe for the actual hitter lurking in the dark street beyond. Angelo looked over at Isabella and noted how calm she appeared and how defiant her eyes were in the face of danger.

"They tell me you ain't much on talk," Garrett said, leering over at Isabella. "That doesn't matter to me. It's your ears I want."

Garrett reached into the side pocket of his coat and pulled out a slice of chewing gum. He unwrapped it and shoved it slowly into his mouth. He inched a couple of steps closer to Isabella.

"I have to give you dagos credit," Garrett said, smiling at Isabella. "You know how to pick the kind of woman a man doesn't mind waking up next to." He turned back to Angelo. "You know the kind I mean, don't you?"

Angelo didn't answer. He kept his temper lever at idle, his anger shoved down deep, well below any visible level. He watched as Garrett stroked Isabella's arm and felt her recoil at his touch. He stayed distant and impassive as Garrett's fingers ran the length of Isabella's face and neck.

"Do yourself a big favor, dago," Garrett said to Angelo, his hungry eyes never leaving Isabella's face. "Make your deal with Wells. Let him make you a rich man. A beauty like you got needs a man around her with deep pockets. She doesn't get that, then before you know it, she goes looking for somebody else. Maybe even a somebody like me."

Garrett held Isabella's look, then brought his hand back down to his side. He lifted the collar on his jacket and stood square in Angelo's face. "You and your partner got till next week to make the smart call. After that, Wells takes it out of your hands and puts it in mine. Which means, next time we meet, it won't be as friends." He tipped the brim of his fedora at Isabella and winked at Angelo. "Enjoy what's left of your night," he said, walking past them and reaching for another cigarette.

*   *   *

ANGELO HELD ISABELLA'S face in his hands, wiping loose strands of hair from her eyes. "Are you all right?" he asked her softly.

"Yes," she said, nodding her head. "I just didn't like him touching me."

"It's the last time that cop will ever touch you," Angelo said. "I promise that."

"How do you know he was a cop?" she asked, curious.

"He had the look and the smell." Angelo's voice had a trace of disdain. "Just because a man is given a badge and swears to follow the law, it doesn't make him honest."

"What are you going to do?" They were walking slowly now, her arm held tightly under his. "About what he said to you?"

"For now, nothing." Angelo stared straight ahead into the dark street. "He gave me a week to decide."

"And what then?" she asked, her eyes searching his face for any sign of concern. "When the week is up?"

"Then, I'll find out if the cop's actions are as strong as his words," Angelo said.

"And what if they are?" She stopped walking and stood in front of Angelo, her hands gripped around his arms. "What if that cop is all that he says he is?"

"Then one of us will be found dead," Angelo said.

8

Summer, 1926

FRANCIS THE PIMP looked across the table at the nervous young prostitute. He reached a hand into the rear pocket of his tan slacks and pulled out a thick roll of tens, bound together by a rubber band. He unfurled the roll, counted out six bills and dropped them on the wooden table. He leaned forward and slid them toward the girl. She was smoking a cigarette with her left hand and curling the strands of her dark brown hair with her right, the nails on both chewed down to the nub.

"You understand what it is you're supposed to do?" Francis asked.

"Believe me, it don't take much to get Pudge Nichols into bed," the girl said. She spoke with a thick, nasal accent, filled with the flat sounds of her Columbus, Ohio, childhood. "At least not for me."

"Once you get him in bed, make sure he stays there," Francis said.

"For how long?" the girl asked.

"Do whatever it takes for as long as it takes," Francis said.

"There's just so much I can do. I mean, Pudge Nichols wants to go, he goes. There's no way to stop him."

"Listen to me, Shirley!" Francis shouted. He slammed his hand down on the table, knocking over an empty whiskey glass. "I don't give a good damn where he's gotta go or what you gotta do to keep him from going. All I know is if you want to keep yourself alive, you put Pudge Nichols in your damn bed and you keep him there."

"I don't like any of this," Shirley said in a little girl voice. "What did you go and get yourself into? Whatever it is, if it means messing with a lit fuse like Pudge, it's going to end up bad."

Francis sat back in his chair, the wood end of a match shoved into a corner of his thin lips. "Pudge Nichols is who they're coming to get," he said. "Not me and not you."

"What if I say no?" Shirley asked, looking down at the sixty dollars. "You're not exactly settin' me up for life, you know."

Francis the Pimp's eyes narrowed and a smile slithered over his unshaven face. "There's more money to be had," he said. "Maybe a lot more. How much is really up to you."

Shirley grabbed the bills from the table and jammed them under the shoulder strap of her dress. "How much more?" she asked. "Enough so I don't have to turn over any more johns?"

Francis the Pimp handed Shirley a hand-rolled cigarette and waited while she put it to her lips. He lit a match, cupped a palm around it, leaned over and placed it against the raw end. He watched as she blew a thin line of smoke at his face.

"After this job, you want somebody to take a taste, you can do it for free," Francis said. "All it takes is a little courage."

"What do I have to do?" Shirley asked. "For the extra money?"

"Will it bother you if Pudge gets killed?"

"I like the guy," she said, "but I'm not in love with him or nothin' like that."

Francis the Pimp leaned his arms and chest over the table and brought his voice down to a raspy whisper. The tiny first-floor room was filled with clouds of smoke, the only window locked tight and shaded. In a dusty corner, a large roach crawled along the baseboard in search of the nearest crumb.

"Then all you have to do is kill him," Francis said.

• • •

THE LITTLE BOY'S face was a frozen and frightened blank as he watched the spilled vanilla ice cream soda drip down the side of the table. He watched as the man sitting across from him pulled his chair back and stared at the splattered stains on his creased pants. "You stupid little bastard!" the man snarled. "Look at what the hell you went and did."

"I'm sorry," the boy said in a quivering voice. "It was an accident."

"It's always an accident with you," the man said, his angry words catching the attention of the other patrons sitting in the crowded diner. "No matter where the hell we are or where the hell we go."

"I didn't mean it, Mr. Tyler," the boy said, fighting back the urge to cry. "It won't ever happen again. I swear it."

An elderly counterman ambled toward the table, carrying a wet dish towel bundled in his hand and a weak smile. "It's just a spill," he said. "In this place, they're about as regular as the rent."

"Just leave the rag," Tyler said. "The boy made the mess and the boy will clean it up."

"It's not his job," the counterman said, still smiling. "It's mine. And besides, I don't think his mamma will be all too happy with either one of you if he walks through the door with his clothes all a mess."

Andrew Tyler stood against the edge of the wet table, anger clouding his eyes and rushing the blood to his face. He was a tall man, in his mid-thirties, with thick dark hair and a quick as lightning temper. He had been a boxer in the army and had gone undefeated in the four years he wore stripes on his arms. He owned an uptown lumber supply company and had been dating the boy's mother for six weeks. He liked everything about her except for the fact that she had a son.

"I said the boy will clean it up," Tyler said in harsher tones. "Now hand him the rag and get the hell back to making milkshakes."

The counterman caught the edge in Tyler's gaze, nodded over at the boy and rested the dish towel on the tabletop. "Just leave it when you're done," he said, turning away. "I'll deal with it later."

Tyler jabbed the boy in the shoulder and smirked when he saw him grimace. "All right, Edward," he said, "start cleaning. And make sure you don't spill any more of it."

Edward, one week past his sixth birthday, reached for the dishrag, leaned over and started to wipe at the milky white flood. He kept his head down and spread the rag out as far as it would go in an attempt to catch all the spillage. The large puddle around his feet matched the one on the table by his elbow. He wanted very much to cry.

"You're doing it wrong," Tyler said, raising his voice. "If you're always going to make a mess, then you better damn well learn how to clean one up."

"I've never done this before, Mr. Tyler," the boy stammered. "I'm doing the best I can."

Without a word of warning, Tyler reached down and yanked Edward off his chair, lifted him into the air, then sent him crashing to the floor. The boy landed with a squishy thud into the center of the puddle, milk covering his blue slacks and black shoes, his face dotted with spots of vanilla ice cream. "Start from there and work your way up," Tyler said, his rage at full vent. "And we're not going to leave here until every damn drop is cleaned up."

Edward looked around at all the faces staring at him, some in horror, others just curious, and he felt the warm tears rush down his cheeks. He lowered his head and began to sob. "Please don't do this, Mr. Tyler," the boy whispered.

"If you're going to cry, there should be a goddamn good reason," Tyler said. He leaned over and landed two hard slaps across the back of the boy's head. The sounds echoed through the hushed diner. He lifted his hand a third time, his fingers now balled into a fist and swung it down toward the boy's face. A hand caught the fist in midflight and held it there.

"I'll give you a better fight than the boy," Pudge Nichols

said calmly. "And I'll try not to spill any ice cream on you while I do."

Tyler stared at Pudge, more than eager to swing his anger toward the intruder. "You have no idea the kind of beating you're in for," he hissed.

"Sammy," Pudge said to the counterman who was now standing directly behind him. "Any damage that's done, send the tab to the Café. I'll see that it's covered."

"It's my treat," the old counterman said. "Just make sure when you're through with him, he isn't in any shape to walk back into my shop."

"A free bust-up," Pudge said, smiling at the much taller Tyler. "Sammy must really like you."

Tyler landed the first punch, a glancing blow off the side of Pudge's head. Pudge stumbled backwards, knocking over two chairs. He felt his lower lip and tasted the warmth of his own blood. "Hey, kid," Pudge shouted over to the boy. "This guy mean anything to you?"

The shivering boy shook his head no.

"That's good to hear," Pudge said.

Pudge immediately jumped into Tyler, hitting him at chest level, sending him to the ground. Tyler's feet gave way under the melted ice cream and the back of his head hit the hard cement floor. Pudge dragged the dazed bully into a corner booth, pushed him down and held him in place with his knees. His attack was relentless, a steady assault of fists, bites, slaps and elbows. Pudge felt Tyler weaken under him from the rain of blows, heard his breathing choked back by bile and shattered bone, but he wouldn't let up. A number of the patrons had left the diner before the fight began. Those few who remained behind held their collective breath, mesmerized by the power and viciousness that was taking place before their eyes. This was the Pudge Nichols they had heard so much about, a few had even read about, but none had ever witnessed up close.

Pudge, breathing hard and drenched with sweat eased himself off the battered Tyler. He picked up a lantern from the center of a wood table. He stared down at what he had done, nodded and smashed the light on top of the prone body, glass shattering against the center of the slow-heaving chest. Pudge looked up and caught his image in an overhead mirror. He was soaked through with another man's blood, his blond hair matted down with sweat, his new jacket torn at the sleeve. Pudge Nichols, victorious once again, smiled.

He walked over to the boy, who had remained frozen in place under the table, reached a bloody hand down and lifted him to his feet. Pudge grabbed a napkin off the table and wiped the tears from the boy's face.

"You never did get to finish that ice cream soda," Pudge said. "You in the mood for another?"

The boy nodded.

"You up to making two fresh ones?" Pudge asked Sammy.

"You'll be drinking them before you know it," Sammy told him.

Pudge put an arm around the boy and walked him over to a clean table. "Don't worry about spilling any," he said, casting a glance over at Tyler. "I don't think anybody's gonna mind if that happens."

· · ·

PUDGE HAD A passion for violence. He had a taste for fight and a thirst for battle that were matched by few in his profession. His fists and his guns had been the engines that propelled him to succeed in the only life he fully understood. Few people knew him well; most feared him and were willing to pay any price to keep him clear of their lives.

But I knew him and I loved him.

Where others saw a sociopath eager to pistol whip a reluctant victim, I saw a man who was quick to smile and offer a young boy a place at his table. I knew he was a man cold enough to kill, but I also knew him to be warm and sensitive to those he cared about. He had no tolerance for acts of betrayal or cruelty and lacked Angelo's taste for the minute details of a business deal. He was a man totally in the moment, who knew only to respond to an action with an action. He was pure gangster.

"Pudge cared whether people liked him or not," Angelo once told me, years ago. "It never entered his mind that what we did left little for people to like. It's always better to like a gangster from a distance anyway. Like a tiger cub in a cage. They always look soft and cute and warm behind those iron bars. Everybody's happy, smiling, waving, taking pictures. But you take away those bars and all that goes away. All that's left then is the fear. That's Pudge. That's every gangster."

· · ·

THE BLACK FOUR-DOOR sedan was parked on a dirt embankment, half a mile from the Cloisters, headlights shining down on the dark currents of the Hudson River. Angus McQueen stepped out of the car's left rear door. He had a bowler hat clenched in one hand and an unlit cigar in the other. He took a few steps forward and turned back toward the tall man sitting behind the wheel.

"You bring something to read?" he asked.

"No," Spider MacKenzie said. "Just smokes and a pint."

"You don't need lights for any one of those," Angus said. "Am I right?"

Spider smiled and clicked off the headlights. He watched McQueen walk toward the rocky edges of the embankment and disappear behind a clump of thick trees. Spider tipped a row of tar-black tobacco onto a thin strip of paper, rolled it carefully between two fingers of his right hand and put it to his mouth. He tipped a match with a sharp flick of his thumb and lit it. He rested his head against the back of the car seat and closed his eyes. Spider held the cigarette in his mouth and kept the flask cradled between his legs.

The voice crept up on McQueen. It came from out of the trees, whisked along by a mild breeze. He knew it would be there, was expecting it from the moment Spider pulled the sedan off the road and out to the directed spot. It is a voice every gangster expects to hear at some point in his life. A voice that often brings with it a dire warning or a fatal bullet.

"Glad you found the time to make it up here, Angus," the voice said.

"The way I heard it, it didn't sound like I had much say in the matter." McQueen had his hands in his pockets, the hat back on his head and the cigar in his mouth, still unlit. He leaned over the edge, peering down at the dark river several hundred feet below.

"Could be all a bluff," the voice said. The man behind it was now a few steps closer, just outside the range of the tree coverage.

"A bluff can take you a long way in a poker game," Mc-Queen said. "It can get you killed if you try it in life."

"Don't worry, Angus," the voice said. "It's all for real. There's a call out for you to die. Put out by Jack Wells himself."

"If you know that much, then you know who he handed the job to," McQueen said. "Am I right on that?"

"Yes," the voice said.

"I pay a lot less if I have to guess the answer," McQueen said. He turned in the direction of the voice and saw a figure standing off to the left, shrouded by the hanging branches of an old tree.

"It's my job, Angus," the voice said, stepping in closer to McQueen. "You're supposed to be my hit."

"I have to give you credit," McQueen said, nodding his head with approval. "You picked the perfect spot. By the time my boy Spider hears the shot, you'll be long past gone."

"He would have heard the shots by now," the voice said. "I'm not here to kill you. I came to hear you make me an offer."

"Just out of curiosity," McQueen said. "What does Jack Wells say my life is worth?"

"Ten thousand," the voice said. "Five's already in my pocket. I get another five when he reads in the paper that you're dead."

"Sounds about right," McQueen said with a shrug. "There's no sense in paying more than street value."

"A hit on Wells would be worth at least twice that," the voice said.

"Not to me," McQueen said.

"He always said you were a cheap bastard," the voice said.

"You got a name?" McQueen said. "Or you expect me to hire you on a hunch?"

The voice stepped up closer to McQueen and lit a cigarette. He was a young man with a pale, pockmarked face and a black mustache that looked penciled on. His lips were thin and his teeth were crooked.

"Jerry Ballister," the voice said.

"You're the one they call Kid Blast, am I right?"

"Never to my face," Ballister said, his dark eyes turning killer hard.

"Life's filled with firsts," McQueen said, a wry smile spread evenly across his aging face.

McQueen came to the meeting expecting a gunfight, not a recruitment plea. His body was relaxed and at ease. He gave a quick look around and was surprised only in that a voyage that began in the slums of England could have ended on such a dark and silent bluff. In the currents of the river below, he knew there floated many of the men whose deaths he had ordered.

"Why do you want to come over to my side?" McQueen asked.

"I figure you to be out of the rackets in a few years, maybe less. You've stashed away enough to make an easy old age for yourself. Wells is in this for the long haul. Let's just say I don't have the patience to wait him out."

Angus stared at the young killer and saw the look of a man who took pleasure from the pain he brought others. "Okay with you if I think about it?" Angus asked. "Get back to you with an answer in a week or two?"

"Take all the time you need," Ballister said. "Wells didn't

put any time limit on the hit, though I expect he wants to see it happen sooner than later."

"Hello, *Kid*," Pudge Nichols said, standing in Ballister's shadow, one gun in each hand.

"What the hell are you doing up here?" McQueen said, as shocked as he was pleased.

"Angelo's never seen the Cloisters," Pudge said, keeping both eyes on Ballister. "Hope we're not breaking up anything too important."

"Me and the *Kid* were just standing around, shooting the shit," McQueen said. "Getting to know one another better."

"Let me guess," Angelo said, stepping out from the shade of an oak tree. "He wants to come over and work with us."

"I don't blame you," Pudge said. "I met your boss."

Ballister turned from McQueen and shifted his gaze to Angelo. "How'd you know I'd be here?"

"They call you Kid Blast, not Kid Genius," Pudge said. "It wasn't that hard to figure out."

"What happens now?" Ballister asked, shrugging his shoulders.

"You wait," McQueen said, stepping up to him. "Until I decide if you're for real. Like Angelo and Pudge. Or just another name looking for a headline."

"You won't be disappointed, Angus," Ballister said. "Believe me."

"I'm never disappointed," McQueen said.

Pudge nudged Ballister with the palm of his right hand. "You're not a partner yet, which makes it time for you to leave."

Ballister looked at the three faces surrounding him, giving each of them a slow nod. "I hope we see each other again," he said.

"We will," McQueen said. "One way or another." He watched Ballister walk back into the woods, then turned to Angelo and Pudge. "You think he came up with the idea to leave Wells on his own?" he asked. "Or did somebody hand it to him?"

"He doesn't seem the type to have a lot of ideas," Angelo said. "Let alone good ones."

"Spider will take it from here," McQueen said. "You boys take the rest of the night off."

"Cold beer and warm women, that's where I'm heading," Pudge said. "You guys want to tag along?"

McQueen stopped short, kicking up small dust clusters at the base of his feet. "I'm married," he said. "And drinking is against the law. Or don't you bother to read the papers?"

The three of them shared a laugh as they walked across the cooling shelter of the Cloisters.

• • •

GANGSTERS THRIVE ON feuds. The feuds are almost always genuine, deadly and last for decades, spilling over into subsequent generations. These underworld hatreds and grudges usually start with the most minor offense and end in the most horrendous forms of death. And they almost always begin in the most innocent of places. "You want to stay away from any function that involves going to a church," Pudge would say. "It's the feeding ground of feuds. It could be a wedding, a baptism, a confirmation, a funeral—I don't care what, it ends up deadly. You sit in the wrong pew. You pay too much attention to the bride, or maybe not enough. You don't bring a big enough gift or you bring one so big it offends the host. You get stuck in traffic and you're late for the funeral mass, that becomes a sign of disrespect. Believe me, inside a church, there is no way a gangster can come out ahead."

My sense of Angelo was that he enjoyed feuds. He had the perfect mental makeup for dealing with them, especially feuds that spanned decades. He seldom exhibited any emotion, keeping both his anger and his respect hidden well below any visible surface. With the exception of his cramped inner circle, no one ever knew those against whom Angelo held a grudge. No one other than Pudge was told when he would strike against an enemy and what form his retribution would take. Angelo was the perfect gangster in that sense, a

silent and deadly terminator capable of waiting a lifetime for
his payback or choosing to launch an attack within a matter of
days. Only he knew when the moment was ripe and the time
at hand.

. . .

PAOLINO VESTIERI WAS asleep in a corner bed, facing the wall
of the small back room. He was in number sixteen, on the
third floor of a run-to-the-ground Baltimore rooming house
catering to a client list working their way south of the poverty
line. The doors were plywood thin and sounds of discord carried through the halls of the five-story building. Paolino was
once a strong man with an insatiable desire for work. But
now, still shy of fifty years, he had surrendered his will to the
facts of his life. He no longer held out any large-scale ambi-
tions, but had settled down into the oddly comforting routine
of a job-to-job and place-to-place existence. He had been
living at the Burlington Arms for six weeks, paying the three-
dollar-a-week rent from his salary as a bootblack at a shoe-
shine concession on the lower level of Baltimore's main train
terminal. He lived alone and had few friends, and would fall
asleep with one hand loosely holding an empty bottle of red
wine. He had not seen Angelo since the day he walked out of
their New York apartment and never made mention to others
of having a son. Paolino Vestieri was living his life as it had
come to be. He was neither bitter nor angry, but simply accepted it as the way it was meant to unfold. In his wallet he
kept only two reminders of a past life—his wedding photo
and a torn picture of him holding his son Carlo above his
shoulders, both with full, bright smiles, the gleaming waters
of the Mediterranean Sea behind them.

Angelo walked into the room and stared down at his father.
His sleep was heavy, the weariness of the workingman com-
pounded by the bottle of wine. Angelo had taken the train
down from New York alone, not needing Pudge, not needing
anyone, for his meeting with Paolino. He sat next to a
window in a parlor car, gazing out at the passing scenery, his

mind racing to conjure up the few warm memories he had of his father. Through the underworld network, he had kept tabs on Paolino as he moved from city to city, knowing he would never venture far from water nor be able to afford anything other than a cheap flophouse. He knew his father was short on money and low on hope. But little of that mattered. Paolino Vestieri needed to be confronted.

The time was now. Angelo was set to begin a new life with Isabella, the wedding less than two weeks away. He did not wish to have that life clouded by shadows. She, along with Pudge, Ida and Angus, knew about his father and Angelo was confident that they would take whatever happened to their grave.

"Wake up, Papa," Angelo said in a strong, quiet voice.

Paolino stirred but did not open his eyes. His breath was heavy from the drink and his body fatigued from the long day spent slumped over other people's shoes.

"Papa, wake up," Angelo said, leaning over to shake him. "I need to talk to you."

"Carlo," Paolino muttered, still half asleep. "Carlo."

"Carlo's not here," Angelo said.

The words forced Paolino's eyes open and he turned on his cot to glance down at the feet of the man in his room. The shoes were expensive, black lace-ups with thick heels. The cuffs of the pants just above them were also black and tailor-made. Paolino looked up and saw his son's hard eyes boring in on him.

"What are you doing here?" he said, quickly sitting up. "Who asked you to come here?"

"No one asked, Papa."

"Then why are you here? To stare at me? To prove to yourself that your way is better? Is that it? Well then, look around, gangster. Have your laugh and then leave."

"I have come for Carlo, Papa," Angelo said. He was calm and confident, standing erect and a short distance from his father. Paolino's thick hair was tousled from his sleep, stacked to one side and coated with shards of gray. His blue work

pants were soiled by shoe polish and grease and his white
T-shirt was smudged with the remains of past meals.

"You have nothing to do with Carlo." Paolino spit out the
words. "You have not even earned the right to speak his
name."

"You made two mistakes," Angelo said. "You murdered
your own son, then you had another one who found out
about it."

"So what will you do now?" Paolino wearily got to his feet.
"Kill me, too? Are you that stupid? Can't you see, gangster,
that I already walk among the dead?"

"I'm here to make your pain go away, Papa. You have suffered enough." Angelo slid a hand inside his jacket, slowly
pulled out a revolver and held it, pointed at Paolino's chest.
He twisted the gun in his hand and clicked open the chamber.
He slid a bullet into one of the empty slots then snapped it
back shut. He stepped forward and placed the gun on a
rickety nightstand next to the cot.

"There is one bullet in it," Angelo said. "It's time to make
your peace and use it."

"Why don't you do it yourself?" Paolino asked quietly.
"Do you lack the courage to end my misery?"

"Yes." Angelo stared at his father. "But for once in your
life, I pray that you will have such courage. I leave it to you,
Papa. Bring it to an end. For both of us."

"I loved my Carlo," Paolino said, tears forming around
his eyes.

"I know," Angelo told him. "And I know you loved me,
too."

He took a slow look around the room and then turned back
to his father. He walked over to the night table and pointed
down at the gun.

"You made a mistake and it did nothing but ruin your life,"
Angelo said. "I am leaving you with a chance to make it
right."

Paolino Vestieri picked up the gun, cradled it in two hands
and sat back down on the cot.

"Good-bye, Papa," he heard his son say.

Angelo walked out of the room and shut the door behind him. He was turning a corner, heading for the first-floor landing, when he heard the shot echo down the thin walls. He sat down on the top step, his head pressed against his chest. His eyes were closed and he bit down on his lower lip.

He sat there well into the late hours and mourned the death of his father, Paolino Vestieri.

• • •

ANGELO GOT OFF the train and saw Isabella standing on the jammed platform, waiting for him. He walked toward her and reached for her as soon as she was close enough to touch. "I am so sorry," she whispered between sobs. "So sorry."

"I hope he finally has the peace he always wanted," Angelo said. "He more than earned it."

Isabella looked up at him, her face smeared with tears. "You have both earned it," she said.

"I gave my father nothing to be proud of," Angelo said. "I became what he most hated. My hand was not on the gun that killed him, Isabella. But in every other way, I was the one who helped pull that trigger."

Isabella stared into Angelo's eyes and stroked the sides of his face. On both sides, harried commuters rushed toward final destinations, dragging luggage and reluctant children in their wake. They stood between them, holding one another, both shedding tears over the death of a good man. Alone in the middle of a crowd.

• • •

"HE COULD HAVE just left his father alone," I said, handing Mary a fresh cup of water. "Let him live out what was left of his life. Treat him as if he were already a dead man. It wasn't as if he was a threat to him or anyone else, for that matter."

"It would go against the way he had been raised," Mary said, speaking with subtle authority. "Against all the tenants of the life he had chosen. His father's death haunted Angelo, probably to this very day. But he had to answer for Carlo's murder. There was no way out, for either one of them."

"Why not give the job to somebody else, then?" I asked, staring over at the dying man. "He could have ordered it done. It would have had the same effect."

"It was personal," Mary said. "And he had been raised to separate the business from the personal. He could never have allowed anyone else to kill Paolino. To him, that would have been an even bigger crime."

"I always thought Paolino's death was just another way for Angelo to finally bury his past," I said. "Help to clear away everything that happened before that day he was taken in by Ida the Goose. He always thought of that as the most important day of his life. What came before it didn't matter."

"There's some truth to that." Mary nodded. "His father's presence reminded him of the life he would have had without Ida or Angus. And those were images he didn't want to keep alive."

"I've thought about his father quite a bit," I said. "I don't really know why it's stayed with me as much as it has all these years. I guess because I could never really figure out whether what Angelo did was an act of courage or just one of cruelty."

Mary rested her cup on the small tray cart behind her, then turned to look at me. "I think it was both," she said.

． ． ． ．

PUDGE NICHOLS SLEPT with his back to the open window, its curtains furling against the early morning breeze. He was naked except for a pair of cream-colored boxers. His muscular body rested on the soft feather mattress, his burly arms curled against a stained pillow. Shirley lay next to him, one arm draped across his back, the other shoved beneath her thin frame. Strands of brown hair flowed down her face and neck. She was awake, her eyes peeking above the curve of Pudge's shoulder, looking at the two men on the fire escape, guns in each of their hands. She lifted her left hand and waved them into the room.

The two shoved aside the curtains and slid carefully through the window, their eyes fixed on their sleeping target. They stood there, poised and steady, their backs to the bathroom, its door slightly ajar. As the men lifted their guns to waist level, one motioned to Shirley, asking her to move away from the bed with a nudge of his head. Shirley slid her arm off Pudge's shoulders, fingers skimming the hard skin. She leaned over and kissed him on the flat of his cheek, the cascade of her hair hiding his face. She moved back and lost all her breath when she saw him look up at her and smile.

"I got a lot to learn about women," Pudge said, the sound of his voice getting the two men's attention.

Pudge rolled off the bed just as the first volley of bullets plunked through the mattress, sending feathers flowing through the air and knocking Shirley to the floor. He landed in a crouch position, the hand that was shoved under his pillow now holding a gun and firing rounds aimed at the two men.

The bathroom door swung open and there was Angelo. He stood, feet firm between toilet and sink, his two guns firing bullets in the direction of the shooters. Within seconds, both men crumpled to the ground, one on top of the other, their suits stained with dark blotches. Pudge walked over and looked down, his bare feet stepping into puddles of blood. He stared up at Angelo and gave him a relieved wink. Angelo glanced past Pudge and saw Shirley standing at the foot of the bed, a gun in her hand. Pudge caught his look and knew it was too late.

The two bullets ripped into the center of Pudge's back. He fell to his knees, still holding onto his empty gun.

Angelo walked out of the bathroom and stepped over Pudge, careful not to slip on the blood-slick floor. He looked at Shirley, the warm gun still grasped in both her hands. Her face was ashen, stunned that she had actually managed to shoot Pudge Nichols.

Angelo looked at her for several long seconds and then lifted his gun and fired a bullet into Shirley's chest. The force sent Shirley crashing back onto the bed, her face up and her eyes closed.

Angelo slid the guns inside his hip holster and walked back over to Pudge. He cradled his friend's head in his arms and rocked him back and forth. "Don't you die, Pudge," he whispered to him in a shaken voice. "Don't you dare die on me. You have to live. You hear me. You have to fight. And you have to live."

Angelo looked around him, on his knees in a room now filled with the remains of the dead. He reared back his head and let out a series of loud, anguished cries for a doctor's help, the words echoing down across the cold, barren walls of the silent tenement.

9

Winter, 1927

ANGELO DELAYED HIS wedding until Pudge recovered from the shooting. He lost half a lung to one bullet and fragments of the other were left just above his rib cage, too close to a vital artery for doctors to remove. He had lost a great deal of blood and teetered close to death for several days. Pudge was confined to a hospital bed for five weeks. Angelo stayed by his side throughout, spending his nights on a thin cot shoved next to the IV bottles. While he watched his friend sleep through his pain, he made the plans that were needed now that an all-out gangster war was at hand. Angus McQueen had ruled the lucrative streets of lower Manhattan since the turn of the century and had fought back many a challenge. But no one had yet come as close as Jack Wells to wreaking havoc on his domain. Wells, using a great deal of care and cunning, had positioned himself to take over the top slot in the city. With James Garrett on his side, Wells had total control over the corrupt branch of the New York City Police Department, using them as enforcers and leg breakers whenever needed. With Jerry Ballister, whose overtures to McQueen had been rebuffed, still on his payroll, Wells had a fearless and now angry trigger willing to go up against anyone at any time. Ballister was a terrifying man because he was willing to die not for money or a cause but because he knew no other way.

McQueen, meanwhile, had made his gang members wealthy. That, in turn, had given them all something a gangster should never have—a feeling of security. A number of his lieutenants were ready to walk away from the rackets, their money safe, their children grown, their bodies intact. McQueen was left with an inner circle that was strong on loyalty but weak on experience. With Pudge not yet back to full strength, McQueen was missing his most feared and dangerous weapon. Spider MacKenzie was a solid soldier but untested in battle. Ida the Goose was retired and too old to call back into the mix.

Which left the outcome of the upcoming war in the young hands of Angelo Vestieri.

·   ·   ·

"HE COULD GO either way," Angus said to Ida on one of his monthly visits to her farm. He had a white cane stick in one hand and his customary unlit cigar in the other. "I don't know if he's cold enough to pull that trigger and walk from it."

"He'll come through," Ida the Goose said as they walked up a grassy slope. "Probably in ways neither one of us has even thought about."

"What makes you so sure? He plans well, but when it comes to the guns, that's usually left to Pudge."

"Trust me," Ida insisted. "The only way for you to win this war is to let Angelo do it for you."

Angus McQueen stopped and grabbed Ida the Goose by the hand. "I've trusted you all my life," he said. "I'm not going to start doubting you now."

"I wish I could come in on this with you," Ida said.

"You got a good life up here," Angus told her. "If I was as smart as the papers say I am, I'd be up here with you. Got more than enough money saved. I could live to a hundred and still have a dollar left over. Been through four gang wars in my time. Came out scarred but still alive and still on top."

"You can't quit it, Angus."

"You're not going to fill me up with that live by the gun, die by the gun broth now are you?" When Ida shook her head, Angus said, "Good. I never bought into that and I never will. I got into the rackets looking to die old and rich, not young and filled with bullet holes. Nothing I've seen or heard since has changed my thinking."

"Then you need Angelo and Pudge more than you think you do."

"And why's that?"

"Because they care more about winning than they do about living. And that kind of thinking is what wins a gang war. If you're so eager to die fat and with a full wallet, let those boys loose and stay out of their way."

· · ·

ANGELO AND ISABELLA walked along the water down by the South Street piers. The night was cold and breezy, an angry wind screaming off the Hudson's waves and running out toward the railroad tenements. They both wore wool coats buttoned to the neck with the collars up and their gloved hands were entwined around one another. Above them the clear dark sky shone with an impressive array of stars.

"Do you mind walking in the cold?" he asked.

"No," she said, shaking her head. "I like the wind against my face. It is so different here than the winters I remember in Italy when I was little."

"I've never been to Italy." Angelo glanced over at Isabella. He was always taken aback by the simplicity of her beauty. Her embrace-me eyes shone like torches against the lapping water beneath them, her cheeks were flushed red by the harsh wind, and her long hair hung over her coat, thick and rich as a horse's mane. But most of all it was her smile that gave his heart pause and eased the nagging pain in his lungs.

"You will see it after we're married," Isabella said. "It's the best place in the world to go on a honeymoon."

Angelo stopped and grabbed Isabella gently by both arms and held her close, gazing into her eyes. "I cannot go with you on our honeymoon," he said. "We will both get on the ship, but I will get off just before it leaves harbor. One of the tugboats will take me back and you'll go without me."

"Angelo, what are you talking about?" Isabella said, pulling free of his hands. "I've never heard of such a thing. No one goes on a honeymoon alone."

"The men who tried to kill Pudge will try again," Angelo said. He still looked at her, but spoke in a firmer, more direct manner. "They will try to kill me, too. I can't let that happen."

"And what will you do to stop them?" she asked, but the expression on her face told him she already knew the answer.

He turned and began to walk, his arm under the sleeve of her coat, their heads down against the bracing gusts of wind. They walked for several blocks, both lost in the deep silence of their very separate thoughts.

"You know what it is I do," Angelo finally began. "I have not tried to hide it from you or your father. It is what I am now and what I will be after I am your husband."

"I knew what you were on the first day we met," Isabella said. "It does not change what I feel for you."

Angelo turned to her and smiled. "Then you know that until this is finished, I will owe you a honeymoon."

"You will also owe my father an explanation," Isabella said. "Wait until he hears about this one."

"He already knows," Angelo said, taking Isabella in his arms. "And he couldn't be happier."

"When did you see him?"

"Early this morning. He's going with you. I gave him my boarding ticket so you wouldn't be all alone for two weeks."

"On my honeymoon with my father," Isabella sighed. "What more could a bride ask for?"

· · ·

"IT'S HARD FOR me to imagine him being in love with anyone," I told Mary as we made our way back to Angelo's hospital room. "Especially enough to want to get married."

"No one really looks to fall in love," Mary said. "It usually happens by accident. But you can teach yourself not to love. I think that's what Angelo did with every woman he met after Isabella."

"Where did you fit in?"

"I was the one in love with him," she said, staring straight ahead at the dark, empty street, the neon store lights highlighting her clear skin and handsome features. "To him, I was someone he felt comfortable having around. I never expected it to be more than that."

"Did you want it to be?" I asked.

"It was never a question of what I wanted," Mary said. "You accept things for what they are. Especially with a man like Angelo. We had a strong friendship. And that was enough."

"Would you have married him if he'd asked?" I held the main entrance door to the hospital open for her.

"Do you know anyone who ever said no to Angelo?" Mary asked as she walked past me into the elevator.

"Not anyone who's still alive," I said.

Spring, 1928

"ARE YOU SURE you're strong enough for this?" Angelo asked as he followed Pudge toward the tenement stoop.

"You can stop nursing me, Ang," Pudge said, bouncing a rubber ball against the concrete pavement. "Even that one-eyed doctor Angus found says it's time for me to get back out."

"I don't think he's a real doctor," Angelo said. "He doesn't have any diplomas hanging in his office."

"He doesn't even have an office," Pudge said. "Either way, it doesn't matter. I'm finished with doctors. Now, let's play some stoopball."

Pudge bounced the ball four times, keeping it low and against his right thigh. He lifted his right arm high, at a sharp angle, and slammed the ball down against the side of the stoop. The ball hit off the curve of the step and shot out on a straight line, two-hopping against a tenement doorway.

"That's good for a double," Pudge said slapping his hands together. "Would have given myself a triple if I were at full strength."

"We're not playing against anyone," Angelo said.

"I need the practice," Pudge said. "For when we do."

．　．　．

STOOPBALL WAS A sacred tenement game. The standard rules were the same as those of baseball minus the bats, gloves, bases, pitchers and a playing field. The length of a game depended more on traffic conditions than players' abilities or the weather. The location of parked cars and trucks, vendor stalls, garbage bins and baby strollers determined whether a ball slammed off the stoop was either a long single or a short home run. A ball had to be caught to be called an out, no matter how many bounces it took. Any ball that bounced off the first floor of a tenement wall was signaled an automatic home run.

Pudge loved stoopball and played it every chance he got. He was always rounding up neighborhood kids, breaking them down into teams and playing games well into the night for a penny a run. In his eyes, the game was the street equivalent of chess and he treated it as an opportunity to both think and relax.

"This one's going over that fire escape," Pudge said, taking a ball out of his back pocket and pointing to a building across the street.

"Try not to hit any old women walking by," Angelo said. He was as casually indifferent toward the game as Pudge was passionate. "And then tell me you're not worried about any of the moves we talked about."

Pudge stopped bouncing the ball, held it in his hand and looked at Angelo. "I haven't worried about anything since Ida put you and me together," he said. "But just know that after this war is done with, it's all going to be different for you and me. This is big-time movement we got planned and *if* we come out the other end alive, it's going to put us in a place we might otherwise never see."

"Are you sure they won't try anything at the wedding?"

"It's not their style," Pudge said, shaking his head. "They want you out of the way and as far as they know, you're going to Italy for two weeks, so that's that. Plenty of time to kill you when you get back. They'll look to hit me and Angus, maybe even Spider, sometime during your honeymoon."

"I invited them," Angelo said. "Just to be sure."

"Invited who?" Pudge asked.

"Jack Wells and his crew," Angelo said. "I had invitations sent to Ballister and Garrett, too."

"To the wedding?" Pudge was incredulous. "Are you serious or crazy?"

"Both," Angelo said. "Maybe you're right and they won't try anything that night. But just to be safe, I like knowing they're someplace where I can see them. And if they behave, then they have a good time at the wedding and Isabella has three more gifts to open."

"You scare me sometimes with how you think," Pudge said, bouncing the ball again and smiling at the simple logic behind such a maneuver. "I would have loved to have seen their faces when they got the invites, that dog-eared cop especially."

"It's a free night of food and drink," Angelo said. "It would be too hard for a man like him to pass up. And Wells and Ballister had only one choice. Turning down the invitation could have been seen as a sign of fear on their part from some of the other crews."

Pudge nodded and bounced the ball again, taking aim at the stoop, ready for his second shot. "Where're they going to be sitting?" he asked as he lifted his arm and slammed the ball hard against the stoop. It flew off on an arc, landing high up against a closed first-floor window.

"I put them at your table," Angelo said as he handed Pudge his jacket.

Pudge stared at him, his mouth slightly open, his fists resting against his hips. "You got a good reason for doing something like that?"

"The doctor doesn't want you to drink too much. He said it's still too soon, your insides need a little more time to heal. I figure with them at your table, you got a lot of reasons to stay sober."

"You're some friend, Angelo," Pudge said, putting on his jacket and leading the way back to his car.

"I know," Angelo said, following behind him.

• • •

ANGELO WAS THE first to do it. Now, in the years since, it has become an organized crime tradition to invite enemies to a wedding celebration. Such a gesture serves a number of often clear, sometimes subtle purposes. The clearest of which is to demonstrate a lack of fear on the part of the gangster issuing the invitation.

"It's all a game," Angelo would tell me. "You always need to have the upper hand, or at least act like you do. It plays to your advantage to have a sworn enemy at a wedding, make him feel welcome and treat him like a close friend. It doesn't cost anything and it keeps the edge on your side of the table. He's got to wonder why you did it and what you're thinking and what else you're planning. All the concern is thrown back at him. All you have to do is make sure the wedding comes off without any problems."

No gangster ever turns down a wedding invitation from an enemy. It is a safe gesture, since a reception is considered off-limits for violence. It gives the two rivals a chance to size one another up in a secure environment and try to assess when and where the next move will be made. "It gets to the point where you almost need a wedding to figure out who's on whose side," Pudge liked to say. "You can tell that by seeing where a particular guy sits, who he talks to and, sometimes, who he doesn't talk to and even goes out of his way to avoid. That tells you that they may have made a pact and they don't want anybody to know. It's really crazy. Some weddings you go to there are more people there looking to kill you than shake your hand. You spend most of your time trying to figure out which way a guy's going to swing. The bride and groom are the last two people on your mind. But that's this business. What are simple things to civilians are always life and death to us."

• • •

THE NIGHT OF May 15, 1928, was filled with music. Isabella, in a white veil and hand-sewn gown, mingled with ease among the hundred and twenty guests, the content smile of the new bride never off her lips. She greeted strangers and familiar faces with equal degrees of warmth, giving the large hall the intimate feel of a small dining room. The hardest of men at the reception were enchanted by her beauty, while their more suspicious wives were won over by her innocent nature. Her friends and family were swallowed up by the emotions of the night, thrilled to have the happiness of another bride to celebrate. They all looked at Angelo as a suitable but dangerous husband. He had their respect, but it grew more out of fear than affection.

Angus McQueen brought a six-piece band down from the Cotton Club and the soulful rhythms of their blues melodies filled the hall and ruled the dance floor. Ida the Goose, down for the weekend from her upstate farm, moved from one pair of arms to another, spirited and free in the company of men with guns. Pudge sat across from Jerry Ballister during the five-hour meal that was highlighted by a seven-tiered wedding cake. The two gangsters seldom spoke and when they did, the words were forced and veiled.

"You got to give the Italians credit," Ballister said at one point. "They sure know how to throw a wedding."

"They're not bad when it comes to funerals either," Pudge said.

"I wouldn't know about that," Ballister said, smiling across the flower arrangement at Pudge.

"Maybe one day you will," Pudge said, returning the smile.

Sitting next to Angelo, Ida the Goose lit a cigarette and poured herself a foamy glass of beer. She looked over at him, sizing him up in his black tuxedo and slicked back hair, and laughed.

"Do I look that bad?" Angelo asked.

"The first time I saw you, I didn't know where the blood stopped and you began. Now, here you are, coming at me right off a movie screen."

Angelo sipped from a glass of water and leaned closer to

Ida. "I saw you talking to Jack Wells," he noted. "You two seemed to hit it off."

"I kept company with his brother a lot of years ago," Ida told him. "He was just a kid, then, following the two of us around like a lap puppy."

"His brother still alive?"

"We broke up about six months before I took over the Café. He pulled an armed heist and got caught. Got a soft judge and was given three years upstate. Should have been an easy stretch, but it wasn't. At least not for him. He took a dive off the top tier of his cell block."

"Pushed or jumped?" Angelo asked.

"What difference does it make?" Ida said. "Dead is dead."

Angelo turned and saw the guests begin to form a line near the front table.

"They're starting to hand out the gifts," he said, sliding his chair back. "I should go stand with Isabella."

"Here's my gift," Ida said, keeping a grip on Angelo's hand. "I've been around a lot of men in my time, good ones and bad, and they all need a place and time where they let their guard down, try to forget their troubles, clear their minds, whatever. In most lines of work, you don't give something like that a second thought. In ours, it could put you on a morgue slab. Jack Wells is no different from any man I ever met."

"Where does he go to forget his troubles?" Angelo asked.

Ida the Goose stood and dropped the rest of her cigarette into the glass of beer. She wrapped her arms around Angelo and kissed the top of his head. "Dog fights," she said. "And he never leaves until the last dog dies."

* * *

THE CROWD PARTED to make room for the new couple and Angelo and Isabella took to the center of the dance floor. They held one another and swayed to the beat of a clarinet solo, Isabella's head at rest on her husband's shoulder.

Angelo knew that, whatever roads his life would lead him down, he would never be happier than he was at this moment.

This was a day separate and inviolable from a lifetime that was to be packed with violence and death. Here, in a crowded hall, filled with the company of friends, family and enemies, Angelo Vestieri, for one full day, found peace.

"I will always love you," he told her.

"I wish you were coming to Italy," she whispered.

"There will be a day for that," Angelo whispered back. "I promise you."

As he spoke he looked over at Pudge's table to see Jack Wells, James Garrett and Jerry Ballister staring over at him. Angelo knew from their hard looks and confident demeanor that if they had their way, the promise he had just made to Isabella would be one he would not live to keep.

• • •

ANGELO STOOD ON the closed deck of the tugboat, watching the ocean liner veer to its left and out of New York Harbor. He drank a cup of black coffee as Pudge steered the boat clear of the high waves.

"At least you *look* like you know what you're doing," Angelo said, still staring at the dark hull of the ship that was taking Isabella back to Italy.

"It's the only thing I ever picked up from my old man," Pudge said. "Before he split for who the hell knows where, and when he wasn't drunk and pounding me around, he drove one of these for money. Sometimes he'd take me along for the ride and I paid attention."

"You think she'll be all right?" Angelo asked.

"She's not the one about to get shot at by a full crew," Pudge said. "That would be you and me. She's gonna get a tan and have lots to eat. She might be a little fatter when she gets back, but my hunch is you're still going to love her."

"You think anybody saw me get off the ship?"

"They can't see what they're not looking for," Pudge decided.

"Spider is parked inside the pier hold."

"Then let's start the honeymoon," Pudge said.

• • •

JAMES GARRETT SAT in the third row of St. Matthew's Church, kneeling down, his hands crossed, his eyes closed. It was late on a Saturday afternoon and the long line of people waiting to have their confessions heard had dwindled down to a handful. Garrett made the sign of the cross and sat back down, waiting for the last sinner to leave. He stared up at the altar with an ear-to-ear grin on his face and ten thousand in cash stuffed inside an envelope in his jacket pocket. He turned to his right and watched a dark-haired woman in high heels part the curtains of the confessional and make her way down the center aisle, her head bowed in deep prayer. Garrett wondered what sins such a woman would commit and how many Hail Marys and Our Fathers had been doled out by the senile priest hearing the five o'clock confessions to ease the burden of forgiveness. He looked to his left, saw the last person on line, an elderly woman with a black shawl over her shoulders and a black scarf bobby-pinned to her head, exit the booth. Garrett slid across the pew, stood and genuflected before the main altar, then walked casually toward the purple curtains to clear his soul of sin.

He leaned down in the dark cubicle and waited for the small window to slide open. When it did, he looked through the mesh screen and saw the shadow of the priest sitting with his back to the wall and his hand to his face. He crossed himself and began his litany. "Bless me Father for I have sinned," Garrett said. "It has been two weeks since my last confession."

The priest coughed into a handkerchief and nodded. "That's not so long," he said. "What sins did you commit in that time?"

Garrett took a deep breath and shrugged. "I lied a few times and cursed a lot more than I should. But it's hard not to when you're a cop and deal with the kind of people I do every day."

"I see," the priest said. "Anything else?"

"That's pretty much the long and the short of it, Father," Garrett said. "A couple of foul thoughts here and there, nothing more to it than that."

"Do you pray every day?"

"Yes," Garrett said. "Maybe not every day, but most days."

"Did you pray today? Before you came here to make your peace with God?"

"Just a few minutes ago." Garrett was curious about the line of questioning. In the darkness of the cubicle, he couldn't make out the face on the other side. He knew it wasn't the regular Saturday afternoon priest. "I gave thanks for the good fortune that's come my way."

"That gives you a clear soul," the voice said. "And all that's left now is for you to receive your penance."

"Let's have at it then, Father," Garrett said, pressing his elbow against the padded envelope inside his jacket.

"Say three Hail Marys," the voice instructed. "And the Lord's Prayer. And then, die."

James Garrett saw the muzzle and the flash pop of a bullet before he felt the sharp burn in his chest. The thick velour curtains that hid Garrett in his cubby parted, letting in shafts of flickering light. The crooked cop, his head resting against the thick wood of the confessional, looked up and saw Angelo Vestieri standing there. The man on the other end of the booth, Pudge Nichols, opened his door and stood behind Angelo.

"You're too stupid to know the rules, dago," Garrett said. "A church is supposed to be off-limits."

Angelo stepped into the booth and put his gun against Garrett's temple. "The Lord works in mysterious ways," he said, then pulled the trigger. Garrett jumped off his seat, slid down and slumped over dead in a corner of the booth. Angelo holstered his gun, reached into the cop's jacket pocket and pulled out the envelope with the ten thousand dollars.

Angelo and Pudge walked to the front of the empty church

and knelt down before the main altar, both blessing themselves. Angelo then took the envelope crammed with money and shoved it into the wooden poor box on his right.

"That should buy a few prayers for his soul," Angelo said.

"Or a year's worth of booze for the rectory," Pudge said. "A good cause any way you look at it."

They turned and walked out of the dark and empty church into the sinking sunrise of a late afternoon day.

• • •

THE MANNER IN which a gangster carries out a hit is just as important as the actual murder. How and where it's done transmits a variety of signals to a warring rival. If the shooting occurs in a place unofficially declared off-limits, it puts an opponent in the uncomfortable position of not being able to anticipate his rival's next move, realizing the person he is up against is willing to do anything at any time to achieve victory. Up until the James Garrett shooting, there had never been a mob-sanctioned hit inside a church. It caused turmoil within underworld circles and sent an instant message to Jack Wells and his crew that this war would be different.

"The crime bosses started to pay attention to Angelo right after the hit on Garrett," Pudge told me. "Before then, I was considered the trigger and he was nothing more than the shadow on my right. With that one move, he changed the rules and put himself front and center. He did it the way he did everything else in his life—very quietly and when you least expect it. One of the reasons hits are so public is to bring more attention to the shooter than to the target. Angelo didn't care about any of that. He didn't want the tabloids to know who he was, but he did want his enemies to know what he did. The key to any victory is to pull off the unexpected. When you can do that, it scares people like no street shooting ever can."

• • •

FRANCIS THE PIMP was asleep on the couch, his head tilted back, his arms hanging by his side. He was dressed in brown slacks, the belt unbuckled around his waist, and a white button-down shirt, his shoes off. The sun was twenty minutes shy of rising and the room was still shrouded in early-morning darkness. The floor around his feet was damp and sticky from spilled beer. Two dirty plates rested in the center of the wooden coffee table, inches from his legs, food remains crusted around the edges.

The man walked around the room, his footsteps unheard by Francis. He carefully placed a chair behind the couch, its back facing the shuttered windows. He stood on the chair and waited out its creaks. He held a thick rope in his hands and flipped one end through the steam pipes that lined the walls of the ceiling. He caught the loose end and curled the edges of the rope into knots and then pulled out enough rope to form a noose. He let it hover just above his head and quietly stepped off the chair.

The man watched the sleeping pimp's chest heave up and down in a deep sleep. He pulled a roll of packing tape from his jacket pocket, stripped off two thick slices, leaned over and slapped them over Francis's mouth. The pimp jumped awake at the touch, but was held in place by the man.

"Stay quiet," the man instructed. "This will only take a few minutes."

Francis shook his head, his eyes bugged out. He flailed his arms up and down and tried to move the man's hand off his chest, but it was fear working against muscle and proved futile. The man grabbed Francis by the front end of his trousers and lifted him to his feet. He turned him around and moved him toward the chair, the noose swinging gently above it. Panic ruled Francis as soon as he saw the rope. He kicked and scratched and shoved against the strength of the man, to no avail. A gloved hand came down and slapped Francis across the face twice, the sting calming the tension.

"Get up on the chair," the man said.

Francis shook his head. Sweat had drenched his face and

the collar of his shirt. He was breathing heavily, and the tape was starting to wilt from the wet streams running down his cheeks. The man reared back and slapped him again.

"Get on that chair," the man said. "You do it right, it'll be over quick. If you make me shoot you, I'll make sure to take my time."

The man shoved Francis closer to the chair. The pimp's legs were barely moving, each step a painful quiver. He helped lift him onto the chair and stood back, a gun now in his hand, pointing at the rope above Francis's head.

"Put it around your neck," the man said. "Nice and tight. That's all you need to do. I'll take over from there."

Francis stared at the gun and lifted his hands above his head, feeling for the rope. He put the noose around his neck, tightened it and began to cry. "I'm sorry," he mumbled through his tears and the tape on his mouth. "I didn't mean for anybody to get hurt."

"But somebody did," the man said.

"It was Jack Wells," Francis said in a clearer voice, pushing at the edges of the tape with his tongue. "He made me and Shirley do what we did."

"You weren't much of a pimp, Francis," the man said. "And you're not much of a man."

"Please, please don't," Francis begged. "I'll work for you. Do anything you want me to do. Just don't let me die like this. Please, don't let me die."

The man looked up at Francis and holstered his gun. He pulled a cigarette from his pocket, lit it and took a drag, letting the smoke filter out through his nose.

"Take care of yourself, Francis," the man said.

He pulled a leg back and kicked the chair out from under Francis the Pimp. The man walked to the couch and leaned against it, smoking his cigarette, watching Francis shake and twirl until his eyes popped and his neck snapped. He tossed the remains of the cigarette onto the dirty dinner plate and left the apartment as quietly as he had entered.

Pudge Nichols's mission for the morning was complete.

• • •

ANGELO RINSED OUT the hand towel and pressed it against Ida the Goose's forehead. She was in her bed, a thick quilt raised up to her neck, fighting the shivers of a high fever. She looked up at Angelo and smiled, smelling the fresh coffee Pudge was brewing in the small kitchen just outside her bedroom.

"I can't believe you got him making us breakfast," Ida said. "God only knows what's gonna end up stacked on a plate with him behind the stove."

"The doctor said you needed to eat," Angelo said. "He didn't say it had to be any good."

Ida took in a deep breath and Angelo could hear the thick bronchial rasp he knew so well rattling around her lungs. He lifted her into a sitting position, making it easier for her to pass air through a clogged nose and dry mouth. She had been sick for nearly two weeks before she placed a call to a local doctor who diagnosed her with a severe upper respiratory infection. He left behind a large bottle of cough syrup and a crumpled bill for services rendered. Angelo and Pudge arrived two days later to find Ida collapsed on the back porch, the empty bottle of syrup by her side. "There was no label on it," Ida said in her defense. "And the doctor didn't say how much I should take or how often. Besides, it had a nice taste and it did quiet down the cough some."

"You're lucky it didn't kill you," Pudge said. "And quiet your cough permanently."

"That would only happen if I drank a full bottle of that poor man's whiskey you boys sell," she said, dismissing them with a wave of her hand.

"We'll take care of you from here," Angelo said. "Stick around till you get well again."

"I don't doubt you're better at it than that sorry excuse calls himself a doctor," Ida said. "And a lot better company to boot."

Pudge came in carrying a platter filled with scrambled eggs, crisp bacon and a stack of toast. Three forks and salt and pepper shakers were crammed inside his shirt pocket. He rested the platter at the foot of the bed and nodded toward Angelo. "I left the pot of coffee and three cups over by the stove," he said. "How about you grab those and I get to feeding Ida."

Angelo walked away from the bed and out toward the kitchen. "Where do you keep the sugar?" he asked over his shoulder.

"First cabinet next to the back door," Ida wheezed. "If not there, look on the bottom shelf of the pantry. If it's not there, then it's someplace else."

"Be easier to go out and buy some," Angelo said from the kitchen.

Ida looked down at the platter by her feet. "Looks like you made enough to feed a full crew," she said.

"What you can't finish, we will," Pudge said, removing the damp cloth from her forehead.

"I'm contagious," Ida said. "Or so the doctor says."

"Yeah? Well, I'm hungry," Pudge said. "And the doctor's not here to tell me otherwise."

He pulled a fork from his shirt pocket and grabbed a piece of toast. He spread eggs and bacon on the bread, then sealed the mix with another slice. He handed the sandwich to Ida who took it from him. She took a big bite. Then she sat back against the pillows, her eyes closed, her face lit with pleasure. "If I knew you could cook like this, I would have had you work the kitchen in the Café," she said.

"Wait till you taste my coffee," Pudge said. "You'll change that way of thinking in a heartbeat."

Angelo came back into the room, three tin cups of coffee in his hands. "I found the sugar," he said. "But not the milk."

"There's none to be found," Ida said, finishing the last bite of her sandwich. "You can always walk over to the barn and pull it out fresh. I'm sure Eloise will oblige."

Angelo handed Ida and Pudge each a cup and sat back down across from the bed. "I'm happy with what I have," he said, holding up his tin, steam rising off its lip.

"You about ready for another?" Pudge asked Ida, pointing over his shoulder to the platter.

"I'm more than full," Ida said.

"Eggs not done the way you like?" Pudge asked.

"The eggs were great." Ida paused to wipe a thin row of toast crumbs off her nightgown and onto the floor. "But the hit on Garrett was even greater." The strength was back in her voice. "A great first move."

"It was Angelo's plan," Pudge said without a moment's hesitation. "He led and I followed."

"It's a helluva start to what's going to be a helluva war," Ida said. "A gangster makes his reputation off wars like these."

"We don't care about reputations," Pudge said as he finished the final piece of bacon. "We only want to win."

"You'll care when you get older and your blood's not so quick to boil over the idea of a fight. A solid reputation can stop a war just as quick as it can start one."

"The shooting is causing Angus some problems downtown," Angelo revealed. "It doesn't look good for a cop to be gunned down, corrupt or not. It looks even worse if it happens in a confessional booth."

"What's it costing him?" Ida wanted to know.

"Double the monthly payoffs to every precinct below Thirty-fourth Street for the next six months," Pudge said. "And we let the cops make some noise in the papers about how they're not going to stand for shootings in churches. It's just until the old ladies feel safe enough to go back in and tell a drunk priest all about their sin of the week."

"The money you lose now, you'll make back when you take Wells out," Ida said. "It all evens out in the end."

Pudge stood and picked up the empty platter. "I'm going to start cleaning up the mess I left in the kitchen," he said to Ida. "Maybe you should close your eyes and get some sleep."

Angelo got up to follow Pudge out of the room, the three empty cups in one hand, but Ida stopped him, reaching out for his arm. "Are you okay with all this?" she asked.

"Yes," he said.

"I guess I trained you a little too well." Her words were inked with sadness. "I needed to make you tough, and to do that I had to chisel away all the soft parts. Maybe I went and made you too hard. It'll serve you well in life, but won't make you much good to anybody else. For that, I have to say I'm sorry."

"What other choice did we have?" Angelo's eyes were hard but his words soft.

"Still, I wish now you had time to just be a little boy, enjoy that even for a short while. Pudge, too. I guess it just wasn't meant for either one of you."

"It all happened the way it was meant to, for me and for Pudge," Angelo said. "I don't regret it. Not for one minute. You shouldn't either."

"That beautiful wife you found yourself," Ida said, watching him walk away. "She still in love with you?"

"She was when I put her on that ship," Angelo said with a half smile. "But I can't say for sure until I see her again. You know what a cruise does to women."

"It's probably why I never went on one," Ida the Goose said.

She stared at the doorway as Angelo passed through to join Pudge in the kitchen. She put her head back on the pillow and listened to the two of them wash pans and dry dishes and argue over what went where. She closed her eyes and wiped at the tears running down her face with the ruffled sleeves of her gown.

• • •

ANGUS MCQUEEN UNDID the leash around the neck of his English bulldog, Gopher, and watched as the dog made a dash for the shrubs and leaves of Washington Square Park. Angus lifted his face up to the noon sun as he walked past empty rows of benches and large old trees, enjoying the solitude of a daily ritual not even a gang war was allowed to interrupt. A short distance behind him, sitting alone with a folded newspaper across his lap, Spider MacKenzie kept his eye on the boss. The lack of privacy was the one aspect of gangster life that never appealed to McQueen.

"I don't need anybody's help to walk a dog," McQueen had said to Spider before he left his office just west of the park.

"I'm just looking to find a nice place to read my newspaper," Spider said.

"Go sit behind my desk," Angus told him, as he slammed the outer office door. "That's a nice place to read."

Angus liked Spider and found comfort in his silent company. He had just grown weary of the precautions and preparations that were needed to survive a gang war. In his career in the rackets, Angus had never initiated a war nor had he ever lost one. He had always been cautious in his routine and daring in his maneuvers, making all the key decisions with a cold eye on detail and a brutal stance against his opponent. This war was different. Maybe it was because he was too old and too rich to care. Or maybe it was just that the taste of this battle didn't sit as well as had past glories. Whatever the reasons, Angus McQueen felt more like a participant than a principal in what was probably his most important battle. As he watched Gopher run back and forth across the sprawling lawn, a thick twig between his teeth, Angus knew, win or lose, this would be his final war.

Angus bent down and picked up the twig Gopher dropped by the side of his paws. He reared back and tossed it past a row of benches and into a clump behind a thick oak tree. Gopher sat until the twig landed and then took off in search of it. Angus watched as the dog ran and disappeared behind the tree, sniffing frantically for the piece of wood. He then walked over to an empty bench and sat down, smiling when he looked across the park and saw Spider move three rows closer, the paper still folded over in his hand. Angus closed his eyes and let the warm sun wash over his pale face and dark suit as he waited for Gopher to return.

From where he sat, Angus couldn't see the dog, but he heard the rustling of the leaves and dirt and that brought an even bigger smile. There was a time Gopher could smell out a stick in less time than it took to sneeze. Now, it looked like the old bulldog was as much in need of a break as his owner. They both should follow the trail Ida the Goose left. Pack your money and your health and take them both out of town long before a bullet ends your day.

The rustling had stopped for several minutes before Angus stood and walked toward the tree in search of his dog. As he got closer, he whistled several times but failed to receive a response.

"Gopher!" Angus shouted out, the sound of his voice only stirring the attention of the rummies asleep under the benches and the young couples entwined on top of them. "C'mon, Gopher," Angus said. "Get your old ass out here."

Angus was inches from the base of the tree when he stepped onto a pile of bloody leaves. The blood was brown, thick and fresh. Angus McQueen turned the corner, his hand on the tree, and stared down at his dog. Gopher was laying on his side, his throat slashed open. He was breathing in painful huffs, white foam forming and flowing down the sides of his jaw, his eyes staring up at a clear sky.

"He didn't put up much of a fight," Jerry Ballister said. "But I would expect that from an English dog."

Ballister stood across from McQueen, the dying dog between them, holding a gun in each hand. "You turned your back on my offer," he said. "For that alone you should die."

Angus beat his fists against his sides, frozen in anger by the sight of his dog, his eyes moist with tears. "You had a beef and it was with me," he said through clenched teeth. "The dog had no damn part in it."

"I figured this way, you wouldn't have to be buried alone," Ballister said, baring his teeth as he cast a glance down at the dog.

Angus bent down on his knees and petted Gopher, the dog's tired eyes looking up at his, his breath coming in shorter spurts. "Shut your eyes, buddy," McQueen whispered, one arm wrapped around the dog's bloody neck. "And let it happen. There's nothing to be afraid of."

Ballister stepped up behind McQueen and pressed a gun against the back of his head. "Except for me," Ballister said.

He fired two rounds into McQueen's head and two more into the small of his back. Ballister watched McQueen fall, then turned and left him there, facedown in the leaves, the front of his body keeping his dead dog warm, the black leash still wrapped around his right hand.

Spider MacKenzie sprinted toward the sound of the gunshots and skidded to a stop when he saw the two bodies. He had dozed off sitting under the sun reading the newspaper and had bolted awake as soon as he heard the shots. He stared down now at the body of the man for whom he had worked most of his life. He swallowed hard, ran a hand across his face and took two deep breaths.

"I'm sorry, Angus," he said in a low voice. "I'm so sorry."

Spider MacKenzie then turned away and walked out of the park to find a pay phone and arrange for someone to come and remove the body of Angus McQueen, the first great gangster of the twentieth century.

• • •

ANGELO WAS BEHIND the bar of the Café Maryland pouring two cups of coffee. He put the pot back on the burner and pushed one of the cups across to Pudge. They drank in silence, the bar empty, the sign hanging off a chain on the front door declaring the restaurant closed. "It was a smart hit," Angelo said. "But a lucky one, too. Spider doesn't take the first nap of his life and he has an outside chance to save Angus and a better-than-even chance to nail Ballister."

"There's no way they got to Spider, if that's what you're thinking," Pudge said, holding the cup from his mouth. "He was as close to Angus as we are to Ida."

"There's always a way, Pudge," Angelo said. "You just have to be smart enough to figure the price. We know Jack Wells is a dangerous man. If the hit on Angus proved anything, it proved that. But we still don't know how smart a man he is."

"Be a good idea to make him dead before we have a chance to find out," Pudge said, downing his coffee in one long gulp. "And the sooner the better. Once word hits the streets that they got Angus, the other gangs will figure Wells has the upper hand and that you and me won't be able to hold the crew together."

Angelo reached under the counter for the coffeepot and poured Pudge a fresh cup. "The crew will hold," he said, dropping the empty pot into the slop sink. "At least long enough to see what we got planned. Plus, they should have it figured that Wells has no interest in them. He's got a big enough crew. It's the turf he's after."

"The funeral's set for Wednesday morning," Pudge said. "Burial will be up in the Bronx at Woodlawn."

"What about the dog?" Angelo asked.

"Nobody's gonna mind we put him in the same grave as Angus," Pudge said. "I'll put somebody on it."

"Is the wake at Munson's?"

Pudge nodded as he drank his coffee. "Starts tomorrow night at eight."

"And Wells and Ballister will come and show their respects?" Angelo asked. "You're sure about that?"

"They have no choice but to be there," Pudge said. "They won't come on the first night, that's for friends and family. But sure as we're breathing, they'll be there on the second, flowers in one hand, hats in the other."

Angelo leaned over and rested one hand on top of Pudge's and stared across the wood at him. "So will we," he said.

• • •

THE MURDER OF Angus McQueen affected Angelo in a much deeper way than it did Pudge. Up until the killing, Angelo thought Angus to be invincible, that fear of the great man was sufficient to keep anyone from getting close enough to bring him down. It was a naive way to think, but fit his character up to that point. For despite Angelo's intelligence and innate ability to read people's motives and anticipate their actions,

Pudge was more the pure gangster. He functioned on gut and instincts, reacting quickly to a slight, knowing that any hesitation could cost him his life and that no matter how strong the shield around him there would always be someone, somewhere, willing to pull a trigger against him.

"Angelo still had an innocence about him, despite his demeanor, despite his actions," Mary said to me. "The death of Angus took that away. The horrific events that soon were to follow helped bury that softness. In his later years, Angelo would only allow it to rise to the surface now and then. Mostly when he was around me and on many of the days he spent with you."

"He told me that he always felt Angus wanted to die," I said. "That he had grown tired of the life and couldn't think of an easier way out. So he walked into the setup and allowed himself to be killed."

"There might be some truth to that," Mary said. "It's hard to tell. They're not exactly the type of men who confide their thoughts easily to others. But I do think that at different stages of their lives they grow weary over the constant battle for survival. Anyone can make money illegally. My father died rich doing it. Pudge made his millions and so did Angelo. That was always the easy part. The isolation, the inner turmoil, the hidden fears, those all take a toll and that's what ultimately brings them to a sorry end."

I walked over to the bed and felt the top of Angelo's forehead. It was cool and damp. "His fever's all but gone," I said, staring down at his sickly face. "I guess this'll be another night he'll prove the doctors wrong."

"It's not by choice," Mary said. "Only by will. He's angry and he'll stay angry until he dies."

"Because he's dying?" I asked.

"Because he's dying in this way," Mary said. "Civilians die like this, with tubes and respirators and people watching over their bedsides. He's living out his biggest fear."

"I spent a few nights in the hospital that time he got shot outside his bar," I said, walking over toward Mary's side of the bed. "I was only a kid then and I was really scared. I didn't think there was any way for him to pull through. The doctors were going crazy, they couldn't figure a way to stop the bleeding. In the middle of it all, he looked over at me and saw me with my head down, crying. 'Relax,' he said. 'I'm not going to be lucky enough to die from a bullet.' "

Mary stood over him and wiped tears from her eyes. "Very few of us get the death we deserve," she said. "So we settle for the one that's chosen. And no one has the power to change that. Not even Angelo."

· · ·

THE INSIDE OF the cabin was dark and the wood-burning stove had long since turned cold. A window was partially opened and welcomed in gusts of chilling early-morning air. Ida the Goose slept on her side, with her back to the door, a heavy quilt covering all but the top of her head. The overhead kitchen light was still on, a bright beacon in an otherwise dark setting.

The heavy footsteps creaked across the bare-board floor. They passed by the kitchen, the tall shadow moving casually toward Ida's bedroom. The footsteps stopped in front of an open hutch and a half-empty bottle of whiskey. Two hands grabbed the bottle, yanked out the cork and lifted it toward the ceiling. Two long, full gulps later, a hand placed the bottle back in its spot. It was nearing six A.M. and the sun was less than ten minutes away from the start of another day.

The feet came to a final stop at the base of Ida's bed. A gun was held in one hand, rubbing against a leg and directly across from Ida's serene face. Ida's eyes opened when she heard the trigger cocked.

"You're the first man to come into my bedroom without an invitation," Ida said, not moving, her eyes on the gun. "And my guess is the last one, too."

"I'm the one that killed your friend Angus," the voice above her bed said. "I got to thinking it wouldn't be fair for him to die alone."

Ida shifted her head slightly and looked up at the man holding the gun. "I couldn't ask to go out in better company," she said. She was fully awake now but still had not moved, except for the fingers of her right hand, which were wedged deep under her pillow.

"I figured you'd be happy," Jerry Ballister said. "Tough old gal like you was meant for better than to die up here in the woods all by herself. The bears be chewing on your bones by the time anybody got around to finding you."

"I didn't tell many people about this place," Ida said. "And I know you weren't one of them."

"You ask the right people the right questions and you find yourself with the right answers," Ballister said with a shrug of his shoulders.

"That usually works if the right kind of money is part of the deal," Ida said. "And the hands reaching for it belong to the wrong kind of man."

Ballister lifted the gun to waist level and aimed it inches from Ida's face. She looked away from the barrel, shifting herself slightly on the bed, the hand under the pillow moving closer to the edge of the mattress.

"There's nothing personal in this for me," Ballister said. "I heard a lot of great stories about you when I was growing up and I used to come drink in your Café just so I could get a look at you."

"Angus always said I attracted the wrong kind of man." Ida lifted her head gently from the pillow. "Didn't know until you walked in just how right he was."

Behind her, the sun had risen and its early-morning rays were warming the sides of Ballister's pale face. Ida shifted her feet and began to kick aside the bottom half of her quilt. "If it's okay with you, I never wanted to die in bed," Ida said. "Let me get to my feet and then you can do what you came here to do."

"Ladies' choice," Ballister said, taking several steps backwards, watching as Ida eased herself up on the bed, her right hand still under the pillow.

Ida sat up and looked around her cabin. It was a warm home, barren of furniture but crammed with memories. It was the place where it all began for her and now, it appeared, where it would come to an end. In between, she lived in a world dominated by men who treated her as an equal, respected her as a friend and feared her as an enemy. To all of them, she was Ida the Goose, the toughest woman ever to walk the streets of New York's West Side.

"You mind if I ask you one last question?" Ballister said.

"Make it a good one."

"Why are you called Ida the Goose?" he asked.

"That's something you're going to have to die not knowing," she told him.

Ida pulled her hand out from under the pillow and aimed a small-caliber derringer at Ballister. She kept her eyes fixed on his as she fired off two rounds. The first shot grazed his arm, causing him to flinch slightly. The second one whizzed by his head and put a small hole in her clothes closet.

Ballister stood his ground. There was no more talk, no more questions. He aimed his gun and shot six bullets into Ida the Goose, the last one landing in the center of her forehead, its force throwing her against the headboard, her legs hanging over the edge of the bed. Ballister holstered his gun, turned away from the dead woman and walked over to a telephone in a corner of the room. He pulled a folded paper from inside his pants pocket and dialed the number of the Café Maryland. He waited through three rings before a familiar voice picked up the receiver.

"You got two friends to bury now," he said into the mouthpiece, then he hung up and walked out of the cabin, leaving the front door open to the sounds of a country morning.

• • •

ANGELO AND PUDGE drove up to the cabin minutes after Jerry Ballister's phone call. Angelo had slammed down the phone in the Café Maryland and turned to Pudge, the empty look on his face telling him all he needed to know. "It's Ida," he said.

The drive, which both had always found so tranquil, now seemed torturous and endless. Angelo looked out his driver's side window and remembered the woman who shaped the man he had become. She had taught them all she knew, fed her lessons daily, preparing them both for this very day. His mind flashed back to when he was seven years old, a few months removed from the street beating Pudge had given him. He was sitting on the far end of the bar at the Café Maryland, eating a hot cup of pea soup with bacon. It was early evening and the room was crowded, drinks were flowing and tempers were all on a short fuse. Two men at a center table tossed back their chairs and pulled out knives, squaring off among the diners and the drinkers. The fury between them was enough to guarantee a bout destined to end in death.

Ida came out from behind the bar. Her hair was hanging along the sides of her shoulders, a gun was jammed in the belt of her long skirt. She walked with confidence and style, head held high, arms swinging at her sides, the patrons parting to make way. Angelo stared at her from his seat at the bar. He could never imagine anyone more beautiful, her face glowing under the hot lights of the Café, her smile causing the hardest of men to give a sheepish nod as she passed. She was an underworld queen holding court in a den of sin. Young Angelo was thrilled as he watched her step between the two men with knives in their hands and murder in their eyes.

Ida looked down at their table. "I worked all morning to make that stew just right," she said. "Be a shame for one of you to die without finishing what's on your plate. Let me have your knives. I'll keep them up by the bar. You still want to kill each other after two helpings of my stew, then come up and I'll give them to you. At least this way, whoever dies does it on a full stomach."

The two men looked at Ida, then down at their food, their anger quelled by the words of a woman. They handed Ida their knives, picked up their chairs and sat back down. Angelo watched as Ida turned away and walked back to the bar. As she stopped to pour a fresh beer, she caught Angelo staring at her. She looked at him with soft eyes, much like a mother would look at a young son, smiled and winked. At that moment, Angelo knew he would be safe and protected in the company of a woman who would let no harm come his way.

. . .

ANGELO AND PUDGE stared down at Ida's body. The blood from her wounds had started to jell around the sheets and blankets. Black flies swarmed over her now cold skin.

"I'll strip the bed," Pudge said in a low voice. "Then we'll put a clean nightgown on her. Nobody should have to see her like this."

"Nobody will," Angelo said. "The only people left she cared about are here."

"She wanted to die in this cabin and be buried up here," Pudge said.

Angelo looked at Pudge and nodded. "I'll get her ready," he said to him. "You find what we need to get a strong fire going."

Pudge stared down at Ida and stroked the sides of her head and face. He bent over and kissed her gently on the lips, then turned and left the room. Angelo lifted the body, his jacket and shirt becoming stained with her blood, and placed her on the floor as he changed the sheets. He found a crisp, clean nightgown in a bottom bureau drawer and put it on her, stripping away the blood-caked one. He laid her head down on a clean pillow and covered her with a thin white sheet. He sat next to her and brushed her hair until Pudge came back in.

"I don't think she would have wanted us to pray for her," Angelo said. "And she hated any kind of good-byes."

Pudge walked over to the foot of the bed and picked up Ida's revolver. He went to the other side of the bed and laid the gun across her chest. "But I think she would have wanted this," he said.

They sat in silence, each on one side of the woman who

had brought them together. They then lifted the top fold of the white sheet and covered her face. As they stood and walked out of the room, they each lit a match and tossed it on top of the kerosene-drenched pile of wood Pudge had assembled in the center hall. They watched the fire start to build, then walked out of the cabin, Angelo gently closing the door, leaving Ida the Goose to her final fate.

They stood outside and waited until the fire was down to embers. By then, darkness had taken over the mountaintop and a warm wind moved the thick smoke into a dense row of trees behind where the main house once stood.

"Let's get going," Pudge said. "We still got another funeral to plan."

• • •

MORE THAN FIVE hundred mourners were on hand to pay their respects to Angus McQueen. They waited quietly in a two-deep line along a dimly lit hallway outside the room where Angus was laid out in his coffin, wearing his finest dark blue suit and striped red tie. Angelo and Pudge sat on two folding chairs, five or six feet away and directly across from the body, looking at the faces of the mourners as they filed past. Many were former Gophers who had started out with Angus at the turn of the century, back in the years when a gang war involved only fists, knives, clubs and street savvy. The toll of those weekly battles showed on their still-young bodies. Scars lined their faces and necks, their ears were gnarled, their knuckles swollen twice their normal size, and many walked with pronounced limps. They bowed their heads in unaccustomed prayer before Angus's body, then turned and shook hands with Angelo and Pudge. Many of the visitors walked around the small room crammed full with mounted floral arrangements to greet the friendly faces of Angus's West Side crew. All the members except for one were present, either in the room, roaming the nearby halls or sitting out front next to their parked cars.

"It's not right for Spider to be missing Angus's wake," Pudge said. "Seeing as how he's only going to be dead once."

"I sent him downstairs over an hour ago," Angelo said as he nodded a silent hello to a passing mourner. "Gave him the money to pay the undertaker."

"It shouldn't be taking him such a long time."

Between the shadows of two passing mourners, Angelo caught a glimpse of Angus's coffin. The old gangster looked serene and regal in his well-tailored suit. Angelo looked up at the faces peering down at Angus and wondered how many of them were indeed his friends and how many would have acted on a whispered order and pulled the trigger that killed him.

"You need more than doubt to kill a man," Angelo said, turning to Pudge. "And that's all we have right now."

"Except for us, only two people knew where Ida lived." Pudge's voice was low and hard. "One's in that coffin."

"If Spider's the one, we'll know it soon enough."

Pudge shook his head. "If you're waiting to get a confession out of him, you can forget about it. I've known the guy most of my life. He won't say boo on Halloween night unless there's a dollar in somebody's hand coming his way."

Angelo turned away from Pudge to look back at the long line of mourners. "What we see, not what we hear, will tell us all we need to know."

· · ·

JERRY BALLISTER, AS expected, walked into Munson's Funeral Home on Central Park West to show his respects on the second night of Angus McQueen's wake. He stood in the center of the long line, his head bowed and his fedora in his hands. Jack Wells was in the backseat of a parked car across the street from the funeral home, smoking a thick Cuban cigar and waiting for his turn at the sympathy wheel. Ballister's appearance was meant to alert the other gangsters in the home that the boss would soon be on his way in. If the majority stayed, either out of fear or respect, then that would deliver a clear signal to Wells that the balance of gang power had shifted in his direction. But if anyone left before he walked in, Wells was situated in a perfect spot to identify the offender. Either way, he saw it as a no-lose.

The rumblings among the crews had already begun. McQueen's death had made some members of the Englishman's two-hundred-man team apprehensive. Few, if any, believed that Angelo and Pudge had either the will or the ability to take on Wells, let alone defeat him and Ballister. The boldness of James Garrett's church murder still held their attention, but was also seen by some to be a costly move that eliminated a bought-off cop. The killing of Ida the Goose, long retired and out of the business, frightened even more members of McQueen's crew. It matched the Garrett shooting for boldness and showed the gangsters on both squads that the beer baron from the Bronx would not accept anything less than a complete victory.

"We broke the rules with our hit on Garrett," Pudge once told me. "Wells came right back and broke the rules with his hit on Ida. That was one of the very few times a woman was marked for a killing, even to this day. A lot of people saw it as a no-class move, given as how Ida was pretty much out of it by the time she and Ballister went at it. But they were too afraid to say anything, since they were all banking on having a new gang boss. I mean, everybody at that funeral was looking for us to fold. They didn't think we had the stomach or the smarts to battle Wells. The word was out that we wouldn't live a week past Angus's funeral. That was his mistake. He gave me and Angelo way too much time."

· · ·

JERRY BALLISTER BOWED down before the coffin of Angus McQueen, made the sign of the cross and mumbled a few prayers. Angelo looked around the room and caught sight of Spider MacKenzie standing off in one corner, half-hidden by a circular wreath, intently watching Ballister's every gesture.

After several moments, Ballister stood and laid a hand on McQueen's chest.

"If you didn't know he was the one that put him in the box," Pudge muttered, "you'd swear he was really upset over his dying."

Ballister turned away from the coffin with a wide smile on his face. He shook hands and exchanged small talk with several of the men in line, making his way slowly toward Angelo and Pudge. Angelo glanced above Ballister's broad shoulders and saw Spider holding his place near the wreath, his hands folded behind his back. "Spider's found himself a good spot to cover somebody's back," Angelo whispered.

"We just have to wonder whose," Pudge said.

Angelo and Pudge stood as Ballister came toward them, his right hand extended, the smile still on his face. His jacket was open and flapping as he walked, exposing two guns buried inside his waistband. A circle of mourners broke from the line and followed close on his heels, covering him on both sides.

"I'm sorry about all this," Ballister said as he shook Angelo's hand, Pudge standing just off to his right. "None of it ever should have happened."

Angelo held Ballister's hand in his and stood inches from his face, their eyes locked. "Life is full of things that should never have happened," Angelo said. "Angus and Ida both learned that long before you ever came around."

Ballister lowered his voice. "She put up a good fight." He grimaced slightly from Angelo's hard handshake, the flesh wound on his arm from Ida's bullet still raw. "Stayed tough till the end. I thought you both would want to know that."

The men standing around Ballister tightened the circle, the air in the room now stale and still. Spider MacKenzie moved away from the flowers and walked to where he was directly behind Ballister, his back to the coffin. Outside, Jack Wells sat in his car and lit a fresh cigar, anxious to bring his evening to an end.

"There's something you should know before you go," Angelo said to Ballister. He reached out and rested a hand on the shorter man's wounded wrist. Pudge held his position, his eyes fixed on Spider MacKenzie, watching a line of sweat form on his upper lip. He caught a quick glance from Spider and in that blink knew all he needed to know.

"And what would that be?" Ballister said, stopping in midstep, turning back to face both Angelo and Pudge.

"We're not coming to your funeral," Angelo said.

Angelo squeezed his grip on Ballister's wrist. Pudge leaned forward and clamped down on the other arm. With their free hand, they each pulled a gun and pressed it against Ballister's stomach. Ballister struggled to get free, but couldn't fight off the holds. The arrogance had melted away and his eyes were wide with fear. Around him, men who seconds earlier were quick to be his ally, held their place.

"You can't do this!" Ballister shouted. "You can't do this here!"

"Why not?" Angelo said. "We're not in a church."

Angelo and Pudge held Jerry Ballister and put ten slugs into his stomach at close range. The line of mourners scattered in all directions. Spider MacKenzie was the only one not to move. Angus's boys held on to Ballister until he slid to the ground, the life lifted from his body. They let go of his arms and let him fall face forward to the carpeted floor.

Angelo holstered his gun and walked over to Spider. "Kneel down and say a prayer in front of your old boss," Angelo said, nodding toward Angus's coffin. "Then take Ballister outside to your new boss and tell him the war's not over yet."

* * *

JERRY BALLISTER'S MURDER shook Jack Wells. With Angus dead and Spider coming over to his side, Wells had every reason to feel the war was his to be won. Ida's killing was meant to toss a final jolt of fear in Angelo and Pudge's direction. While he never questioned either their toughness or

determination, Wells was convinced that they were too inexperienced to withstand the pressures of an all-out war. The
best they could hope to achieve, he believed, was a negotiated
peace that would allow them, working together with a
random array of gang members still loyal to McQueen, to
keep the proceeds from selected minor territories.

"A gangster gets used to having things go his way," Pudge
would often say. "That's because for too many years, they
usually do. You go in and make a move on somebody else's
territory, his business, maybe even his wife, and nobody does
anything to stop it. So it becomes habit. You want, you take.
But then comes the time when it's not so easy to reach out and
grab. When you go to take a bite and somebody bites back.
When that starts to happen, you begin to question your judgment and you hesitate before you plan another move. And
that weakens you. That's what Jack Wells was feeling sitting
in that car outside the funeral parlor, knowing he had just let
his top triggerman walk into a death trap."

• • •

ANGELO AND PUDGE sat at a back table in the Café Maryland,
one drinking hot coffee, the other cold milk, both looking
over the ledgers Angus had left behind.

"You gotta speak a foreign language to make these out,"
Pudge said, slamming one thick binder shut in frustration.

"I do speak a foreign language," Angelo said, holding his
glass of milk close to his mouth. "And *I* have no idea what it
means."

"Maybe we don't have to know how to read them," Pudge
said, leaning back in his chair. "We'll just let the pencil man
explain it to us. He's been doing Angus's books for more than
twenty years, if he don't understand what these ledgers say,
nobody else will either."

"I don't need these books to tell me this war is cutting into
the money we take in," Angelo said. "And that's making a lot
of the guys on the crew nervous. They don't seem to care

much about losing their lives, but being twenty dollars off on their weekly take hits a raw nerve."

"Face it, if you're not making big money, what the hell's the point of being in the rackets," Pudge said with a shrug. "They'll get over their snit soon as the war ends."

"You think they even care who wins it?" Angelo placed the empty milk glass to the left of a black ledger.

"A few do, I guess. The ones who came up with Angus and knew Ida back when this place was new. The rest just want to work for whoever's out there willing to pay them. The only loyalty they know is buried inside their wallets."

"It's not what I thought it'd be like," Angelo said. "When I was a kid, being in here, around Ida and Angus and the people they knew, made me feel safe. It was where I belonged and I wanted nothing more than to be just like them."

"And you got your wish," Pudge said. "What'd you expect after all this time? You are just like them."

"I'm not," Angelo said, looking over at Pudge. "And neither are you. They wouldn't have pulled the moves on Garrett and Ballister the way we did. They had more heart than to think up something that cold."

"We did what needed to be done."

"Killing people comes too easy to us and that scares me a little. And that what I do doesn't bother me after it's all over scares me even more."

"This ain't like pumping gas or working behind a counter," Pudge said. "You can't just punch out and walk away from it. This is who we are, Angelo, and this is what we do. And now that you're giving it so much thought, let me give you something else to think about."

"What?"

"That if we're lucky and we stay around the rackets long enough, then we're only going to get better at it," Pudge said. "And I can't believe that any of it gets any easier to live with."

"This is the part Angus and Ida forgot to tell us about," Angelo said.

"I think this is the part they couldn't tell us about," Pudge said, leaning across the table for the coffeepot. "Maybe it's just because they didn't know how. Maybe it's something you have to live through and figure out on your own."

. . .

THE FRONT DOOR to the Café swung open and a boy in a wool cap and knickers stood in the shadows of the entryway, his right hand still clutching the knob. "A man down the block asked me to come in here and give you a message," the boy said in a confident, out-of-breath voice.

"The man have a name?" Pudge asked, looking past the boy to see if anyone else was lurking.

"Jack Wells," the boy said.

"Come in and close the door behind you," Angelo instructed.

The boy did as he was told and then walked toward them, his eyes scanning the empty tables, his brown lace-ups echoing on the hardwood floor. He stopped in front of Angelo and Pudge, folded his arms across his waist, looked down at the table and stared at the half-empty bottle of milk.

"What's your name?" Angelo reached behind him and pulled a clean glass off a shelf.

"George Martinelli," the boy said, his eyes still focused on the milk.

"Have a glass if you're thirsty," Angelo said. "And then let's hear what Wells asked you to tell us."

George poured the contents of the bottle into the glass and drank it down in three long swallows. "He wants to set a meeting with the both of you. You pick the place and the time, just so long as it's off-limits to both crews. He'll be alone and he expects you to do the same."

"He say anything else?" Pudge asked, pushing his chair back and clasping his hands behind his head.

"The sooner it happens, the better, was the last of it," George said.

"You live here, in the neighborhood?" Angelo asked the boy.

"Around the corner, the apartment just over the butcher shop," George said with a nod. "My dad works there in the back, slicing up hindquarters."

"Go home now, but I'd like to see you back here tomorrow morning."

"What for?" George asked.

Angelo pushed his chair back and stood, looking down at the boy with empty eyes. "I'll let you know when I see you again," he said.

Angelo walked away, his head bowed, toward the back room behind the bar. Pudge stood and put a hand on the boy's shoulder. "How much did Wells pay you to deliver his message?" he asked.

"He didn't pay me," George said. "And I didn't ask him to."

"So why do it at all?" Pudge asked. "You don't look the type that scares."

"I'm not," George said, turning away from the table to face Pudge. "I just always wanted to come into this place, but I never had a reason."

"Is it like what you thought it would be?" Pudge asked as he slid his chair back into its slot.

"No," he said. "It's not even close to what I thought."

"Nothing ever is." Pudge moved toward the back room to join Angelo. "If you're as smart as you act, you might do yourself a favor and learn that lesson now. It'll end up saving you a lot of grief down the road."

• • •

ANGELO CRACKED OPEN a peanut shell and stood staring up at a bearded lady sitting on a large throne, a midget in blue tights on her lap. He was next to Pudge, both of them squeezed in among the crowd filling the basement of the St. Nicholas Arena, all there to gaze at the Carbone Brothers Circus's traveling freak show.

Pudge shoved a hand into Angelo's large bag of peanuts and pointed up to the bearded lady. "You think somebody like her ever gets laid?"

"I don't see why not," Angelo said. "You take it past the beard, she's not that bad-looking."

Pudge tossed the peanuts into his mouth. "It would be worth the dough just to see a naked woman with a beard. I mean, you don't even need to take it any further than that, unless she's hiding something we haven't seen before."

"You can worry about her later; she'll be here all week," Angelo told him. "Let's deal with Wells first."

"He's running late." Pudge glanced at his pocket watch. "For a guy who likes to have meetings, he doesn't seem to be in too much of a hurry to get this one started."

Angelo looked beyond Pudge's shoulders, past the faces packed tight in front of each booth, and saw Jack Wells hand a ticket stub to a young man in a red jacket and black top hat. "He just came in," Angelo said. "I told the kid to have Wells meet us over by the sword swallower. That's where he's heading now."

Pudge turned and caught a glimpse of Wells, walking with his hands in his pockets, toward the booth in the farthest corner of the basement. He nudged an elbow in Angelo's side and the two of them began to edge their way slowly through the crowd. "You think that guy's got himself a gimmick going?" Pudge asked over his back. "Or does he really jam those blades down his throat?"

"Everybody's got a gimmick going," Angelo said, tossing his bag of peanuts into a packed garbage bin. "Why would sword swallowers be any different from the rest of us."

•   •   •

JACK WELLS WAS dressed in a rumpled blue suit, the jacket stained with coffee drops and cigar burns, the wrinkled pants desperate for a pressing and the shoes scruffy enough to be thrown out with the morning trash. "He looks more like a rummy than a gang boss," Pudge said to Angelo.

"That's *his* gimmick," Angelo said. "He gets your attention by the way he dresses. Wants you to take him for a soft push. But we've already seen his other side. And no matter how this meeting goes, we'll probably see it again before one of us dies."

"This is where you guys decide to hold a meeting?" Wells asked, frowning, as both Angelo and Pudge walked up to him. They stood by an iron rail separating them from a thin, long-haired sword swallower. "Every other place in town taken up?"

"We wanted you to feel at home," Pudge said. He ignored Wells's outstretched hand, staring instead at the man in the red leotards as he reached into a brown canvas bag for a handful of swords, each one a different shape and size. "Besides, the circus kicks back a cut to our crew. This gives us a chance to see how good the business is doing."

"From the size of the crowd in here, there must be a lot of money to be had in freak shows," Wells said, putting his hand back down by his side. "But there's no money at all to be had in a gang war."

"You should remember that the next time you go ahead and start one," Angelo said.

"The move had to be made." Anger and defiance filled Wells's voice. "I did all I could to avoid it. But Angus refused to listen, refused to admit that he couldn't go it alone anymore, that he needed to bring in fresh partners."

Angelo stepped close enough to smell the cheap cologne splashed across Wells's unshaven face. "What do you want?"

"Let's bring it to an end," Wells said. "We both lost people we didn't want to see die. There's no need to go through it anymore. There's no profit in it and there's no win in it."

"I don't think you want to walk away from it empty-handed," Pudge said. "How big a cut are you looking for?"

"Before the war started I expected to take over all of Angus's action." Wells stared up as the swallower gulped down two blades.

"And now?" Angelo kept his eyes only on Wells.

"Twenty-five percent the first year," Wells said. "It goes up five percent a year after that with a forty cap. You get to take over Angus's crew and I keep what's left of mine. I can't make you a fairer offer than that."

"You'll pay your end of the protection payroll?" Angelo asked.

"Take it out of my weekly cut." Wells turned to face Angelo. "I'll trust you not to take more than you need."

"And what do we get from you?" Pudge now turned his back on the swallower to lean against the rail.

"Ten percent off the top on all my beer and policy business in the Bronx. I'll kick it up to fifteen after two years. That should add between eight hundred and a thousand dollars a week to you and your crew, ballpark figure. Maybe a little higher around the holidays."

"What if we say no?" Angelo asked. He hid his disdain of Wells with professional care, burying it behind a relaxed, indifferent pose. He had learned enough to know that the business and personal ends of his life, though always linked, needed to be dealt with as if they were separate entities.

"Why would you?" Wells shrugged. "You come out of this running a top-level crew and with a lot more money in your pockets. I walk away with a bigger cut of what I had before this all started. I don't see any losers standing here."

"What about the ones not left standing?" Pudge asked, his anger just barely below the surface.

"If it was them instead of us here, the same deal would be cut," Wells said. "Now I didn't come all the way down here just to see a dwarf get shoved inside a lion's mouth. I came looking to walk away with a peace deal. So before I start munching on peanuts and popcorn, I need to know if we're putting away the guns."

"Enough people have died, on both sides," Angelo said, giving Pudge a quick glance and a nod. "The war's over. At least from our end."

Jack Wells took several long seconds to look at their faces. "That's good," he finally said, reaching out his arms to both of them. "Now, instead of enemies, we're partners. Which is the way it should have been from the very start."

When Wells turned and disappeared into the crowd, Pudge looked at Angelo. "I don't like the bastard," he said. "And I trust him even less. I should have pulled one of those swords outta that guy's mouth and shoved it in his heart."

"He doesn't give you much to like or trust," Angelo agreed.

"So how long do you suppose this peace treaty is gonna last?"

"I hope forever," Angelo said. He slipped his hands into his pants pockets and looked up at the sword swallower bowing dramatically as all those around him cheered and applauded. "Or at least until it's time for one of us to die."

• • •

GANGSTERS USE THE months or years between gang wars to prepare for the next big battle to come. In their business the only way to further a career or strengthen a position is through death. Gang bosses decide to wage a fight for any number of reasons—the love of another mobster's wife, the desire to take over a rival's turf, the need for more money for their crew, anger over a perceived insult. The reasons usually are slight, providing scant cover for a visible greed. Like many executives in the corporate world, a gangster is consumed with an insatiable desire to possess what belongs to someone else. Unlike legitimate power brokers, however, mobsters are not satisfied with a mere Wall Street–backed takeover, no matter how lucrative. They will not rest until they live to see their opponent buried.

"It's been a truth about us from day one," Angelo told me, many years after his meeting with Jack Wells. "No gangster is ever happy when he's at peace. The main reason he's in the business is to eliminate his enemies. I've read stories about some of the great gangsters and I read where people say that they were so smart, they could have run big corporations instead of being criminals. Maybe some of that's true. But no gangster, great or not, would ever give up what he has to go into the business world. He wouldn't be able to follow the same set of rules. If I'm in charge of General Motors, then that means I want the guy who runs the Ford Motor Company dead, no matter how long it takes. And then once I see him put in the ground, I take over that company and make it part of mine. That's the biggest difference between a gangster and an executive. They may think about killing the guy they're up against. We go right out there, in the middle of the day if we have to, and we do it."

10

Summer, 1931

THE PEACE BETWEEN Angelo, Pudge and Jack Wells lasted more than three years. In that time, both squads secured enormous profits and were placed in strong positions to reap even more. The underworld was thriving while the rest of the country was in the grips of the Great Depression, with more than eight million Americans out of work and in desperate need of cash. While 2,294 banks were closing nationwide, New York gang bosses increased the interest they charged on cash loans to three percent a week. The labor force was losing, on average, three workers a day, and movie theaters were showing daily double features to provide a fantasy refuge for those without jobs. Meanwhile, the country's most powerful gangsters had mapped out a plan that would eventually broaden their enterprise into a national crime syndicate that would be structured in such a way as to maximize profits from every possible venue, legal or not. As Dick Tracy made his first appearance in the *Chicago Tribune*, eager to do battle with the underworld, real gangsters were lording over a democratic kingdom whose very foundation seemed to be on the verge of collapse.

"It was our time," Pudge liked to say of those years. "Maybe the greatest time ever to be in the rackets. Everywhere we turned, there was money to be made. That's why we all made the move to take our business national. It gave what we did a structure and made it all the easier to take money that we earned illegally from gambling or booze and spread it out to legal setups like transportation and banking. Back in those years, even as young as we were, anybody in the rackets who had himself any kind of a brain knew that if we kept it all going the way it was, sooner or later the whole country would belong to us. But for that to work, you needed a lot of patience. And there were too many gangsters who didn't have that. I guess that's true wherever you go, no matter what sort of racket you're in. There's always somebody in the middle of the pack who just can't wait."

· · ·

ANGELO AND ISABELLA walked down lower Broadway, holding hands, stopping every few feet to look at the displays in the store windows. The last three years had been good ones for Angelo. He and Pudge had solidified their hold on Angus's crew, expanding the core group to where it now numbered more than one thousand salaried members. Unlike the other gang leaders, Angelo and Pudge were not exclusionary gangsters. They were the first to accept Jews in their ranks and ventured out to upper Manhattan and the outer boroughs to recruit selected members from the more organized of the black gangs. Both actions were done solely for business, not social, reasons. "Black gangsters wanted a piece of the action at a time when no one wanted a piece of them," Angelo said. "To get in, they were willing to handle twice the work with a smaller cut of the profits coming their way, which meant more in our pockets. We brought in the Jews for an even better reason. They were prime-time killers. They would go anywhere, at any time, and didn't care who they had to shoot. And like the blacks, they did it more to get the attention, knowing that, in our business, it's reputation not race or religion that eventually brings in the big haul. A lot of those Jewish shooters we first hired later went out on their own and formed Murder, Inc. That's when their price went up, but even then, they were still more than worth it."

Angelo and Pudge were both quick to embrace the notion of a national crime commission and drew up and sent out an array of proposals as to how it could best be implemented. They were part of a new generation of American gangster, moving to the faster pace of a money-driven century and taking full advantage of every opportunity. Where past gangsters were once content to bribe a wide array of police officials, they now were in a position to run their own candidates for political office and have their own judges appointed to the bench. The underworld ran the wards, secured the banks and controlled the import and export of all goods that crossed the ocean and passed state lines.

"It was like the industrial revolution for crooks," Pudge would tell me. "For whatever the reasons, during those years, we were left on our own. The feds were just starting out and couldn't find their ass with either hand. The local badges were just looking for a bigger payoff. And John Q. had his hand out for anything we could give him. We had it all and we ran it all and it didn't look like anybody would ever be able to touch us."

The business relationship with Jack Wells was also running on a smooth track. Wells had solidified his power base and gained some respect among his peers for the war he had waged against McQueen. He had expanded his beer distribution ring beyond the Bronx to where it now reached as far north as Toronto and as far to the west as Scranton, Pennsylvania, willingly kicking back a small share of the large profits to Angelo and Pudge. The two sides still did not trust each other, but as long as the money kept coming in, there was no reason to fear the outbreak of new hostilities. Angelo knew that another confrontation with Wells was inevitable. There was too much past blood between them for a final war not to be fought. Angelo was, for the time being, content to let the false peace between them run its course.

. . .

ISABELLA PAUSED WHEN she saw Pudge, a large teddy bear shoved under his right arm, walk toward her. "For the baby," he said. "I wanted to be the first to get the kid one."

"Thank you." She took the bear from him. "I'll be sure to put it where he can see it." Isabella was nervous around Pudge. He relished his role of gangster, took more pleasure from it than her husband did. It was always easy for her to forget who Angelo was and what he did for a living when she was in his company. She could never do that with Pudge.

"I know you don't much care for me," Pudge said. "I can't say I blame you. You're a smart woman and I never could get them to go for me."

"You are a good friend to Angelo," Isabella said. "I will always respect that."

"I won't let anything happen to him," Pudge said. "I swore my life on it. That holds true now for you and for his baby."

"If you can keep my husband alive, then you will be a good friend to me as well."

"My job's been getting easier as he gets older," Pudge told her. "He's very good at what he does."

"It might be better if he weren't," Isabella said. "It might lead him to start looking for some other work to do."

"Stuff like that's always nice to think about," Pudge said. "It never has anything to do with the truth."

"And what is the truth?"

"There's no other way for either one of us."

"Why are you telling me all of this?" she asked.

"So you won't ever hate him," Pudge said. "I don't want you to look at your husband and have you see the gangster looking back. The way you do when you look at me."

"I know him in different ways than you do," Isabella said. "And what I know I can never hate."

Pudge nodded. "Then he's a lucky man," he said.

. . .

"WHY DO WE need to choose a crib so long before the baby is born?" Angelo asked Isabella as they stood in front of a window display featuring an extensive array of hand-sewn rugs.

She turned to him, smiled and rubbed a hand gently across his face. "Angelo, the whole *room* should be ready before the baby is born," she said. "Unless you want him to sleep with us."

"Why do you always say him and never her?" He covered the top of her warm hand with his.

"Because I know it is your son inside me." She looked down and patted the slight bulge in her belly. "He's too quiet not to be. All the other mothers tell me that their babies kick and punch. Not mine. He sits inside there and thinks. Just like his father."

They turned away from the window and continued on their walk, their hands automatically reaching out and clasping. "We haven't talked about what name to give the baby who's getting all this new furniture," Angelo said.

"That's not going to be too difficult," Isabella said. "If I'm right and it is a boy, we will name him Carlo, after your brother."

Angelo stopped and turned to stare at his wife. He put his arms around her and they embraced, holding each other under a brutal afternoon sun, Angelo's face buried in the crook of her neck, overcome with a rush of emotion. "I love you," was all he could manage to say.

"We should go," she whispered into his ear. "I told the man at the furniture store we would be there no later than one."

They walked in silence for several blocks, still holding hands. Angelo was anything but a gangster when he was in Isabella's presence. She brought to the surface feelings of warmth and kindness that he had long ago learned to suppress. When he was around her, Angelo never gave any thought to his business ventures or the motives behind the actions of his enemies. He gave in to the façade of the happy husband eagerly awaiting the birth of his first child, finding a degree of solace in the relaxing nature such a pose afforded.

"How did you find out about this store?" Angelo asked.

"A friend of my cousin Graziella told her about it," Isabella said. "He builds all the cribs by hand and they last forever. No matter how many children we end up having."

"I never thought I would want a child," Angelo said. "I was always afraid of the idea."

"What are you afraid of?" Isabella asked.

"I don't know what kind of father I'm going to be," Angelo said. "I only know the kind of father I don't want to be."

"You won't be like your own father. That won't happen with you." She had listened to enough of his early-morning nightmares to know how that fear haunted his sleep and tormented his soul. "You are not the same kind of a man."

"In many ways I'm worse," Angelo said. "What will my son think of what I do?"

"I don't know."

"I don't want him to be what I am," Angelo said firmly. "I want him to be a good man."

"He will be," Isabella said with resolve. "I promise you that."

He looked at her, nodded and smiled, lifting the lid off his dark mood. "In that case," he said, "we will have as many children as you wish."

She leaned her head against his shoulder. "Do you know, I've never even held a newborn in my arms? I'm going to be so nervous coming home from the hospital."

"We'll get Pudge to hold him. Nothing ever makes him nervous."

Isabella lifted her head off Angelo's shoulder and laughed. "Why does he like to be called Pudge?" she asked. "What's the matter with his real name?"

"He hates it," Angelo said. "He's hated it since I've known him. Lucky for him, there're not many people left who even remember his first name. So, let's keep him happy and let him be a good Uncle Pudge to our baby."

"But *you* know his name, don't you?" Isabella asked, looking at her husband and smiling.

"Yes," Angelo said, smiling back at her. "I know it."

"Will you tell me?" she asked, stroking a hand across his face. "Please."

"I've kept it a secret for over twenty years." He gently tugged his wife toward the entrance of the furniture store she had been so eager to see. "I think it can at least wait until after we have picked out a crib for our baby to sleep in."

•   •   •

THE SALESMAN WAS short, bald and had a round thick paunch hanging over his belt. His hands were small, like those of a child, and his mannered voice bordered on feminine. He smiled when Angelo and Isabella approached and, with great care, wiped at the dampness on his forehead with a folded napkin. The large showroom was filled with an assortment of furniture, from cabinets and bureaus to beds and dining room sets. It was a poorly lit room, heavy drapes blocking out the view from the street and shaded lights casting minor shadows along its corners. It took several minutes for Angelo's eyes to adjust his vision from the harsh glare of the bright sunlight outside. When he was able to focus, he noticed that except for the two of them and the salesman, they were alone in the store.

"It's close to lunch hour," the salesman said, quick to read the concern on Angelo's face. "If you'd come here earlier this morning, I wouldn't have been able to help you, we were so crowded."

"Are you the man who builds the cribs?" Isabella asked, her eyes searching the room for the furniture she wanted.

"No, madam," the man said with a respectful nod. "He's not at work today. But, luckily, many of his cribs are here. I keep them in the back of the showroom. Would you like me to take you over to see?"

"I would like that very much." Isabella smiled over at Angelo and urged him to follow along. "And so would my husband."

The man bowed slightly and led the way toward a rear corner of the room. Angelo watched his agitated walk and the circle of sweat forming around his starched shirt collar. He saw the man nervously glance into the near-darkness, half-expecting someone to pounce out and surprise him. Angelo squeezed Isabella's hand, grabbed his gun from his hip holster and dropped it into his jacket pocket. He stopped walking and pulled his wife to his side.

"We have to get out of here," he whispered to her. "And we have to get out now."

"But we haven't seen any of the cribs."

"Now, Isabella!" Angelo said in a louder, firmer voice.

• • •

THE TWO MEN came out from behind the shadows of a large brown hutch, their guns drawn and aimed at Angelo's back. The salesman disappeared around a bend, hidden behind massive bureaus and ornate desks, walking head down and with a purpose. Angelo heard the footsteps pound on the carpeted concrete and the click of a chamber spinning slowly inside the barrel of a gun. He turned to Isabella and saw a look of hopeless terror engulf her face. In that brief moment of eerie silence, Angelo's mind focused on a rainy day, when he handed a young woman with a magnetic smile a piece of fresh fruit.

"Behind you!" Isabella screamed.

Angelo whirled away from her face and turned to confront the men coming at them, his gun in his hand. They began to run at him, shooting as they moved, the bullets coming his way in loud and rapid succession. Angelo stood his ground, aimed his gun, and emptied it at the two men sent to kill him.

It was over in less than thirty seconds, but for Angelo Vestieri, every movement seemed to fill out a lifetime.

• • •

ANGELO SQUINTED AT the overhead lights. He shifted his eyes slightly to the right and saw Pudge sitting in a chair, his hands balled into fists, staring at him.

"Don't talk," Pudge said as soon as he saw that his friend was awake. "Just listen to what I have to say. You took three slugs, nothing serious. One grazed your head and knocked you out for a few hours. That's why it's all bandaged. Another ripped through your shoulder. And the last one got you in the leg. You'll be out of here in about a week, maybe less."

"Where's Isabella?"

"I said don't talk, goddammit! At least not until I finish everything I have to say." Pudge's voice started to crack. "Nod if you understand."

Angelo nodded and closed his eyes.

"The two shooters were hired by Jack Wells," Pudge said. "The setup was to get you into the place. They paid off somebody from the neighborhood to get Isabella all excited about going there. Wells owns the building and anybody who works in the store is too afraid not to do what he tells them."

Angelo opened his eyes and reached out a hand. Pudge took it and held it tight. "You did good with the gun, Ang," he said. "One of the shooters died on the spot. The other one is two floors down from us in critical. They were only supposed to shoot you. They didn't figure on Isabella stepping in the way, trying to save you from getting hit."

Pudge was barely able to speak now, his strong body trembling. "I'm so sorry," he managed to say. "I swore on Ida's grave that I wouldn't let anything happen to you. Or to Isabella and the baby. I should have been there with you. I should have smelled it out, but I didn't."

Angelo still said nothing. He didn't have to. His eyes asked the only question that needed asking.

"She's dead," Pudge said. "Isabella is dead."

Behind them the city skyline had darkened, as night came

in to close out what had, only hours earlier, been a beautiful summer day.

"Take me to see her," Angelo said.

Pudge lifted his head and shook it. "Your wounds are too fresh. If I move you, they'll only open up again."

"I want to see my wife," Angelo whispered. "Take me."

Pudge wiped his face with his jacket sleeve, took a deep breath and nodded. "You're going to have to move as fast as I do, because if they see us, they'll try and stop us."

"Shoot them if they do," Angelo said.

• • •

"LIFE GAVE ANGELO a lot of reasons to be cold," Pudge once told me. "But Isabella getting killed was the capper. He spent the whole night crying over her body. Hell, we both did. And then, just like that, he stopped and turned away. And all that he ever lived for, from that moment on, was making his enemies suffer. He had lost too many people he loved and the best way he knew to stop that from happening was to never love anybody again. Instead, he went out and made other people lose whatever and whoever they loved. It wasn't about business or revenge anymore. It was about hate and it's what probably helped turn him into an underworld legend. But it's hard to be a legend *and* a man. The Angelo who was in love and happy and waiting for his baby to be born was gone forever."

11

Winter, 1932

ANGELO AND PUDGE waited in the dark hallway, by the back door, in the rear of the warehouse. They were both still shivering from the long walk across town, the arctic blasts of air coming off the river cutting through their thick winter coats. They had parked their car over by the edge of the pier, preferring the cover of the empty streets as a safety shield against anyone who might be following them.

Angelo walked with a slight limp; his right leg, from the kneecap down, was still numb from the nerve damage caused by the bullet. But he ignored the pain and kept up with Pudge's accelerated pace. Angelo had spent the entire summer and a good portion of the fall recovering from his wounds and from the loss of Isabella, living in the top floor of a sparsely furnished Upper West Side apartment. Except for Pudge, who visited every day, he allowed himself no company. He spent the bulk of his day sitting in a thick leather chair, staring out past the row of tenement buildings toward the vast expanse of the Hudson River. Once a week, he was driven out to St. Charles's Cemetery on the eastern end of Long Island, where he spent a silent hour in front of his wife's grave. He had insisted that her funeral be a private affair, limited only to friends and family. Neither Jack Wells nor Spider MacKenzie bothered to make an appearance at the wake, and the flower arrangements they had sent were left out with the trash in a side alley. For the time being, Angelo informed all members of his crew that they should conduct their business in the usual manner, and that any encroachments Wells made on their turf be allowed to happen without any fear of reprisals. For his part, Wells moved slowly, content for the moment to nibble away at the pieces of Angelo's domain. As the months passed, Wells grew bolder, convinced that the accidental killing of Isabella had stripped Angelo of his taste for battle and his desire to maintain control of the New York rackets.

"If I had known that killing his wife would have buckled the guy the way it has, I would have done it long ago," Wells told Spider MacKenzie after learning that his crew had taken over another chunk of Angelo's Manhattan numbers business. "The way he's acting, he's as dead as she is."

Spider nodded and, as usual, said nothing. He had sold out to Wells for a bigger cut of the profits and a greater sense of mob power; now that he had both, he stood there wishing he had never made the move. Spider MacKenzie was not fit to be a leader in the new underworld order. He had neither the taste for brutality nor the cold character a crew boss needed to rule, and he could never shrug off the murder of a former friend's wife. He was aware that such faults would eventually lead to his demise and he didn't seem to care. Angus had once told him that the price of a betrayal was too steep for most men. It had to be lived with every single day of their lives and few could handle such a burden. Spider MacKenzie knew he was not one of those few.

· · ·

THE FRONT DOOR to the warehouse swung open, letting in blasts of light and cold air. Spider reached a hand out to the wall nearest him and flicked on a switch, turning on a long row of overhead bulbs. He slammed the door shut behind him and turned to lock it. He looked around the enormous room filled with whiskey crates newly arrived from the Canadian border and marked for distribution. MacKenzie walked toward the rear of the room, his hands in his pockets and his head down. Angelo and Pudge stood with their backs against the cold wall, pulled their guns and watched as Spider's shadow moved closer to them. As he turned a corner, Spider paused to pull a row of keys from his pants pocket. He stopped by a metal door leading to the warehouse basement, bent down and inserted a key into the lock. The thick bolt clicked and Spider swung the door open. He peered down a dark set of steps, then his body stiffened as he felt the cold barrel of a gun press against the base of his neck.

"You must really rank up there with Wells," Pudge said, reaching into Spider's waistband and pulling out his gun. "I mean, for him to trust you with the keys to his stash."

"You guys running low on whiskey?" Spider asked. He was careful not to move, keeping his arms at his side, his hands extended. "All you had to do was ask. We would have sold you a few cases."

"It's always better to take than to receive," Pudge said.

"Turn on the light to the basement," Angelo said, standing directly behind Spider. "Then start walking down the steps."

"There's nothing down there but a small office and a furnace," Spider said. "We only keep the whiskey on the main floor."

"We're not taking inventory," Pudge said, shoving the gun barrel deeper into Spider's neck. "So just do what Angelo tells you."

Spider nodded as Angelo and Pudge followed him down the basement steps.

"Our trucks should be here in a few minutes to start moving out the whiskey," Pudge said. "From the size of the haul, it's gonna take them a good two hours to clear the place out."

"I want the whole floor emptied," Angelo said. "Have them break open any cases that can't fit inside the trucks."

"All except for one bottle," Pudge said. "That one we gift wrap and mail to Wells. He's gonna need a drink when he hears about this."

Angelo walked into the small office next to the warm furnace. He looked around at the file cases and long stacks of ledgers wedged against the corners of the room. "This is where Wells keeps all his distribution records," Pudge said. "The folders in those cabinets have all the names and dates, how much each haul costs and how much it brings in."

Angelo picked up a ledger and leafed through the pages. "Who tipped you about all this?"

"A balls-on-his-ass gambler who owns Sam's Deli, about three blocks down. Wells has been eating brisket sandwiches in there since he first had money in his pocket. But he won't handle any of Sam's action because he knows the guy's nothing but a deadbeat. So for the last year or so, Sam's been betting with a runner from our crew. Last week, I found out Sam was into us for about nine hundred dollars. I cut the difference and in return got him to spill what he knew about this place."

"There's at least thirty thousand worth of whiskey in those crates," Angelo said. "Maybe more. It's not nice to keep those kind of secrets from your partners."

"Wells started working out of this building when he first got into the rackets," Pudge said. "That was back in the early years, probably before he ever even heard about Angus. He's got his big distribution warehouse over on Gun Hill Road. That's the one we're supposed to know about. This one, he tries to keep a lid on. Likes to think of it as his good-luck spot."

"His luck just changed," Angelo said, tossing one of the ledgers onto the small desk in the center of the office. "And not for the better."

• • •

THE FURNACE DOOR was open and the room was filled with clouds of white smoke. Angelo sat on a wooden chair, his back to the stairs and to Spider, casually throwing ledgers and crammed folders into the mouth of the fire. One floor above, he heard the muted voices and the heavy footsteps of Pudge and his men loading whiskey crates onto the backs of flatbed trucks. His face and shirt were dripping wet from the stifling heat, but Angelo went about his task of destroying the carefully maintained records and receipts of Jack Wells's beer and whiskey business.

"You better think about what you're doing, Angelo," Spider said, his voice tired and hoarse. "When Jack hears about all this, it'll be sure to start another war."

"We never finished the last one," Angelo said. He threw another packed folder into the center of the flames and walked over to where Spider was laying with his head against the final step. "We'll start doing that today."

"By doing what, burning his records and stealing his whiskey?" Spider asked. "That's not the smart way to hurt Wells."

"You're his number-one man now, Spider," Angelo said, bending down and staring into his former friend's eyes. "He listens to you. Comes to you for advice. That kind of clout carries a lot of muscle, the kind a top gang boss doesn't like to lose. So killing you, that would hurt Jack Wells, wouldn't it? Hurt him a lot?"

MacKenzie looked up at Angelo, his face filled with regret and relief. "You'd be doing me a favor," he said. "I should never have walked away from what I had with Angus. It was where I belonged."

Angelo stood and stared down at Spider MacKenzie, the fire from the furnace warming both of them and casting the room in an eerie glow of dancing shadows. He tightened his grip on the gun and held it away from his side. He took a long and silent breath and calmly fired three bullets into Spider's upper body. Then Angelo shoved the gun into its holster, turned and walked back toward the furnace to burn the last of the records.

• • •

A GANGSTER MUST always be prepared to kill a friend. It is one of the many open secrets of the business, since it is the truest test of his ability to rule and command the respect of his crew. To eliminate a sworn enemy requires little more than opportunity, luck and the willingness to pull a trigger. But to end the life of someone once considered close, regardless of any previous betrayal, requires a determination that few men possess. "We never talked about that end of it, me and Ang," Pudge once explained to me. "I guess we didn't want to have to ever think about it. We loved each other more than brothers. But if business called for it, I don't doubt for a second that he would have pulled the trigger on me, just as I'm sure I would have pulled it on him. I'm not saying we would have been happy about it or that we wouldn't have cried about it after it was over, but we would have seen it through. I don't see as how we had any other choice. No gangster does."

I knew they were killers, but I never felt in any danger when I was in their company. As a child, I would listen to the stories and appreciate their sense of mystery and adventure. As an adult, I would never allow myself the luxury of judging them, but would sometimes question my own lack of concern over their willingness to bring a life to an end. It is not easy to love those so quick and eager to kill. Angelo's children, for example, having learned the truth about their father, were too frightened to ever want to be allowed close. It was a door they refused to open. But for me it was different. I was raised in the life and was well aware of its murderous rules. To do otherwise, meant to turn my back on the two men I loved more than any other.

● ● ●

MARY HAD SAT silently for many minutes, her eyes on Angelo, her mind swayed by the memories she had conjured up during our long night together. Behind me, the early-morning sun was bringing the city to life, while outside the room the nurses were in the midst of a shift change. "He was so afraid to get close to anyone," she finally said, looking back up at me. "Anyone he ever got close to had ended up dead."

"He was close to you," I said. "At least I think he was, from the way you talk about him. And you're still alive."

"There are many different ways to die," Mary said. "Sometimes words can inflict more pain than any bullet. Angelo understood that."

"Is that what he did with you?"

"*And* with you," she said.

"Then why are we here?" I asked. "Why are we the ones who still care?"

"Maybe he didn't take all the love we felt for him away from us," Mary said, her beautiful face suddenly twisted and sad.

"Why not?" A rush of anger added an edge to my words. "If he was so tough, so ruthless, why couldn't he make us hate him enough to wish him dead?"

Mary pulled back her chair and walked toward the large door in the corner of the room. Her head was down and her hands were at her side, her walk still poised and dignified. "Maybe he didn't want to," she said with her back to me. "It could be as simple as that."

Then she walked out into the hall, the thick door closing slowly behind her, leaving me alone with Angelo in the stillness of the dying man's room.

•   •   •

THE ALBINO WOLFHOUND locked its thick jaw around the pit bull's muscular neck. The crowd of men surrounding the dirt pit cheered and tossed more money into the huge box next to Jack Wells.

"Double my action, Big Jack," a large bearded man in bib overalls and a hunter's coat shouted. "And gear yourself to watch your favorite pit bull die."

"Be a pleasure to take your money," Wells shouted back. "And if he loses out to an albino dog, then my old Grover deserves nothing short of death."

The small barn was smoke-filled and crowded. Sixty men stood in a tight circle around a split-rail fence, watching and wagering on the blood sport of dog fighting. Once a month, regardless of the time of year or what else was going on in his life, Jack Wells ventured up to an empty Yonkers farmhouse to rule over a series of matches featuring the fiercest dogs in the tristate area. Kegs of beer and empty steins lined the walls and full bottles of whiskey were available at discount prices, as the screaming wagers often reached as high as five thousand dollars a battle.

A dog needed to die in order to lose. It was going on two years now, but Jack Wells's pit bull, Grover, named after his favorite American president, Grover Cleveland, had yet to lose a match, tasting only—and literally—the warm blood of victory. Between bouts, the dog was fed the finest cuts of raw beef. He was given a daily bath in a mixture of pure bleach, hand soap and dry ice to keep his skin rough to the touch and hard to cut. He also had his front incisors filed and sharpened daily. Grover was allowed no displays of affection, his mean streak kept fresh for his monthly battles in the dirt ring. He was locked in a large mesh cage in the back of the barn on the days he wasn't scheduled to fight, prodded regularly with long sharp sticks by the attendants paid to care for him. Each night, before his supper, a long leather leash was strapped around Grover's neck and he would be taken to the fields outside where he would chase down ten live rabbits let loose for him to kill. The inhumane treatment served its intended purpose. Grover was the meanest dog in the ring and every owner feared putting his best up against him. "If the guys on my crew were half as tough as that dog," Wells would often brag, "I'd own more than a chunk of the city. I'd own half the damn country."

. . .

WELLS HELD A lit match against the end of a cigar as he watched Grover spin from the wolfhound's grip and clamp his strong jaw muscles on one of his hind legs. Grover ground his teeth down hard and the sound of a bone snapping could be heard even above the loud noise of the crowd. Wells blew out the match with a thick white line of smoke and smiled, sensing yet another in an unrivaled string of victories. He turned to his right and caught the eye of the wolfhound's owner. "Do your dog a favor," he shouted across the room, "shoot him dead now, before my Grover starts tearing him apart. A couple of minutes more and you won't be able to sell his carcass to the dog food buyers."

The man, in a three-piece suit and bowler hat, dropped a handful of money to the floor, turned and walked out of the barn. The crowd edged in closer, standing in silence, staring down at the bloody slaughter taking place just beneath their feet. The wolfhound was lying flat on the ground now, his white coat drenched in blood, half his torso torn away. Grover was in a foam-induced frenzy, biting and chewing frantically, ripping at exposed bone and flesh. "This match is over, Wells," a man from across the fence shouted out. "Call it and let the poor beast die in peace."

"It's over when I say it's over," an angry Wells shouted back. "And that's not gonna happen until I see my dog standing over a dead one."

Angelo Vestieri waited in the rear of the crowd, his back against a stack of fresh-cut hay, watching as Wells held court over an odd mix of farmers, hunters and hoodlums. He had been there for the bulk of the evening, safely hidden by the thick backs and raised arms of men eager for a closer look and a larger wager, his lungs burning from the smoke fumes he inhaled. He knew that this fight would be the last one for the night and that soon the crowd would begin to disperse, walking away with what was left of their money and their dogs. He also knew, as Ida the Goose had told him years earlier, that Jack Wells would be the very last to leave the barn.

It was close to dawn when Jack Wells stood in the blood-stained pit of the barn and counted his winnings. Grover, tired and bitten-up, stood by his side, drinking from a large bowl of cold water, white foam as dense as lard still running down the sides of his mouth. Wells folded the bills and nodded a final good-bye to the last straggler, a middle-aged farmhand carrying a bandaged rottweiler out a side door. He leaned down and ran a hand slowly across Grover's back, checking the severity of his wounds.

"It's gonna take more than a couple of bites to put you down, tough guy," he said to the dog, his soft voice swelled with a parent's pride. "I'll get you fixed up and then we'll come back here for one last go-around. After that, you can call it quits and have your way with as many bitches as you can handle."

Grover growled and continued to lap at his water with a casual indifference. The dog's eyes had a vacant look, his nose was stuffed with mucus and blood, and his breath was still hot and moist. Small pools of blood had formed around his four paws.

"It took me awhile, but I finally figured you out," Angelo said, stepping out from the back of the barn, standing now under the overhead lights, facing Wells and the dog. "You're the kind of guy who orders the kill but never gets his hands bloody. Likes to let others lead his fights. Even his own dog."

Wells looked up at Angelo's words. Grover showed off a mouthful of teeth and gave out a low bark, more routine than menacing. "I didn't know you were a fan of the dog fights," Wells said. "I hope you didn't lose too much betting heavy against my boy here."

"I'm not," Angelo said. "And I didn't."

"It would be nice if I could offer you a little something to drink," Wells said with a shrug. "But my booze supply is on the low side this month. I don't know if you heard about it or not, but one of my Bronx warehouses just took a big hit."

"I don't drink," Angelo said. "And I don't make a move on my partner, unless he gives me a reason."

Jack Wells kicked aside a rock and stepped closer to Angelo, his bleeding dog now resting his head next to the water bowl, his watery eyes giving way to sleep. "I'll tell you what," he said. "I'm gonna give you a chance to walk away from all of this. You're young still, probably saved a good chunk of the cash you made. Here's your shot to quit the rackets, leave with what you got and leave alive. Best deal I'm ever gonna put on a table for anybody."

"I love my work," Angelo said. He spoke in a calm and steady voice, both hands in his pants pockets, his eyes staring over at Wells. "And I'm too young to retire."

"You're too young to die, too," Wells said. "But as sure as there's buffalos on nickels, I'm gonna see you dead."

Angelo took a slow look around the barn, gazing at the bales of hay stacked three deep and at the horse stalls, shuttered and clean. He turned to his left and peeked through the fence, droplets of blood still dripping off its rails, the brown dirt mixing in with the spillage of bone and fluids. "What better time than right now?" he said.

Wells bent to his waist and rushed into Angelo, who braced himself for the hit, arms out to his side, his feet spread wide apart, the heels of his black shoes digging into the thick dirt. Angelo grunted as he wrapped his arms around Wells, raising a knee into the smaller man's stomach. The two fell together, crashing through the loose bolt of a horse stall. Wells flailed away at Angelo's head and chest, full-force blows raining down on his rib cage and cheeks, causing him to gulp for breaths of air. Angelo squeezed a handful of dirt between his fingers and tossed it into Wells's eyes, momentarily blinding him, then he tossed Wells off his stomach and jumped to his feet, his chest burning with pain, blood flowing out one side of his mouth.

"You're not good enough to take me down," Wells said, his breath coming in short puffs. "And you never were. If you wanna know the truth, your wife would have put up a better fight."

Angelo flew off his feet, the weight of his body crashing down hard against Jack Wells, ramming his back up along the side of a wooden pole. He then began to throw punches in a blind fury, attacking Wells from every possible angle, landing flush rights and lefts to his head, swinging his right knee repeatedly and viciously into his groin and stomach. It didn't take long. Wells crumbled in a slow heap to the ground, his legs folded over one another, his head falling forward and to one side. Angelo continued hitting and stomping him, his shoes moving in a slow rhythm from the dirt floor to Wells's face, their tips tinged with lines of blood. Sweat blanketed Angelo's angular frame. The knuckles of his hands were shed of all their skin and coated with rich, thick red streaks.

A long, muscular arm reached up from behind Angelo and brought an end to the assault.

"He's had it," Pudge said, whispering into Angelo's right ear, a firm grip on his chest and arms.

Angelo was breathing heavily, the air wheezing its way out of his mouth, his hair matted down, his face bright crimson. He glanced over his shoulder at Pudge and nodded. "Help me toss him into the pit," he said.

Angelo grabbed Wells under the shoulders, Pudge lifted his legs and they walked his prone body out of the horse stall. They stopped in front of the split-rail fence and Pudge kicked open the spring latch with his foot. They tossed Jack Wells down into the center of the dog fight ring and watched him land on his back, his head bouncing off the hard dirt. He lay there spread-eagled and dazed, at rest in the ooze of bone, blood puddles and the split-open carcasses of dead animals.

Pudge pulled two guns from his waistband and handed one to Angelo. They did not wait for Wells to speak. Nor did they say a word. Neither Angelo nor Pudge had any interest in pleas or sentiment or declarations of revenge. They were interested in one thing only, so they stood above the dog pit and emptied their revolvers into Jack Wells, twelve bullets in all. As soon as they were done, they tossed their guns into the pit and turned away.

The war was over.

• • •

"There're some horse blankets over in that corner," Pudge said to Angelo as he stood above Grover, the dog still bleeding and moaning in pain.

"What do we need with a dog?" Angelo asked, walking

past the stacks of hay and reaching into the darkness for a thick brown blanket. "Especially one that'll probably bite us first chance he gets."

"We could always use another friend," Pudge explained. He took the blanket from Angelo, kneeled down and gently wrapped it around the dog. He stood, holding Grover close to his chest. "And if we're ever in a pinch, we know he can fight."

Pudge started to walk toward the double doors leading out of the barn. "We'll drive him down to that doc that used to take care of Angus's dog. If anybody can fix him straight, he can."

"The dog's a killer," Angelo said, following in Pudge's shadow, turning to give Jack Wells a final look. "Thought I'd mention it, just in case you forgot."

"So are we," Pudge said, stopping and turning to face Angelo. "Just in case you forgot."

12

Spring, 1934

IT WAS THE spring when Clyde Barrow and Bonnie Parker were gunned down on a dirt road fifty miles east of Shreveport, Louisiana, bringing to an end a two-year string of armed robberies that had netted them a top haul of $3,500. Later in the year, John Dillinger would walk out of a Chicago movie theater, his arm wrapped around the woman who had betrayed him to the FBI agents who would soon shoot him dead. His body was found with nothing more than pocket money jammed inside the slit of an old wallet. Later that summer, the U.S. Army turned over Alcatraz Island in San Francisco Bay to the Bureau of Prisons where it would eventually house Al Capone, George "Machine Gun" Kelly and "the Birdman," Robert Stroud. All three front-page public enemies would die broken men.

It was also the spring in which twenty-eight-year-old Angelo Vestieri and thirty-one-year-old Pudge Nichols ruled over the largest and most profitable gang in the New York underworld. It was a distinction that earned them millions in untaxed dollars and two seats on the nine-member National Crime Commission they had helped establish three years earlier. They shared in their power equally, trusting only in one another, allowing no entry into their private domain. They steered clear of publicity and tabloid exposure, fearing that such notoriety would propel Justice Department investigations into their activities. Angelo studied the habits of the industrial and business leaders of the day, and sought to follow their ways. He read the *Wall Street Journal* and the *New York Times*. He devoured books on business and banking techniques and read as many biographies of world leaders as time permitted. Pudge loved to work with numbers and had an intuitive knack for investments. He utilized both of these strengths to further swell the gang's portfolio. They were modern-day gangsters determined to rule their violent world with the unbeatable weapons of fear and finance.

They were taught the skills of laundering money from Park Avenue realtors and bankers who were allowed to frequent their brothels free of charge. They then quickly turned those lessons into an intricate and well-structured revolving door of cash that transferred the illegal gains of prostitution, gambling and whiskey into the safer havens of real estate and business holdings. "We didn't want anyone to know how much we had and how much we owned," Pudge once told me. "That kind of information makes people jealous and, in our line of work, leads to somebody getting shot. So we bailed out a banker in financial trouble, took over a piece of his bank, sealed our records and kept our main holding companies listed under other names. And then, every eighteen months or so, we would switch them all around again, names and all. If anybody came looking, it would take months, even years, before they could track one dollar of the cash back our way. We took over control of the town and nobody even knew it was gone."

Their personal lives, as they had been from the very beginning, constituted the only area where Angelo and Pudge chose to travel separate paths. Pudge had an open aversion to marriage but an insatiable passion for women. Such desires left him free to pick from among any of the four hundred call girls working for his crew. He lived in a top-floor suite of the Madison Hotel on West Forty-seventh Street and kept a stockpile of suits and shirts hanging in the closets of a half-dozen brothels throughout the city. This not only allowed him to spend the night anywhere he wanted, it avoided creating any clear pattern to his routine.

"We were both loners," Pudge would often say. "But we handled it in different ways. After the war with Wells, I learned to be a little more cautious. I drove my own car and never parked it in the same spot twice. I never let a woman, no matter how much I liked her, spend the whole night with me. I'd been shot once in bed with a broad and I wasn't gonna let that happen a second time. If I was in a business meeting and got offered a drink, I made sure I wasn't the only one with a glass in his hand. It's little things like that that help keep you alive in the rackets. If you can live that way and not let it make you crazy, then chances are you're gonna be around for a long, long time."

$\bullet \quad \bullet \quad \bullet$

ANGELO LIVED ALONE in Ida's old railroad apartment, one floor above the Café Maryland. The walls of each room were lined with framed photos, a still-life tribute to those few whom he loved. The dining room belonged to Angus, usually in bowler hat and flashy tuxedo, strolling in style down the West Side streets he owned for so long. The living room was all Ida, looking down from her perch across the bar of the Café, the flower of her fetching beauty in full bloom. In one photo, taken when she was at the height of her gang power, her eyes glistened against the shaded overhead lights and her wondrous smile was warm enough to keep out the cold. Angelo's small office in the back of the apartment was lined with ledgers, log books and company portfolios, all of them surrounded by shots of a quick-to-smile Pudge, who was always eager to ham it up whenever he knew a camera was in focus.

The bedroom was where he kept his photos of Isabella.

It was the one room he always paused before entering, the weight of her loss still haunting his every action. Except for Pudge, no one was allowed into the apartment, and even he never dared set foot into the bedroom. Angelo's only company on most of those nights was Grover, the pit bull Pudge had rescued from the Jack Wells shooting. Angelo and Grover would eat their dinner together, both content with the silence, listening to the music from the bar downstairs filter up through the cracks in the hardwood floors. Angelo suffered from insomnia and very seldom slept through the night. Instead, he would walk the dark side streets of the neighborhood around the Café, Grover, scar tissue etched across most of his body, dutifully by his side. When he did attempt to get some rest, he did so sitting in a leather rocking chair next to the bedroom window, book in hand, staring down through tireless eyes at the passing traffic below, his framed wedding photo at rest on his lap, Grover curled up by his feet.

"He was the most powerful gangster in town," Pudge said to me. "And hands down the saddest. In a crazy way, I was jealous of him. I would never know what it was like to be that in love with somebody. Angelo had that in his life. Yeah, it was only for a short time, but that's more than most people manage to get their hands on. Then to lose her the way he did, made what they had between them only that much bigger. But he never wanted to hear talk like that. He just wanted to be allowed to miss her as much as he did. That was the one part he knew nobody could pull away from him. He never talked about her, never mentioned her, kept everything they had together locked inside. All those nights he spent alone up in his room, with that crazy dog we found, I think he looked at it as his time alone with her. Kept her alive that way, at least in his head. Who knows? Maybe kept himself alive, too."

. . .

ANGELO KNELT IN front of the marble tombstone, his warm hands resting on top of the chiseled rock. It was early Sunday morning and the sun was just beginning to cast its glow across the vast expanse of the hilltop cemetery. He had left the city while it was still dark and made the ninety-minute drive alone, stopping only to pick up two bouquets of fresh-cut flowers from an all-night market. Isabella's grave was close to the shaded comfort of a large, weeping willow, its old, thick branches helping to ward off both the sun and the rain. He had cleared away the dried flowers and brushed aside the brown leaves that covered the front of her grave. He was alone in the gated grounds, the quiet that engulfed him broken only by the heavy whistling of a strong wind.

He rubbed his hands gently against the sides of the stone and leaned back on his heels, his coat spread out across the dirt and gravel. He picked up the fresh flowers and put them into the two vases in front of the grave. He folded his hands, holding them down by his waist, and bowed his head, but not in prayer. Angelo never prayed, choosing not to believe in a God cruel enough to allow death to come to a young bride and her unborn child. He raised his head to the sky and felt warmed by Isabella's silent presence and allowed himself the rare luxury of a smile.

Angelo leaned forward and, with eyes closed, kissed the two names that were chiseled onto the thick granite. The first belonged to his wife, Isabella Conforti Vestieri. The second was that of the son he would never see, Carlo Vestieri. He then reached into his pocket and pulled out a large, round peach, much like the one he had given Isabella the first time they had met. He placed it in the center of the headstone, between the two flower vases.

Angelo bowed his head and then stood. He turned and walked quietly out of the cemetery, slowly making his way down the hill, back to his waiting car.

He was a young man in mourning, stripped of a love he would never again be allowed to touch.

He was a wealthy man, tapping into the millions that were to be had in a hard country so willing to give to those who were so eager to take.

He was a man of power, controlling the lives and destinies of thousands, many of whom he would never even meet.

He was an enemy to be feared and a friend who would never betray the strength of that union.

He was an astute man of business who saw opportunities years before they materialized.

He was a stone-hearted killer quick to eliminate any enemy who presented the slightest threat to his empire.

He was Angelo Vestieri.

A gangster.

BOOK TWO

Home of the Brave

some say we are responsible
for those we love
others know we are responsible
for those who love us
—Nikki Giovanni, "The
December of My Springs"

13

Fall, 1964

ANGELO VESTIERI FIRST came into my life during the seventh game of the World Series between the New York Yankees and the St. Louis Cardinals.

I had just turned ten and was living with my fourth foster family in two years. My new parents were a tight-lipped, middle-aged couple who rented the rear apartment in a second-floor walk-up on Twenty-sixth Street and Broadway. They seemed happy enough to have me around and were even happier when the monthly checks they received from the New York State Department of Social Services to pay for my food, school and boarding arrived in the mail. I never took any of the family transfers personally, having learned to accept them more as the business transactions they were rather than as the long-term parental stability they were publicly perceived to be. I knew their tolerance for me would end as soon as my foster parents came to the realization that the burden of a child didn't balance out the comfort of a steady check. I was labeled an orphan at birth and was considered a ward of the state, and was soon aware that staying with a family, no matter how indifferent or cruel, was a hands down better option than life inside an institutional home.

I hadn't been lucky enough to be picked by an Upper East Side couple eager to bring a son into their deep-pocketed world or by wanna-be parents from a leafy suburb who would thrill at the sight of a young boy at play in their spacious backyard. Every orphan dreams of such good fortune, but then reality takes root and you wake up and know that you are nothing more than the ward of John and Virginia Webster, a railroad conductor with a gambling problem and a housewife who drinks more than she should. And you accept it and live with it as best you can, knowing that one night the phone will ring and you will be sent off to yet another set of parents eager to add to their family. At least for a few months.

I was walking back home from another new school, my books bundled under my right arm, my feet aching from the tight P. F. Flyer hand-me-down sneakers I had been given that morning. It was early October and the warm winds of summer had long since faded, replaced by the frigid blasts of fall. I was hoping to get to the apartment in time to catch the last few innings of the seventh game on the small radio Virginia Webster had given me for my room. I loved baseball and I especially loved the Yankees and listened to as many games as I could during the season. I had never been to the stadium, but could easily visualize its magnificent scope and dimensions in my mind as I listened to the familiar voice of Mel Allen bring each play to life.

I turned the corner on Twenty-eighth Street and passed a bar with dark windows and a well-lit sign. I stopped briefly to take a quick look inside and could make out a few figures drinking, smoking and talking, their heads collectively lifted up to a small television perched several feet above the stacks of bottles. I placed my books down by my feet, cupped my hands around the window and peered inside. The World Series was on the TV and even though I could barely make out the moving forms through the thick glass, I stood there mesmerized, watching the players whose names and most minute statistics I had committed so clearly to my memory. Only one of the families I had ever lived with had enough money to have a television of their own, and they would turn it on at night long after they thought I had fallen asleep. The players lived and played their games in my imagination. They were brought to life by the occasional glimpses I got of them in a newspaper photo, or by sneaking looks at the baseball cards of the other boys at school or by the images I could make out from the cold windows of shadowed bars.

"What's the score?" the man asked. He stood above me, his height blocking out the late afternoon sun.

"I only just got here," I said without turning to look at him. "I can't make out too much, but I think the Cardinals are up."

"Why don't you go in?" the man asked. "Watch the game from where you can see it?"

"No point in doing that," I told him. "I'll only end up getting tossed out by the guy working the bar."

"Maybe this bar will be different," the man said.

I saw his hand reach for the doorknob and turn it open toward him, letting out the sounds of the ball game along with the sweet smells of fresh-brewed coffee, grilled burgers and tap beer. I looked up and saw his face for the first time. He was tall, bigger than most men I had seen, muscle-thin, and dressed in creased black slacks, black jacket and a black shirt buttoned up to the collar. His hair was jet dark and was brushed neat and straight back. His eyes were clear and didn't show much life or movement as they looked back down at me. His face was clean-shaven and unmarked, a young man's look on a middle-aged body.

He held the door open and waited. "Am I going in alone?" he asked in a voice that was low and strong, comfortable with giving out commands and not taxed from overuse.

"Maybe I'll get to see Mantle hit one out before they toss me," I said as I picked up my books and walked past him into the bar.

• • •

THERE WERE SIX men inside and they all stood when they saw us walk in. The bartender stopped wiping down the wood, bent down and pulled a pitcher of milk and a chilled glass from the small fridge by his legs. I led the way, the man behind me keeping one hand on my shoulder, his right leg dragging slightly as he walked.

"This kid wants to see the game," the man said. "Find him a good spot and bring him some food. And only throw him out if he roots for the wrong team."

The other men all laughed and smiled. One came over and led me to a table directly across from the television set. "We got fresh lentil soup cooking," he said. "How about a bowl of that and maybe a cheeseburger and some fries?"

I sat down, laid my books on the table and nodded. "That'd be great, thanks," I said. "But I only got a quarter on me."

"Then I won't expect much of a tip," he said and walked away.

The man from the street stepped over to my table and looked at me. "Enjoy what's left of the game," he said. "You can come in here anytime you want. No one will toss you out unless you give them a reason to."

"Thanks," I said. "And don't worry, if I do come in here, it won't be to cause you any trouble."

"I don't worry," the man said.

He nodded and turned away. He walked slowly toward the bar and grabbed the glass of milk the bartender had just poured for him and then disappeared around the bend and into a back room.

That was my first meeting with Angelo Vestieri.

• • •

WHEN I MET him, Angelo was fifty-eight years old, and was said to be the most powerful gangster in America. The long ago war with Jack Wells had hardened his grip on the New York rackets, and the battles that followed only helped increase his reach. He and Pudge had managed to survive the physical and legal threats. They eluded the government hunts that came to a head during Senator Estes Kefauver's televised subcommittee hearings in the early 1950s. And they did not bend to the unrelenting pressure placed on organized crime by Robert F. Kennedy during his tenure as U.S. Attorney General.

The four wars they fought in the years after their battle with Wells had grown in common perception to where they were now a part of mob folklore. But their boldest move came in 1939, four years after the Wells war, and was soon after christened by the tabloid writers as "The Night of the Vespers." It was, by far, the goriest event in mob history. In one swift and brutal move, Angelo and Pudge orchestrated the murder of thirty-nine of the top-ranking figures in organized crime.

"Getting rid of that many people in one night was something nobody had ever done before and the odds are pretty stacked against anybody ever doing it again," Pudge would often tell me as we sat across from each other, eating linguini drenched in a thick and spicy fish sauce. "In less than twelve hours, we got rid of all of the people standing between us and the sky. Nobody saw the move coming, and even the people we needed to let in on it never figured it would pan out. But Angelo, he had it all mapped out in his head. He had worked on the plan for two years, had it measured down to the smallest detail and he only told people what they needed to know. None of the shooters had any idea how big the job was. Each one of them thought they were out on the only hit. It was a pure and brilliant move. Thirty-nine gangsters died, all in one night. And that's how Angelo Vestieri became a legend."

•　•　•

THE NIGHT OF the Vespers was the most violent twelve hours in mob history. It was a story I would always ask to be told when I was a child. It was better than any bedtime tale I could find in a book, because its bold power and cold-blooded precision were all true and not bred from any imagination. In the days prior to the night in question, Angelo and Pudge, young, brilliant and brutal, were ranked in the second tier of the nation's criminal elite as ordained by the National Commission. The men on the list above them, spread out as far west as Chicago and Cleveland, but mostly centered in New York and New Jersey, ran crime on a day-to-day-basis. Their rulings were law and were meant to be followed. All the men were older and far more experienced in the ways of the racket business. It would take decades for Angelo and Pudge to move up the corporate criminal ladder in order for them to be in a position where their decisions were the final ones.

Neither one was willing to wait.

"We picked from the top thirty shooters in the country," Angelo said in a tone more common to a Wall Street takeover. "Gave them each a job and paid them in full before the hit was made. One contact, one meeting. It was made clear to them that if they failed, they, too, would die. Me and Pudge split the other nine. Then we moved out to do what we do best. By the next morning, I was ranked number one and Pudge was number two and we didn't have to wait for anybody anymore. We were now in charge."

Among the nine killings attributed to Angelo and Pudge were two men, Tony Rivisi and Freddy Meyers, who once worked as killers for Jack Wells and moved up to Buffalo after his death. Within a year, they ran most of the action coming out of upstate New York and were ranked in the mid-thirties by the commission. The mob rumor mill had always linked their names to Isabella's shooting. "Angelo never said if they were the wheel men or not and I never asked," Pudge told me. "But he made it very clear that those two belonged to him. And he killed them as if it meant something to him. They were both found in a downtown slaughterhouse, a hook shoved into the back of their necks, their bodies gutted like a cow's, their eyes taken out. That last thing was an Italian superstition that meant they would never find their way to peace after they died. And if they were part of the team that led to Isabella's death, they more than earned their pain."

．　．　．

I SAT IN the bar, ate everything they put in front of me and watched the Yankees lose the seventh game of the World Series to Bob Gibson. I pushed my chair back and gathered my books, ready to leave and walk back to the reality of my world. I checked the clock above the bar and saw that it was already ten minutes past the time the Websters liked to sit down to eat their dinner, something that was sure to agitate them both. They were as dependable as a sunrise, eating all three of their meals at the same time each and every day, never veering from their routine. I had been living with them for three weeks and this would be their first meal without me since my arrival.

A muscular older man with thick forearms and a relaxed smile walked up to the table carrying a blueberry pie. "You're not gonna leave without having dessert, are you?" He rested the pie on the center of the table and raised two fingers to a man sitting with his back to the bar. "Tommy'll bring us over a couple of forks," he said. "You should have at least a taste. It's a fresh pie. Just took it out of the oven."

"I'm going to be late for dinner," I said, glancing down at the empty platter and soup bowl that was on the table.

"Seems to me you just had your dinner," the man said, gently pushing back a chair with his foot and sitting down. "And besides, if you're already late, the worst you can be is later. Tell you what? I'll even toss in a fresh cup of coffee, help you wash down the pie. Now I know nobody is gonna make you a better offer than that. At least not today they won't."

I smiled at him, pushed my chair closer to the edge of the table and sat back down. Tommy from the bar came over and handed him two forks. "You want plates with that?" he asked.

"No," he said to Tommy, shaking his head. "We're good as is."

He handed me one of the forks and looked down at the pie. "Time to dig in," he said. "And let's not be shy about it."

He cut at the pie with his fork, broke away a large chunk and jammed it into his mouth. He looked across the table and motioned for me to do the same, watching with approval as I repeated his move. Tommy came back, this time carrying a small tray that had a pot of coffee and two cups on it. He placed the tray next to the pie and walked back to his seat at the bar. The man lifted the hot pot by its black handle, filled the two cups and pushed one toward me. "Milk and sugar are up by the bar," he said, leaning back in his chair. "Go up and help yourself."

"I've never had coffee before," I said. "This is my first cup."

"Then get used to drinking it black," the man said. "The less you need in life, the better off you're gonna find yourself."

I sipped my coffee, the bitter taste coating my tongue and warming my throat, and watched as he drained his cup with three fast gulps. "What do they call you?" he asked, brushing the empty cup off to one side of the table.

"My name's Gabe," I said, holding the cup away from my face.

"Pudge," he said, thrusting a thick hand across the table for me to shake. "Pudge Nichols."

I shook his hand and watched as my fingers disappeared inside his formidable grip. He was dressed in charcoal gray slacks and a black V-neck sweater, the collar of a crisp white T-shirt visible underneath. His thick hair was as white as fresh vanilla ice cream and he had a half-moon scar just below his left eye. He wore no jewelry and kept his watch around a belt loop on his pants. Pudge was sixty-one when we first met, but had the upper body of a ranking middleweight, his muscles flexing whether he was at rest or moving with graceful ease across a room.

"Are you the owner?" I speared another piece of pie and looked around at the well-kept bar.

"I'm one of them." He leaned back against his chair, his hands flat on the surface of the table. "The other one is the tall quiet guy who let you in to watch the game."

"He never told me his name."

"If that's something he wants you to know," Pudge said, "then he'll be the one to tell you."

"I should get going," I said, pushing my chair back. "It's

pretty dark out now and the people I live with might start to think that something happened to me."

"You need somebody to walk home with you?" Pudge stood next to me, his hands at rest by his side. "Have them back up your story, just in case things start to look like they're gonna get out of hand?"

"Thanks anyway," I said, shaking my head. "They won't care enough to be asking me lots of questions."

"Does that bother you?" Pudge asked as he walked with me toward the front door of the bar.

I stopped at the door and opened it, letting the cold autumn night air rush in and mix with the stale odors of the bar. I thought about what he'd asked, then turned back to look at him when I had the answer. "Not yet," I said.

Pudge nodded at me and turned away, the door closing slowly behind him. I stood outside the bar for several minutes, my eyes closed, a smile on my lips, savoring the final seconds of a day I knew I would never forget. I then lifted the collar of my jacket, lowered my head and began the slow walk back to a place I knew I didn't belong.

. . .

FOR THE NEXT several weeks, I made it a point to walk past the bar on my way home from school each afternoon. I stood on the opposite corner and tried my best not to be noticed, content to watch the quiet comings and goings of bar activity. I was hooked after just that one memorable afternoon. In a youthful imagination charged by living most of my life in isolation, the importance of that day took on a greater significance than it would have for another boy who came to it from a more normal background. It was the first time I had been treated as an equal by any adult. Instead of entering into a strange place as an intruder, I was made to feel wanted as well as welcomed. Such feelings are a rare treat for a foster child.

I had lived my life as an outsider, forced to look at my limited view of the world through other people's windows. I was too young to know it at the time, but gangsters live their life pretty much in the same manner. The only difference is that they *choose* to close off the outside world, content to live within the spaces they have designated as their own. And they very seldom allow a civilian a peek through the glass. For one brief and glorious afternoon, I had been allowed such a peek.

I had been leaning against the lamppost for over an hour when the first drops of rain began to fall. I looked up at the dark clouds overhead and, after taking one final look at the bar, turned to leave. I was walking alongside a row of parked cars, my head down, dreading yet another dreary night that lay ahead, an uncomfortable evening of stolen glances, heavy sighs and forced chatter between myself and my foster parents. With the rain coming down harder, wetting through the shoulders of my windbreaker, I knew my time with my new family would be a short one and that eventually my fear of living in an orphanage would become a reality. I walked past the red taillights of a black Lincoln Continental, the lines of water running down the sides of the trunk and rear fenders giving it a glow, reflected in the glare of an all-night diner across the way. I was about to come up to the driver's side door when it swung open, blocking my path.

I stopped and turned to look inside, the car's interior lights illuminating the face of the tall man behind the wheel, casting him in half shadows, but not enough that I didn't recognize him. He was the same man who had led me into the bar that day to eat a meal and see a baseball game. He looked up at me, one leg outside of the car, his foot hugging the edge of the curb. His eyes were the color of night and his hands were resting on the bottom of the steering wheel as he watched the water run down my face and the sides of my neck.

"If you're going to spend most of your time on the street, an umbrella wouldn't be that bad of an idea," he said.

"I don't mind the rain all that much," I said. "And anyway, I don't live too far from here."

He eased his leg back inside the car. "In that case, I don't need to offer you a ride."

I shook my head. "You never did tell me your name," I said. "That day you let me into your bar."

"You never asked for it." His eyes scanned the rearview mirror for any visible activity behind him. "If you had, I would have told you to call me Angelo."

"If I don't move soon, I might drown out here. And I'm getting the inside of your car wet, which can't be making you too happy."

"It's not my car," he said, ignoring the water dripping off the top of the door onto the interior. "But before you go, I want you to do something for me."

"What?" I leaned in closer to better hear his low voice against the sound of the rain.

"Tell the people you live with that you'll be home very late Monday night. Tell them you'll be out with me and for them not to worry."

He slammed the door shut and kicked over the engine. He flicked on the headlights and pulled out of the parking spot, his tires denting the center of the flowing curbside puddles. I watched the car brake at the corner, make a sharp right and disappear from sight. I was soaked through from head to socks and had begun to shiver. I walked down the four quiet, poorly lit streets back to my foster parent's apartment building, giving up the losing battle to shield myself from the downpour. I knew that when I got inside, the lights would be out and they would both be locked silently behind their closed bedroom door. There would be a cold meal waiting for me on the small kitchen table and maybe a hand towel draped over the back of a chair. I would take off my clothes in the hall and leave them there in a wet heap, so as not to have a heavy water trail follow me through the apartment. I'd lock the door behind me, rush into my room in the rear and jump into bed, drying my body and trying to get warm as I huddled under a double layer of thin white sheet and thick quilt blanket.

I also knew that on this night, I would fall asleep with a smile on my face.

. . .

MOST GANGSTERS NEVER live long enough to see retirement
or prison, and if they're lucky, they don't see the bullets that
seal their early doom. But the ones who were smarter and
more brutal were often the ones to live long enough to see the
late-day sun. Carlo Sandulli ruled his New York crew until his
death from a heart ailment at eighty-five. In his entire life he
never once used a telephone and stayed clear of the modern-
day habit of doing business out of social clubs, which were
under the vigilant eye of federal agents. Giacamo Vandini
gave orders through nods and hand gestures, the death of an
enemy decided by the flipping of a palm. Chicago crime
legend Jerry Maccadro ruled with a Roman fist until his mid-
eighties, defiant to his final breath. "It takes a lot to make it to
old age in the rackets," Angelo said. "You need good luck
when it comes to your health and you have to be smart about
how you go about your life. You also have to make sure all
your enemies end up in cemeteries. The older you get, the
deadlier you have to be and you use age to your advantage.
You make it a strength. Most of us are more dangerous the
longer we live. If we didn't care about dying when we were
young, we're not going to be too concerned about it when we
have two feet in our own grave."

Pudge had matured, softened with age. He was a rare gangster, one who never married or sought out the comforts of
family. He enjoyed his life, the freedom and power it afforded
him. His reputation in mob circles was still fierce and deadly
enough that few dared challenge him. He was still quick to
kill and just as quick to charm. He had grown into a favorite
uncle who was warmly welcomed by those whose path he
crossed.

A favorite uncle who also happened to be a remorseless
killer.

Through the years, Angelo had shuttered his small world
even tighter, limiting his contact to just a handful of those he
trusted. He now reigned over an organized crime universe

changing with the times, forced to confront younger members eager to embrace the lucrative allure of drugs. He knew only one way to calm such a desire. He and Pudge were the Babe Ruth and Lou Gehrig of gangsters, still in the game years after most other players had either retired or died, and still sharp enough to lead their world in hits.

•   •   •

GORILLA MONSOON HAD Johnny Valentine in a headlock, stomping his large foot on the ring mat each time he tightened his grip. The packed house inside Madison Square Garden booed Monsoon as he sneered at them, mocking Valentine's meager attempts to pin him. I was sitting in the center of the front row, facing the middle of the large ring, wedged in between Angelo and Pudge. I had a container of popcorn on my lap and a Coke in a paper cup next to my right foot.

"You think Monsoon's going to be able to take him?" I asked them, keeping my eyes focused on the action above me.

"You talking about real life, then it's not even worth the question," Pudge said with a shrug. "But inside of that ring up there, there's no way they're gonna let Monsoon leave here with his arm raised."

I turned away from a vicious-sounding Monsoon body slam to the mat and looked at Pudge, Valentine flat on his back grimacing in pain. "What do you mean?" I asked. "Are you saying the match is rigged?"

"This is wrestling, little man," Pudge said. "It's supposed to be rigged. They have it all worked out even before they slip on their trunks. Everybody's in on it, from the referees to the crowd."

I looked around me at the nine thousand men, women and children, most of them standing up from their seats, screaming out words of encouragement to their favorite wrestler, booing when a move or a call didn't go their way, and then came back to Pudge. "What about them?" I asked him, pointing at the rows across from the ring. "Do they all know, too?"

"Everybody knows," Pudge said. "And if they don't, they should."

"Doesn't that take away from the fun?" I asked.

Pudge shook his head, continuing with the life lesson, one that was similar in setting to the early schooling given them many years ago by Angus McQueen. "Why should it?" he asked. "You still root for the good guys, boo the bad ones and go back home having had yourself a good time."

I looked up and saw Johnny Valentine swing Gorilla Monsoon off the center ropes, then catch him, squeezing his arms around the much bigger man's waist, locking his fingers across his spine, forcing him to tilt his head back in pain. The house cheered its approval as Valentine's seemingly powerful hold forced Monsoon's knees to buckle and his lungs scream for air, his bulky arms hanging limply by his side. The referee lifted one of Monsoon's arms and watched as it fell back down like an airless balloon. He did it a second time with the same result. A third time would officially bring the match to an end.

"Looks like it's all over," I said, holding a handful of popcorn. "The big guy looks like he's going to faint."

"It's too early for it to end," Angelo said with a casual indifference. "They haven't given the crowd enough for their money yet. When they do, that's when it will be over."

"And then who'll win?" I looked over at Angelo, the popcorn crammed into a corner of my mouth.

He looked back at me, his eyes cold and distant. "It doesn't matter who wins. If Valentine wins, the crowd goes home happy. If Monsoon wins they get upset. But by next week they're back rooting and yelling as loud as ever."

"That's the only thing that counts," Pudge added. "That they come back every week."

"You can learn a lot about life by watching a wrestling match," Angelo said. "Rigged or not. You got your good guys and your bad. You got those that are friends and those that are enemies. But then, the wrestler you think you can trust the most turns against you, betrays you to another group and leaves you out there by yourself. And all that does is make you want to come back looking for revenge. It's all there for you to see, Gabe. It might be buried under the theater of it, but if you look for it, you won't have too hard a time finding it."

"Is that why you guys come to the matches?" I asked, taking a sip from my cup of Coke.

"We got our lessons from a different ring," Pudge said. "If there's anything that needs to be learned here tonight, it's you who's got to learn it."

"You can choose and be like the people that are sitting around us," Angelo said, his hand placed gently on my knee. "Now, if that's the direction you go in, then you only need to treat tonight for what it is, a little bit of fun, a break in your routine. But if you decide to come away from it with something more than another night out, then pay attention to what you see. It may come in handy one day or it may not. Either way, you make the time spent work in your favor and not against."

I turned away from Angelo and looked up to watch Johnny Valentine put a neck grip on Gorilla Monsoon and, after several minutes of cries and groans, force him into submission and bring the match to an end. The audience erupted into wild cheers as Valentine strutted around the ring, his arms raised to the lights above. Pudge nudged an elbow against my side, leaned over and shouted into my ear. "I'll give you better than even money the two of them are having dinner together after they leave here tonight."

"What if somebody sees them?" I asked. "Won't they get into any trouble?"

"For having dinner with a friend? That day ever comes around then we'll all be in big trouble."

I smiled at Pudge then turned to look at Angelo but all I saw was an empty seat. "Don't worry," Pudge said, sensing the question I was about to ask. "Angelo's not one for crowds. He'll be at the restaurant when we get there."

"Which restaurant are we going to?" I asked as I took

Pudge's hand in mine and followed him down a ramp that led out of the arena.

"There's only one kind of cooking that goes down easy after sitting through two solid hours of wrestling." Pudge made a right past the ramp and out through a set of double doors. "And that's Chinese. How's that sound to you?"

"It sounds great," I said, walking at twice my normal pace in order to keep up with Pudge's accelerated speed. "Well, I don't really know how it sounds. I've never eaten Chinese food."

"It looks to me like we got to take you from the top to the bottom, little man." Pudge turned his head toward me as we both stood on the corner of Fiftieth Street and Eighth Avenue. "Try and make up for lost time and teach you everything you need to know. Does that sound like a good deal to you?"

"Yes," I said and then I lifted my arms and wrapped them around his neck. It was the first time in my entire life I had ever hugged anybody, let alone a man, and I never wanted to let him go.

Pudge returned the hug and then lifted me off my feet and carried me the rest of the way to the restaurant, keeping me safe and warm, shielding me from the cold harsh winter winds.

. . .

GANGSTERS FEAR LEADING a normal life and do all they can to denigrate such an existence. They are constantly pitting their chosen lifestyle up against that of a working man and must walk away from such discussions needing to feel superior. They find themselves compelled to justify, in the simplest of terms, the reasons they are career criminals and they willingly color the truth in order to reach a conclusion that bends in their favor. They do this with all that they see and hear, coating it with the brush of a harsh lesson in order to give weight to the reality of their world.

That is why treating me to a night of wrestling meant more to Angelo and Pudge than a few hours of fun. It was a way to illustrate to me how life really functions, that someone per- ceived as being good can easily shift toward evil and that no one should be trusted beyond the moment. They would im- pose such lessons on me throughout my childhood years, re- gardless of where we went or what we would see together.

"Find me any gangster and keep in mind he doesn't know shit about the theater, but he'll tell you that his all-time fa- vorite play is *Death of a Salesman*." Pudge told me that as we were sitting through yet another production. "Now, I know it's a lot of other people's favorite play, too. But they like it for the writing or maybe for the acting. Gangsters don't care about any of that. Instead, what we walk away with after watching it, is how living the decent life and following all the rules and working hard every day of your life in the end does nothing but screw you and leave you for dead. Willy Loman is every gangster's biggest fear. He lived his whole life for nothing but empty pockets and then his only way out was to wrap a car around a tree trunk and hope the insurance com- pany came through with the cash. If that's what an honest man can hope to get at the end of the road, then you can have it and keep it all, with interest."

• • •

I WALKED OUT of my last class of the day, my book bag filled to capacity, eager to get out and meet Pudge at the pizzeria around the corner from the school. It was near the end of my second month as a transfer student at St. Dominick's at Thirty-first Street where my foster parents had placed me, hoping a parochial education would do more for me than a public one. While I had adjusted to the heavier workload and the stricter rules imposed by the Catholic Brothers who taught us, I still had no real friends, keeping a safe distance from the others in my grade. I never knew when I would have to move again and did not want to risk becoming part of any group I would have to be torn away from, despite the many assurances I got from Pudge that this would be my last stop. My stubborn stance didn't seem to pose much of a problem, though, since the others students still did their best to avoid me. By now, I had spent enough time alone that I had grown comfortable in the role, content to watch from a distance the friendly antics that went on between the other kids around me. My background was well known to the students and teachers in my grade. There are few secrets that can be kept from the peering eyes and acute ears of a tenement landscape, and mine was no exception. By staying silent and keeping to myself, I simply gave them all a little less to talk about, knowing that would only further fuel their curiosity.

· · ·

I SLAMMED DOWN on the iron bar and opened the red wood door that led out to the street. My foot touched the top step when a hand reached out and pushed me forward, causing me to lose my balance and drop my book bag. I caught myself with one hand on the railing, the other scraping against the center of a concrete step. I looked up and saw a circle of boys standing above me, all smiling and waiting for me to get back to my feet.

"Which one of you pushed me?" I asked, wiping the blood off my hand on the knee of my pants.

A pudgy kid with an oval face and thick red hair flipped a toothpick from his mouth and walked down a step. "You're looking at him, orphan boy," he said, standing with his feet square apart, his closed hands at his side. "I saw that you were in a hurry so I thought that maybe I'd help speed you along."

The cluster behind him laughed and snorted their approval, while a skinny Hispanic kid gave him a gentle nudge on the shoulder. The pudgy boy's name was Michael Cannera and I had seen him a few times in the playground during lunch and recess, and I was in a religion class with him, but we had never exchanged a word. He seemed the leader of his pack and was always pounced upon by the Brothers who were quick to dole out their brand of punishment with a leather hand belt. He was on the hunt for a fight, more out of pleasure than any sense of dominance or threat to his little domain. I had seen him in a few of his street-corner battles, usually matched up against smaller kids, and he always came out of the scrap bloodied but a winner. I also noticed that regardless of who he was up against, his back was covered by at least three of his buddies, ready to jump in if asked. As I looked at him glowering down at me, I knew I was nothing more to him than a convenient target.

He already had one advantage over me even before any punches were thrown. I was a state-sponsored foster child and as such had to be on my best behavior, both in the home I was sent to live in and at the school I attended. A street fight, especially one on school grounds, was sure to be brought to someone's attention, and that could easily earn me a ticket out to a state home.

"It's not a problem," I said, as I leaned down to pick up my book bag. "I wasn't looking to get in anybody's way."

Michael walked down two steps closer to me, his face locked in a tight sneer. "Only a punk would turn his back and walk from this," he said. "Is that what you are, orphan boy? That must be what happens when you gotta go and pay somebody to make believe they're your parents."

"Why don't you go and look for trouble somewhere else?" I said, lifting my bag and turning my back. "You're not gonna find any here."

"I don't let anybody tell me what to do," he snarled, running with full force down the remaining three steps. "Especially no little punk ass orphan boy."

He landed square against the center of my back, the blow pushing the air out of my lungs and causing me to lose the grip on my bag. I landed face first on the sidewalk, Michael leaning against my shoulders, his weight holding me down, his fists landing blows across my neck and head. I lifted my head and tried to regain my focus, tasting the thin lines of blood that were dripping into my mouth from a slash under my eye. My bag and books were scattered off to my right, one of them resting flat on its spine, its pages flapping open in the wind. I stretched out my hand and reached for the nearest one, a thick geography text resting on its side, up against the base of a thin tree surrounded by a dry patch of dirt. My upper body was burning from the storm of punches pounding down on it. I closed my eyes and grabbed for the book, gripping my fingers around its pages, using my free hand as a balance.

The pace of his punches was slowing down, his energy sapped by his explosive assault. I could feel him rocking back on his heels, one hand grabbing the crook of my collar and lifting my head off the ground. He was breathing hard and heavy, his mouth swallowing gulps of cold, fresh air. I leaned forward on my right shoulder and tightened my grip around the book. I turned and swung it against the side of the boy's pudgy face. I caught him flush on the ear, the edge of the book catching a corner of his eye, and sent him tumbling off my back and onto the sidewalk, where he landed on his side. I rose to my knees and began to throw my own punches against the boy's face and chest. One hard blow caught the center of his nose, sending a wide spray of blood flying onto my shirt and face. I reached down to my right and picked up the geography book and brought it down hard against the boy's nose and mouth. I didn't stop until the flat of the pages were lined red with his blood.

I tossed the book to the ground and got to my feet. My back and shoulders burned and were weighed down with pain. I stood over him, watching as he ran his fingers across the front of his face, his nose red and clogged, blood running out of the corners of his mouth.

"Is this what you wanted?" I asked him, surprised at how quickly my own violent instincts had surfaced. I turned away just to make sure none of his friends were looking to make a move against me. They were all where I had last seen them, on the top steps of the school exit, huddled together, the eager smiles wiped from their faces. "Is it what you and your pals expected to see?"

He spit out a mouthful of blood and glared up at me. "This has got a long way to go till it ends," he said.

I was breathing fast and shaking with anger. It had gone past the bleeding pudgy boy and his crew of friends. My rage was no longer only directed their way. It was now aimed at all those anonymous faces in all those hallways of all the schools I had ever attended. The ones who pointed at me and whispered words I pretended not to hear. I was a marked child and a focus for their scorn. Many of them came from homes where violence behind closed doors was commonplace. A few were the children of divorce, distanced from one parent because of hatred and discord. A few more were illegitimate but were able to dodge freely past the stigma that often came attached to such births. I was the foster child tossed into their poor puddle and was forced to bear the hatred and fear such a position imposed. Foster children are seldom welcomed into working-class neighborhoods by other kids. They are seen as oddities and threats, not to be trusted and never to be liked. It is why so many foster parents try and keep it a secret. We are not taken in because we are loved or needed. We are taken in because we come with a monthly check attached to our names.

I released all the anger that had built inside me through all those years as I kicked Michael, ripping into his sides and back with the full force of both legs. My black shoes found their mark with each swing, the round tips cracking against bone or bending into rolls of flesh. "No!" I shouted down at him after each kick had landed. "It ends here! It ends now!"

I heard his friends come down the school steps, walking together, watching as their once brazen leader tried to crawl away and hide in a safe corner, next to a row of garbage cans. I continued to kick at him, the pent-up venom spewing out of me in one rush of pure, unrestrained violence. My body was washed down in a chilled sweat, as a small crowd of passersby stood around me, having stopped to stare, mumble and gawk at the bloody scene that was taking place. I landed a solid kick just under his rib cage and heard him grunt and cough, a bloody trail marking the path he had crawled from the sidewalk to the edge of the school building. I reared back, primed to land another hard blow, when a thick arm grabbed me around the waist and lifted me off my feet and away from the boy.

"You won your fight, little man," Pudge said into my ear. "Why don't we just leave it at that?"

I turned to look at him and nodded, watching the sweat drip from my forehead down onto the sleeve of his jacket. "I didn't go looking for it, Pudge," I said. "They'll probably go and tell the Brothers otherwise, but I wasn't the one that got it started."

Pudge released his grip on me and walked over toward the kids gathered on the school steps, slowly looking at each of their faces. "Pick up your friend and take him to a place where he can get cleaned up," he told them. "If it were me in your spot, I would make sure it was a place that knows how to stay quiet about this kind of business. The less anybody knows about what happened here, the more it'll look good for all of you."

The boys slowly made their way past Pudge, fearfully avoiding his gaze, bent down and lifted Michael to his feet. The front of his shirt was a wet sheet of blood and it stuck to his skin like tape, his head hung down and off to the side, and he had trouble putting weight on his legs. I watched him being dragged away and now, with my anger dissipated, wished I had walked away from this fight much as I had so many of the others before it. I looked down at the ground and saw the thick blotches of red that were the only remnants of what had happened. The crowd around us had quickly dispersed, moved along as much by Pudge's menacing presence as they were by the end of the action.

Pudge tapped me on the shoulder and nudged his head toward the scattered books behind me. "You better pick those up and follow me out of here," he said.

"I'm sorry, Pudge. I didn't mean for any of it to happen the way it did. He was just looking for a fight and I was stupid enough to give him one."

Pudge stood above me and watched as I picked up my books and shoved them back into my school bag. "He was the one that was stupid. He came out looking for the easy mark and by the time he figured out how wrong he was, he was running a couple of quarts low on blood."

"He'll get a few stitches and some bruises," I said. "Then the worst is over for him. He lives here in the parish. Nothing more can happen to him. That's not true for me. I'm a foster. Soon as they find out who beat him, I'll get tossed out of school and be living in another place by the first of next month."

"Don't be too sure about that," Pudge said, walking alongside me toward Tenth Avenue. "People keep their talking to whispers around here."

"It's happened to me before," I said, my head down, the pain in my neck and shoulders radiating to my back. "At one school I went to it wasn't even over a fight. I got invited by one of the kids in class to go over and watch TV at his place. His mother sees me there and freaks out. She goes in to see the principal the next day and tells him I'm causing problems for her son. Since they gave money to the church regular each Sunday and my fosters were looking for an excuse to dump me, out I went."

"That's old news," Pudge said with a shrug. "You weren't with me and Angelo then. You're not alone anymore. We'll make sure nothing like that happens here."

I stopped and turned to Pudge, dropping my book bag by my feet, the knuckles of both my hands red and swollen. "Why?" I asked him. "Why do you even care about somebody like me?"

Pudge put an arm around my shoulders, ignoring the painful grimace on my face. "Because long before you came around, little man, somebody found me and Angelo and took care of us. Maybe now it's our turn to do the same."

"Well, I hope you're getting something out of it."

Pudge lifted his hand off my shoulder and pointed a finger across the street at Maxi's Pizzeria. "I love pizza but I hate to eat it alone. So with you around, I don't see how that's going to be a problem anymore."

We both crossed the street against the rush of the on-coming traffic, the smell of oven-fresh pizza filling the air while the memories of a brutal street fight slowly faded.

14

Summer, 1965

I SAT AT the center of the small kitchen table, wedged in between John and Virginia Webster, the three of us sharing a fried steak and tomato dinner. We ate in silence, our eyes focused on the new white portable television set in the corner that was tuned to the evening news. The Watts section of Los Angeles had erupted into a full-scale riot as ten thousand African-Americans burned and looted a five-hundred-square-block area and caused more than forty million dollars worth of property damage. Fifteen thousand cops and National Guardsmen were called in to bring a halt to the rage, and by the time it was brought under control there would be thirty-four people left dead, four thousand arrested and two hundred businesses whose doors would never again open.

The scene played out before us like an eerie horror movie as the TV cameras panned angry black faces shouting slogans or tossing rocks and bricks into burning buildings. On the other side were stoic white faces desperate to do whatever was necessary to stop the killing of a neighborhood. I sat there, riveted to a moving portrait of an America I could never imagine, listening to the muted commentary of the off-camera reporters, wondering what could drive an entire section of a city to such a level of hate.

"Only a damn nigger would go out and set fire to his own home," John mumbled, chewing on a mouthful of steak, staring at the TV screen. "And then they go after the stores and shops right where they live. They don't care and they never did. You give them half a chance, they'll burn the whole damn country down and blame us for doing it."

"Who's us?" I asked, turning away from the set to look across the table at my foster father. John Webster was a big man, two hundred forty pounds packed solid on a six-foot frame, with a quiet manner and a perpetually sullen demeanor. His outlook on life was mostly negative, finding blame for his own economic plight not his lack of education or initiative but on the encroachment by various ethnic groups into what had once been an all-white workforce.

"Who do you *think* us is?" he said. "White people. They do all the burning and we get all the blame. Like it's my damn fault they were born the way they were."

"Maybe they got good reasons for being as angry as they are," I said. My eyes were on the small screen as I watched a supermarket get swallowed up by the flames of lit torches, as young black kids in T-shirts and jeans ran from the police, smiles of victory on their faces. "You just don't do what they're doing without holding in a lot of hate."

"I don't want to hear any sorry talk about those people at my table," he said, an angry jolt in his voice. "They were born no good and that's how they'll die. You want to come up with excuses for them, do it someplace else. I won't allow it under my roof."

I turned away from the set and stared at my foster mother who, as usual, stayed quiet and distant, locking whatever thoughts and feelings she might have deep inside her sad and shriveling body. I pushed my chair back, stood and began to clear my place at the table. John lifted his mug of beer and downed it to the suds and looked at me and smiled. "If you're that fond of them, maybe I can make a call down to social service and see if they got a family of niggers that's willing to take in a white trash boy who spends all his spare time running errands for gangsters. I bet even a dumb nigger's got enough sense to stay clear of a loaf of poison like that."

I saw Virginia grimace at her husband's harsh words, but still she stayed silent. I placed my dishes in the sink and ran cold tap water over them, my back to the simmering anger of John Webster and the relentless violence that was still exploding off the small television screen. I thought it best, for the moment at least, to try and ignore both since there wasn't much I could do about either. I had no respect for John Webster and, in the months I lived in his apartment, under his forced care, he never gave me reason to show him any. He was a bitter and angry man, using the hardships of his life to justify the bubbling hatred he only occasionally allowed to surface. I never saw any of those emotions in either Angelo or Pudge. They seemed at ease with who they were and looked no further than themselves to solve the problems they confronted. Unlike John Webster, Angelo and Pudge didn't have the time or the wasted desire to break the world down into a black and white confrontation. Instead, they glimpsed it from a distance, allowing access only to those few they could trust and putting up barriers to all outsiders. They didn't look to the color of a man's skin to decide whether or not he could be trusted, but rather they sought out the tone of his intentions before they even bothered to acknowledge his existence.

"It's not smart to be a racist, especially in the rackets," Pudge once told me. "In fact, it's just the opposite. The bulk of organized crime, at least when me and Angelo first got in, was made up of Italians, Irish, Jews and blacks. Four groups that were forced down this country's throat at one time or another. And there are still a lot of people who wish we would just disappear. We know what it's like not to be wanted, to get tossed aside. The difference is, when you're a gangster, people may still hate you and want you dead, they just don't say it out loud. They shut up because they're afraid of what we'd do to them. So believe me, little man, if you're looking for a racist check out the banker down the corner or the guy taking in millions on Wall Street. Don't look to us. On that score, more often than not, we plead not guilty."

As I scrubbed my dishes clean, I also wished I could better

comprehend the reasons for the riots, find some justification for the destructive actions that were taking place, but I didn't quite know how to put into words what it was that I felt in my heart. I understood what it was to be weighed down with excessive amounts of anger and resentment and to be deemed insignificant by those around me. I didn't know if I would ever let my inner hatreds take me down the same road the rioters were now embracing, but I did know that if I didn't find my way out of the Webster household, that I, too, was capable of a violent explosion.

"Are you finished eating?" I asked John Webster, reaching over to scoop away his dinner plate. While I had washed my dish and the cooking pans, he had finished another beer and changed the channel on the television away from the riots, tuning instead to the week's choice for *The Million Dollar Movie*, *Godzilla* with Raymond Burr.

He pushed the plate toward me and gave me a hard and angry look. "Those hoods you waste your time with," he said, letting a stomach full of beer help fuel his desire to talk, "you ask me, that bunch is just as bad as the niggers." He snapped the can opener down on a fresh Piels, a small white bubble of foam creasing over the top. "They get to live the easy life by stepping on the backs of hard workers like me. What they want they just go out and take. That's the only way they know how to live. If you're not too careful, you're gonna turn into one of them before you know it. If you haven't done it already."

"Since when do you care how I turn out?" I picked up his plate, walked it over to the sink.

"I never have." John Webster shrugged his shoulders and poured the beer into his empty mug. "I never made it a secret that we took you as a foster because it was nice to have some extra money. Neither one of us wanted kids and we still don't."

"That's enough, John," Virginia said, speaking her first words of the night, her worn face flushed red. "There's no need to be cruel. Maybe you should just finish your beer and watch the rest of the movie."

John sat across the table and stared at his wife, drinking his beer, his temper doing a slow simmer. "I was just trying to be honest with the boy. Just trying to give him some idea of where his real place in the world is. Out there and in here."

"From what I heard, you did that just fine." She slid a Marlboro out of its pack and put it up to her lips, then shifted sideways in her chair, leaned back and turned on one of the gas burners on the stove and lit her cigarette. "But now it might be a good idea to let it all drop."

"Looks like you got the lady in your corner," John said to me with a nod toward his wife. "Which doesn't surprise me too much, since it was her idea to take you in. That was back in the days when she wanted to see what it was like to be a mother. What she didn't count on was in hating it as much as she does. Am I talking the truth here or not?"

"You're doing nothing but running your mouth," Virginia said, blowing a thin line of cigarette smoke across the table. "And I'm asking you to please stop it. It's not something we should be talking about in front of the boy."

I dried my hands on a dish towel and rested my back against the edge of the sink. "I haven't heard anything I didn't already know," I told them, placing the towel on top of the stack of drying dishes. "What I don't know is why you kept me here as long as you have."

"That's not a question for me to answer," John said, pushing back his chair and walking toward the bedroom in the rear of the apartment. "That's something you need to ask your gangster friends about. Maybe they'll be up front and tell you the truth. But I wouldn't go and bet a paycheck on it."

My emotions ran through a rinse cycle of anger, confusion and relief. I didn't know exactly what he was talking about, what Angelo and Pudge had to do with my staying with them, but I did know that I had long overstayed my lukewarm welcome. While we were both aware of our feelings for one another, it was still an awkward silence that fell upon us as we stood in the center room of the railroad apartment. I walked away from the sink and past the shadows of my foster parents, reached a hand up to the coat rack, pulled down my Yankees warm-up jacket and unlocked the cracked wood door. "You can keep the clothes," I said as I opened the door and left.

I walked slowly down the flight of tenement steps, turning my back on an old life and heading out to begin a new one.

· · ·

I HAD FINALLY found a home. It was a place where I belonged, where my actions would not be scrutinized or questioned daily, where I was never viewed as an outsider forced to exist under the care of a pretend parent. I had my own room, the freedom to come and go as I pleased and a clear understanding that I would be held responsible for my actions. I was a child living life in a land filled with adults and I eagerly embraced all the implications of such an adventure. I was also made privy to a slice of the world that few as young as me would ever be allowed to see, and its influence would forever skewer the way I viewed society and my place in it.

That night, as I walked from the Websters' apartment building down to Angelo and Pudge's bar, I knew the current course my life was on was in desperate need of a change. I was also aware of my limited options. If the two of them had turned me away, I knew I would eventually be found by state authorities and placed in an upstate orphanage for the next seven years. Few, if any, come out of such places sound, and I knew I would not likely be one of them. I was not mentally equipped for a street existence, and the handful of kids I knew who had that life had either ended up hooked on drugs or were found dead in an alley. Knowing that, it was clear that my only hope rested on the whims of the two most dangerous gangsters in New York City.

I spoke to both of them together and I spoke quickly. "I'll do whatever you ask," I said, still wearing my windbreaker inside the air-cooled bar. Angelo and Pudge sat at a back table, their faces lit by candles and the glow from an overhead television, looking up at me, their hands folded in front of them. "And I won't ever be a bother to you. I'm not even around for most of the time, anyway, and I can run errands to pay for the food you give me."

Angelo lifted a glass of milk to his lips and took a slow sip. His olive-colored eyes glowed in the flame from the candle and his thin, unlined face betrayed no emotions. He placed the glass back down on its coaster and wiped his mouth with the edge of a folded napkin. "I have a wife and two children," Angelo said, his voice as always low and rich. "I only see them when I have to. Why do I need to see you every day?"

"I didn't know you had a family." I tried to hide the surprise in my words. "You never said anything about them before."

"You never said anything about living here before," Angelo said. "At least not to me."

"You both have been real good to me," I told them. "And I know I came in here asking a lot. So, if you say no, it won't change the way I feel about you and about this place."

"Where's no take you?" Pudge asked. His voice was much softer than Angelo's, his body less rigid. "Other than not here."

"On my own for as long as that lasts," I said with a shrug. "Then probably up to a home."

"And does something like that scare you any, having to live in one of those places?" Pudge asked, leaning closer in to the table.

"I try not to think about it too much," I admitted. "But when I do, then it does."

"I hope you're not afraid of dogs," Angelo said, finishing his glass of milk and looking down at the white pit bull nuzzled against his leg. "Because any spare room we might have, you have to share with Ida. And she likes to have people around her even less than I do."

I looked down at the dog whose eyes were as dark and distant as her owner's and turned back to Angelo. "Does she bite?" I asked.

"She sees an opening, she takes it," Angelo said with a certain pride.

"She's also used to getting her own way," Pudge said. "Wouldn't surprise me much to see her take the bed and leave you sleeping on the floor."

"Hands down, I'd take her floor over the bed I just left," I said.

Angelo slid his chair back and stood, stepping over the dog and turning his back to me. "You'll need to get a leash," he said looking at me over his shoulder. "She walks with me without one, but I don't think she'll do the same for you. Which means she might get lost and if that happens then you'd need to do the same."

Pudge watched Angelo open the back door and disappear into the darkness of his small office, then turned to me. "You got any clothes with you or stuff you want to bring up to the room?" he asked.

"Just what I'm wearing," I said, trying to contain the relief I felt at being accepted into their company.

"That should make your moving in a snap, then," Pudge said, pouring himself a fresh glass of grappa.

"The Websters are probably going to call social services in the morning," I told him.

"They're not going to call anybody." Pudge waved his hand dismissively. "On paper and as far as anybody else is concerned, you're still staying with them. Me and Angelo stay invisible. All it means for you is that every once in a while you may have to scoot over there, whenever one of the social welfare people come bopping by. They'll keep your room the way it is, make it look like you still live there."

"Why would they do that?" I asked. "They couldn't wait to get rid of me."

"You they can live without," Pudge said. "But money is something they need and if they want to keep it coming in, they'll play along with whatever we ask."

"John Webster said the only reason the two of them kept me long as they did was because of you two."

"Drunks never lie," Pudge said.

"When can I move in?" I looked around the bar, fighting back the urge to both cry from happiness and smile out of relief that what I had wished seemed ready to come true.

Pudge stood, walked over to me and put an arm around my shoulders. "Soon as you go out and get her a leash," he said, pointing down to Angelo's sleeping white pit bull. "The quicker you make Ida your friend, the better off you're gonna find yourself. Don't expect it to be easy. Who she doesn't know, she doesn't trust. Just like us."

• • •

"I NEVER DID figure out why he took me in the way he did," I said to Mary. She was standing in a corner of the room, staring down at the busy streets below, her arms folded around her chest.

"He probably looked at you the same way that Ida the Goose had looked at him," she said, her eyes not moving from the bump and shove of the teeming traffic. "You needed someone to take care of you, just like he once did. I don't think it was any more complicated than that."

"I can figure why Ida did it," I said, walking over closer to Mary. "She had no one else in her life. Angelo had a wife and two kids and, from the way he acted, he couldn't care one way or the other if he ever saw them."

"The family he had just wasn't the family he wanted. His wife lived in a big house on Long Island and the two children were sent to the best schools. They had plenty of friends and activities to occupy their time. And that's what made them happy. Angelo had Pudge, those horrible dogs he loved having around and, then, he added you. And that's what made him happy."

"He never talked about his wife," I said. "I met her a few times before she died. She was nice enough and didn't seem upset that he wasn't around her much. They just didn't have anything going on between them. She might as well have been another customer in the bar."

"What they had was once called a marriage of convenience," Mary said, in an accepting tone of voice. "A business deal of sorts. Her father was an Irish gang boss in Nassau County and Angelo and Pudge were looking to expand into his area."

"So they made a deal, that part's easy to understand," I said. "What I don't get, if one of them needed to get married, then why not Pudge instead of Angelo?"

Mary placed a hand on my arm and smiled. "Pudge would never agree to it," she said. "He loved life too much to settle down on a business deal, regardless of the circumstances. Angelo saw it for what it was and that's the way he dealt with it."

"And the kids? Why bother having any?"

"It was all part of the agreement," Mary said. "If her father was going to hand over half his business to Angelo, he wanted more than a married daughter in return. He wanted grandchildren playing in his backyard."

"I don't even remember her name," I said. "It's been so long since I even thought of her."

"Gail," Mary said. "Gail Mallory and she was a good woman who deserved better than to have a father who bargained her off to a husband who didn't love her."

"After Isabella, it would have been difficult for Angelo to fall in love with any other woman," I said. "It would have been too hard for him to accept."

"He came close one other time," Mary said, turning her back on me, content once again to search through the traffic passing by on the avenue beneath us. "At least as close to love as Angelo would ever allow himself to get."

"Who was it?" I asked, stepping closer to Mary, the morning sun warming both our faces.

"Me," Mary said, lowering her head, her delicate hands holding on to the edges of the radiator.

Winter, 1966

ANGELO WATCHED IDA walk along the side of the pier, stopping every few feet to stare out at the emptiness of the Hudson River. I was next to him, my hands shoved as deep into my wool jacket as they could go, the collar lifted to cover as much of my ears as possible. Angelo never seemed to notice weather, dressing the same regardless of the time of year. The pain from his lungs grew worse as he got older and no climate could help ease the torment each time he took a breath. His face had hardened with age, crease lines now wedged in along the eyes and lips, giving him a more lived-in look and adding to the threatening menace that could accompany an otherwise innocent glance. He was now in his third decade as a mob boss and, despite the millions he had accumulated, gave no indication of walking away from the life he had embraced.

"Being a mob boss, especially one as big as Angelo was, is the same as being the king of a small country," Pudge would tell me. "He ranked right alongside Luciano, Giancana, Trafficante and Genovese in terms of underworld power. When you are that strong, you find yourself with people around you willing to give up their life in order to save yours. Then you got those who would flip you over and work to have you killed, so they could look good for the next king that comes along. You got all this money coming in but, at the same time, you got soldiers working the streets griping about how little they get to take out of the big pot. People fear you until you're dead and then they forget you as quick as yesterday's breakfast. But no king ever walks away from it. However they die, on the throne or in the street, they do it with that crown still sitting tight on their head."

I stood next to Angelo as a large river rat floated past, both of us watching Ida bark down at the murky waters below. She was crouched on her rear legs, poised to make the leap and nab her prey.

"Do you think she's going to jump in?" I walked closer to the dog, trying to put myself in a position to reach out for her if she did.

"If it were a cat, maybe," Angelo said. "Then she'd have a chance. All she's going to get chasing after a river rat is wet."

"Pudge says that the two of you used to swim these waters when you were kids."

"We did that and a lot more in this river." He stared off into the horizon, the harsh winter wind turning his cheeks a shy red. "Ran our first whiskey boat out of this harbor and got our first taste of bootleg money. Almost got killed down here in a shoot-out with Johnny Ruffino's crew right before the war. I got clipped in the leg and fell into the water. Pudge jumped in and dragged me out."

Angelo nudged me on and we continued our walk, Ida moving in step behind us, her nails making a scratching noise coming off the cobblestones. My Sunday morning walk with Angelo was part of my weekly routine and had been since I moved into the room above his bar. It was our time alone together and always culminated with breakfast with Pudge in an Eleventh Avenue diner. I think Angelo looked forward to the walk as much as I did, though neither one of us ever said anything about it. The ritual was always the same. I asked as many questions as I could cram in, looking to learn as much about him as possible. He gave up only as much information as he thought was needed and changed the topic whenever the subject touched an area he didn't want to enter.

"Were there really German submarines out here during the war?" I asked, stopping next to Ida and pointing a finger just beyond the edge of the pier.

"If there were, I didn't see them. The newspapers made a lot of noise about it back then and people got scared because they believed what they read. That made a few guys in the government nervous and when that happens they reach a hand out to us."

"What did you do?" I said, looking away from the pier and up at him.

"We got together and we cut a deal," Angelo said. He reached a hand into his pocket and pulled out a chew treat for Ida and tossed it at the dog's paws. "The government left us alone to do whatever business we had out here and in return we told them we would get rid of any German subs that we found floating around the New York waters."

"But you said you never saw any subs," I said.

"So we made a lot of money without having to worry about the feds being on our backs." Angelo ignored the strong gusts of wind that were whipping past the pier posts. "Besides, I never said there weren't subs in the waters. I just said we didn't *see* any of them."

"Did you even bother to look for them?" I asked.

Angelo looked at me and shrugged. His slicked-back hair rested defiantly in place against the wind's heavy onslaught and his handsome face was as rigid as stone. "It would've been a waste of my time," he said. "Finding submarines was not something I knew how to do."

We crossed against the traffic on West Forty-fourth Street, heading uptown, when I saw the car move in place behind us. There were three passengers in the four-door black Ford Comet, two in the front looking forward and acting casual, the one in the back sitting sideways facing the street, wiping a hand against his face and forehead. I looked up at Angelo and knew he had seen them long before I had, probably when they first turned the corner, against the light.

"You know where Pudge is, am I right?" He looked

straight ahead, his body relaxed, his voice poised and in control. "Don't turn your head. Just answer."

"Yes," I said, my voice cracking from the cold and from fear.

"When I tap you on the shoulder, you run to him and tell him where we are. Until you get back, me and Ida will try and hold these guys off as best as we can."

"Why can't I stay and help you fight them?" I asked, ignoring his request and stealing a glance at the car that was creeping up closer to us.

"I've done this before," Angelo said. "So has the dog. You haven't. On top of it, Ida doesn't care to run from a fight. It goes against her bloodlines. So she'd be plenty pissed if I sent her out to get Pudge."

"Are they here to kill you?" I tried hard to stop my body from shaking.

"That's what somebody's paid them to do."

The guy sitting on the passenger side and the one leaning against the door in the back both lowered their windows, replacing thick miniclouds of cigarette smoke with fresh gusts of cold air. The Comet had come to a slow stop just three cars down from us, its engine running in idle, all four of its doors unlocked. I turned away from the car and looked up at Angelo. "The diner's only two blocks from here," I said. "Why don't you run with me?"

"It's not what I do," he said in a soothing voice. "And not who I am."

I stared up into a pair of eyes that were as dark as a crow's wing and nodded. Without another word, I turned and ran, sprinting up the street as fast as I could go, leaving behind Angelo and Ida to deal with three paid killers.

Angelo and Ida walked toward the Ford Comet. He was close enough to see their faces, which were nervous and streaked with sweat in the winter air. His experience told him he wasn't up against top-drawer professional talent. Prime shooters would not have wasted this much time getting ready to gun him down. They would have simply driven up, fired and sped off. So, whoever put up the money for these three did so in order to get Angelo's attention, make him aware that he was out there. If, in the process, these three left him sprawled and dead between two parked cars, then so much the better.

Angelo was several feet from the passenger side door when he saw his backup Cadillac turn at the corner and come up behind the Comet. There were four of his men in the Caddy, each one of whom would kill at the simple nod of their boss's head. Angelo glanced back at the three in the Comet. The two in the front had guns in their hands, the wild cowboy in the backseat had two cocked and ready. But they froze, their fear too strong for them to lift the guns and fire, the drugs and drink that had fueled their ride to this point not able to help them take it to the next step. Angelo looked into each of their faces, his eyes telling them what he already knew. They had left earlier that morning with pockets filled with money, eager for the kill and a chance to make a name in a business where murder is the fastest way to advancement. Back there, they were tough and hard and wanting nothing more than to be gangsters. Now, in the cold and the wind and the harsh light of reality, they were three scared young men, pumped up by bar talk and each other, confronting a man they had only read about in the papers or caught a glimpse of on television. They knew him the way a child knows about a baseball player after reading the statistics on the back of a trading card. He had been tagged Bones Vestieri by the tabloids, for all the bodies he left in his wake, and the name stayed as the decades passed. He was a mob boss from a time when wars lasted for years and only the toughest were left to stand. He was a real gangster standing in front of them, with a growling white pit bull by his side, neither one of them afraid to die.

Angelo's four men surrounded the Comet, their guns at their side, ready to be emptied into the bodies of the three shooters. Angelo leaned into the car and looked at each of them. He placed a hand on the car door, his jacket open and flapping in the wind. "I get a name," he said into the smoky interior, "and you live. If not, then you'll die wishing you had never made the deal that put you here."

"Marsh," the one closest to Angelo, sitting on the passenger side, said. He tried to keep up his tough-guy front but was betrayed by the crack of fear in his voice. "Jimmy Marsh was the one who paid us."

Angelo looked into the young man's eyes and saw a boy with a gun on his lap. He was dressed in black leather and jeans, smelled of whiskey and couldn't control the shaking of his hands. "Who knows this Jimmy Marsh?" he asked his four men.

"I do," the tallest of the group said. He was young, handsome and had been with Angelo since he, too, was a child, abandoned in a tenement hallway by a drug-addicted mother on her last fix. "He's a small-timer pulling meat market heists for quick cash. If he's got himself a crew, they can't be any better than the ones he sent here this morning."

"Find him before he has his breakfast, Anthony," Angelo said. "And kill him before I finish mine."

"What about the three in the Comet?" Anthony asked.

"Help them find the highway," Angelo said, his eyes on the men in the car. "And if you ever see any of them in my neighborhood again, kill them, too."

Anthony nodded and led the other three back to the open doors of the Cadillac. They got in, slammed the doors shut and followed the Comet as it eased its way down the street and onto the ramp of the West Side Highway, filled with young men who thought they were heartless enough to want to be gangsters.

. . .

I SAT IN Angelo's armchair, my feet curled up under me, watching Robert Stack as Eliot Ness put *The Untouchables* through their paces. Angelo and Pudge sat on the couch across from me, relaxed yet focused on the anticipated take-down of the television gangster.

"They make this guy Ness out to be a one-man band," Pudge said with a dismissive wave of his hand. "How good could he really have been? They brought him in from Cleveland."

"He was good enough to catch Al Capone," I said, my eyes still on the large-screen black-and-white set.

"Time caught up with Capone," Angelo said. "A fed named Eliot Ness just happened to be there."

"You can be headline material for just so long," Pudge said. "Sooner or later, people get tired of reading about you. They want to read about the next new gangster. That's when the cuffs come out and the judge slams the hammer down."

"You want to make a career in this business, you do it quiet," Angelo said. "The only people who know you're in it are the only ones who need to know. Anybody can get their names in the paper. You don't need talent to do that. But keeping your name out of them is a skill. You have that, you get to play in the game for a long time."

I loved to watch TV or go to the movies with Angelo and Pudge. Before they came into my life, I hadn't watched much television and was aware of the popular shows only from what I picked up in passing conversation. Movies were my safety valve, as they are for most foster children. I would escape into the cool confines of an old movie house and find the solace I sought from the emptiness of a nonexistent home life. The movie theater also served as an avenue for safe adventure, where I could lose myself for two hours in the heroic exploits of others. Angelo and Pudge, as did every gangster I ever met, also had a love for the movies and the small screen. We more or less shared the same tastes in what we liked and in what we sought to avoid, which made it easy for us to sit through anything together, our viewing nights always ending with dinner in a back booth at Ho-Ho's restaurant on West Fiftieth Street.

Gangsters hate science fiction and romance. They would rather be shot dead in an alley than sit through a game show. "Tell me what a game show is?" Pudge would demand whenever I was brazen enough to turn one of them on. "Better yet, let me tell you what it is. It's gambling, plain and simple. They take two people, put a mike in front of them and bet they won't get the right answer to whatever it is they ask. If they do, they get paid. If they don't, they walk away empty. So how come, when a guy in Hollywood does it, they call it a TV show, but when we do it here, without the cameras and the mikes, they call it a crime? That's really *The $64,000 Question.*"

Gangsters love stories that are set either in the Wild West or during the height of World War II and are avid fans of thrillers, silly comedies and high-class horror. Above all else, however, gangsters love crime movies and police shows. Angelo and Pudge both would get a big laugh as they sat back and watched Hollywood's idea of what they did for a living, their every move glamorized and overdramatized. "Most of the time, the movies and shows are so far off base it's not even worth the time it takes to sit through them," Pudge the critic would often tell me between bites of an egg roll. "Rod Steiger as Al Capone goes beyond stupid. The same goes for that guy Neville Brand on *The Untouchables.* Now, Robert Stack, I'll give you, looks like a fed, but so what? You still don't pick up anything from watching any one of them work. Not like you did with somebody like Cagney. Him you could study, take what you saw him do and bring it out to the street with you and not have to worry about getting gunned down. A couple of the other old-timers had it figured out the right way, too. George Raft was one. Paul Muni and John Garfield were two more. But Humphrey Bogart didn't make the final cut. None of us ever bought him as a tough guy. We never paid for his sell. To us, he always came across as a rich boy acting tough, which, from what I understand, is what he was in real life."

"I like *M Squad* better than *The Untouchables,*" I said, spreading my legs out and resting them on the coffee table.

"Which one is that?" Pudge asked, pouring himself a fresh cup of coffee.

"It's the one with Lee Marvin," I said. "He plays the tough detective."

"I go for that one, too," Pudge said. "You believe a guy like that, ex-marine, war hero, wounded in action. I could see him slapping the cuffs on me and tossing me in the back of his squad car."

"I can't blame you on that one," Angelo said with not-so-subtle sarcasm. "If I had to make a choice, I'd much rather be arrested by an actor than a cop. It would make it a lot easier to deal with."

"You know who I don't buy as a cop?" Pudge asked.

"Who?" I smiled at him, enjoying what for us passed as family conversation.

"That old fat guy from *Highway Patrol*," Pudge said. "Tell me his name again?"

"Broderick Crawford."

"That's the one." Pudge sat up on the couch, animated and filled with a fan's passion. "I mean, seriously, how old is that guy that they still let him drive around in a car chasing after people? He should be retired, sitting on a nice stretch of beach somewhere, scratching the chicken fat on his belly. If a cop that old were chasing me, I would never stop. Keep my foot pressed heavy on the gas and keep driving until his nap time came around."

"I wouldn't complain too much," Angelo said. "The older the cop, the better it is for us. Young cops want to go out and make a name for themselves. Best way for them to do that is to bring down either you, me or maybe both. Old cops just want to go home and put in enough time to cash a pension check. And the best way for that to happen is to stay away from trouble. Their mind is sitting on a condo down by the beach. It's not on the next boost you and me have planned."

I sat back, happy to watch Angelo and Pudge link everything we saw on TV or in the movies straight back to the life they led, turning it all into yet another lesson for me to learn. I was now an accepted member of their family and with that came the burden of filling the void in my knowledge with their take on life and the honest, if skewered, view of the world they brought with them to even the most mundane of daily events. Angelo and Pudge boiled everything down to a basic scenario of black and white, right and wrong, profit and loss. They had fought off the challenges and survived and thrived for decades in a brutal business that was free of reasonable compromise and short on peaceful resolution. They did it by combining street savvy with a fearless determination that their will would not be thwarted, regardless of the odds and the opponent. They obeyed only a set number of structured commandments and never strayed far from those beliefs.

Over time, their numerous lessons would eventually take hold and their strong theories would be very much a part of my thinking and way of looking at the life around me. I would become like them, a bona fide member of their small society. I knew that whatever path my life took, it would be determined by the formidable will of these two men I had come to see as parents. No other solution would be acceptable to them. They were not interested in raising just a son. Much like Ida the Goose and Angus McQueen before them, Angelo and Pudge were just looking to raise a gangster.

And so, night after night, I would watch them, their faces a blurry haze from the glow of the television set, close my eyes and smile. I was on the eve of my thirteenth birthday and I couldn't think of anything else I would much rather do than grow up and be one of them.

Be a gangster.

* * *

I GLANCED AT my watch and turned to Mary. "I was thinking of heading back to my apartment, grab a shower and change into some fresh clothes. Maybe even take time to catch a smile from my kids and a kiss from my wife. Will you be here when I get back?"

"Yes," Mary said. "I may leave for a bit to do the same, but I won't be gone long."

"He'll be okay," I said, looking down at Angelo as he slept in his bed, the green monitors blinking and beeping around him. "The day nurses check on him every hour or so."

"Can he hear anything at all?" Mary asked. "Is he even aware that we're here, talking about him?"

"The doctors say no," I said. "They said his brain and body are barely functioning and that he's living moment to moment."

"And what do you say?" Mary asked me with a sweet smile.

"I think he hears what he wants to hear and tunes out what doesn't interest him," I said. "And I think he's happy that you and I are here together."

"But you still don't know where I fit in," Mary said.

"It just comes down to a question of time. Eventually you'll tell me everything you came here to tell me."

"That sounds more like Angelo talking than you," Mary said with a slight tilt of her head. "As much as you may want to try and fight it, a lot of who and what he is has rubbed off on you."

"I'll pick up some soup and sandwiches for us on the way back," I said, ignoring her comment. "I shouldn't be long. Two hours, three at the most."

"Take as long as you need," Mary said. "I wouldn't mind having some time alone with him."

I nodded and headed for the closed door. I turned to watch Mary walk over to Angelo's bedside and pull a chair closer to him. She sat down, rested a hand on top of his and stroked the side of his face with a gentle motion.

15

Fall, 1968

I WAS FOURTEEN years old when I was sent out on my first official job for Angelo and Pudge. It was a cash pickup at an actor's rented brownstone in the East Seventies. The actor was late on a cocaine payment to an uptown dealer who had given up on any chance he had of collecting his money, so he'd sold off the debt to Pudge, willing to take half as opposed to nothing.

"You heard of this guy before?" Pudge asked me. "I mean the name, it sound familiar to you?"

"I've seen him in a few things," I said. "He's in that big action movie that's out now. I don't like him all that much."

"That's good on all counts," Pudge said. "You and Nico aren't going to see him to do a breakdown on his acting. You'll be there to pick up the cash he owes. Now, he's Hollywood and used to getting most things for free. Angelo and me ain't Hollywood and we're used to getting what's owed us. So, something's gotta change and we're way too old to start now. Nico will be there to make sure he doesn't give you more than a little lip when you go to collect."

"What do I do?" I asked.

"You be polite at all times and never get angry, no matter what he says to your face," Pudge said. "Leave the heavy work to Nico, he'll know what to do if it comes down to that. You're there to take the cash, put it in your pocket and leave."

"What if he doesn't have it on him?" I asked. "Not many people have twenty-one hundred dollars lying around the house."

"Then it's gonna be a bad night all around," Pudge said, standing to leave. "We'll be outta cash and he'll be outta luck. No winners anywhere in the circle."

"I won't let you down," I said.

"It never crossed my mind you would. There's a folder about this bum up on your bed. Look it over before you leave. The more you know about your target, the more it keeps you in control. Be ready to go when Nico comes to get you."

"What should I wear?" My face turned beet red and I hoped the question didn't come out sounding as stupid as it felt.

Pudge came walking over toward me. He put both his large hands on my two shoulders, leaned over and kissed me on the cheek, the smile on his face as wide as I'd ever seen it. "You don't think the blue jean, T-shirt and sneaker look is gonna be enough to make him shit his pants?" he asked. And before I could answer, "There's some new clothes for you, on your bed, next to the folder. Wear those. It won't make him respect you any more than he's going to, but at least you'll look the part. This actor's gonna be laughing when he sees you. You go in like a kid, then he's got no reason to be scared. You go in like a man who wants his pockets filled with money that's owed him, you'd be surprised how fast that sense of humor disappears. A good gangster, no matter how young, old, tall or short he might be, always runs the room. *Always.*"

Pudge's smile was long gone and he held that look on me for several seconds. Then he turned and walked quietly out of the room. I sat down on the soft upholstered couch and closed my eyes, trying to drown out the muted sounds rafting up from the crowded bar below. Above me, the floorboards creaked as I heard Pudge walk across his room and turn on the record player. He slid a Benny Goodman album on the turntable, rested the needle on the third cut, "Sing, Sing, Sing," and turned the volume on high, knowing I was downstairs and wanting me to hear it. I sat back on the couch and smiled, my eyes still closed as I listened to Gene Krupa's ground-swelling drum solo mix in with Goodman's magical clarinet. Almost every career criminal I've ever met has a song of choice they play before they go out on a job. It is an important part of their ritual. "Sing, Sing, Sing" was Pudge's favorite song and it could always be heard blasting out of his stereo system whenever he and Angelo needed to attend to a crucial and often deadly piece of business. By playing it now, he was confirming the importance of my first job and his confidence that I would not fail in my task. It was also a way of handing his song down to me.

From now on, it would be what I would play whenever I prepared to head out to help quench a gangster's insatiable thirst for blood and money.

· · ·

THE ACTOR, THIN, pale and shirtless, sat forward on a leather chair, slapped his hands together and laughed just like Pudge said he would. He was facing a glass coffee table, its top covered with coke spoons and empty silver tins. He was wearing dirty jeans and white socks, a pair of Dingo boots tossed casually off in one corner of the well-decorated main room. Nico stood in a far corner, his hands folded across his waist, staring silently at the back of the actor's head.

"Tell me again why you're here." the actor said.

I stared down at him, his blue eyes glazed and trying to focus in on me, his hands shaking as they reached for a half-filled bottle of red wine. "Like I told you, you're twenty-one hundred down from the drugs you bought and you need to pay it off," I said. "Tonight. To me."

The actor put down the bottle, kicked his head back and let out a loud laugh. "That's what the fuck I thought you said," he shouted, nearly choking on the mouthful of red wine he had just swallowed. "You see, when I'm in New York, I get my coke from Charley Figueroa. I don't get it from some midget dressed for a funeral. You hear what I'm saying, shithead?"

I shot a glance toward Nico and he shrugged his massive shoulders, eager to move forward and do some damage. I pulled a key from my black Perry Ellis jacket and showed it to the actor. "I didn't ring the bell to get in here," I said. "I used this key that I got from Charley Figueroa. But that's not all he gave me. He also gave me your drug debt. That's the twenty-one hundred I've been talking about. Now, just so you know the full story, I'm supposed to leave the key here and take the cash with me."

"Would you settle for an autograph and a kick in the ass?" the actor said, still laughing, turning around to glance at Nico, seeming to notice him for the first time.

"No, sir," I said. "Just the money. Once I have that, there's no need for you and me to ever see each other again."

"I figure you to be about fourteen, maybe fifteen, tops," he said. "Now, I've handed the kind of money you're asking for to girls your age, but at least I got to fuck them first. So why don't you get the fuck out of here, the both of you, before I stop finding this whole bit funny."

The actor leaned over the coffee table, picked up a razor and pieced together a line of coke from the residue spread across its top. He placed his nose right on the glass and inhaled, a grunt and a cough mixed in with the final snort. He wiped the base of his nose with his hand and looked back up at me. "I know he don't talk," the actor said, jerking a thumb toward Nico. "But I know you both can hear." The actor stood in the center of the room, his hands cupped around his mouth. "I'm gonna go take a short nap," he screamed. "When I come back out and see your faces still here, I'm going to kick some fucking guinea ass!"

He turned and headed for the rear bedroom, walking with an unsteady gait. I looked at Nico and nodded. I glanced around me, past the clothes and empty food containers strewn throughout the expensive room and found an empty dining-table chair. I pulled it out, turned it toward Nico and the actor and sat down. I wasn't at all nervous. Instead, I remember an incredible rush of excitement flowing through me, the power

I had over the situation burying any fear. I knew that violence would be inevitable, the actor would allow no other resolution to occur, and I was oddly comfortable with all of it. Though such a feeling surprised me, it also pleased me. For now I knew that if the gangster life was the path my life would lead me down, I could live with its results.

"That fuckin' Charley," the actor mumbled to himself. "Selling me out to some little punk kid."

"You can sleep all you want," I said. "We'll be here and we'll stay here. Until we get what we came to get."

The actor turned and came walking toward me, his temper lit beyond excess by the cocaine floating through his system. He stood over me, staring down, his blue eyes blazing with anger, his hands bunched into fists, his thin, hairless chest heaving up and down. "Who the fuck are you talking to that way?" he screamed at me. "Do you have any idea who the fuck I am?"

"You're a bad actor with a bad habit," I said, fighting to keep my voice calm, the back of my black button-down shirt soaked with sweat. "But that doesn't mean anything to me. The money does."

The actor took several deep breaths, his eyes bulged out so far they looked as if they would pop. He was blinking furiously and rubbing his hands against the sides of his dirty jeans. He bit down hard on his lower lip, cracking the skin and drawing blood as he leaned in closer, a foul mix of cocaine sweat and body odor causing me to flinch. He lifted his hand up and brought it down against my face, slapping me with the length of his fingers, the blow stinging and causing my left eye to tear. I looked up at him and saw a man long past the point of reason, running now on drug-fueled adrenaline. "I don't let nobody talk to me that way!" he shouted. "Nobody! You hear that, you little motherfucker! You hear that?"

He lifted his hand again, ready to strike me with another blow. Nico caught the hand as it came down, inches from my face. The actor looked up at him and gritted his teeth. "Do I have to kick your ass now, too?" he said.

"Yes." Nico spoke his first words of the day, still clutching the man's hand. "Before you start, let me just get a few things out of the way."

"Like what, asshole?" the actor said.

"Like your hands," Nico said.

He lifted the actor's wrist back and with the slightest of tugs, snapped the bone. The sound was like that of a shoe stepping down on a twig. The actor screamed out in pain and fell to his knees, his head bent down against his chest, tears rushing down his face. Nico lifted a foot and rested it against the actor's neck for leverage and then took each finger in his hand and cracked it like a fortune cookie. He let go of the mangled hand, its fingers bent and broken, and watched it fall to the carpeted floor like a dead weight, the actor lying there, moaning out in pain.

It was the first time I had seen a gangster at work. It was the calm with which Nico attacked more than the brutality that struck me. It was one thing to be told stories about violence and quite another to bear witness to a man's pain. I swallowed hard, felt warm bile rushing up to my throat and knew I needed to remain calm and not let what I had just seen affect the way I spoke or moved. I got up from the chair and squatted down next to the actor. "Get the money," I said to him. "It's all I want, and then I'll go. But if you say no again, I have no choice but to leave you alone with him."

"On the bureau in the bedroom," the actor said in between sobs, his eyes fixated on his busted hand and wrist. "My wallet's in there. There's cash in it and next to it. I don't know how much, but there should be enough to cover what you need."

"I hope so," I said, standing and nodding to Nico. He stepped over the actor's body and walked off toward the bedroom. The actor crawled to the couch, lifted himself up and sat down, leaving his limp hand, now starting to swell, on his thigh. We stared at one another until Nico walked back into the room and handed me the cash.

"It's all there," he said.

I took the money, folded it over and stuffed it into my jacket pocket. "Then we're finished here," I said to the actor. "Your debt's been paid."

"I need to go to the hospital, have a doctor take care of my hand," the actor whispered. "Put a cast on it, ice it down; something to make it better."

"That's a good idea," I said, then I turned to follow Nico into the foyer and out of the brownstone.

"Help me get dressed and get me there," he pleaded. "It's the least you can do for me."

I turned back, looked at him, and shook my head. "Get there on your own. Call one of your friends and have him come get you," I said. "That's not what we do."

"You little fuck," the actor said, the pain from his hand now reaching high up into his arm. "All you do is hassle people for their money and bust them up. That's what you do."

I didn't respond. There was no need. But that's not all I do, I wanted to tell him. I also go to high school.

• • •

NICO WAS DRIVING on the West Side Highway, heading downtown when I asked him to pull the car off to the side of the road.

"You okay?" he asked, turning on an overhead light to get a better look at my face.

"I will be," I told him. "Soon as I throw up."

He got off on the Seventy-ninth Street exit and parked the black Cadillac alongside a stone embankment overlooking the Hudson River. I eased out of the passenger seat, leaned forward and vomited, my body coated with sweat, my new clothes splattered with stains. I stared down at my hands, holding them under the glare of the lamps illuminating Riverside Park. They were trembling uncontrollably and were unable to grip even the door handle on the car. The calmness I felt in the actor's apartment had long since abandoned me. I looked up and saw Nico standing over me, one hand resting gently on my back.

"I've never been this sick before," I said, wiping my mouth against the sleeve of my new jacket.

"You never been out on a job before," Nico explained. "This happens to everybody the first time. You'll get used to it. It gets to the point where it comes as easy as taking a breath."

Nico Bellardi leaned against the rear door of the Cadillac and lit a cigarette. He was tall, about six foot two, and carried a solid two hundred sixty pounds across his massive frame. He had a rich, thick head of dark hair, speckled by touches of white at the temples and along the sides. He was in his late thirties, always impeccably and stylishly dressed and spoke only when he felt the need. He was Pudge's top enforcer and the most trusted member of his crew.

"I wasn't scared in there until the end," I confessed. "That guy had enough drugs in him, he could have killed you and me and not figured it out for three days. And when he came over and slapped me, I should have come back at him. Instead, all I did was sit there and sweat. If you hadn't bailed me out, I'd still be there catching a beating."

"Your job was to leave with the money," Nico said. "Mine was to help you do that. The way I see it, we both did what we went there to do."

"If it was just you alone, having to go in there without me, what would have happened?"

"If the money was there, I would have come out with it," Nico said, shrugging his shoulders and pulling on his cigarette. "But the actor might have had more than some broken bones in his hand to worry about. Without you in the room, I might have left him for dead. So what you did was make sure we got the cash and, better yet, that we left behind somebody who's not going to tell anybody about it."

"How long you been doing this?" I asked. "You know, going out on jobs for Pudge?"

"About ten years now," Nico said. "He spotted me in a street gang I was running with and pulled me out. A guy like me, all he can do if he works in the rackets is be the muscle.

Little chance to ever be a boss. But I make good money and they treat me right. If I was still kicking with that gang, I'd be on my second swing upstate by now, doing multiple years of straight time. Instead, I'm paying off a mortgage and I get a new car every two years."

"You have a family?" I asked, standing and leaning over the wall, breathing in the air coming up off the river.

"Came close a few times to sliding that ring on my finger," Nico said. "But I broke away before it got that far."

"How come?" I asked, watching as he stepped up alongside me and stared over at the uptown traffic.

"There's gonna be a night, no matter how good you are at this, when you just don't make it through a job. It's one of the first things I learned. And I never wanted to have somebody I cared about be on the other end of a phone call where they'd have to hear something like that from a stranger."

"Thanks for helping me out tonight," I said to Nico. "I really appreciate it. Maybe the next guy Pudge sends you out with won't be as bad at it as me."

"There won't be a next guy," Nico said.

"What do you mean?"

"I've been made *your* guy," Nico said. "When they send you out on jobs like these, you'll be going there with me."

"Not too exciting for you, working with somebody who's probably going to throw up at the end of every job."

"Don't look for me to knock it," Nico said, walking past me and back toward the driver's side of the car. "The pay's good and the hours are easy. And judging by what I saw today, you're only going to get better at this end of the game."

Nico jumped in behind the wheel and slammed his door shut. He watched as I stepped toward my side and did the same. He gently slipped the Cadillac into drive and moved back onto the West Side Highway, easing the car into the speed lane and heading downtown toward Angelo and Pudge's bar.

"Will the radio bother you?" he asked, clicking it on. "You can pick the station, won't make any difference to me."

"Anything except opera's fine," I said, leaning back against the headrest and shutting my eyes. "If you tuned in to some rock 'n' roll, I wouldn't be upset about it."

"Rock 'n' roll it is," Nico said, pushing buttons on the console with his right hand and steering with his left, moving up and down the dial until he found the station he wanted.

We rode the rest of the way in silence, both of us listening to Sam Cooke, Frankie Valli and Little Richard, my jacket pocket filled with crisp hundred-dollar bills collected from an actor with a debt. I opened my eyes and looked out at the illuminated city as it sped by and I smiled.

My first day as a gangster had been a success.

• • •

THE GIRL WAS walking up Thirty-first Street, a leather belt wrapped around her books held tightly across her chest. She was dressed in her school uniform, black-and-white checkerboard skirt and white blouse, topped by a blue winter coat with a hood attached. She had short brown hair and hazel eyes, and her feet were clad in white socks and a pair of shiny lace-up Buster Browns. She was alone, her head down against an early afternoon wind, her coat unbuttoned and flapping to the breeze.

"There she is," Nico said to me. "The girl of your dreams. Now comes the hard part. Making those dreams come true."

"Are you sure this is a good idea?" I asked, sitting on the hood of a car, my feet resting on a bumper, the girl walking toward us from the other side of the street. "I mean, what if she says no?"

"I don't see how you have any other choice." Nico stood next to me, his hands in his pockets. "Not unless you want me to be your date at the school dance."

I looked over at Nico with a weak smile. "You're always bragging about what a great dancer you are. Maybe I should give you a chance to prove it."

"You need a Ginger not a Fred, and that's not something you're going to find on this side of the street," Nico said. "So get going."

I sighed, slid off the car, straightened my jacket and ran a hand through my hair. "Is there anything else I should know before I go?" I asked, my eyes focused on the girl as she walked past the dry cleaner and turned to glance in our direction.

"If you remember her name, it would give you a leg up," Nico said. I gave him a playful shove, checked the passing traffic and walked at a fast clip toward the girl in the checker-board skirt.

She saw me coming, flashed a sweet smile that made my face flush and said, "Hi, Gabe. What are you up to?"

"Not much, Maddy," I said. "Just talking with my friend." I pointed over my shoulder and saw her cast a glance at Nico, his foot up on a fender, a lit cigarette in his mouth.

"He's a pretty big guy," Maddy said, crinkling her nose. "Looks like he plays football."

"He likes to play all kinds of sports," I said.

"Did you finish that French report yet? I haven't even done the reading for it. I had such a hard time picking my topic."

"I can help you with it, if you want," I managed to get out. "French and History are the only classes I'm any good in. I can barely stay awake for the rest of them."

"That would be great," Maddy said. "I mean, if you have the time."

"I can make the time," I told her. "How about after school Friday in the library? That'll give you some time to finish the reading."

"It's a date," she said. "Friday, three-thirty, in the library. I'll sneak in some candy. That way we won't get too hungry while we work."

She started to walk away but I screwed up my nerve, my fists clenched nervously by my side. "So . . . speaking of dates . . . are you planning on going to the gym dance Saturday night?"

"I'd like to," Maddy said with the kind of coy smile that comes so easily to teenage girls, "but no one's been around to ask me yet."

"Would you go if I was the one who asked you?" I tried to swallow with a mouth dry enough to hold sand.

"I'd love to go with you, Gabe." Her smile disappeared as quickly as it had come. "I really would. But I can't."

I was red-faced now and confused by her quick refusal. "What, are you waiting for somebody else to ask?"

"No," Maddy said, shaking her head.

"Then I don't get it. Why can't you . . ."

"I can't go with you, Gabe," she cut me off. Then, starting to walk away, she said, "Please just leave it at that."

I reached out a hand, grabbed her by the elbow and held her in place. "Whatever the reason is, I'd like to hear it. I don't know, maybe there's something I can do to help change it."

Maddy looked at me and then over my shoulder at Nico, still in his place by the parked car, talking bets now with Little Angel, a neighborhood loan shark. "My father would never say yes to it," she said. "And there's nothing you can say, nothing you can do that will ever change his mind. It's just the way he feels about you."

"The way he feels about *me*?" I didn't bother to mask my anger or surprise. "There's no way he could feel anything about me. I've never even met the guy."

"It's not about you, Gabe," Maddy said. "It's the people you live with."

I'll never forget the rush of emotions that flooded through my body at those words. It was a mixture of anger and humiliation. Anger that the men I knew and loved were not considered good enough for her or her family. Humiliated because even then, I understood why that was so. Things had changed since I'd come to live with Angelo and Pudge. But I was still on the outside looking in. I was still in a world that was somehow soiled, yearning to cross over to one that was nice and new and clean.

Maddy must have seen my agony, because she said, quite gently, "My father works hard, very hard to take care of his family. He takes a lot of pride in that. Goes to church on Sunday mornings with my mom and coaches Little League games on Saturdays. The only time I ever see my father get angry is when he talks about your friends. He says they live off other people's hard work and ruin every neighborhood they go into. And he says you're a part of them, Gabe. So as much as I like you, I can't go to the dance with you."

I shoved my hands in my pockets, looked at this beautiful girl and nodded. "I would never ask you to do that," I said. "I've learned to stay away from places where I'm not wanted. I'm sorry I bothered you, Maddy. I won't do it again." I stepped off the curb, waiting for the traffic to clear.

"My father's a good man, Gabe," Maddy called out after me.

"He hates people he doesn't know and has never even met," I said, looking over my shoulder at her. "If that's the way a good man is supposed to act, then I'll stay next to the bad guys where I belong."

I waited for an opening and ran across the avenue, away from Maddy and back over to the smiling faces of Nico and Little Angel.

Back to my side of the street.

          · · ·

ANGELO LEANED AGAINST the edge of the rooftop and watched as his flock of pigeons flew in a wide circle above his head. There were two large buckets of feed by his feet and a dripping garden hose curled alongside the coop. I tossed a pail of soap and water into the coop, grabbed a mop and started to scrub it down. There was a portable radio resting above the coop's wires tuned into the Italian news hour. I listened to the announcer discuss the latest fiscal crisis to hit Naples. There were times when I felt I knew more about what was going on in a country I'd never seen than I did about events in my own city.

"I wanted to say so much more to her," I said to Angelo. "I wish I had. I just didn't want to hurt her feelings."

"What more was there for you to say?" Angelo asked me. "Nothing would have made her go against her father's wishes. She's been brought up well, how could she betray his respect?"

"I still could have told her some things," I said, leaning down heavily on the mop, trying to clean out all the corners of the coop. "Not so much to change her mind but maybe to help open her eyes a little bit."

Angelo walked over to the coop, reached up above my head and turned off the radio. "Open her eyes to what?" he asked.

"That Little League field for one thing." I rested the mop against a pole and looked at him. "You know, where her father coaches the kids every Saturday? Well, I could have told her that there wouldn't be a field there for him to coach on if you and Pudge hadn't put up the cash and built it."

"And they would have said we did it with money that wasn't ours. Money we took from the pockets of the poor. They'll always find a reason not to accept us, Gabe. And they're right. That's just something you're going to have to learn to live with."

"It was only a dance," I said, walking toward the ledge to pick up the hose. "It wasn't as if I asked her to marry me."

"To you, it was only a dance," Angelo said. "To the girl's father it was the start of something that he couldn't allow. He's an honest man and he would never run the risk of crossing the line into our end. He knows who we are and what we do, and wants nothing to do with any of it, either for himself or for his family."

"But I see men like her father all the time," I said, spraying water into the coop, washing down the soap and the dirt. "They're always nice to you and Pudge on the street. They make it their business to stop and ask how you're feeling and wish you well. And I see them come into the bar and ask for your help to get them out of some jam they're in. If they don't want anything to do with us, then why do they do that?"

"Nothing we do for them is done for free," Angelo said. "They know that the minute they walk into the bar, even before they ask. They have to pay if they want that favor to be done, with money or service. I'm not the first person they come to for help. I'm the last, and I cost them the most."

"So if it's all going their way, then they don't want anything to do with us." I dropped the hose and reached for a broom in the corner, resting against the side of the roof door. "But the second there's any kind of trouble they can't get out of on their own, they forget all about what horrible people we are and come running in and beg for our help. If it was up to me, knowing how they really feel, they could come in and cry all they want. They wouldn't get the right time."

"You don't go into the rackets to make friends," Angelo said, looking up at a cloudy sky, watching his pigeon flock circle the edges of the West Side piers. "You go into it to make money. If you want people to think nice thoughts when your name's mentioned, be a priest."

I swept the last of the water out of the coop, watching as it ran down the roof toward a rusty drain pipe. "I left the dry rags downstairs," I said. "You want me to bring something to drink on my way back up?"

"For yourself, if you like," Angelo said. "I'm good the way I am."

I nodded and opened the door leading back into the building. As I made my way down the old wooden steps, one hand on the rickety railing, I went over what Angelo had just finished telling me. I was not troubled by what I had learned. I had grown used to being alone and keeping my thoughts and feelings to myself. I had long ago learned to be my best source of counsel and realized that aside from Angelo, Pudge and, to a lesser extent, Nico, it would be best to continue that practice for the rest of my life. Such a skill had been nurtured during my early years as a foster child, when there was no other solution but to stay silent and pretend not to hear the words clearly aimed in my direction. It would prove to be the perfect start to living my life inside the darkness and silences of a gangster's home.

I realized I was the perfect child for Angelo and Pudge.

I would never betray the trust they placed in me nor speak

to anyone outside their scope about anything beyond what needed to be discussed. The incident with Maddy and her father only helped to reinforce and solidify the belief that I was part of a powerful and feared group of men. They did not care about being liked by those around them, were not concerned with the trappings of family, and had little regard for an American value system they had long ago learned to scorn and exploit. They were wealthy men who did not flaunt their money nor seek to make the climb up the rung to a higher class. They solved their problems with warnings and with violence and initiated any business takeovers with guns and force. They were an ingrained part of twentieth-century America, their hands wrapped around every form of commerce, legal or not, yet they operated openly and freely.

They were hated by the law enforcement community and tolerated by the public. In many ways, they ruled the country they had come to think of as their own. I was now an accepted part of their world and, for that, I was glad.

"We always knew how people really felt about us," Pudge once said to me. "It's not like anybody tries to keep it a secret. We just didn't care, one way or the other. We didn't want to be liked by them anyway. That's one of the reasons we became gangsters in the first place. When we got to this country, they were the ones holding all the jobs, the money, the power to get things done and, believe me, not one of them went out of their way to share, especially not with anybody fresh off an immigrant ship. So we made a play for the power and did whatever we had to do to hold on to it. And they hated us for doing that. They'll never want anything to do with us. If they need a favor they'll take it. They want to do business, they'll work it out. But that's as far as it goes. Don't let anybody tell you different. The door that leads into their world will always be locked and bolted to people like us. Always."

· · ·

I WAS CARRYING a bucket full of dry rags in one hand and a cup of coffee in the other when I stepped back onto the rooftop. I looked around for Angelo and finally spotted him sitting on the ledge, his legs stretched out, his face tilted up to the sky and his eyes closed to the warming sun. He looked at ease with himself and at peace with his surroundings. I put the bucket down and started to dry off the stalls in the wet coop, sipping my coffee as I worked. I went about my job quietly, comfortable with the silence that was around me, broken only by the occasional wail of a siren or a car horn honking seven stories below. I liked being in the coops with Angelo and enjoyed being allowed to share in the caring of the birds. He always seemed to me to be much more relaxed around his pigeons and his dogs than he was in the company of people. Like most men in his profession, he put more trust in the behavior pattern of animals than he did in another human being's word. On his rooftop, his flock of birds flying overhead, Angelo Vestieri could close his eyes and allow his mind to drift off and explore the wells of his memories. He did not need to be a gangster in their presence, his body always on the alert for a slight or the first sign of a betrayal. On his roof, he could let down his shield and take refuge from the battle.

I had finished drying the coop and was filling the feed tins with seed and water. I glanced down and saw Angelo's shadow behind me. "I'm just about done here," I said.

"Good." He looked up again as the flock was swooping in, circling the tenements in a tight pattern. "They should be coming down in a few minutes."

"They've been out for a long time," I said, following the birds in their flight. "They must like it better when it's cold."

"You're good with them." Angelo walked into the coop, reached down into the feed bucket and began to help me fill the tins. "And they've responded well to you. The same is true for Ida. I think now she likes you better than she does me. That's a good sign. It's harder to get an animal to trust you than it is to get a man to do the same. Animals are smarter, they can sense if you're out to do them harm. A man has to get hurt a few times before he learns. If then."

"It doesn't take much to make them happy," I said. "A

clean place to live, regular food and a little attention. You treat them fair and they'll do the same back. They'll like you based only on that, not on who you are, where you live and who you live with."

"Not like that girl's father." Angelo stepped out of the coop as the pigeons came in as a group, roosting and cooing on the outside of the cages. "He's more like most of the people you'll meet. They decide that they know all they need to know about you before they even sit across the table. More times than not, that kind of thinking works to your advantage. Sometimes, like with you and the girl, you end up being hurt. But, with time, it passes."

"Did anything like that ever happen to you?" I asked, following him out of the coop, the pigeons rushing past me in a mad rush to get at the seed.

"That's a question for Pudge to answer," Angelo said. "He's the ladies' man, not me. I'm happy enough spending time with the birds and with Ida."

"What about your family?" I asked, realizing I was crossing into territory never before entered in our conversations. "Your wife and kids. Don't you miss being with them?"

Angelo closed and locked the pigeon coop and glared down at me for several interminable seconds. "I've learned not to miss anybody," he said in as cold and distant a voice as I'd ever heard him use. "And I've also learned to never ask a question whose answer I didn't need to know. I think it would be a smart move for you to start to learn to do the same."

Angelo turned his back on me and walked slowly over to the rooftop door and disappeared into the darkness of the stairwell. I leaned back against the pigeon coop and looked up to the sky. The sun was buried behind a mass of dark clouds and a light rain began to fall.

16

Summer, 1970

IT HAD BEEN two months since four students were killed by National Guardsmen at a noon rally at Kent State University in Ohio, protesting a war that no one claimed to want or understand. As I entered the middle of my high school years, the world around me seemed poised to explode. Student terrorists, backed by upper-middle-class money, were in Greenwich Village brownstones building makeshift bombs aimed at overthrowing a system they had grown to detest. Airlines were being hijacked at regular intervals from New York, Tel Aviv, and London, as scores of armed men and women argued with loud voices for peace as they left the bodies of the innocent in their wake. A U.S. Army lieutenant, William Calley, would soon stand trial for killing twenty civilians in My Lai, a place I never knew existed until I read the body count in the papers. And in New York City, as in the rest of America, a generation dedicated to free love and peace had latched onto the expensive and addictive taste of cocaine and were causing havoc in the silent circles of organized crime.

Angelo and Pudge hated the turmoil, clashing as it did with the shuttered world they had so carefully built for themselves. They viewed with a cynical eye the words of peace that flowed so easily from the mouths of those who seemed bent on disruption. They were troubled by an unending war whose existence even they as gangsters could not justify. And they had no trust in the leaders of the time, looking past the soothing words and seeing a set of eyes eager to grasp for a power they claimed so much to disdain. "It was a tough time," Angelo said. "For the country and for us. Usually, we do well in times of trouble. But not back then. It shook our business like no gang war ever could. Young people everywhere were giving the back of the hand to the rules of society. It was just as easy for young gangsters to ignore the rules of the mob. There were days when I began to believe this country was headed for a mass revolt. I don't know what we would have had if something like that happened. And nothing good came of any of it. We're still paying the price for the troubles those days brought."

During those years, I split my time between high school and preparing for a future as a gangster. I did my best to keep the two worlds separate, not knowing if I would be able to handle it if they collided. I attended a private school, was a good student, enjoyed History, French and English classes and kept my friendships to a minimum. School officials knew I lived with Angelo and Pudge and either one or both always made a point of showing up for functions and advisory meetings. I never missed having real parents. I don't think anyone could have loved me as much as the two men who had given me a home. Angelo had passed on his love of reading to me and I constantly had a book in my hand. Thanks to Pudge, who devoured the daily papers and weekly newsmagazines, I would plow my way through the crime and sports sections. The teachers at school built a learning foundation based on the classics. I followed my own boyish instincts with the works of Alexandre Dumas, Jack London and Rafael Sabatini. Angelo and Pudge furthered my education through even more colorful stories. Through them, I learned all about the formation of Murder, Inc. and the murder at the Half-Moon Hotel. I knew how the mob owned certain fighters and weight divisions and cleared out their purses long before the matches were even fought. I read about the great baseball players of the past and was told how many of them had links to organized crime. I knew all about Willie Sutton and every bank he ever held up and Two-Gun Crawley and his famous Upper West Side hostage siege, which had been the basis for the James Cagney movie *Angels with Dirty Faces*.

No young man could ever ask for a better education.

I longed for nothing. Prime tickets to Broadway shows, concerts and sporting events were mine for the asking. In a decade when most teenagers were in tattered jeans and dyed shirts and chose to wear their hair long, I wore imported Italian jackets, polo shirts and had my hair razor cut fresh every week. I was being raised apart from my generation, viewing what was going on around me as spectator rather than participant. While the teenagers whose faces I scanned on the evening news attended peace rallies or walks for women's rights, I went to the racetrack with Angelo and Pudge and came home with a tan and my pockets filled with winnings. As young men burned their draft cards and women tossed their bras into the trash, I went out with Nico and collected overdue money from those with limited choices on where to draw the cash to feed expensive habits.

I've always looked back at those years with warmth and fondness. I was living during a period of America's greatest political and social upheaval and I was at my happiest. I had found my peace by embracing the life of a young gangster. It was easy for me to think of myself in those terms, but, in truth, I was still a decade removed from the real possibility of joining the life. I was allowed glimpses into the dark world and was able to enjoy the perks it offered, all of it meant to make it attractive and alluring. But I was never put in the position where I was forced to make the moves of a gangster, decide a man's fate, be there at the fatal moment when bullet was put to bone. I had been spared that for a later time, when I knew there could be no turning back and when I lacked no other choice. Occasionally, I would allow myself to think of my life in those terms. It was the only time I felt any fear.

. . .

THE DECADE-LONG PEACE that had existed for Angelo and Pudge was rapidly coming to an end. New ethnic gangs were rising up to challenge the authority of the old order and, fueled by the massive income generated by the drug business, were both well-armed and well-financed. A two-hundred-fifty-member black crew based in the Brooklyn flatlands and led by Little Ricky Carson, a twenty-three-year-old one-time college football all-American, was taking in close to $100,000 a week in pure profit from their street-corner coke business. They called themselves the KKK, the Kool Knight Killers. In the late spring, they had formed an alliance with Pablito Munestro and his three-hundred-strong Colombian ring that was working out of Washington Heights in upper Manhattan, both groups looking to stretch their turf and their wallets. Hispanic gangs were making a move on the streets of the Bronx and a renegade band of Italians, the Red Barons, wanted to make the borough of Queens their private drug playground.

Within the ranks of their own crew, Angelo and Pudge could sense the seeds of discontent. The whiff of large amounts of drug money waiting to be made was proving to be too strong to ignore, especially for the younger members who were still a few years removed from earning top gang dollars. Angelo and Pudge were both aware that the drug trade could no longer be ignored. In the spring of 1947, they had suggested to the gangster's ruling body, the National Commission, that a penalty of death be issued to any member caught working in the trade. The request was voted down.

"Nobody was going to go for it," Pudge said to me. "We knew it even before we put it on the table. A gangster will walk away from a lot of things and he'll kill for the dumbest of reasons. But he's never gonna walk away from money and he'd never kill anything or anybody that could bring it to him. Everybody sitting at that table knew that sooner or later they would be in the drug business. And they would either get very rich or they would live in a jail block for fifty years, no parole. To them, that was a chance worth taking."

.   .   .

BY THE SUMMER of 1970, Angelo, at sixty-four, and Pudge, sixty-seven, began preparations for their sixth and final gang war together. Even at this late date, we lived without any telephones, since both believed them to be a gangster's worst enemy. "Point out a gangster who likes to talk on the phone," Angelo would often say, "and the odds are good that you'll be pointing inside a prison cell."

A portion of the work was done on the streets, utilizing a rotation of pay phones located on corners all within a ten-block radius of the bar. Angelo and Pudge never made any of the calls themselves, and when either Nico or I was asked to make one, the conversation never made much sense to anyone but the person at the other end. The bulk of the plan was being slowly implemented in the string of rooms above the bar. There, the two of them would sit through many a night and bring to life the maneuvers that would ultimately lead to someone's death.

In all my time living with them, I had never before seen them with this much focus, their body language never relaxed, even their moments of silence carrying an edge. "You get ready for war the same way a fighter gets ready for a championship match," Pudge told me one night as we were taking Ida on one of her long walks. "You gotta have your mind and body in top shape. Now, it's been a long time since either me or Angelo have had to get down in the street and fight for what we believe belongs to us. And we're going up against opponents we don't know too well and haven't seen too much of. That's why the training and the preparation have to be just right. We can't leave any openings, no room for mistakes. In the ring, that's what gets you knocked out. In our game, it's what gets you left for dead."

• • •

ANGELO SAT AT the kitchen table, his back to an open window, a bowl filled with pasta and peas cooling in front of him, and poured himself a large glass of bottled milk. Pudge sat across from him and nibbled on a breadstick, his broiled veal chop and potato dinner shoved casually to one side, a thick stack of papers filled with names and affiliations replacing it amid the knives, forks and wineglasses. I sat next to Nico on the other side of the table, both of us cutting into a steak pizzaiola platter.

"Just when you think you've learned all the names of the new crews that are out there, a dozen fresh ones pop up," Pudge said, shaking his head and running a pencil down the list. "They can't keep it straight among themselves. How the hell are we supposed to do it?"

"The money trail will lead you to the boss." Angelo glanced down at his untouched pasta dinner. "That part never changes."

"Still, we've never gone up against gangs like this before," Pudge said. "This guy Little Ricky shoots a pregnant woman in the head in a disco because she steps on his new boots. Leaves her for dead and keeps right on dancing. That's not killing for business. That's doing it because you like it. You go after a guy like that, you gotta hit him quick. Especially at our age."

"It's the dope inside him that makes him think he's brave and can't be touched," Angelo said. "It also makes him stupid, and that's where we look for our opening and we make the age difference work to our benefit. Let him think we're old and feeble."

"He wouldn't be half-wrong," Pudge said, putting his pencil down. "I haven't held my gun in ten years, let alone shot at somebody. These days I feel more like Chester than Matt Dillon. But what the hell does it matter anyway? Any of these guys we put to sleep ends up replaced by someone just the same. It's like Vietnam for us to get into this. The more of them you kill, the more of them you gotta fight."

"You could walk away from it," I said, not knowing if it was proper for me to speak or not. "It's not like you need the money. And I've heard you both say how you don't like the way the business is turning. Maybe now would be a good time to get out."

"This isn't like any other corporation that's out there," Pudge said. "There's no pension plan, no stock options, no bonus. In this business, the only buyout you get comes with a pair of bullets. Besides, I haven't had any action for some time and I miss it."

"What would you have us do instead?" Angelo asked. "If we were to walk away from it."

"Whatever you end up doing, it'd be better than getting killed by one of these people." I wasn't backing down from my position. These were the two men who raised me and loved me and I didn't want to see either one end up in puddles of their own blood, their photos splashed across every tabloid for weary commuters to stare at while sipping their morning coffee.

"I guess you're not picking us in the pool to win, then," Pudge said, a thick hunk of veal hanging off his fork.

"I don't want to see you die."

Angelo rested one of his hands on top of mine. "We can't walk away and retire to a little villa in Italy. Every day we'd be there, we'd know that we turned our backs on our way of life. Over time, that would be a much harder death than any bullet could ever bring. I know that's not how you'd want to see us die either."

I looked to Nico for support. "Sometimes the best way to go into a fight is thinking you can't win it," he said, glancing over at Angelo. "That's what helps give you the edge. Somebody a lot smarter than me told me that just before we went into the last war we weren't supposed to win."

"Then I want to help," I said. "If you're going into this, I want to be a part of it, too."

"You're at this table," Angelo said. "That already makes you a part of it."

"But you get no taste of the action." Pudge jabbed the sharp end of his fork at me. "You're not ready for that yet."

"Were you ready the first time?" I asked with a hint of teenage defiance.

"The decision for us had already been made," Angelo said. "It was what we were expected to do. You have other choices in front of you and there's still time before you need to decide."

"We didn't have a choice when we were kids and we don't have a choice now that we're old men," Pudge said. "We have to fight. But you don't need to come into this end of it, at least not now. And keeping you out keeps you safe."

"When will I be ready?" I asked, looking across at both of them.

"That's something you'll know even before we do," Angelo said. "But until then, sit back, listen and learn. These are lessons that are only taught once."

"This kid that runs the Red Barons asked to meet with us," Pudge said, finishing off his veal chop and getting back to the business at hand. "He says his crew will take out the Colombians for us, in return for a cut of our real estate action."

"What's his name?" Angelo asked, sipping his milk, his eyes still on me. "This gang boss of theirs."

"Richie Scarafino," Pudge said. "Nico's having a folder worked up on him. But what we don't know about him we can guess and probably be right."

"I'll have it done no later than tomorrow," Nico said. "But don't expect to find too much in it. He hasn't been around that long; he's just a few years older than Gabe here. He comes from a working family and at the start he used some of their money to fund his own crew."

"He learned his tough from watching movies and television," Angelo said. "This kid's about as Italian as a Waldorf salad. He's never seen a real fight, just street-corner bully action. Those Colombians are born with the tough and they'll kill any of the Red Barons that don't run from it."

"So what do we tell him at the meet?" Pudge asked. He tossed the veal chop bone across the room and watched as Ida scooped it up then got on all fours to gnaw away.

Angelo pushed his chair back and stood, the cool breeze coming off the open window hitting his back. "We agree to give him ten percent of our real estate business with a five-million-dollar cap," Angelo said. "And then we tell him to go out there and fight the Colombians."

"What if he gets lucky and beats them?" Pudge asked. "Then we're out five million and stuck with a partner we don't need or want."

"He's already out of luck, Pudge," Angelo said. "He's up against us."

．　．　．

THIS WAS GOING to be a war over the future direction of organized crime, and every one of those roads led to the drug trade. Cocaine and heroin were the new hot commodity and every young gangster on the street was looking to carve out a piece of the lucrative action. The older bosses, including Angelo and Pudge, had held the line for years, content to earn their money off what they knew best and felt were the most secure forms of crime—loan sharking, extortion, prostitution, hijacking and gambling. To them, the drug business remained a fierce unknown, much as Prohibition had been to an earlier generation of gang leaders. "Look, gangsters are a consumer's best friend," Pudge said. "We've always looked to make our money off of what people want but know they can't have. It used to be booze. Then it was gambling. Now it's drugs. We have to change as the demand changes, just like any other business. We had no problem with that. It was just a long time between cookouts for me and Ang, and in the back of our minds, we both wondered if we were up to it. These new guys played hard, like we did. To beat them, we had to be harder and smarter. It's a tough thing to be both for your whole life."

The new gangs threatening old-line mob authority were deadlier than any of the groups I saw on television professing to want to overthrow the establishment. They were quick to kill and cared little for the rules that had lasted for decades. They were from different ethnic backgrounds and looked to rise up the ranks fast, indifferent to the fact that they were not welcomed into the ordered environment of organized crime. "In that sense," Angelo said, "they were a lot like we were many years ago."

I didn't think they could win. As tough as Angelo and Pudge were, they had coasted on reputation for far too long. These new crews had no feel for what they had accomplished and no regard for the weight their names carried. To them, they were old men blocking their way to a fortune. I didn't want them to fight, but I didn't know how to keep them out of it. I sensed the same doubts from Nico, but he was too much the loyal soldier to speak out. He also had a lot to gain in the event they were victorious and he would do nothing to risk that possibility. I knew of their aches and pains and how, despite strong exteriors, they were slowly losing another war, the one with age. I wanted them to die in a way that I knew they would hate. As old men in the comfort of a warm bed in a safe home. What Pudge always called "a gangster's nightmare" was my greatest wish for both of them.

• • •

I STOOD IN the near darkness of the Brooklyn Aquarium and watched a shark slink its way past the thick glass. Angelo watched the shark move with sleek precision and turned to me. "They usually attack straight on," he said with admiration. "Come in fearless, no matter who it is they're up against. They're the gangsters of the sea, keep what they want and take what they need."

"How long before it all starts?" I walked away from the

glass, the gleeful cries of running children echoing off the carpeted walls of the packed aquarium.

"It's chess not checkers," Angelo said. "The first move's your most important. Somebody will make it soon enough."

"I can do more than you're letting me do," I said in a low voice. "You're calling in every member of your crew, but you're not looking to me. And you can't say it's because I'm too young. You were a lot younger when you went out to fight."

We were about to walk past a long wooden bench facing a school of various shapes of jellyfish. Angelo reached out a hand and gently grabbed my elbow. He was always conscious of those around him, constantly scanning faces, trying to discern young couples out on a weekend trip from federal agents working a surveillance job. "Let's sit for a bit," he said. "Give the crowd a chance to thin out."

"You want a drink?" I asked. "They sell water and soda in the gift shop."

"We'll get some on our way out." He stared at the jellyfish quietly for several moments and then turned to me. "You like to hear the stories," Angelo said. "And I'm glad. You need to know who we were and who we are before you can become a part of it. But there's another part to it, to us, a darker one. And that's what will tell both of us if the life is for you or not."

"I don't know if I can kill somebody," I said, anticipating his concerns as well as my own. "There's been some rough stuff on some of the jobs I've been out on with Nico, but nothing that came close to something like that."

"It's not the killing," Angelo said. "It's living with it. You have to make it become a part of your life, like reading yesterday's newspapers. There's a lot of people out there think they can do that, but not many can. If you're one of them, you have a chance to be a great gangster. If you can't, you can still be a good man. You just can't ever be both."

"What do you want me to be?" I asked him.

"A good man isn't much help to me," Angelo said. "But

you'll stay out of this war, sit back from it, watch and learn. If we make it through, then we'll continue on our way."

"What if you don't make it?" I stood and faced him. "What if going into this war kills you?"

"Then the lessons are over," he said. "And that leaves you with no other choice but to be a good man and lead an honest life. That might be the best thing I ever did for anybody."

"You don't have to die for that to happen," I said.

"Yes I do," Angelo said.

Angelo then stood, patted a warm hand across my face, turned and walked slowly away, deeper into the bowels of the crowded aquarium.

. . .

RICHARD SCARAFINO LEANED his head against the side of the dirty redbrick wall, a toothpick jammed into a corner of his mouth. He was rail thin, tall and wore a tan jacket that hung loose off the shoulders and arms. He slid his hands into the front pockets of his jeans and spit into a small puddle to his right. He was twenty-two years old and in charge of a renegade crew of thirty-five that was no longer content dealing pot and cocaine to college freshmen. He turned around and nodded to a man sitting on a full garbage can, smoking a cigarette. "He's coming out of the bar now," Scarafino said. "Him and that fucking dog."

Tony "Mesh" Palucci tossed the cigarette behind the trash and walked over toward Scarafino, standing just behind him, both hidden by the shadows of the alley. "Look at him," Tony Mesh said. "Walking without a worry in the world. Like he's some kind of king."

"So long as he stays alive, he is the king," Scarafino said, watching Angelo and Ida walk along the far side of the street, both of them shielded by the passing traffic and the crowd of people milling around. "It's up to us to change that."

"Then why are we wasting time?" Tony Mesh said. "Why don't we just take him out?"

Scarafino looked behind him and stared into Tony Mesh's

glazed brown eyes. The two were first cousins and had grown up together, both raised by Richie's mother in Commack, Long Island. They had each served full tilts in upstate juvenile homes on rape and robbery convictions and had started their criminal careers by boosting foreign-made cars parked along Queens Boulevard during afternoon rush hour, selling them off to chop shops in the Bronx, up near Yankee Stadium. Tony Mesh had a snap temper, a quick trigger and a seventy-five-dollar-a-day heroin habit. He lifted weights every day and drank Jack Daniel's mixed with milk to help soothe an agitated stomach.

"If we're gonna take on this guy and his crew, then let's be smart about it," Scarafino said. "Coming at him with our guns out is what he'd expect us to do. He may look old to you, but don't let the look fool you. That's why we clip off his guys one at a time, always staying under the radar, as far from blame as we can get."

"But if he goes down, his crew walks away looking for a new boss," Tony Mesh said with a shrug. "Maybe they might even come work for us."

"What do you do, wake up in the morning and take stupid pills?" Scarafino asked, annoyed. "The only place his crew will ever lay eyes on us will be at our funeral. They're old world. When their boss goes down, they're gonna be looking for the triggers that did him in. But when the time is right, if we play it right, he'll agree to sit down and talk to us. That's only if he sees he's better off with us on his side."

"And what's talking to him gonna get us?" Tony Mesh asked, turning his back on Scarafino and walking toward the garbage cans. "A boss like him is gonna take one look at you and me and see nothing more than a couple of skells. Might have somebody put two in our heads right there at the meet, that's how pissed off he might get. You ask me, we got a better shot at him out here in the open. But then again, what do I know? I'm stupid."

"Look, he may not think it and he may not know it, but a guy like him needs a crew like ours." Scarafino looked away from Angelo and at his cousin. "It's up to me to help him figure that out."

"How's that add up?" Tony Mesh asked, lighting a fresh cigarette and blowing a thin line of smoke into the darkness. "Him needing us?"

"You sit on top for as long as Bones Vestieri and you get comfortable in that chair," Scarafino said. "You may not want to get your crew all bloodied up fighting a war nobody wants to fight. That's where we fit in like a shoe. He'll find out enough about us before the sit-down to know that, if nothing else, we can handle the blood end of the business. We'll knock heads with the Colombians or with that black crew up in the Heights. All we want is a chance to pull a trigger for him. In return, he cuts us a piece off the pie."

"That all sounds good to the ears, Richie," Tony Mesh said. "And if it happens, I'll be more than happy to tag along and play whatever song he asks me to play. But if, instead of a warm welcome, he stiffs us with the cold shoulder when we sit down across from him, what then?"

Richie Scarafino leaned back against the wall and waited for Angelo and Ida to return from their walk. He took in a deep breath and let it out slow, his eyes closed, his hands slapping in rhythm against his thighs. "Then he'd be the stupid one, not you," Scarafino said.

· · ·

PUDGE SAT IN a thick red leather chair, a large mug of coffee on the side table to his right. He looked over at the slender black man sitting across from him, his arms stretched out along the back of the leather couch, and leaned forward to place a hand on his leg.

"It's not something that can be avoided, Cootie," he said. "None of us asked for this, but it's here now and now is when we have to deal with it."

Cootie Turnbill gazed out the large double windows to the left of the couch. There, four stories below his brownstone, he could see the streets of Harlem begin to show signs of early-morning life. These were the streets that Cootie Turnbill had controlled since the end of World War II, splitting all the profits from his numbers, booze, trucking and carting businesses fifty cents on the dollar with Angelo and Pudge. The arrangement had earned millions for all of them and, except for the occasional tussle, had kept the neighborhood free from any gangster wars. Little Ricky Carson and his KKK crew were eager to bring all that to a quick and vicious end.

"What the hell kind of black gang boss names his crew after the Klan?" Cootie asked Pudge. "That supposed to be their idea of cute?"

"Cute or not, they got their eyes marked for your streets. They only know how to do that one way, and talking about it isn't it."

"They're a big crew packing big guns." Cootie pulled a cigar from the front pocket of his velvet robe and held it gently in his hands. "Shoot people they have no beef with, just to show that they can. They talk more about dying than they do about living. We've tussled with some crazy bastards in our time, Pudge, but I don't think any one of us has seen the likes of these."

"They're no different than we were starting out," Pudge said with a shrug.

"You and Angelo up for this?" Cootie asked, resting the cigar on the coffee table separating him from Pudge. "It's been a long time between dances for all of us. Won't take long for Ricky Carson to find that out, if he hasn't already."

"It's been a while since we got our nails dirty," Pudge said, leaning back in his chair. "No doubt about it. But I don't see it as a question of choice. It needs to be handled. Now, will your crew be there for us, the ones up here as well as the ones you got stashed down in the Bahamas?"

Cootie Turnbill smiled at Pudge and clapped his hands together. "Even with the guns from down there, Carson's crew beats mine by at least two to one. Seems like every black kid with a gun and a driver's license is on his team."

"They got the numbers but not the experience. We don't need to outgun them. We need to outthink them. If that happens, we might get lucky enough to sneak away with a win."

"Before you came up here, I was thinking back to the first time the three of us teamed together in a war," Cootie said, his stylish short-trim Afro specked with puffs of gray, the bottom of his handmade slippers leaning against the sides of the coffee table. He was fifty-eight years old now, still with a handsome face and a relaxed manner. Hidden below the calm surface, buried by years of comfort, wealth and security, sat the first black gangster to be accepted into organized crime's ranks. He was also one of its most ruthless killers. He was a low-tier numbers runner on Pudge's payroll when he stepped between Angelo and the blade of an assailant's knife in an East Harlem bar on a humid summer night in 1942. The man reached out and slashed Cootie across the chest, slicing open his shirt and several layers of skin. Then he moved to finish off the dazed and wounded Angelo who was lying on the ground by his feet. Cootie pulled a handgun from his hip and pressed the nozzle firm against the man's throat. Staring into the man's eyes, he pressed on the trigger and put two bullets through his throat and out the back of his neck.

"Skin Reynolds and his demented crew," Pudge said. It was as if they were talking about a favorite family picnic. "They came at us out of nowhere, and if they were only as good as they thought they were, they would have handed us our ass in a glass jar. There's no way we take that war without you in it, Cootie."

"We got them all but Skin," Cootie said, resting his head against the back of the couch. "He ran a little too fast, even for us. Thought he was better off taking a ten-year stretch in Sing Sing than going up against our guns. But it didn't work out like he planned. Hadn't even finished doing six months before he was found dead in his cell block."

"Some plans can do nothing but fail," Pudge said. "Let's hope that the one we got isn't one of them."

"What is the plan?" Cootie asked, resting a hand on his old friend's shoulder.

Pudge looked at Cootie with a knowing nod. "The same plan we've had since we started in this business. We're way too old to come up with something new."

"No need to repeat it then, because I know it by heart," Cootie said. "Live to kill. It's what we know and it's how we go."

. . .

PABLITO MUNESTRO STARED down at the two head shots lying on the center of his bed. He was wearing a denim shirt and snakeskin boots, his pants curled up in a corner of the large, airy room. He leaned back against two thick fluffy pillows and grabbed a half-empty vodka bottle off the night table. He took a long, throaty swig from the bottle, then tossed it to a man in a gray suit and black felt hat standing to his right.

"Are these the two everyone is so afraid to piss off?" he asked, pointing at the photos and looking at the faces of the four men standing in front of him around the bed. "These two old men?"

"No one is afraid of them, Pablito," a young man in a zippered running suit said. "But they are worried about who'll come in their place if anything should happen to them. The Italians don't figure to sit back and let us walk all over their turf."

"That's too bad," Pablito said. "Because unless they all want to die, that's their only choice."

"If there's a way to move in on the Italian's action without a lot of guns," the young man said, "then that's something we might want to look into."

"The Italians ain't gonna hand over shit," Pablito said. "They need to see bodies stack up before they start to think you're serious."

Pablito Munestro was thirty years old and a millionaire several times over, moving in a swift and lethal manner from the impoverished back streets of Cali, Colombia, to a duplex apartment in an Upper East Side condo. He had a solid build and was magazine handsome, with long dark hair falling to his shoulders, tender eyes and a smile that could warm the most indifferent of women. He was blind in one eye, the result of a childhood playground accident, and controlled a drug empire that earned in excess of $50 million a year. He was the first of the Colombian dealers to target entire families for death if any one member was tagged an enemy of his crew.

His mother pulled up stakes and took her family out of the slums of Cali and moved them to the promised land of Florida when Pablito was a toddler. It was there that he began his drug career as a ten-year-old boy, running money between pickup drops for a Miami-based drug boss named Diego Acuz. He killed his first man when he was twelve, and by the time he was fifteen had a full crew of a dozen dealers, most of them twice his age, dealing coke for him out of a burrito-and-beer stand in South Beach. On his eighteenth birthday, Pablito took over the Acuz crew by pumping three bullets into his boss's head and then piloting a twenty-three-foot sailboat forty miles off the Florida coast and dumping the body into the chilly, shark-infested waters. He had been in New York less than two years and had already wiped out four rival gangs. His sights were now set on Angelo and Pudge's powerful crew and their millions in yearly income. Pablito was ranked tenth on the FBI's Most Wanted list and wanted nothing more than to be the biggest gangster to run the table in America's largest city.

"We'll be ready to move by Monday," the man in the suit, Pablito's older brother, Carlos, said. "The Italians asked for a meeting at a restaurant in Queens across from the Fifty-ninth Street Bridge."

"Ours or theirs?" Pablito asked.

"Neither," Carlos answered. "We had it checked out. It's an independent. No ties to any crew."

"Go in heavy, just in case," Pablito instructed.

"It's only a first meeting," Carlos said. "I don't expect

them to try anything. The word we get on them is that they move only when they have to, and when they do, it's slow at its fastest."

"That's the word they want you to hear," Pablito said, looking up at his older brother, the two photos gripped in his right hand. "Forget all that and remember who it is you're going up against."

"We outgun them, outnumber them and outrun them," Carlos said with a puffy confidence. "There's no place for them to go that we can't reach."

Pablito grabbed a gold cigarette lighter off the end table and snapped it open, his eyes staring down at the thin line of fire. He picked up the two photos from the bedspread and ran the flame under them. He held them as they burned. "All that will sound a lot better to me after I know that these two have both been buried," he said.

Then, Pablito dropped the burning pictures at his brother's feet, jumped from the bed and walked out of the room.

· · ·

ANGELO AND PUDGE walked quietly in the wooded area, their heads down, the sun hidden from view by the thick tree coverage above. I followed close behind, watching as Ida sniffed her way through the rough, looking to surprise a squirrel and enjoy an early lunch. We had left the city in the middle of the night, Angelo doing a rare turn behind the wheel, Pudge up front next to him. I sat in the back with Ida's heavy head resting on my knee. Bobbie Gentry's throaty voice filled in the silent gaps as she sang "I'll Never Fall in Love Again" on the car's eight-track system. Outside, the city landscape quickly slipped past, replaced by the small-town feel of upstate New York. We stopped twice to gas the car and walk Ida and once to grab a quick coffee and buttered-roll breakfast. Angelo was clearly more at home navigating the eight-cylinder jet black Cadillac down the hard Manhattan side streets than he was winding his way through two-lane back-country roads.

"Where are we going?" I asked them at the halfway point of the trip.

Pudge turned around, resting one of his thick forearms across the dark brown leather upholstery. "To pay our respects to an old friend. It's something we do whenever we can. And we thought now was a good time for you to join us."

I nodded, my hand gently rubbing the muscular rib cage of the sleeping pit bull next to me. "That go for Ida, too?" I asked.

"We don't even get in the car without Ida," Pudge said. "If those gangs out there only knew who really runs this crew it would go a long way toward saving them a lot of blood and bullets. A twenty-two-steak rack of beef would seal the deal in less than an hour's time."

"How much longer?" I asked. I was not enjoying the ride. The looming gang war circled us like an unwanted houseguest.

"An hour," Pudge said with a shrug. "Maybe less, if Angelo can kick the engine up past sixty."

"Speed kills," Angelo said in his low voice.

. . .

"THIS IS IT," PUDGE said to me, stopping in front of a small headstone in the center of a large clearing. "This is where Ida lived out her last years. Had a cabin right about where we're standing."

I looked over at Angelo, watched him kneel in front of the headstone and bend down to kiss it, one hand gently stroking its side. The markings across the front bore only the words "Ida the Goose" and a chiseled rose. Pudge walked over and stood behind him, Ida following in his steps, her nose to the ground. Pudge reached into a side pocket of his jacket, pulled out a pint of Four Roses and rested it alongside the headstone. I stood off to the right, my hands in my pockets, respectful of their private moment with the woman who had raised them. The area around the grave had been allowed to grow wild in the years since Angelo and Pudge had burned the cabin to the ground, with Ida's body still inside.

We wound up sitting around Ida's headstone eating chicken cutlet sandwiches on fresh Italian bread. I shared one bottle of red wine and one of water with Pudge, while Angelo washed his sandwich down with a quart of milk. Ida the pit bull was content to munch out of a bowl filled with grilled beef and sliced provolone cheese. We didn't do much talking that afternoon. I understood that they had both chosen to say their good-byes to Ida the Goose before what could easily be their final battle.

"Ida fought in the first gang war of this century," Pudge said with a hint of pride. "It was for control of the Bowery. It went on for about two, three years. In those days, a war could last a lifetime."

"She made her reputation during that war," Angelo said, staring at the headstone. "She walked into a bar on Little West Twelfth Street, which was enemy turf to her, and went right up to the gang boss's table. Told him he had two choices. One was to back down, the other was to die. He looked up from his poker hand and laughed right in her face. She didn't even blink. Pulled a gun and put three slugs in him, killed him right where he sat. Turned around and walked out as easy as she had walked in."

"She always said it was a damn shame he had to die that day," Pudge said. "She had caught a look at his poker hand. He was sitting there holding three queens and a pair of sevens. I guess when you don't have the luck, you don't have a rat's chance."

"It's really pretty here," I said, looking around at the massive trees and the hills and mountains that circled them. "Quiet, too. Would you ever think of moving up here, like she did?"

"This is our cemetery, Gabe," Angelo said. "Ida's buried here. So's Angus, over by that big oak tree facing the mountains. All the dogs we've ever had are scattered around here, too. And when the time comes, me and Pudge will be put here. That's the part that you'll take care of, making sure we're buried where we want to be."

"I know it's not something you want to think about, little man," Pudge said, leaning closer and resting a hand on my shoulder. "But it's something we want to make sure gets done. We need to be with our own kind."

"That goes for the dog, too," Angelo said. "All her relatives are here, she'll feel right at home."

I looked out across the clearing and saw Ida running wild in the high grass, switching speeds, resting on all fours when tired, free from the confines of the city streets. "How about me?" I asked, my eyes holding on the hard-charging dog.

"There's a place for you." Angelo stood and walked past me, heading down the slope toward the parked Cadillac. "If you want it."

"You got a full life to live and plenty of other decisions that'll come along with it," Pudge said. "But if the road you take leads you back here, you'd be more than welcome."

"Thanks," I told him.

And at the time, I meant it.

• • •

"THOSE WERE DANGEROUS days," I said. I was sitting on the edge of Angelo's bed, my hands resting on my legs, looking across the room at Mary. "I was missing a lot of school, not because they needed me to do anything, but because I felt I should be around in case they did."

"I wish you would have had a normal high school life," Mary said, leaning back in the chair and crossing her legs. "A young man should be worried about pimples and dates, not a gang war planned out in his living room."

"The double life never bothered me," I said. "So I skipped a few dances and didn't get to go out for the football team. I don't think I missed all that much. They both wanted me to lead as normal a life as I could, but I found it all so boring when I wasn't with them."

"Were your friends afraid of them?" Mary stood and walked past me and toward the window.

"A few were. They didn't say so in words, but you could

tell from the way they acted. Then there were the ones who wanted to be my friends just so they could meet Angelo or Pudge. Wanna-bes, I guess. I pretty much steered clear of them."

"What about girlfriends?" Mary turned to look at me over her shoulder, her eyes arched. "Were there any?"

"I was more like Angelo than Pudge in that department," I said with a shy shrug. "There were girls I liked and wanted to ask out, but I never did. Maybe it was because of the one time I got burned and didn't want it to happen again. Or maybe I just wasn't any good at it."

"Did you ever talk to either one of them about it?" Mary said. "Ask for some advice?"

I leaned over and poured myself a cup of water. "There were a lot of things we never talked about. Angelo's family, my life before I met them, other people in their lives. We only discussed what they felt was important for me to know. The rest of it was kept separate. It was as if all that mattered was the three of us being together."

"Did either one of them ever mention me?" Mary asked. She was standing above me now.

I shook my head. "No, they never did. But you must have been around. You know too much about this gang war, things I had never even heard before, not to have been."

"I was around." There was a new hardness in her voice. "I was there for all of it."

"Doing what?" I asked.

"Making sure you were safe," Mary said.

• • •

THE DARK BLUE Mercedes-Benz made a sharp turn around the corner of 111th Street and First Avenue, its four doors swinging open as soon as the car came to a hard stop in front of a crowded pizzeria. Three young black men in long rider coats stepped out, each with a gun in his hand, and stood next to the open doors, waiting for the final passenger to emerge. Little Ricky Carson, short and muscular, eased himself out of the backseat, lowered the collar of his long rider, shot his cuffs and, his head up, walking with a slight limp, stepped through the small entrance. He went in alone, his three men holding their guns at their sides, their backs against the pizzeria glass, staring at the passing faces on the street. He waited for the two burly men blocking his way to step aside, offering them nothing more menacing than a smile.

"Let him in," said the owner, who stood next to a stainless-steel oven.

Little Ricky Carson nodded as the burly men reluctantly cleared a path and walked up to the man by the oven. The pizza chef was tall and overweight, but carried the extra girth well, dressed in catalog slacks and a black button-down shirt. His head was shaved bald and glowed off the overhead lights. Up close he smelled of imported cologne. His name was John Rumanelli and on the streets outside his pizzeria, he was a man to be feared. He was a ranking member of Angelo and Pudge's crew and controlled the East Harlem neighborhood where he was born forty-two years before and where he still made his home. He never carried a gun and, other than a short juvenile turn when he was seventeen, had a clean yellow sheet.

Rumanelli watched Carson walk up to him and stand alongside the counter. "You come a long way for pizza," Rumanelli said. "The place in your end of town burn down?"

"We're hip to a lot of things, but, truth is, black people know close to nothing about making pizza," Carson said, locking eyes with Rumanelli. "We think pepperoni plays first base for the Yankees."

"It all has a way of evening out," Rumanelli said, his body language tense and on alert. "I don't have any dancing trophies on my dining-room shelves, if you know what I mean."

Rumanelli nodded to a thin, balding man on the other side of the counter, who grabbed a plain slice from a tray next to a row of stacked boxes and tossed it into the top tier of the triple-deck oven. "Have one ready for you in less than a minute," he said to Carson. "You want a drink to wash it down with?"

"Not right now," Carson said, keeping his eyes on Rumanelli.

"What about the boys on your crew?" Rumanelli looked past Carson to the three gunmen in front of his shop. "They might want to eat something before they start putting a finger to those triggers."

Carson ignored the question, lifted his hands as the bald man slid a hot slice of pizza on a paper plate across the countertop. "I hear you're pulling down a little over ten large a week out of here," he said, "and none of it comes from selling anything with sauce on it."

"You and my accountant on a first-name basis now?" Rumanelli asked.

"How much of that do you kick back to Vestieri?" Carson asked. He folded the slice of pie and took a large bite, small puffs of steam coming out of his mouth like cigar smoke.

"Enjoy your slice." Rumanelli turned away from Carson. "Have as many as you want. It's my treat. Then, when you're done, take your three *paisans*, get in your Benz and drive back to the minor leagues. Never show your face here again. If you do, your next slice of pizza will be delivered to the morgue."

Little Ricky Carson flashed a ghetto smile and let the slice of pizza fall from his hands. He pulled a revolver from the side pocket of his long rider leather coat and aimed it at Rumanelli's back. "You might be right," Carson said. "But it won't be any pie coming out of this shit hole."

Rumanelli turned his head back toward Carson and caught the first bullet in his right shoulder. The next two caught him in the chest and sent him sprawling on his back, two chairs and a table knocked aside as he fell. The three gunmen were now standing in the pizzeria doorway, each one aiming a gun at the crowd standing around Carson. Little Ricky stood above the fallen Rumanelli and barely bothering to glance down at him, pumped a final bullet into his chest. Carson then lifted his smoking gun and aimed it at the bald man standing frozen behind the counter. "You know Bones Vestieri well enough to talk to him?" Carson asked.

The bald man nodded. "I can talk to him."

"When you see him again, tell him I kicked off to get the game started," Carson said. "It's his ball now."

Little Ricky Carson looked around at the faces staring at him and dropped a hundred-dollar bill on the countertop. "See to it that anybody wants a slice gets one before they leave," he said. "On me."

He lowered his head, gun resting at his side, and walked out of the pizzeria, his three gunmen moving backwards and following him out. They got into their car, the engine running in idle, slammed the open doors shut, put it in gear and drove away. The rear tires left smoke and rubber in their wake. Inside the car, sitting deep in the thick leather of his new Mercedes, Little Ricky Carson shook his head and laughed, a young gangster filled with a sense of power. "That son of a bitch deserved to die just for having the balls to call that shit he served pizza," he said. "The people in there, if they think about it for a while, they'll realize I did them a big favor. Saved them all from an ulcer."

The laughter of the four was drowned out by the music from a Sly and the Family Stone eight-track blasting out of the four speakers as the car disappeared into the heavy traffic heading onto the Willis Avenue Bridge.

• • •

I SAT IN an Italian restaurant on West Fifty-fourth Street, just a few blocks north of the hospital, waiting for Mary. The long nights by Angelo's bedside were starting to take their toll. I wasn't spending as many hours at my advertising firm as I should have been, leaving the bulk of the work in the hands of the young staff I had assembled. My family life was suffering as well. I would rush through a meal with my wife and kids, always with an eye on the dining-room clock, afraid that I wouldn't be there for Angelo's final moment. After so many long years, I was allowing him to once again consume my days and nights.

I initially feared that his illness, combined with our years of separation, had robbed me of the opportunity to show him what I had made of my life. I wanted to tell him of my business and how successful it had become. I had started my advertising agency with nothing but a phone, a legal pad and a cheap, small rented office on the Upper West Side. I had worked it hard, putting in countless hours and a determined effort, until it had grown to a multimillion-dollar business that was now spread across two floors on Madison Avenue with a partner office in Los Angeles. I also needed him to know that I was a good husband in love with a woman who was both my wife and my best friend. A woman I needed to talk to every day and to see every night. I wanted him to know what an even better father I had been to my two children, who would soon be old enough to embark on lives of their own. I wished he had been there when we had laughed and played in the park or when they celebrated their birthdays, faces smeared with cake, or when they had made it through yet another middle-of-the-night emergency room run. But then, reality would grab hold of the moment, and I felt that maybe he didn't need to see any of it and that he didn't need to hear any words from me. He already knew it all.

I would expect nothing less from Angelo Vestieri.

I had taken the lessons Angelo and Pudge taught me and made use of them in the civilian world that now claimed me. I admit there were a number of occasions when I desperately wished to be back in the life, if only for one brief moment. There I could easily reach out and squash an enemy, or get my revenge against a business betrayal, or eliminate a friend who had broken a trust. But those were only moments of fantasy, played out in the silent corners of my mind, for no one but me to see and hear. Instead, I took the cunning and guile of the mob life and utilized it to my advantage, playing the political games and maneuvers of the modern business world with a skill I would not otherwise possess. I would often pause and hear Angelo and Pudge's voices whisper to me, their words of purpose pointing me toward yet another in a string of victories. In that sense, I would never be free of them. They were too much a part of my life. And I held on to them as tightly as I could.

I sat at a center table in the warmth and comfort of the restaurant, nursing a cold glass of mineral water, waiting for Mary. I was forty-two years old and had turned my back on a place that had embraced me from my earliest years and chose instead to live in one that I had entered as an outsider. In all my time spent in Angelo and Pudge's company, there was never a moment when I didn't know where I stood in their eyes. Their emotions and motives were clear and out in the open, the days free from hidden agendas and deceits. With the exception of my family, I knew I could never allow myself to feel that way with anyone else. I would never find the civilian world to be as trusting as the criminal one. I had been schooled and loved in the company of killers, but had chosen to make my way inside a more treacherous arena. But I believed that what I had achieved had been silently guided by Angelo and Pudge's strong and willful hands. They had been the ones to lead the way and clear my path.

17

Fall, 1970

ANGELO WAITED THREE months before he made his first move in the war.

In that span of time, his crew took heavy hits, attacked from all sides by the combined forces of Little Ricky Carson, Pablito Munestro and, to a lesser extent, Richie Scarafino and the Red Barons. The initial meetings mutually agreed upon by all parties had resolved nothing and only further heightened the tensions that existed between the crews.

The three attacking gangs were wreaking havoc on Angelo and Pudge's profit margins. Weekly earnings were down by half and the younger members of the gang were starting to panic, listening with eager ears to outside overtures. While his rivals slammed his business with a gleeful and fearless abandon, Angelo went about his daily routine, never straying far from the bar and his long afternoon walks with both me and Ida trailing close behind, defiantly daring anyone to attack in the open.

Pudge, meanwhile, busied himself working the streets, keeping up the crew members' morale and assuring concerned parties that all was not lost. But Pudge was much less patient than Angelo and his nerves were starting to fray. He was eager for the action to begin. "Angelo would be willing to wait until he was close to death for his opening," Pudge told me over those long, frustrating days. "I gotta admit that sometimes it gets to me, sitting around, watching our body count add up, losing as much money as we are and doing nothing about it."

"A lot of times, too long can get to be too late," Nico complained. "They're already saying he's lost the stomach for the fight, that he doesn't care enough to protect what belongs to the crew. The talk on the street is that he's never been weaker."

"Those are nice words for me to hear." Pudge smiled for one of the few times during that period. "That makes me think maybe he really knows how to win this damn war."

"I've never seen him like this before," I said. "It's almost like he's not even with us, he's so distant. Sometimes it's scary to be around him."

"Angelo puts the moves in place in his mind before he makes them on the street," Pudge explained. "It's what's always worked for him. It's just that now we're up against the kinds of crews we've never seen before. They make up their rules on the fly and don't look too far beyond the win. That's their big advantage going into all this. Unless we do a total wipeout, they can't help but come out with a gain."

"Whatever happens, I hope it happens soon," Nico said with a shake of his head. "I'm down to less than forty men in the Bronx and half of the Queens crew is laying low. These guys are looking to gun down anybody even close to us. If Angelo doesn't make his move before too much longer, he's not gonna have any turf left to defend."

Pudge poured himself a cup of fresh-brewed coffee. "They've taken their shots at everybody in our crew," he said as he walked out of the room. "Everybody except me and Angelo. We can walk down an empty street unarmed and nobody ever dares come near us."

"You're no threat to them without a crew backing you up," Nico said. "They eliminate them, they eliminate you."

"Maybe that's it," Pudge said. "Or maybe there's a little part of them that's still too scared to make a full play. And if that holds to be true, then we got them by the short hairs."

"I hope that's not the whole plan," I said.

"That's the plan for now," Pudge said.

. . .

TONY MESH STEPPED over a thick pile of shoveled snow and cleared a path to get to the driver's side of his four-door Plymouth. He was wearing a coffee-colored army jacket, tan pants, L.L.Bean rubber-soled boots and a rain-soaked Yankees cap. A cigarette hung off the center of his mouth. He opened the door, scraping its bottom against ice and slush, and hopped in behind the wheel. He tossed the cigarette into the middle of the street and slammed the door shut. He blew warm air into his cupped hands and looked around at the empty boulevard, still reeling from a long night of snow. He checked the time on his Three Stooges wristwatch and smiled, knowing he was less than an hour away from the big time.

He had been Richie Scarafino's main muscle these past three months as they had both cut a slow carve through Angelo and Pudge's aging crew. Now, finally, they were making the direct move against the two top gangsters, something Mesh had been pining for since the start of the one-sided war.

"Believe me when I tell you they don't have the stomach for it anymore," Mesh said to Scarafino as they sat in the back of a cousin's restaurant off the Brooklyn waterfront, in the flush hours of their early planning stage. "They got way too much money to care and too little time left in their lives to waste it fighting with us."

"I wish I had a pocketful of nickels for every time I heard that Bones Vestieri and Pudge Nichols were ready for the dirt farm," Scarafino said.

"They're getting hit from three sides, Richie." Tony Mesh slapped a palm on the white-clothed table for emphasis. "This ain't no one-on-one goomba war like they've been used to fighting. This is three crews, all packing large, looking to do nothing but kill. Against that, they can't win. I don't think any of the big-time crews could. They're going to get hit like they're in the middle of Pearl Harbor."

"Yo, professor, try not to forget who ended up winning that fight," Richie said, taking a sip of espresso. "Look, let the Colombians and the smokes go their own way. We stick to my plan. We hit the outside of their crew and work our way in, the way we've been doing. So far, not a peep from either Vestieri or Nichols. So if we keep going, when you do go out to whack them, you'll face a lot less muscle than we could've faced. And if, like you say, they've both lost their taste for the action, then the takedown becomes an in-and-out job, with us still ending up with a large chunk of the business."

"I'll work it any way you want, Richie," Tony Mesh said with a resigned shrug. "I'm just looking to get us up to the top rung at a faster clip."

Richie Scarafino leaned across the table and put an arm around Tony's wide shoulders. "And I love you for it," he said. "But let's climb that ladder one step at a time. Trust me, we do that and we'll enjoy it a whole lot more."

· · ·

THE HOMELESS MAN standing alongside the idle Plymouth shook Tony Mesh out of his thoughts and brought him back to the moment. He was holding a black cup, his face buried under dirty rags and a wool cap. His hands were stained dark with dirt and oil, and he was wearing a soiled pair of pants that were held up by half a belt and a long roll of thick cord. His feet were covered by torn desert boots, their soles wrapped in tinfoil.

He rapped on Tony Mesh's window with two cracked knuckles and held his empty cup against the glass. "Whatever you can spare," he mumbled.

Tony Mesh rolled down the window and peered up at the homeless man, his short-fuse temper already set to go. "How about you find an empty lot and curl up until you freeze?" Tony Mesh said to him.

The homeless man kept his head down, slowly shifting one

of his hands to an inside pocket of his torn navy pea coat. "Just trying to make it through the day, pal," he said, his head still down, voice even lower. "Not looking for trouble, just a warm spot in my stomach."

"All you're gonna get out of this spot is a hard kick in the ass," Tony Mesh said sullenly. He pulled a fresh cigarette from his shirt pocket and pounded it against the steering wheel. "Now go take yourself a long walk before I stop being so nice."

"You got an extra one of those?" the homeless man asked, standing up against the door, his back blocking the sideview mirror.

Tony Mesh looked at the homeless man, shook his head and opened the driver's side door. "You don't have to worry about the cold weather killing you," he said as he stepped out of the car and stood inches from the homeless man's face. "You don't get away from my car, I'll kill you." He unzipped his army jacket and showed the homeless man the .38 special he kept on a hip holster.

The homeless man shoved Tony Mesh up against his car, keeping his hand inside his jacket pocket. Tony Mesh's eyes searched the homeless man's face, surprised at his strength, unable to break the hold, his back crammed along the panel next to the open door. The homeless man pulled his free hand out of his navy pea coat and came out holding a fully loaded .9mm. He jammed the nozzle of the handgun under Mesh's rib cage, his eyes suddenly alive, shedding the street drunk's downcast demeanor and replacing it with an assassin's confidence.

The homeless man waited as Tony Mesh's hand slid out of his jacket. He then held the cup he was holding up to Mesh's face. "Are you crazy?" Mesh asked, staring down at the half-filled cup. "I'm not gonna drink what's in there."

"You can drink or you can bleed," the homeless man said.

Tony Mesh looked with eager eyes up and down the wide avenue, the streets still empty, the stores not yet open. The homeless man moved closer, shoving the barrel of the gun harder against Tony Mesh's body, smiling when he saw the lines of sweat forming along the sides of his face and neck. "I'm not drinking poison," Mesh said, his right eye twitching, his upper lip trembling.

The homeless man tossed the cup over Tony Mesh's shoulder and watched it land and spill across the Plymouth's front seat, a thin line of blue liquid flowing out and dripping onto the brown rug. The homeless man stared into Tony Mesh's eyes and leaned into him, pinning his arms at his side. Then, with a professional calm, he pumped three slugs into the center of Mesh's erect body, each shot causing the younger man's head to tilt back. He held Mesh in place until he saw the blood run down the sides of his mouth and his eyes begin to flutter and drift, the soft coat of tears masking the drain of his life. The homeless man checked the street for pedestrians, then stepped aside to gently place Tony Mesh back inside his car, positioning his hands on the steering wheel and leaning his head back against the leather rest. He reached across his body, picked up the discarded cup and brought it up to the dying gangster's lips. He poured what remained of the poison liquid down Tony Mesh's throat and threw the cup back down to the car floor. "This way you get the best of both," he said.

The homeless man slammed the door shut and started a slow shuffle walk up the avenue, leaving behind Angelo Vestieri's first victim of his last war.

• • •

IT WAS HALFWAY through the five o'clock mass when I looked away from the altar and saw Angelo sitting in a back row of the church. There were no more than thirty other faces sitting in the high-ceilinged cathedral, most of them elderly, their rosary beads wrapped around trembling hands. I was working the mass alone, serving as altar boy to Father Ted Donovan, a middle-aged priest who brought a driving passion to both his sermons and the Sunday afternoon touch football games that were organized for the kids of St. Dominick's parish. I rang the bells and bowed my head, wondering why Angelo was there. I had been an altar boy since my grammar school years and this was the first time I had seen him at one of my masses. As with most gangsters, he had little regard for the demands the Catholic faith made on how their subjects chose to live their lives.

"They were in the rackets centuries before the first gangster was even born," he once said to me, dismissing the very notion of religion with a slight wave of his hand. "They got a big-time money operation going and the perfect cover. Who better to partner up with than God?"

"They do a lot for the poor," I said, watching him pour hot milk into a large cup.

"They give them a warm place to sit for one hour a week," he said, looking up at me as he poured. "And even for that, they expect some coins in the basket. To me, that's not help. That's taking advantage. They do the same thing to the poor that we do, except the interest rates they charge aren't as high. You want to go inside a church and say a few prayers, don't look to me to stop you. But don't be fooled. It's a business, just as cold as ours."

I had always found comfort inside a church, seeking my silent refuge across its empty pews. I would light a daily candle to St. Jude, the patron saint of lost causes and, ironically, cops as well, and would, on occasion, walk the stations of the cross, retracing the steps of Christ leading to the crucifixion. But mostly, I would sit in a back row, taking in the familiar smells, watching the sun slant through the decorated windows, and allow my mind to wander and rest. It was the place I sought out when the delicate balance of my life would prove too difficult to bear. It was not so much peace I sought as an escape. Inside the dark walls and high ceilings of St. Dominick's, there were no gang wars that needed to be fought and there were no high school pressures that had to be faced. There were just quiet moments where life stayed still and allowed me the luxury of catching up to it.

I slid in the back pew alongside Angelo and sat facing the

main altar. He patted me on the leg and nodded. "You did good up there," he said. "From what little I understand of it."

"There's not much to it," I said. "If you can sit and kneel, you can pretty much handle the job."

"I'm sending you to Italy for the summer," he said, his eyes looking up at the large wooden cross hanging down from the center of the church. "Soon as you're done with school."

I looked away from the altar and turned to face him. "Why?" I asked, raising my voice slightly. "I can't leave you in the middle of . . ."

I stopped myself from saying anything further. But Angelo continued my thought, speaking quietly but leaving no room for argument.

"The war will be at an end long before we see summer. One way or the other. But either way, you're going to Italy."

"I know I'm not much of a help," I said.

"You're going to learn more about our way of life," he said. "That way, maybe one day, you'll be a bigger help."

I sat back, took a deep breath and realized what Angelo was telling me. I was being sent to Italy to be further schooled in the gangster ways, and I knew, even then, that if I boarded that plane, my life would be set on its path and any say I would have in its outcome would be tossed aside. I would be in too deep, be too ingrained in their ways to want to seek out any other. All that was needed was for me to take that one final step and earn the missing degree in my criminal education.

"Who's there to teach me?" I asked, watching an old woman kneel in front of a statue of St. Anthony, her head bowed in prayer.

"You'll stay with a family on a small island just off the coast of Naples," Angelo said. "I've been doing business with them since before the Second World War. They'll treat you as one of their own. All you have to do is listen to what they say."

"Why don't you come with me?"

"Because vacations are bad for business. But you won't be

going alone. I'm sending Nico. He'll make sure you don't run off with the first girl who smiles your way."

"Who's going to be there to keep an eye on him?"

"He's old enough to call his life his own," Angelo said with a slight shrug.

The sun came down on us in warm slants, leaving half our bodies buried in shadows as the flickering glow from the candles danced on the walls of the large church. I watched the women dressed in black whisper their daily prayers for the dead, the color of their clothes reflecting their mood. Up at the main altar, a young priest began to prepare for the last mass of the afternoon.

Angelo tapped me on the leg and nodded. "Let's get out of here before they pass around the basket. I've lived this long without giving them any of my money. Not looking to start the habit now."

"There are things I want to say to you but I can never figure out how," I said, looking over at him. "I've practiced them hundreds of times when I'm alone, but I just can't seem to get the words to come out straight when I'm with you."

"It's easier to talk to Pudge. He's got a way about him that makes people tell him things. With me, they tend to stay quiet. Maybe because I encourage it."

"I don't ever want to do anything to disappoint you," I said, my words coming out slow and measured. "I want you to be proud of me and to never regret the choice you made in taking me into your home."

Angelo stared at me with warm, dark eyes, but he didn't speak, the sunlight bouncing off the hard lines of his face, and he kept his hands still and folded across his lap. I knew this was the kind of talk he liked the least, but it was important for me to finally tell him. There was so much more I wanted to say, but I didn't know if it would draw him closer to me or force him to take a careful step back. He was not a man who made a show of his emotions, and he understood that such reticence only added to his mystique. He also had an in-bred mistrust for those who were quick to open up to others and reveal their innermost thoughts. "If you know what I think, then you know *how* I think, and that could be enough to give my enemy the edge he needs," I once overheard him telling Pudge. "Besides, there should be a private place in your heart that no one should know about, no matter how close you are. A place no one should ever be allowed to see."

Pudge was always quick to laugh off such talk, preferring to let you know how he felt and what he believed even before you had the time to ask. While such an attitude made Pudge an easier man to be around, there was a magic to Angelo's silence. I felt that simply by being allowed in his company he was handing me entry into a very dark but very special world.

"I don't love easy," he finally said. "And I don't disappoint easy. It has helped keep me alive, even on days when I didn't care if I died. That's a part of me that won't ever change. But I know you won't do anything to disappoint me. You haven't yet and I don't think you're ever going to start."

"I don't know what it would have been like for me," I blurted out, tears unwillingly falling down the sides of my face, "if you and Pudge hadn't come along. I feel like I have a place where I belong. And I know that I'll do anything not to lose it. Or to lose you."

Angelo leaned over and for the first time in my life kissed me on the cheek and forehead. "Let's get out of here," he said, "before they sign us up as priests."

I wiped at my tears with the sleeve of my shirt. "Wouldn't be such a bad thing," I said. "Pudge says wearing the collar is the perfect cover. He says you'd make money hand over fist if you planned it right."

"Don't kid yourself." We stood and eased our way out of the pew and turned our backs to the center altar. "The church bosses would never let Pope Pudge past the front doors. They'd eat him up. That's a crew that could give us lessons."

• • •

PABLITO MUNESTRO SAT in a center booth of the crowded restaurant, one hand wrapped around a large glass of rum and the other resting on the thigh of a tall brunette in a black maxi skirt and high heels. His older brother, Carlos, was wedged in next to him on his left, edgy and nervous, anxious for the meeting to begin.

"This doesn't seem the kind of place that serves pizza and meatball wedges," Carlos said, looking around at the oakwood walls and thick leather booths. Turn-of-the-century crystal lamps lined the sides of the large room and candles in Venetian-glass holders rested in the middle of each well-adorned table. The diners surrounding the booth were well-dressed, well-mannered and rich, old money blending in with the new millions being made on Wall Street.

"It's a neutral," Pablito said, his eyes on the brunette as he leaned in and kissed her gently on the neck. "We can talk without having to worry about anybody trying to pull any shit."

"It'd be nice to see the Italians do something other than talk," Carlos said with a disgusted wave. "We've been walking all over their crew and they haven't raised a hand up to push us back. The *cops* are giving us more problems. Now that's a day I thought I'd never live to see."

"We agree to whatever they ask," Pablito said, looking away from the brunette and taking a long swig from his drink. "Especially if they come in looking to make peace. From our end, it's nothing but empty words. By the time you put up your Christmas tree, we'll have full control of their outfit."

Carlos paused as a waiter placed a large plate filled with a New York strip steak and grilled vegetables in front of him, then threw a glance to the wine steward, who rushed over to fill the three empty glasses with a Mouton Cadet. The young Munestro cut into the medium-rare meat, shoved a hunk into the corner of his mouth and looked at his watch. "He's already ten minutes late," he said. "I should shoot him just for that."

"Don't get agitated," Pablito said, placing a hand on his brother's arm. "It hurts the digestion. Eat your meal and worry about the Italians when they're sitting down across from you."

Pudge walked in alone, shook hands with the maître d', whispered a few words into his ear and was then led over to the center booth. He nodded at both brothers, smiled at the brunette and slid into his seat across from them. He was wearing a dark blue sports jacket over a pale blue polo shirt and dark slacks and rested his arms on top of the starched white tablecloth.

"You were late and I was hungry," Carlos said, pointing the sharp end of his knife at the remains of his meal. "But don't worry, I'll make sure it goes on your tab."

"I know you and I know your brother," Pudge said, looking at Pablito and nudging his head toward the brunette. "But her, I don't know."

"It's not important for you to know her," Pablito said. "Whatever you came here to say, I got no trouble with her hearing it. But if you find you got a problem with that, order a drink, finish it and get the hell out."

Pudge turned to look at the brunette, giving her a smile and a nod. "I've never asked a woman to leave a table in my life," he said. "I'm too old and she's too beautiful for me to start now."

A waiter walked over to the table and put a scotch straight up in front of Pudge, a sparkling glass of mineral water alongside it. Pudge lifted the glass and held it out across the table. "To your health," he said.

"Screw that," Pablito Munestro said, ignoring the toast. "I want to know what you're ready to hand over to me. Once that's made clear, I'll let you know how we stand with it."

"The way I see it, anything I put on the table is not going to be enough," Pudge said, resting his glass next to the candle. "The two of you came into this looking to take it all. Anything less is a walkaway."

"A live man with empty pockets always comes out ahead of a dead one," Carlos said.

"These last three months, your crew has taken control of almost twenty-five percent of my weekly business," Pudge told him. "And you did it without asking anyone's permission. You just reached out and grabbed."

"Fuck permission. Where are we, in school? Got to raise our hand to get what we want? Don't waste my time, Grandpa. Take Carlos's offer and get out while your eyes are open and you can breathe without pain."

"I can't go back to Angelo with that," Pudge said. "It would put him in a really bad mood and I'd have to hear him piss and moan for weeks. Trust me, that's not something I want to have to do."

"We're taking it all." Pablito leaned against the edge of the table, his voice lower, his eyes on Pudge. "We're not even leaving a crumb on the floor for the two of you to fight over. The entire operation, from numbers to trucking, is gonna be run by my crew. If you're smart, go home, pack and leave."

Pudge sat back in the thick leather booth and took a slow sip of his scotch, put it down and picked up the glass of mineral water. He drank the water down in long, thirsty gulps, looking past the two Colombians over to the booth behind them where two young men in business suits were enjoying a quiet meal, their table littered with stock tabulations and legal pads. "I got two first-class tickets to Miami in my jacket pocket," Pudge said. "Take them and go back to where you came from. Make sure your crew leaves the same day as you. If you say no to my offer, then there's nothing I can do to keep either one of you alive."

"Who the fuck you think you're talking to, you washed up piece of shit!" Carlos shouted at Pudge from across the table. "You come here to scare me, you old goat? You think your tough talk can scare somebody like me? Somebody like my brother?"

Carlos stood up, stared down at Pudge, raised his right hand and slapped him hard across the face. Pudge took the five-finger blow, ignored the glances from the other patrons, and smiled up at Carlos. "I didn't come here to scare you," he said in a calm voice.

Pablito and Carlos reached into the sides of their jackets,

their fingers on the handles of high-caliber revolvers. The brunette next to Pablito pulled a .38 special from behind her back and jammed it against Pablito's temple. The two businessmen in the next booth turned and held two .44s against the back of the Colombians' heads. "I won't stay for dinner," Pudge said, sliding up and out of the booth. "The food here's too rich for my stomach. Old guy my age has to watch what he eats."

Pudge smiled at Pablito and Carlos, then nodded at the brunette and the two businessmen with guns. He walked through the main room of the restaurant, never turning to look back, as he heard the gunfire and watched the patrons scatter and scream. When he reached the front door, Pudge shook hands with the maître d' and patted him on the shoulder. "I hope to see you again soon," the maître d' said to him.

"Not until we do something about the noise in here, Frank," Pudge said, smiling at him. He waited as the maître d' held the door open, then walked up the three short steps to his waiting car, a brisk breeze from an early fall night blowing against his face.

· · ·

THE TWO PLANES taxied down the dark runway, their lights low, rumbling toward an old hangar on the outskirts of a small Long Island airport. I sat next to Nico in a car at the rear of the hangar, Angelo in the backseat, his eyes fixed on the planes coming his way. Alongside us, cars were parked three deep, lights and engines down, each with a driver and a detailed set of instructions. The two-engine prop planes had come in from Canada, each of them weighed down with forty heavily armed men, on loan to Angelo from affiliated crews nationwide. They were on a forty-eight-hour turnaround and would be back on their own streets in less than three days.

The planes came to a stop, their engines idling as the side doors slid open. A small team of airport personnel placed wooden blocks under the wheels and lodged ladders up against the doors. A long line of men in coats and hats, each one carrying a black leather case, stepped off the planes, walked to the waiting cars and got in. As soon as each car had its full complement of passengers, it kicked into gear and sped out of the airport hangar.

This was my first exposure to this level of organized crime power. I had not yet grasped the reach that gangsters like Angelo had, the fact that through a series of clandestine phone calls and early morning meetings, they could muster an army from cities throughout the United States, an army determined to eliminate any enemy at their door. It was a power few had and fewer still knew existed. By the time those men reboarded the waiting planes for the return flight back north, every member of Pablito Munestro's crew would be left for dead. What time remained for the assassins would be spent working to wipe out the renegade Red Barons team, holed up in Queens and Nassau County safe houses since the night Tony Mesh's body had been found.

"Wait five minutes after the last car pulls out," Angelo said to Nico, both of them standing in the rear of the hangar. "Then we head back to the bar. Pudge should be waiting for us by the time we walk in."

This was the danger and the power of Angelo Vestieri that so many feared, and for the only time in my life I felt uncomfortable in his company. I was even more uncomfortable in the knowledge that he would know. A true gangster can smell out a person's strengths and weaknesses in a matter of minutes, but what they can sense most of all, what their bodies are most attuned to, is the scent of fear. I also knew, standing there next to Angelo inside an airport hangar that had been turned into an assault center, that I could never be a great gangster. Angelo was indeed one, any small doubts that I may have had were scraped away by this impressive show of force. He had planned and maneuvered a total elimination of his enemies. He had sacrificed the lives of many of his own men, hiding his coldness and ruthless abilities under the protective cloak of an aging boss. It was a battle plan few would ever be able to match.

Angelo tapped me on the shoulder with the edge of his folded-up newspaper. "Does this bother you?" he asked, watching the last of the cars drive out.

"A little." I nodded, turning toward him in the dark interior, his face half-lit by the lights off the underbelly of the two empty planes. "I know who those men are and I know what they're here to do."

"But you *don't* know who those men are." Angelo leaned forward, one hand on my elbow. "And you don't know what they're here to do. Which means there's no reason for you to be scared."

I stared back at Angelo, peering into the semidarkness, realizing that I had been brought to the hangar to be taught an important lesson. Of course, he could never just tell me directly, that was not his way. And I was never certain if what I surmised was the lesson he was trying to teach. Even now, I hope that I was wrong. Because after that night, what I thought was that regardless of how much Angelo loved me or how devoted we were to one another, he would not hesitate to have me killed if I posed the slightest threat to his domain. In all the lessons of the gangster life he would give me across the span of many years, this unspoken one would have the most lasting impact. And it was on that night that I also first wondered, during those long, quiet moments standing inside an empty hangar in a small Long Island airport, if I would ever be able to do the same to him. Was I filled with enough hate to order the murder of someone I cared about? Had I been touched enough by death to be rendered a cold witness to it? I honestly did not know. What I *did* know was that if I could not, to Angelo I would be a failure. In the real world, such failings are viewed as blessings.

To a gangster, they are a curse.

"What happens now?" I asked Angelo, my mouth dry, my neck and back cold with the sweat of a young man's terror.

"What's meant to happen," he said in a distant voice. He

turned back toward the open rear door of his Cadillac and got in. I followed in his steps, shutting the door behind me. Nico slid the car into drive and slowly pulled out of the airport hangar. Outside, as a heavy rain enveloped us, I sat back, closed my eyes and tried to erase from my mind the horrors I imagined.

. . .

THE OLD WOMAN gently eased the key into the door lock and slid it to her right. The thin wood door creaked open and she nudged past it, two plastic bags filled with milk, eggs, cheese, bacon and fresh parsley in her gnarled hands. "Richie?" the old woman shouted toward the back rooms of the quiet apartment. "Richie, c'mon, wake up. I bought some breakfast. I'll make us a nice frittata and a pot of coffee. Let's go. Get out of that bed."

The old woman rested her bags on the small kitchen table and walked toward the end of the railroad apartment where her only son, Richie, spent the bulk of his mornings, locked in his room, sleeping off another night of drink and dope. Anna Maria Scarafino had no illusions about her son. She knew he dealt drugs and was in business with people who ended their day with murder. She was well aware that the crisp twenty-dollar bills he often stuffed inside the front pockets of her apron were wrenched from the pried-open hands of hardworking people. But she had long ago resigned herself to such a fate, soon after her husband, Gennaro, took off with the Irish widow with the shapely legs and the longshoreman's pension half a dozen years ago. Since those bleak days, other than her son Richie, no one else had come forward to help pull the family cart. And if the rent and grocery money he gave her came from someplace other than a weekly paycheck, she had learned to turn a blind, if not so innocent, eye to it.

Anna Maria pulled a cigarette from out of her housedress, lit it and kept walking through the well-kept rooms. "Richie," she shouted down the hall, exhaling a thick puff of smoke out her nose and mouth. "What is it with you? Are you deaf, now?"

She turned a small corner and stood at the entrance to her son's room. She turned the handle on the door and tossed it open. Her eyes moved from the empty bloodstained bed up to the wall, the cigarette falling out of her mouth, her hands clasped hard against her lips, squelching both a scream and a violent urge to vomit. There was Richie Scarafino, her only son, born two weeks premature, hanging from his bedroom wall, four thick nails pounded into his hands and feet, thick clots of blood bubbling off his cold skin and running down the blue paint and onto the white sheets. The dark end of a twelve-inch butcher's knife poked out of the right side of his rib cage. His eyes were beaten shut and his head was hanging to one side. Anna Maria fell to her knees, bowed her head and cried over the mangled body of her boy, Richard Scarafino, a young man who wanted so very much to be a gangster. She stayed that way for the rest of the morning, her low, painful moans echoing off cold, uncaring walls now streaked with the stains of death.

• • •

I STOOD NEXT to Pudge, both of us gripping the railing on the top deck of the Circle Line cruiser taking us down the Hudson River. I stared out at New Jersey, the spray of the salt water cooling my face. Around us, young couples held hands and older ones sat on wooden benches under warm blankets wrapped around their legs.

"I like being out on the water," Pudge said.

"I'll always remember that boat you rented for me and some of my friends last summer," I said, leaning closer to him. "You told us all we were going to catch a hundred lobsters each."

"I lied. But at least we had some laughs."

"We don't do much of that anymore."

"What did you think a war was going to be like, Gabe?" Pudge asked.

"I don't know what I expected." I shrugged. "I didn't think so many people would have to die."

"And it bothers you?"

I didn't answer, except to ask another question. "Doesn't any of it bother you?"

"No," Pudge said. "Not now when I'm old and not when I was young and starting out. I always knew it was a part of what I had to be. And I was okay with it."

"I used to love being a part of it all," I said, choking back the urge to cry. "Now, I'm more scared than anything else."

"You love the power," Pudge said. "What you don't love is what you have to do to keep that power." He hesitated, not wanting to say the wrong thing. "Angelo thinks you can be one of us. And he'll do everything to make that happen."

"But you don't think that?"

"Don't get me wrong," Pudge said. "You got the head for it and the respect for it. But you're too nice. And there's no room in our life for *anybody* nice."

"What happens if Angelo comes to think the same thing?"

"That's when it'll get rough," Pudge acknowledged.

"And you'll go along with whatever he decides to do?" I asked.

"I don't pick anybody over Angelo, little man. Not even you." Pudge's eyes were hard now and strangely distant. For the first time, he scared me. "That'll be your war to win," he whispered. "Or lose."

• • •

PUDGE PARKED HIS car under the highway overpass and walked toward the dark, abandoned pier. Overhead, the passing cars rattled the road foundation, for decades now in desperate need of repair. He walked up to the pier entrance, stopped, looking to his left and right for any sign of activity. The combination of a full moon and the reflected lights that came down off the cars rushing out of the city cast the outside of the pier in a hazy glow. The old battered doors were shuttered and the moorings were rusty and loose. In its younger days, this very same pier was clogged with ocean liners and cargo haulers, bringing in thousands of dollars each week in swag earnings for Angelo and Pudge. The money they had earned working off the piers had given each of them the capital to expand into other business ventures. Pudge walked forward and shook his head, saddened to see yet another remnant of his youth reduced to rubble.

The Mercedes came at him at a high speed from his left. The headlights were off, the tires squealing on the cobblestones. The shadowed silhouettes of four men sitting inside the car were all that Pudge could make out. He faced the oncoming car, his back to the splintered wood of the pier's front doors, his hands resting flat against the side of his legs, the fingers of each gripped around a cocked gun. Pudge took a deep breath and waited, the car now close enough for him to see the driver's face. He relaxed his body and then threw himself to the ground, rolling to his right, coming up on his knees, facing the right side of the car, his arms held out, the two guns up and firing bullets into the tinted windows. He saw the driver's head slump against the wheel as the Mercedes crashed into the pier door, its front end bursting through the weathered old wood.

Pudge kept walking toward the car, firing bullets with each step. When one gun emptied he tossed it into the river behind him, reached into the back of his trousers for a third and pumped six fresh bullets into the interior. He stopped when he reached the rear door of the car, looked down with experienced calm at the four dead men scattered inside like broken dolls. He put his guns back inside his jacket, turned around and it was then that Pudge Nichols, a gangster his entire life, knew he had made a fatal mistake.

"That wasn't too bad for an old white man," Little Ricky Carson said, standing there in his standard long rider coat. Three men were behind him as backup.

Pudge turned to look back at the four bodies in the smoldering Mercedes. "Is that how you treat your crew?" he asked. "Put them in the middle of a setup situation?"

"I hope I stay as tough as you, when I turn old," Little Ricky said, his hands in the deep pockets of his coat.

"I wouldn't waste money betting on it," Pudge told him.

And then Pudge swung the Mercedes door open and dove inside, landing on top of the two dead bodies in the backseat. He searched frantically through the insides of their coat pockets, found two guns, turned on his side and started firing. Little Ricky reeled from the line of fire, diving against the pier door, an alley cat scurrying from his late-night prey. The three gunmen pulled semiautomatics from inside their long coats and, with legs apart and arms braced, started firing a steady stream of bullets inside the dark Mercedes. Pudge braced one of the dead men up and used him as a shield, firing wildly in the direction of the three men. He felt the heat of the bullets whiz past him, several cracking the car windows behind him and a few lodging in the thick leather upholstery. He dropped one empty gun and reached into the pocket of the dead man next to him for a fresh weapon. Wrapping one hand around a .44 bulldog, he turned away from the three gunmen, trying to open the door on the other side of the car. As he lifted the handle, he felt a piercing burn in his shoulder and was sent crashing forward, landing facedown on the dirty street. He leaned against the rear tire, blood rushing out of the wound and down his back, and checked the gun in his hand as a wave of bullets popped holes into the Mercedes exterior. Pudge used his feet to lift himself up, turned and fired three quick volleys, hitting one of the gunmen square in the chest, then shifted his attention to the second gunman. He aimed the large gun, the pain in his shoulder sinking down into his back, and put pressure on the trigger. He squeezed off one round, catching the shooter just below the jaw. Pudge watched him fall, then turned to the third gunmen, who was walking toward him now in a bent position, moving his gun from left to right, looking to get off a final shot. Pudge closed his eyes and knew he was one bullet away from making it a battle between himself and Little Ricky Carson. One bullet away from walking clear of a trap he should have been smart enough not to get

caught in. Pudge had been around enough of these last moments to know that they would have little to do with skill. It
was now all about luck and how much of it he had left.

As Pudge Nichols felt the cold barrel of the gun lodge
against the base of his neck, he knew that his long streak had
come to an end.

"Fun's over, old man," Little Ricky Carson said.

• • •

THE SUN CAME in through the cracked wooden slats, highlighting the grease and the rummy shacks huddled in corners
of the pier. A long line of pigeons draped the upper planks,
sitting perched and cooing. Angelo Vestieri stood in the center of the empty port of entry, dirty river water splashing onto
his new shoes and wetting the edge of his cuffs. He looked
down at Pudge Nichols's body, bound and tied to a thick
wooden board. I stood off in a corner, leaning against a shaky
wall, my head resting against the wet wood, my hands covering my face, trying not to let Angelo hear me cry.

"Nico, let me have a knife," Angelo said. He bent down
and ran a hand across his friend's face, staring at him, his eyes
hard but moist, his hands shaking in the filthy shadows of the
abandoned dock. He slowly moved his fingers down each
of Pudge's many wounds, some of which had already been
gnawed at by the water rats that patrolled the piers. Pudge had
been shot several times, but it was the blade of a knife that
had ultimately killed him.

Nico came up behind Angelo and handed him the knife,
then walked back into the shadows, leaving the two men their
final moments together. Angelo clicked open the switchblade
and cut the thick cord away from Pudge's body. He worked
his way from chest to feet and, when he was done, closed the
blade and tossed the knife into the murky waves. He gently
shoved his arms under Pudge's body, lifted him to his chest,
rose to his feet and began his slow walk out. I followed him,
Nico in step alongside me. I had never seen a dead body

before, let alone that of someone I loved, but I was numb to any reaction other than sorrow.

I touched the top of Pudge's head, cold and wet from the long night floating in the hull of a port he had once brought to life. I wanted so much to tell him that I would miss him more than I could even imagine. I never needed a brother or a sister or a mother as long as Pudge was around. He always made it his business to be everything to me that Angelo could never be. Now that was all gone.

"We'll stop at the bar first," Angelo said. "Get Pudge some clean clothes. Then, we'll go up to Ida's farm and bury him the right way."

I knew he didn't even know I was there at this moment. I knew he was alone in the company of the one man in this world he could call a friend.

I also knew that after this day Angelo would never be, could never be, the same. His final link to the past had been stripped away.

• • •

I LOOKED OVER at Mary as she took a bite of her Reuben sandwich and wiped the corner of her lips with the folded end of a cloth napkin. I took a long drink from a glass of mineral water and shrugged my shoulders. "That was the worst day of my life," I said to her. "Losing Pudge in that way is something I don't think I've ever recovered from. It showed me a side of their world that I just didn't want any part of. Being with people you love and being able to do what you want, not having to worry about money or work, that was fun. But the reality of it is that those periods only last a short while. Most of the time you're trying not to get either yourself or the people around you killed."

"Pudge didn't want that life for you." Mary rested her elbows on the counter, ignoring the cigarette smoke from the table behind her.

"Maybe," I said. "When I think back on it and remember all the things he told me, they applied as much to the outside world as they did to his. That was his way of teaching me there weren't too many differences between the two, and that I had to get ready to face one of them."

"Who were you closer to, Angelo or Pudge?" Mary asked, pushing her platter off to one side of the ceramic tabletop.

"Pudge was always easier to talk to," I told her. "He's the guy you went to after a first date or a first kiss or pretty much a first anything. And whatever you had to say, he made you feel good about it. I wanted to be more like Pudge. But inside, I felt more like Angelo. I didn't act like him or treat people the way he did and, God knows, I talked a lot more than he did. But I felt closed off from the world, much like he was. And I always felt different from those around me, as if I was holding a secret that no one else could know. Maybe more of him rubbed off on me than I thought."

"He had a stronger personality than Pudge," Mary said, sitting back in her chair. "He didn't have to say as much to have an impact. Plus, you didn't have as much time with Pudge. He died when you were still a boy. And what other people thought never really mattered to Pudge, as long as their thinking didn't affect the way he lived his life. Angelo looked to force his will on others, align them to his way of thinking. It was a part of his power and he was very good at it."

"You talking from experience?" I asked, signaling a hovering waiter for a check. "Or just as a casual observer?"

"I'm talking as a victim," Mary said, a slight crack to her voice. "Just like you."

. . .

COOTIE TURNBILL SAT across from Angelo, finished off the last of his bourbon and took a long, full drag on his cigar. Sitting around him, each holding a drink and a lit cigar, were his three main lieutenants. Sharpe Baylor was the youngest of the trio, a thirty-five-year-old hard case who controlled the streets for Turnbill's team. Gil Scully handled the crew's money, his clean hands capable of washing thousands of illegal dollars, turning them into solid investments overnight.

Then there was Step, who had been running rackets out of Harlem since the early 1930s and had been Cootie's partner since the start of World War II. Angelo sat across from the four, his hands resting flat on top of his desk, an untouched glass of milk sitting on a coaster to his right. "There isn't time to think this over," he told them. "I need a yes or a no now."

"Carson's adding muscle every day," Sharpe Baylor said. "The hit on Pudge added seriously to his presence on the street. The word we get back is that the young guns all believe he's one bullet from the top spot. That means, right now, we're looking at a crew that's at least four hundred deep. Maybe more."

Step stood and walked over toward Angelo's desk. "It hurt me a lot to see Pudge go out the way he did. If my vote means anything, then we go out and start shooting down some of these bastards."

"Before I put out my vote, I'd like to ask you a question," Gil Scully said, his voice the least emotional of the group. "I want to know why a tough boss like you needs to reach out to a gang of niggers?"

"I'm a gangster," Angelo said. "That's the same as being a nigger. In this room or in any other, I don't see the difference and I never have."

"How you want it to break down?" Cootie Turnbill asked, placing his empty whiskey glass on the side of Angelo's desk.

"I don't want anything from the new action he's picked up or what he had before it," Angelo said. "That's yours to give out."

"We'll need your guns in this as well," Gil Scully said. "Alone we about match up. Your boys give us enough timber to send them off."

"I've told Nico to walk with you on every step," Angelo said, lifting the glass of milk to his lips. "Whatever you need—men, guns, cars, money. It'll be there."

"You ain't the type to sit back and let other people run your fight card," Step said. "You'll want a place on the ticket. Now tell me, where's that place gonna be?"

Angelo stared at Step and nodded. "Do what you want with Little Ricky Carson's crew," he said in a low, powerful voice. "How they die, and where, is your business. Except for one. No one but me touches Little Ricky."

"Humor an old friend, Angelo," Cootie Turnbill said. "What if we take a pass on all this? Sit down with Little Ricky and cut our own deal with him. We do that, where does that leave you?"

Angelo pushed his chair back and stood to face the four men. "On my own. And believe me when I say that alone or with you, I'll make sure every member of that crew, from Little Ricky on down, ends up dead."

Cootie cleared his throat. "A handshake seals it," he said. "I don't see a need to take it further. Especially coming from one nigger to another."

• • •

THE THIN YOUNG drug dealer sat in the hard-back chair in the center of the empty room. He was stripped down to a T-shirt and boxer shorts and was shivering from the overhead fans that were blowing a cool wind down at him at full speed. He had been in the room for more than an hour, placed there by the three strong arms that had dragged him out of his bed in the middle of the night and tossed him into the backseat of a large car.

"You guys ain't been to enough movies," he said to them at one point during the one-hour ride downtown to the warehouse. "If you had, you woulda known that you blindfold a guy after you lift him. This way when he comes gunning for you, he won't know which way to go."

The driver, a large man with a hard body, shook his head. "Take it all in," he said to the dealer. "Take some pictures if you got a camera. It won't matter. Everything you see is the last time you're gonna see it. So, knock yourself out. If nothing else, it'll make the ride go faster."

The drug dealer jumped in his seat when he heard the dead bolt on the center door snap open. Angelo Vestieri stepped through the doorway and made his way slowly toward the dealer, a gun in his right hand. He stopped when he was directly in front of the dealer and stared down at him. Nico followed him into the room and stood off to the side.

Since the agreement with Cootie and his crew, there was only silence and death surrounding Angelo. True to their word, Turnbill let loose his well-organized mob with a vicious fury not seen since the big gang wars of the 1930s, and combined with what was left of Angelo's gang, they inflicted heavy losses on Little Ricky Carson and his troops. As the body count rose by alarming numbers, Carson looked for an escape route out of the war and arranged for his brother, Gerald, to meet with Cootie, hoping to see if a truce could be arranged. He got his answer when one of Sharpe Baylor's hit men left Gerald's decapitated body hanging by the shoulders on the electric garage door chains for Little Ricky to see when he left the next morning to check on his overnight business.

Angelo rested the barrel of the gun on top of the drug dealer's knee and pulled the trigger. The sound of the bullet going through flesh and bone was displaced by the dealer's screams. He sat in the chair, rocking back and forth, his eyes looking up to the tin ceiling, his mouth filled with spit and foam. Both of his hands were wrapped around his leg, blood gushing through his fingers and down the sides.

"I ask one question," Angelo said, waiting until he knew he had the dealer's attention. "And I want one answer. If it's the right one, all you have to worry about is one more bullet. But if it's not, this will be the worst last day of any man's life. Are you ready for my question?"

The dealer didn't speak, but through the sweat pouring down the sides of his face and the tears welling in his eyes he managed a nervous nod. Angelo took a step closer to him, put out his hand and gripped the dealer by the chin. "I know you do your work for Little Ricky," Angelo said in a voice as cold as a winter grave. "I know you sell his drugs and you kill people he asks you to kill. I know the two of you grew up together and have stayed good friends. I know he likes and trusts you. What I don't know is where I can find him. And that's the one question I want you to answer. Where can I find Little Ricky Carson?"

The drug dealer swallowed hard, more out of fear than need. The hesitation was enough for Angelo to lift the gun and bring it down on the dealer's other leg. He pressed it against the soft flesh of the man's thigh and pulled the trigger. The dealer's screams came from out of a hidden place that was welled solid with pain and misery. He rocked violently back and forth, alternating pitiful moans with massive shrieks, his puffy eyes looking up to Angelo for relief. But Angelo shook his head. This was not a day for relief.

"You scream loud," Angelo said. "Talk the same way."

"He's in a building on the Upper West Side," the dealer sputtered, the space around his feet thick with blood. "Top floor. He keeps it quiet. Most of his top guys don't even know about it. When he doesn't want to be found, he cribs up there."

"Don't make me guess the number of the building," Angelo said.

"I got it on a piece of paper in my wallet. In the pants your boys took off me. Don't remember it right off."

Angelo glanced at Nico who nodded back and walked down the length of the long warehouse floor to where the dealer's clothes were stacked in a corner pile. Nico pulled a black leather wallet out of the back pocket of a pair of crisp jeans, scattering its contents on the floor until he found what he wanted. He held up a folded piece of yellow paper. "It's an address," he said. "And an apartment number."

Angelo's dead eyes moved from Nico back down to the dealer, whose upper body was trembling, his lower half washed over with blood. "I gave him up, just like you asked. Gave you what you wanted, didn't I?"

Angelo nodded, lifted the gun and rested it on the dealer's forehead. He looked down and saw the young man's eyes bulge, his lips moving but lacking the ability to form words. He held up two bloody hands against Angelo's rich dark suit and tried to push him away. Angelo squeezed the trigger and blew out the back of the dealer's head, sending him crashing to the floor in a rubbery heap. He slipped the gun into his pocket and walked over to Nico. He put his hand out and looked down at the yellow piece of paper Nico handed him.

"Let's go," he said, crumpling the paper and tossing it behind his back. "I want to make sure Little Ricky's best friend didn't die a liar."

.   .   .

I SAT IN the backseat next to Angelo, Nico driving at a fast clip through the side streets of Washington Heights. We had spoken very little since Pudge's death. His burial on Ida the Goose's property in Roscoe had been a somber affair attended by only a handful of mourners. Neither Angelo nor Pudge cared much for those large, flower-drenched funerals that were so often a highlight of a gangster's newsreel footage. They thought those events were only put on for show, to give the appearance of power and deprived such moments of the privacy they deserved. "Tell me this," Pudge would often ask me, as he sat and read about the exorbitant funeral of a rival. "If he was the guy with all the power, then how come he's riding in the lead car, stuffed inside a coffin?"

I looked out at the crowded streets as they rushed past, eager young faces in sweaters and skirts mingling with old women pulling shopping carts filled with a few days of groceries. I turned away to look at Angelo, his head against the leather rest, his mind lost in the moment, his eyes ignoring all the activity taking place around him. The weight of Pudge's death had taken its toll. Angelo already felt that he was a danger to anyone he drew close to, that he was cursed to bring a painful death to those who took the time to befriend him. I was starting to sense that such fears were now being directed my way.

"I'm sorry you had to see him die the way he did." It was the first time Angelo had spoken to me about Pudge since his death.

"I know it's crazy, but I always thought he was like Superman," I said with half a smile. "That nothing could kill him, nothing would bring him to a stop."

"Now you know better," he said.

I didn't say anything to him. He was wrong. I didn't know better. I still felt the same way about him.

We sat in silence as Nico drove. Then suddenly, Angelo started talking again. The edge was gone from his voice and there was an eerie gentleness to his tone. "Me and Pudge, we built what we have from scratch," Angelo said. "We put it together with our blood, with a lot of people's blood. You can't take something like that and give it away. It's a part of what I am and it deserves to be handed down. And not just to some guy from another crew who did me a favor. What we built should go to someone who will build off it and make it even more powerful."

I stared at his profile, his head rising slowly, his eyes settling on my face and knew that the someone he had in mind all along was me.

．　．　．

I WASN'T SUPPOSED to have seen any of it. I was not meant to have been at the middle-of-the-night pickup of Little Ricky Carson from the rear bedroom of a six-room Manhattan apartment. I should have been at home and not standing there next to Angelo, watching a mask of chilled fear penetrate Carson's once solid confidence. I should not have heard the only words Angelo spoke to him in that room. "Never give an old man an extra day to live," Angelo said to Carson, in a manner cold enough to cause a shiver. I should not have been there for any of what followed, none of it was meant for my eyes. I was still a boy and even Angelo sought to spare me from the sight of another man's murder. Even if it was the man who had killed Pudge.

"I *have* to come with you," I said to Angelo earlier that evening. "I want to be a part of this. I *need* to be there."

Angelo shook his head. "No," he said.

"Why not?" I asked, walking on tentative ground as I questioned a decision.

"A man will die tonight," Angelo said. "And that's all a boy needs to know."

"I belong with you," I said, standing up to him, fearful but defiant. "At least for this part of it."

Angelo sat in a lounge chair, hidden by the shadows of his desk lamp, the only sound the raspy breath coming up from his lungs. "I leave in an hour," he said. "Be ready."

He reached up and turned off the light, blanketing the room in total darkness.

• • •

WE WERE STANDING on the roof of a seven-story building on Columbus Avenue, the night sky brimming with stars and a half moon. Off to my right, the lights of Lincoln Center cast their studied glow on thickets of the exquisitely dressed out for a night of age-old music and refined conversation. I looked down at them, as they mingled near the doors, cramming to get in, each one careful not to get scuff marks on their designer shoes, and I wondered how many could even believe that a few short blocks away a man was about to die.

The thick door leading up to the roof slammed open and Little Ricky Carson was thrown headfirst to the hard tar ground. He landed on his hands and knees, scraping his chin as he skidded to a halt. "Help him up," Angelo said to Nico. "And bring him over by the light."

Nico lifted Ricky by the collar of his silk bathrobe, pulled him off the ground and carried him over to where Angelo waited. Carson shook off Nico's grip, straightened out his robe and smiled at Angelo. "This all the crew you got left?" he asked, still flashing a hint of bravado. "One piece of muscle and a boy? Guess I did you a lot more damage than I thought."

Angelo reached into his jacket pocket, pulled out an old black-and-white photo and showed it to Little Ricky. It was a faded shot of two young men, their arms wrapped around each other's shoulders, wide-eyed and smiling into the camera. Even in the shaded darkness, shadows bouncing off a series of hanging bulbs, I recognized it. It was a picture of Angelo and Pudge as young men, taken on the day each bought his first suit. Angelo kept the photo in a small gold frame on top of his bureau, next to a head shot of Isabella and another of Ida the Goose. Many times, I would sneak into his room and stare at the pictures, trying to imagine what the young Angelo Vestieri had been like.

Angelo nodded to Nico, who walked over and handed him an open four-finger knife. Angelo stabbed the knife into the photo. "This is a gift," he said in a voice that was as calm as it was frightening. "From Pudge."

Nico reached behind Little Ricky, grabbed both his arms and held them tight against his back. Angelo plunged the knife, with the photo facing out, deep into Little Ricky's shoulder. Carson tossed his head back and let out a pained howl, his legs slumping and losing their strength. Angelo turned away from Carson and looked over at me. "Get the ropes out of the box," he said. "And bring them to Nico."

I ran to the edge of the roof, reached down into an open cardboard box and pulled out three large circles of thick cord and brought them to Nico. As I turned away, I felt Angelo's hands around my shoulders. "You've done your part," he whispered. "Now, go downstairs and wait in the car."

"I came to help," I said.

"You have," Angelo said.

I stared over at Carson, watched him start to tremble as Nico bound his hands and feet with the cord. What was left of his courage was doing a fast fade, replaced by the simplicity of human fear. His fate was now in gangster court, where the verdicts were reached quickly and where the punishment more than met the crime.

"I'll be downstairs," I said, glaring at Carson with scorn.

"You'll see everything better from the car," Angelo said, pushing me toward the door leading down the tenement stairs. "Trust me."

. . .

I SAT IN the front seat, gazing up at the roof through the open window, Ida nuzzling her large head under my arm. I knew enough to know that Angelo would do more than simply kill Little Ricky Carson. He would send a stern message, clear and forceful enough that it couldn't be ignored. Carson's death would not serve merely as punishment for what he'd done to Pudge. It would be a warning shot to the dozens of other crews that were amassing money and strength, telling them to be content with what they had and to stay away from what belonged to others. Little Ricky Carson's death was to be both revenge and emblem. And there was no one alive who was better at that than Angelo Vestieri.

I jumped when I saw the burning body hanging off the edge of the roof, held aloft by a dozen feet of cord. Little Ricky's torched corpse swung back and forth in the fall wind, lighting up the night. Angelo and Nico had tied a noose around his neck, drenched his body in gasoline and tossed him off the side. It was Angelo who reached down and dropped the lit sleeve of a shirt on the top of Little Ricky's writhing head and shoulders. The sleeve had been cut from the shirt Pudge wore on the day he died. I looked up and saw Angelo peering off the roof, the hot flames casting his face in a red glow, as he stared at the man whose death would finally bring an end to a long and draining war.

Within minutes, the fire wound its way to the base of the cord, causing it to snap and send Little Ricky Carson's charred remains in a straight drop down to the empty pavement. The crumpled body lay there and sizzled, frightened screams and the distant blare of fire and police sirens following fast in the wake of its crash. I stared over at Carson's corpse, at the smoke rising off the burnt clothes and skin. His limbs were still twitching and thin lines of flames were burning through the holes in his face. I was shaken by what I had just witnessed, horrified by the forced brutality of it all. Yet I was glad to have been there and seen Pudge's death properly avenged. This was the part of a mobster's life I most appreciated. I hungered for the taste of revenge and reveled in the thrill it left in its wake. Most everyone dreams of getting even, but they lack either the ability or the desire to bring such inner hate to life. I was one of the lucky ones. I had been raised by a man who was a master of the payback, expecting nothing more from life than to punish a scorned enemy and right a wrong.

And on this day, I was allowed to be a part of it all.

As a crowd gathered, I slid over to the passenger side of the car, waiting for Angelo and Nico to make their way down from the rooftop. I leaned across the dash, pressed down on the key and kicked over the ignition. I opened the glove compartment, rifled through Nico's tapes until I found the one I wanted, and shoved it into the slot, turning the volume up. I rested my head back and shut my eyes, Ida sitting curled and warm by my side, both of us listening to Benny Goodman and his quartet rumble their way through "Sing, Sing, Sing."

18

Summer, 1971

I WAS WALKING on the long strip of white sand beach, Nico alongside me, the hot Italian sun warming our backs, turning our dark tans even darker. I looked out at the calm waves splashing gently onto the shore as an army of pale white sailboats glided by in the distance. We had been staying on the small island of Procida for two weeks now, in the top floor of Frederico and Donatella Di Stefano's three-story pink stucco villa, twelve miles from the mouth of the harbor. I had initially dreaded the thought of leaving the States and my accustomed New York life, but as I walked next to Nico, both of us with white towels draped around our necks, I couldn't think of ever finding a better place in the world. It was an island of peace, filled with warm people who took enjoyment from the simple moments of each day. The main industry was fishing, with the occasional tour bus making the local rounds. The houses were made of stone and dotted the shoreline, surrounded by fresh pine trees and lofty hills. The women dressed in colorful cotton dresses and wooden clogs, hand-sewn shawls crammed inside straw purses, set to ward off the chill of an early evening walk. The men wore work pants and sandals, short-sleeved shirts open halfway down to their stomachs, arms and necks burned brown by the sun, the rest of their bodies as white as newly bleached sheets. The island boys seemed to run in gleeful packs of six, their days devoted to long swims, napping under a sun hot enough to broil meat and topped off by a stop at the outdoor movie theater, which presented a new feature each night, usually a dubbed American import. They all smoked and chewed gum and were infatuated with any products from the United States. And of course, they were obsessed with women, their southern Italian blood working at a hormonal boiling point that put the awkward moments of my teenage years to shame. "These kids would screw a rotting tree," Nico said to me one afternoon. He was sitting in an outdoor café and sipping an iced espresso. "You give them a woman and a fresh bowl of pasta and it's like handing them a million dollars. When I was their age, all I wanted was for the Dodgers to win the World Series."

The women who captured the attention of the boys were divided into two categories. Of immediate interest were the *stranieri*, offshore beauties who came to Procida on their summer break, eager to escape the draining city life to the north. These women, regardless of age or marital status, were marked prey, pursued by the young men of the island as if they were rare and unique treasures. A summer romance was a most sought-after prize and any teen fortunate enough to be part of such a situation earned the pride and respect of his pack. The sexual conquest of an older woman was viewed as an important first step to an island boy's arrival into manhood.

The island girls were treated in a different manner. These were the giggling teens a few years removed from becoming young brides and mothers. They were treated with respect and their beauty was acknowledged with whispers and glances. Most of the island girls were engaged by their sixteenth birthdays and wed before they turned twenty. "Be careful how you handle yourself with the local girls," Nico told me one warm night. "What to you might be an innocent gesture, could be a whole other ball of wax over here. They grow their own on this island and they watch out for their own. You find a girl you like, think twice. If not, you might find yourself a married man by week's end."

Living on Procida was like being tossed back into an earlier century. The moral code was rigid, unbending and upheld. A woman was expected to be a virgin on the day she married and needed to prove it not only to her husband but to the locals as well. This was done by hanging the bloodstained wedding night sheets out the window at daybreak. If her husband was unable to complete such a task, the marriage could be annulled, and if it wasn't, a cloud hung over the couple that wouldn't pass for decades. The Catholic Church held a great deal of power, but the priests seemed less formal and much friendlier than their counterparts back home, their Sunday sermons filled with joy and laughter rather than gloom. The priest and the crime boss were the two most trusted men on the island, the ones everyone turned to if a problem needed to be solved or a difficult decision made.

"I heard this story the other day from Frederico's driver, Silvio," Nico told me, turning his face up to the warm sun. "Happened during the war. One of the locals went off to fight the Germans, or maybe it was the English. Whoever it was, he was gone. The island was hit pretty hard back then, all of Italy really, and money was hard to come by. His wife finds herself with three kids and no income and, as far as she knows, her husband's lying dead on some battlefield. Anyway, she starts turning tricks to help feed herself and the kids."

"She became a prostitute?" I asked, the sun blinding my attempt to look up at him.

"How else was she going to make money?" he asked. "Be a hit man? She did what she had to do to feed her family. Then the war ends and guess who comes marching back home?"

"Her husband?"

"Bingo," Nico said. "He's on the island about fifteen minutes when about a hundred of his closest friends tell him how his wife had kept herself busy at night while he was away. The guy, understandably, wants her dead. He wants a divorce. He wants her out of his life. Tell you the truth, he's so pissed off, he don't know what he wants."

"So what's he do?" I asked, eager to hear the rest of the story.

"He goes and sees the local priest," Nico said, now facing me, his back blocking the sun from my eyes. "They go over the whole story and when they finish, the priest sits back, lights a cigarette and sets him straight."

"Sets him straight how?"

"He tells him that if he leaves this wife and goes out to look for another, how the hell's he gonna know the new one wasn't a prostitute, too. So the priest says, 'At least at home, you got a prostitute you know. Why go out and take a chance on one you don't know?' The guy nods, stays pissed for a few more years, but stays with his wife."

"Are they still together?" I was walking again, my feet cooled by the licks of the waves.

"Not only are they still together, they went and had another kid. Beautiful girl about your age. So, there you have it, two people who loved each other were kept together, all because some smart old priest knew how to think. See if you get that kind of advice in New York, from one of those dry-ass Irish drunks."

"Not for free, anyway," I said.

. . .

I SPENT MY mornings with Frederico Di Stefano. He was a stout man in his late sixties, with a thick head of white hair, trimmed white handlebar mustache and a leather face, lined and aged from years under the southern Italian sun. I sat with him at a table that was shaded by a thick overgrowth of grapevines. His villa was edged on top of a hill and had an impressive view that overlooked the sea and the mouth of the harbor. Behind us, a dozen acres, lined solid with vines and poles, sliced down the slope of a hill, the land worked on by a quiet army of laborers. It was in this still, graceful and majestic setting that Frederico began the lessons that were meant to further prepare me for a life in the underworld. He would come out the back door of his kitchen, carrying a silver tray filled with cups, plates, a large pot of hot espresso and a basket of fresh rolls. He poured us both a cup of coffee, always serving it without sugar, and sat across from me on a thick hand-carved wooden chair. His English was accented but fluent, helped along by a two-year stay in London where he had been sent by relatives when he was ten to combat an early battle with cancer. He left behind a diseased kidney and a deep affection for all things British except tea. "I hear people say the English are a cold people," he told me. "In my experience, I never found it to be true. They love life, embrace it, understand it in ways few cultures do. But, unlike us Italians, they keep themselves at a distance, and let you know as much as you need to know. Just like you must learn to do."

"Was your father in the life?" I asked him, gripping the heavy cup with both hands and drinking the hot espresso the way he had taught me, fast and in less than five gulps.

"My father and his father and, before him, his father," Frederico said with a shrug. "It is the only life we have known. The ways of this island and the ways of the camorra are the ways of my family."

"Have you ever wished that wasn't true?" I asked, reaching for a roll and a jam spread. "That you weren't locked in to one way of life?"

"When I was younger, about your age, I would stare out at the water's edge and follow the big ships as they passed by on their way to Germany, France, even America," he said, looking down the slope at the blue seawater of the harbor below. "In those moments I would wonder what it would be like to be free enough to board such a ship and travel to lands I had only heard others talk about."

"Why didn't you go?" I asked him. "You know, once you were old enough not to need anybody else's okay?"

"Such thoughts are the sole property of young boys," he said, pouring us both a second cup of coffee. "They must not get in the way of what it is a man must do with his life. To turn my back on that would have been a betrayal to my family and to myself."

"How will I know if it's for me?" I leaned in closer to him, my eyes searching out the calmness in his, hoping to find answers to my questions as much from his expressions as from his words. "I don't know my family history. As far as I can tell, I'm the first to come into this life and I come to it with my hands empty."

"The moment will find you," Frederico said, resting a muscular hand on my knee. "It will point you in the direction your life will take and then you will make your choice. It might be the right one or it might be the wrong one. That part you may never know, not even up to the day you rest your head down on your deathbed."

I sat back in the wood recliner and gazed around at the peaceful surroundings. "I've felt at home since my first day here," I told him. "Not just at your house, but walking the streets, seeing the people, hearing them speak in another language. It all looks and sounds so familiar to me. It is almost as if I'd been here before."

Frederico lifted his eyes up to the sun, his face and neck an interlocking mass of curves and lines. "That alone should help ease the doubts in your head," he said, standing and reaching for a heavy, curved walking cane hanging off a vine. "And maybe the talks we have each day will help take care of the rest."

I put the cups and plates back on the tray and walked with Frederico through the vineyard, listening as he continued the lessons that were designed to prepare me for a life of crime.

• • •

"I THOUGHT I was hooked," I said to Mary, casting a glance over at Angelo. "I forgot about everything else and started to think that maybe this was the way for me. Frederico made it sound so romantic, it was like I was reading from an old book filled with adventure stories. In those stories, they were always the good guys, forced into action because of some injustice. It was never talked about as a business. Only as a way of life."

"It was all done to paint you a picture they wanted you to see." Mary's voice was kind, a warm coat placed over each word. "That was the only purpose of the trip."

"I often wonder if what happened that summer was an act of betrayal or a clear signal to me to find another way," I said to her. "Or was it even a betrayal? It could have just been Angelo, working behind the scenes, to make it all happen the way it did."

"I wish I had the answer," Mary said. "That's one secret he shared with no one. Not even me."

* * *

WE WERE IN a small windowless room with an overhead light hanging from the ceiling, standing around a large oak-legged pool table. A small circular table and two chairs were jammed into a corner. Nico bent over and slammed his cue stick against the three ball, sending it rolling into a side pocket. He walked over to the table, picked up a glass of Sambuca Romana and swallowed it in one gulp. "That was a great shot," he said. "Even if I do say so myself."

"You can say so all you want," I said with a shrug. "Nobody else is going to make a big deal out of it."

"My dollar to your nickel, I make the next three shots," Nico said, picking up his cue stick. "Are you up to it?"

"It should be a thousand lira up against a hundred lira," I said. "I haven't seen a nickel since I got off the plane in Rome."

"It's a bet, then," Nico said, leaning against the side of the pool table, lining up his next shot.

I sat down behind him, my back resting against the cool wall, the flowered paper soft on the skin. I grabbed Nico's pack of Lord cigarettes, pulled one out and lit it. He lifted his eyes from the pool table. "When did you pick that up?" he asked.

I took a long drag from the English cigarette. "It's hard not to smoke around here. Everybody's got one in their hand and an open pack in their pocket. Should I have asked you first?"

"You don't need my permission, Gabe," Nico said, rubbing chalk on the end of his stick. "I'm here to keep an eye out and do whatever it is you might need. If either of us needs to ask for permission, it would be me."

"You're my friend, Nico," I said, putting out the cigarette in a small Martini and Rossi ashtray. "That's the only way you should think of me."

"Don't misunderstand my words," Nico said. "I love you like you were my little brother. But I also know my place and my role. That's to be your shadow and your guide, make sure you get back home in the same shape you were in when you got here. And that's the way it's going to stay, until the boss tells me otherwise."

"Okay if I ask a question?" I said, looking up at his handsome face drawn serious by the direction our conversation had taken. "You don't want to answer it, you don't have to."

"Ask away," Nico said.

"Let's say none of this works out," I said, walking around the pool table. "After all the lessons and the years with Angelo, I decide the life's not for me and I turn my back to it. What if, then, Angelo calls you in and asks you to take me out? Would you do it?"

Nico took a deep breath and exhaled slowly and stared at the wooden floor. "Yes, I would," he said.

"No matter how you felt about me?" I said.

"All that matters is what the boss wants," Nico said. "The boss rules until the boss dies."

I reached behind me and grabbed Nico's cue stick and handed it to him. "It's your shot," I said. "You miss, you lose."

He took the stick and nodded, bending over to line up the balls. I turned around, walked back to the corner, sat down and watched Nico run the table.

• • •

I WAS STEPPING out of the water, a last wave washing over my back, when I saw her. She stood under the shade of a wide blue beach umbrella, drinking an Orangina and sharing a joke with a friend. She was wearing a two-piece bright yellow bikini, her tan as dark as old coal, long brown hair running straight down to her shoulder blades. She was sixteen, had clear, mountain eyes and a smile that could light up a stadium. She turned her head and looked my way. I had never seen anyone as beautiful in my life. I was still a few months shy of my seventeenth birthday and my manner with girls could still best be described as awkward. Compared to the advanced sexual activities of the young men of the island, I was as inexperienced as I was inept. I stood by the water's edge, wiped my face dry with my hands and stared back at the girl under the umbrella.

She left her shaded spot and walked over toward me, her long legs gliding gently along the rich, hot sand. She stood across from me and put out a hand to shake. "I am called Annarella," she said in slow halting English, her voice as sweet as the sounds of the chirping birds I woke up to each morning. "How do you say? Anna? Is that correct?"

"Yes, that's correct," I said, trying not to stammer over my Italian words. "My name is Gabe. I'm an American."

She nodded and smiled, my hand still gripping hers. "I know," she said. "You are staying with Don Frederico. I have seen you there many times."

"Do you live near there?" I asked, freeing her hand. Up close her brown hair was streaked with golden strands, bronzed by their months under the hot sun.

"Not far," she said. "You can walk from my house to his in less than *cinque* minutes." She spread out the fingers of her right hand and showed them to me.

"Five," I said. "*Cinque* is five."

"*Sì, sì,* five," she said, biting gently on her lower lip. "I forget sometimes. I do not have much occasion to speak English. Most of the tourists on the island are Germans."

"I haven't seen many tourists since I've been here," I said. "Must be a slow year."

Anna leaned her head to one side and laughed, sounding more like a young woman than a teenage girl. "On Procida every year is a slow year," she said.

I felt at ease in her company. She had Pudge's ability to turn a five-minute stranger into a five-hour friend. "I was going to walk the beach," I said to her. "Would you like to come? Your friend can come along, if she likes." I pointed over Anna's shoulder at the girl she had been talking to when I had stepped out of the water.

Anna turned and shouted a good-bye to her friend and then looked back at me. "Her name is Claudia," she said. "She has to go back to her job at the bakery, prepare for the lunch business. But I will walk with you."

We walked up and down the long white main beach of Procida most of that morning, the waves cooling our feet, talking and laughing, filling the soft breeze with the innocent chatter of youth. And it was during that long, slow walk that I began my first summer love.

I saw Anna every day after that. We went to movies at the open-air theater, where I discovered she loved Clint Eastwood Westerns as much as I did. We went swimming after my morning lessons with Frederico and would race through the water out to the farthest anchored boat. I marveled at her speed, each lift of her arm and kick of her leg adding an extra length to an insurmountable lead. We would rest against the side of a small boat, Anna wiping the hair from her eyes, me looking for more air to pump into my dry lungs. "I won't leave this island until I beat you in a race," I said to her one morning, my fingers gripping the side of a rowboat as if it were a lifeline.

"That means you will die here a happy old man," Anna said.

I took her to her first dinner date, at a restaurant on the beach that served only seafood. She wore a white dress that night, short at the knee and sleeveless, dark shoes with a half-inch heel, and a blue button sweater her grandmother had knit for just such an occasion. Her hair hung off her shoulders like strands of soft thread. She wore no makeup and her face gleamed from the lights of two candles centered at our table.

"Is it okay for you to have wine?" I asked, sitting across from her, the menu resting flat by my side.

"This is Italy," she said with a light-up-the-night smile. "Wine and water is all we drink. I've had it with dinner since I was in diapers."

"Good," I said, sliding the wine list over to her end of the table. "Then you'll know what to order."

We went on day trips off the island, visiting the neighboring resorts of Capri and Ischia. We took long drives down the Amalfi coast, Nico a constant guide and companion. We stopped for a lunch of grilled sardines in a small café outside Salerno and spent a few pleasant hours mingling with German tourists walking the grounds of the lost city of Herculana. We were taken to the top of Monte Cassino, a monument of honor that Italians considered sacred ground. It was also the site of one of World War II's most brutal battles. "Many people died where we are standing," Anna said, her olive-colored eyes moist. "Many not much older than we are."

"They were soldiers and they were told to fight," I said, putting a hand on her shoulder.

"That's a silly reason to die," she said, walking with her head down, the sun beating off her tan neck.

"I haven't heard many good reasons for young men to die," I said to her. "Not here and not in America."

Anna stood in the middle of Monte Cassino and turned to look at me. "When do you go back to your own country?" she asked.

"The first week in September," I said.

"Will you ever come back?" Anna had her head down, resting against my chest, her warm body feeling as much a part of mine as my own heart.

"I can't make any promises," I whispered, my hands caressing her silk hair. "All I can do is try."

Anna lifted her head and brought her lips to mine and we exchanged our first kiss, standing in the middle of what once had been ground where brave young men had died.

• • •

NICO WAS SPREAD out on the bed, his hands folded behind his head, watching as I dressed for my first dinner with Anna's parents. "You sure wearing black is the way to go?" I asked, glancing at his reflection in the mirror.

"Most of the people on this island dress in black," Nico said. "Every day of their lives."

"They're all widows," I said.

He jumped from the bed, walked over to me and straightened out the collar of my shirt. "Relax. It's only a dinner."

"It's dinner with Anna's parents and I want it to go right."

Nico sat back down on the bed. "I have to tell you, I didn't know what to expect when we got here. Didn't have a feel for how you'd take to the people and their ways. Being on this island is like being drop-kicked back a few centuries. Now, here it is, two weeks later, and you're practically a native. Then, on top of it, you go for a swim and you end up with the best-looking girl on the island on your arm. You have to admit, it beats working as a busboy in the Catskills."

"It's like being in the middle of a dream you never want to see end."

"Those are the ones you always remember."

"There's something I need you to do," I said. "Before dinner."

"I already ordered flowers for her mother, if that's what you're going to ask," Nico said, slipping on a tan jacket.

"It's about Angelo," I said.

"What about him?"

"I tried to get him on the safe phone," I said. "But no one picked up. That's the first time that's ever happened. There's always somebody there to cover that line."

"The guy might have gone to get a cup of coffee," Nico said, heading toward the thick wood doors leading out of the room.

"They're not allowed to leave the phone booth. Those are Angelo's rules and those are your men on that line."

Nico stood at the door and held it open. "Don't make a big deal out of it, Gabe," he said. "I'll have it checked out."

"Have it checked out tonight," I said to him.

"Consider it done." Nico put a hand on my shoulder. "You got nothin' to worry about but mom and pop!"

. . .

ANNA SAT ACROSS from me, dressed in a blue-and-white dress, her hair held from her eyes by two angel pins, her face bright and beautiful. Her father, Eduardo Pasqua, was to my right, sitting at the head of the large dining-room table. He was a tall man with a full, dark beard and a bald head, who carried himself like the successful wine merchant he had been ever since he took over the family business from his father, Giovann Giuseppe. The other head of the table was reserved for Frederico, who was there as a friend and to formally introduce me to the Pasqua clan, which also included a shy older brother, Roberto, and Carla, a precocious six-year-old, who giggled whenever she glanced my way. Frederico's wife, Donatella, dressed in a simple dark blue dress that showed off her aging beauty, sat next to me, her warm hand patting my clammy knuckles whenever I fumbled over a word or botched an Italian phrase. Nico sat across from Anna's mother, a tall, stunning woman with short black hair and an easy laugh, his smooth charm quickly putting her at ease.

As custom dictated, I had presented Anna's father with a gift, one meant to symbolize my good intentions. The gift had to be one that could be used by the entire family; since I didn't have the slightest clue as to what to get, I left the delicate choice up to Frederico. "Eduardo is a proud man," he told me one morning a few days before the dinner, "and he will require a gift that reflects that pride. All the same, we cannot overdo it, because that would insult him. So, it must be one which touches his heart."

"I guess that rules out a dozen roses and a bottle of wine," I said with a shrug.

"Wine he has in abundance," Frederico said, lighting a cheroot and walking alongside me through his groves. "Flowers his signora can pick at will from her garden. Both would be appreciated, but neither would leave them breathless with the joy of your gift."

"Do I give them the gift as soon as we meet?" I asked, a bit overwhelmed by all the rules that needed to be followed.

"No, you must wait," Frederico said, resting a hand on my shoulder. "Until after the *secondo piante, come si dice?*"

"The main course," I said with a nod.

"*Sì*, the main course," Frederico said. "After that, you will make mention of your gift."

"What if he doesn't like it?" I asked.

"Then, *mio caro amico,* we will all at least have had ourselves a good meal," Frederico said. "We will then simply drink our coffees, smoke our cigars and go our way. Still a pleasant night."

"You have so many rules for such a small island," I said.

"We are set in our ways, that is true," Frederico said, looking at me and waving a stubby finger in my direction. "But it makes life so much easier. You always know what is expected, be it a marriage, a funeral or a simple summer meal."

"Then, we better make sure the gift we give is the right one," I said, staring at Frederico. "Nothing less than perfect."

Frederico laughed and shook his head and picked up the pace of his walk. "It is," he said, moving a few lengths ahead of me. "Trust me, *mio caro,* it is truly perfect."

• • •

I CUT INTO a thick slice of lasagna, trying to eat and digest several conversations ongoing at once. Eduardo made sure my wineglass was never empty and he smiled whenever we spoke. I glanced at Anna every few minutes and occasionally caught a comforting look back. I watched as she brought in large platters of food and cleared back to the kitchen the ones that had been emptied. The mood was holiday festive, with Frederico, by far, the happiest of all at the table. The rugged old Don ate until he was full and drank way past sober, knowing all along that he had helped secure such a wonderful gift that Anna and her family would be left speechless with joy.

We had given them a horse.

A prime-quality, two-year-old palomino named Annarella. She had a shiny gold coat, white legs and tail and a white pyramid mark on her face. The gift was as much for Anna's mother as it was for her father, since both loved to ride and were thrilled to own such a fine animal, especially given the fact that it was a rare find in their part of the world. It had taken Frederico a week to have the animal bought, shipped and delivered as he worked quietly, without the use of either phone or telex, to spread the request.

"Are you sure this is what her father would want?" I asked Frederico, standing in the center of his well-lit barn, watching as the palomino took an apple from my palm. "He has a dozen horses in his stables. Why would he want another?"

"Those are workhorses, to help pull the wine carts into town," Frederico said, gently stroking Annarella's mane. "This is a champion and will give him a whole line of champions. This one they all can ride with pride."

"Don Frederico's right on the money," Nico said, admiring the horse from a distance, looking at her legs and muscular front. "If it were up to me, I would have picked up two. One for here and one for the States."

"I didn't know you liked to ride," I said to Nico, letting Annarella rub her nose against my back.

"I've never been on one in my life," Nico said. "I let *others* ride. Like jockeys at the track. A horse like this can bring in millions."

"Her millions will be earned in the pleasure she will bring

to the Pasquas," Frederico said. "You have done well here in such a short time. You have taken to your lessons like a serious young man and have learned to respect our ways. I pray they stay with you for the rest of your life. If they do, I will feel as if I have completed my task."

I walked over to Don Frederico and embraced him, kissing him respectfully on both cheeks. "I won't ever forget you," I said. "Or this place. I'll always remember my days here in your company."

"Then we are both honored," Don Frederico said as he lowered his head, took Annarella's reins and led her back inside her stall.

• • •

THE DINNER WAS nearing its end, as a final glass of Strega was poured for the table.

"Go now, young man," Eduardo said to me after I had downed the bitter drink. "Your time among the old is at an end. I'm sure Anna waits for you, and if she truly is her father's daughter she does so without patience."

"Thank you." I eased myself casually out of the large room that was just down the hall from the dining area.

"Non ce di che," Eduardo Pasqua said with a slight tilt of his head.

"Can I ask one small favor?" I said, reaching for the doorknob. "It would mean a lot to me if you said yes."

"Then ask," Eduardo said. "And I will do my all to see that it is done."

"Can I let Anna take the palomino out for her first ride?"

Eduardo Pasqua looked at me for several long moments, then slowly nodded his head. "She will like that," he said, his voice cracking slightly. "And I will like it even more."

That night, under the smiling glow of a full moon, Anna Pasqua rode the palomino up and down a sand strip on an empty beach of a small vacation island in the middle of the Mediterranean Sea. I sat on the cool sand, my hands folded against my knees, and watched her glide gently past me. The wind stretched her long hair out like a full-blown sail, her hands were loose on the reigns, the splash of the water rose up and wet her dress and the sides of her bare legs. She rode bareback, occasionally leaning over to whisper words that only the horse could hear. In those moments, nothing else mattered and no other place existed. Despite the chill of the night air, my face and arms were warm to the touch and a calm washed over my body.

It was a night I never wanted to see end.

. . .

MY PEACE WAS shattered the next morning. I turned in bed, my face warmed by the early sunlight. I opened my eyes and saw Don Frederico sitting on a wooden chair, his back to me, looking out at the sea lapping gently against the wet sand. "Get dressed and meet me on the terrace," he said, as soon as he heard me stir.

He walked with silent footsteps out of the room and onto the patio. I raced to do as he asked, tossing on a polo shirt and a clean pair of jeans. "What's wrong?" I stood in front of him, the rising sun washing over the cool tiles of the small terrace outside my room.

"There was an attempt made on Angelo's life," Frederico said. His eyes gave weight to his anger. "He was betrayed by one of his own."

"Is he okay?" I could feel my hands and legs shake as I spoke.

"Angelo is a man with many lives. He was shot at twice, both bullets missed."

"Who was behind it?" I asked, stepping closer to the old man.

"I do not know the name of the man who shot at him," Frederico said. "I only know who it was that ordered it done."

I put my hands on Don Frederico's wrists and held them,

helping to brace myself against the rolling shock of emotions I felt. "Who?"

"Nico," Frederico said.

. . .

"IT DIDN'T MAKE any sense," I told Mary, walking alongside her down the hospital corridor. "I had just spent all these weeks learning lessons about honor and loyalty and friendship and then I find out someone Angelo and I both trusted tries to have him killed."

"It would be hard enough for a grown man to understand," Mary said. "It's harder on a seventeen-year-old boy."

"I was living in a world that doesn't allow you to stay young for very long," I said. "I was a kid in the middle of my first summer love when I had to make an adult decision on whether Nico lived or died."

"You could have waited until you and Nico were back in America," Mary said. "Then have Angelo deal with it."

"That wasn't part of their plan," I said. "I had to handle the job on Nico. It was one more lesson I needed to learn."

"You could have said no, Gabe," Mary said, stopping next to a water fountain, bending down to take a long drink. "You could have always said no."

"I didn't know any other way but to say yes. It was how I'd been taught. How I'd been raised. There wasn't any choice in the matter."

"There's always choice," Mary said with defiance. "Especially when someone's life is being decided on. Did you ever think for a moment that you were wrong? That Nico was only part of an even bigger plan that had been designed to keep you where they wanted you kept?"

"Yes," I said, staring back at her. "But I wasn't sure, at least not enough to hold back from what I was asked to do."

"That's the decision of a gangster, Gabe," Mary said. "Not a boy."

"I had to be both," I said and turned away from Mary, walking slowly back to Angelo's room.

. . .

NICO CAME OUT of the trattoria and stepped into the early morning rain. He was holding a coffee in one hand and a panini in the other. A red Fiat was in the alley next to the trattoria, parked front end first, rear wheels lodged up against a small curb. Don Frederico sat with two of his men in a rowboat moored to the pier, directly across the street.

"You told me once you were never cut out to be a boss," I said to him as I stepped around the front of the trattoria. "What changed?"

"I don't see anything that's changed," Nico said, tossing the bread to the side of the street. "You and me, we're both still in Italy and, back home, Angelo's still the boss. It all looks the same to me."

I put my hand into the pocket of my black raincoat and felt for the gun there. "You could have made the move yourself," I said. "Gone up against him on your own, instead of sitting here and sending out somebody who botched the job. That's the move a real boss would have made."

"Is that what they let you think you are now?" Nico asked, lighting a cigarette. "A boss? Or is that something you came up with all by yourself?"

"I thought we were good friends, Nico," I said.

"I work in a business that doesn't allow for friends," Nico said in a sharp tone. "Add that to the lessons the old man taught you. When you go into this as a way of life, then nobody's your friend. And I mean nobody."

I took a deep breath and swallowed hard, sweaty fingers gripping the gun in my pocket. Nico let the cigarette drop from his mouth and ran a hand into the open flap of his jacket. I reached to pull the gun out of my pocket, my hand shaking, heavy sweat mixing with drops of rain running down the front of my face. Nico could have had me at any time, there was no question about it, but he hesitated. His eyes never left mine and his .38 came out much slower than it should have. I heard the first bullet land, saw Nico fall to one leg, and I knew I was shaking too hard to have fired it. I looked to my right and saw one of the men from Don Frederico's boat, a rifle in his hand, firing round after round into Nico's body.

I walked over to Nico and lifted back his head. His eyes were blurry and a thin line of blood flowed out of a corner of his mouth. I didn't have to ask the question. All I had to do was look at him and he answered it for me.

"I'm too old to start killing kids," were his final words.

I stepped away from his body, turned and walked across the street. I got back into the rowboat and sat next to Don Frederico. I watched as the gunman dragged Nico's body from the front of the trattoria and into the alley, lifted him and tossed him inside the front seat of the red Fiat. Don Frederico turned to the man rowing the boat and nodded. The man rested the oars against his knees and picked up a black homing device with a green button in the center. He pressed down on the button and turned his head away from the dock.

The explosion rocked the alley, sending the red Fiat hurtling into the air and landing back down with a flaming thud. The glass from the trattoria shattered and cascaded out onto the street. We were about twenty feet from shore and I closed my eyes to the heat of the blast. I dropped the gun into the bottom of the boat and sat silently next to Don Frederico.

"Gennaro will take you to the airport," he finally said to me as we neared the shore. "You should have more than enough time." Then he pointed toward a dark blue Mercedes that was waiting for us. "Your suitcase is in the trunk. The tickets are on the backseat. Flight seven-eighteen, scheduled to depart at noon."

"I will miss you," I said.

"We will live in each other's memories." Don Frederico gave me a warm embrace. "Both happy and sad ones."

I rubbed my hands across my face, my shirt wet from the rain and the sea, my fingers smelling of dried blood. I turned away from the old man and looked out at the passing Neapolitan scenery, at a place and a people I had come to love in such a short time.

I would see neither of them ever again.

. . .

I WAS NOW well prepared to be a career criminal. I had the proper training and a natural feel for the business. I had a respect for the old-liners like Angelo and Don Frederico. I had been a witness to both murder and betrayal and had my appetite whetted for acts of revenge.

I just didn't have the stomach for any of it.

I didn't want my life to be a lonely and sinister one, where even the closest of friends could overnight turn into an enemy who needed to be eliminated. If I went the way Angelo had paved, I would earn millions, but would never be allowed to taste the happiness and enjoyment such wealth often brings. I would rule over a dark world, a place where treachery and deceit would be at my side and never know the simple pleasures of an ordinary life.

It was during that nine-hour flight back to New York that I decided I wanted to live my days far removed from the evil realm of the criminal. I had to walk away from both the life and from Angelo. I didn't know how he would react, or if I could muster the courage to confront him and tell him how I felt. I was good enough to be a gangster, that I knew. I just didn't know if I was tough enough to tell Angelo that I didn't want to be one.

I tried to sleep but was too restless. I didn't touch any of the food. I stared out the small window at the wide ocean that passed under the wings and vowed not to be swayed by Angelo's forceful personality, and to have the conviction to follow my decision to its natural end. I knew he would give me time to recover from all that had happened in Italy. But I also knew that each day that I allowed to pass would ensnare me deeper into his web and make my escape a much more difficult one.

In the midst of my thoughts, I remembered back to when I

was eleven and sick with a severe respiratory infection. My fever capped out at 105 degrees and no number of blankets could keep me warm. It was on one of those nights that Angelo came into my room, tossed an electric blanket on top of a mountain of quilts and laid down next to me. He rubbed a cool towel against my forehead and rested a hot water bottle on my chest. He whispered the words to an old Italian ballad, "Parle me d'amore, Mariu," in my ear until I had fallen asleep. He stayed by my side until the fever broke.

That was the Angelo few were ever allowed to see. The Angelo I would never fear and always love. The Angelo I needed to find in order to tell him what was in my heart. I sat back and shut my eyes, waiting out the slow descent into JFK and the return to what I had once embraced as a normal life.

• • •

ANGELO SAT ON the edge of a garden chair and let his fishing line hang loose off his left hand, the early-morning sun warming his face and neck. I stood behind him with my back against a wooden mast, the small boat floating free in the middle of Long Island Sound. I had been home for three weeks and this was our first time alone together. The anxiety and unease I felt after Nico's death and my abrupt departure from Italy had not yet vanished. In less than a month I was set to enter college, at a university within walking distance of the bar. I was eager for that day to arrive, seeing it as my first big step toward distancing myself from the criminal world. Angelo viewed my decision to attend college with indifference. He would have preferred not to have to wait another four years before I could begin working full-time by his side. But he also knew that a crime boss with a combination of street knowledge and a degree could prove to be a most lethal weapon to have at his disposal. And so, he stayed silent on the matter.

During those weeks, I kept my own company, choosing to take long walks after my evening meal, turning down frequent requests to go to movies, ball games or the theater. I was in a transition period and sought my comfort in the silent moments such a time afforded. Angelo kept his distance, allowing me as much free ground as I needed. I could feel his eyes on me whenever I walked through the bar. Occasionally, we would look at each other and nod, quick furtive glances meant to convey understanding and concern. He knew Nico's death bothered me and that my time in Italy had changed me, but not entirely in the ways he had hoped. I was heading down a new path and needed to navigate my way through its waters alone. A boy's teenage years can be difficult ones. Mine were made more so, weighted down as I was with the additional burden of attempting to free myself from the addiction of the gangster life.

He stood in the middle of my room, a few feet from my desk, hands in his pockets, hidden by the shadows. As usual, I saw him long before I heard him, looked up, then checked the clock next to my lamp. "Everything okay?" I asked, my eyes eager for more sleep, tired from hours spent reading and watching television.

"Good as it's ever going to be," Angelo said.

"It's almost two," I said. "Not even Ida would want to be walked this late."

"I put some clothes on your bureau. Wash up and put them on. I'll be waiting outside in the car."

"Where are we going?" I asked, as he turned to leave the room.

"I thought we'd pick up something for dinner," he said.

．　．　．

"I DIDN'T KNOW you liked to fish." I looked out at the emptiness of Long Island Sound. "You never mentioned it before."

"I've never done it before. What little I've done so far, I hate."

"So why are we out here? This boat's packed with new fishing poles, gear and enough worms to last a year."

"We need time to talk," Angelo said, dropping the fishing

line at his feet. "And the little I know about fishing is that it's quiet."

"Talk about what?" I was suddenly defensive.

"About you," Angelo said. "And about what happened to you and Nico in Naples."

"You know everything there is to know."

"But you don't. Or at least you're not sure. And I don't want that to boil up inside you like it seems to be doing."

"There isn't anything I need to know," I said with a shrug.

"You need to learn how to live with what happened."

I reached into a packed cooler and pulled out a can of Coke and a quart of milk. I handed Angelo the milk and sat on the wood planks, popping open the soda.

"It was me he wanted dead," Angelo said. "Not you."

"I couldn't kill him," I answered. "Even knowing what they said he tried to do, I still couldn't do it."

"That's because you didn't believe the hit on me was for real. And you still don't."

"How do you survive it?" I asked suddenly, leaning closer to him. "How do you go through every day alone, knowing there's nobody you can talk to, nobody you can really ever trust. How do you do that and not go crazy?"

"I don't think about it." Angelo looked off into the distance. "Not any of it."

"And what do you think about if not that?"

"I think about Isabella," he said. It was the first time I had ever heard him mention her by name. "She's alive to me, even after all these years. She keeps me happy, inside, in places where no one can see."

"If she had lived . . ." I started. He had opened the door and I was eager to enter and ask as many questions about her as he would allow. But now that I had the opportunity, I wasn't sure what I wanted to ask. As always, however, Angelo knew.

"I would have been a better man if she had lived," Angelo said, a soft break to his voice, "but not as good a gangster."

"How long did it take for you to work that out?" I asked.

"I'm still working it out. She's the only piece of me that's alive. Nobody else sees it. Nobody else knows it. But I see it and I feel it. Every day I can touch that part of her that's in me. Some days she's clearer than others. You've been around me long enough to tell when my days are dark."

I nodded and glanced past him at the waves hitting the side of the boat. "Did it help taking care of the ones who shot her?"

"No," he said, shaking his head. "You feel good that they're dead, but they're just triggers without faces. And it's not killing you're looking for. It's keeping alive what you once had in your arms."

"Do you ever see her? Isabella? I don't mean like a ghost. I mean as if she were real, as if she were still alive?"

"Lots of times. In different places. I'll catch a glimpse of a face crossing the street or a head turning my way at the track. Sometimes I'll even see her on a TV show, walking in the background. And each one of those women looks just like what Isabella would have looked like if she were still alive. To my eyes, anyway."

"I'm sorry," I said, my hand on top of his as it gripped a railing.

"You have a difficult decision to make," Angelo told me, clenching his other hand over mine. "Take all the time you need to find your balance and your place. Get through college, if that's important to you. In time, you'll come to me and tell me what it is you want to do."

"I already know," I said.

He looked up at the sun, wiped his brow with a silk handkerchief and ignored my last statement. "I think it's time we took this boat back to shore."

"I said that I already know what I want to do," I repeated. "And maybe it's time for you to hear it."

Angelo took a long drink from the milk container and nodded. "Tell me, then," he said.

"I love you for all that you've done for me." The words came out slowly, buffered by the passing wind. "All that you've taught me."

Angelo tossed the quart of milk against the side of the boat and stood, his dark eyes glaring into mine. "*Tell* me," he said, in a voice crammed with danger.

"I want out," I finally managed, sweat running down my back, my hands holding on to the mast for support. "I can't be what you want me to be. I don't want to look over my shoulder the rest of my life, waiting for a bullet that I know will eventually come. I don't want to run a crew, not knowing who I can trust or who's planning to move against me. And I don't want to end up an old man sitting in a boat, without anyone in the world I could call a friend."

"I thought you were my friend," Angelo said, the words filled with venom.

"I am," I said. "But I'll always be more than that, too."

"Not if you leave," he spit. "It's your choice, what you do with your life. But remember, with choice there's also risk. You've been protected by me all these years. You turn your back on me now, you go out there alone. And that's something you've never tasted before."

"I have no idea what it's going to be like for me in the real world," I said. "But I do know what it'll be like for me in *your* world. And I don't want any part of that."

"Then you don't want any part of me." For the first time in my life he looked at me with hate in his eyes, and it staggered me. "Once we get to shore, it ends between us."

I was suddenly overcome with an urge to cry, realizing how cruel and hurtful my words must have sounded. "I won't ever betray you."

"You just did," Angelo said.

"I'm choosing to lead my own life." I could hear the defiance coming back to my voice. "That's all I've done."

"And I'll allow you to do it," Angelo said. "That will be your punishment. You'll be set free and left alone. The world you've known since you were a child will disappear just as easily as it appeared."

"I didn't mean for it to end this way," I told him.

"But it did," he said, then turned his back to me.

Neither one of us spoke during the five-mile ride back to shore. I knew what happened that morning would never be forgotten by either one of us. He had allowed me entry into a part of his life he had kept sealed all these years and I had returned the kindness by crushing his greatest desire. After this day, neither one of us could ever fully trust the other again. I knew that many years would pass before I would see him, if I ever did, yet I wondered if he would really stay out of my life.

The most dangerous gangster is the one willing to kill what he loves the most, and there was none as dangerous as Angelo. He had no other choice. It was the only way he knew how to live.

• • •

"YOU MAY NOT know him as well as you think," I told Mary. "You may not even realize all that he's capable of doing. All of it in the name of love."

Mary let go of the IV pole and came over to me. "You're wrong about that, Gabe. There isn't anything he did that I don't know about. Especially when it came to you."

"What right do you have to know anything about me?"

"All the right in the world. It was the one thing Angelo could never deny me."

"Why?" I asked.

"One of the reasons I came here was to see you, and not just to tell my story but to listen to yours. There's still more that needs to be told and I need to hear that from you. Then, when that's done, I'll leave you with the end of mine."

"I hope it's worth it," I told her, forcing myself to stay calm.

"It will be," Mary said. "That I promise."

19

Summer, 1980

I WAS STANDING in the middle of the conference room, listening to my coworkers laugh about their weekend, when she walked in. She wore a gray suit with the skirt cut several inches above the knee, a white ruffled blouse and brown shoes with three-inch heels. Her hair was light brown and curled and she had a pretty teenage face on a shapely woman's body. She had a brown leather carrying case in one hand and a cup of coffee in the other, some of it spilling out from the bottom of a white paper bag. She walked with a slight swagger as she headed directly toward me.

"I'm Janet Wallace," she said, putting out a hand for me to shake.

I held her hand and pointed to one of the leather chairs surrounding the table. "Grab a seat. We were just about to get started. I'll introduce you as we go along. We're not the best-looking group in town, but we pay the rent, have some laughs and, every once in a while, come up with a campaign that people like and remember."

Jeff Magnuson, my thirty-one-year-old creative director, sat to her right and reached for her coffee. "How about we share that?" he asked.

"How about we don't," Janet said, pulling the cup back. "It's my first cup of the day."

I sat across from the two and introduced the rest of my

team. "Jack Sampson is my art director," I said, nodding toward a bald, overweight man in his mid-forties eating a bagel with scallion cream cheese. "He's starting a new diet . . . tomorrow."

"I'd offer you half my bagel," Jack said. "But it doesn't sound like you're the type who shares."

"I'm not." Janet smiled.

"And this muscle-bound gym rat pacing behind me is Tim Carlin," I continued. "He writes most of our copy, usually while he's bench pressing over at the West Side Gym."

Tim lifted a large plastic bottle of papaya juice in her direction and Janet nodded in return. "And you've talked with me on the phone," I went on. "I'm Gabe and they're all nice enough to let me run the place."

"Two more weeks and there'll be a takeover," Jeff said to her. "I'll probably end up running the agency. Which still leaves you time to rethink that coffee."

"I'll take my chances," Janet said, holding the cup close to her lips.

"I must have missed a memo," Tim chimed in. "What is she doing here?"

"You never read the memos," Jack said. "If you did, you'd know this young lady is the new hatchet that Gabe's been nice enough to bring in to threaten our job security."

"They're always a little surly before lunch," I explained, looking over at Janet. "We're a little behind on the Bradshaw account. On top of that we've got a GM deadline that's less than two months away and we could use a boost on the Compaq print ads."

"And you're the one who's going to give us all that?" Jeff asked.

"As much of it as you can handle," Janet told him.

I sat back and watched as the banter between my group and Janet moved along at an accelerated pace. It was their way of welcoming her to the team. I had offered her a full-time job and been turned down. She liked the life of a freelancer, content on going from place to place, deciding when and where she wanted to work. She signed on for a three-month stay, enough to help get us past our overloaded schedule. She was smart, had a first-class portfolio and seemed suited to the tight quarters of a busy agency.

"Why am I always the last to know about hires?" Henry Jacobs, the company business manager stood over me, hands on his hips, demanding an answer.

"Because you always tell me we can't afford another hire," I said.

"That's because we can't." Henry shook his head in frustration. "But you go ahead and hire them anyway. Why even bother having a business manager if you're going to do that?"

"You're the only one who knows what the soup of the day is at Bun 'n' Burger," I said. "And that's a skill I can't run this company without."

.   .   .

ANGELO HAD KEPT his word. He had given me back my life. I moved out of my room above the bar and was quickly taught the lessons that came with living in the real world—college loans, part-time jobs, small apartments with large rents, cheap cars and even cheaper meals. I had not chosen the best time to embark on a life of my own. The country was in the midst of a recession. Interest rates would soon hit an eye-blinding 21.5 percent, with inflation topping out at 12.4 percent, and President Jimmy Carter was seemingly unable to bring a halt to either one. It was a struggle, but one I enjoyed. While I still, on occasion, longed for the excitement and the sense of power my previous existence held out, I was now able to spend my days and nights free of that world's dark shadows. I had been taught since an early age to hate the civilian world. I was told it was a treacherous environment whose rules were not meant to be followed, and that the only route to success in such a place was by using methods and means that would make the most hardened of criminals take a step back. "You have to watch your every move," Angelo had told me over and over. "The guy you think is a friend is the one that's making the jump to screw you out of a promotion. Then you go and bust your back on a job and some plodding ass-kiss makes nice with the boss and walks away with the credit."

"Sounds a lot like what you do," I said. "I don't see much of a difference."

"The difference is that with us, you're always on the look-out for that. That's what we're supposed to do. But out there, with the diplomas on the wall and the nice offices, the game's written to be played different. Only it's not. Believe me, they're no better than any hood. I don't care who comes up and tries to tell you otherwise."

As happy as I was being on my own, I did miss Angelo. I longed for his company and his words of advice, but he had shut all doors leading to that path. During my time away, I tried to see him on several different occasions, but was al-ways turned back by one of his crew. Treated just like any other civilian.

But I also knew I wasn't totally free. Not as long as Angelo was still alive. I had lived in his company long enough to know there was still one more move left. I didn't know when it would come or from what direction, but I knew to be ready for its arrival. I could not allow myself to be lulled by his de-cline into old age or be blinded by his silence. I could never lose sight of one of the most important lessons I had been taught in all our years together: Watch out for the gangster who wants you to think he's weak. That's when he's at his most dangerous.

• • •

I HAD WORKED my way up the agency ranks and now, four years after college, I was in control of a growing ten-member firm. The start-up money was not much of an issue. While Angelo's financial door was sealed shut, Pudge had left me a sizable active trust fund that I was allowed to borrow against, providing I could show cause. I found it satisfying that it was Pudge, from the silence of his grave, who provided me with the cash that helped me keep clear of Angelo's reach. The rest of the money was put together through a loan, secured from a bank that had a long-standing history of working with start-up companies. I relished the idea of building a team, pursuing an idea, conceptualizing it and bringing it to life, be it a thirty-second spot or a full-color spread in a high-end magazine. I hired men and women who not only were good at the work they did but took pleasure from it. I wanted my workers to be sincere in their efforts and I sought to keep office politics and company rumors to a minimum. I was proud of my group and we moved quickly from small accounts with local merchants to six-figure deals with large corporations. It was a good working environment and a safe refuge from Angelo's haunting glare.

Yet I always felt his presence. It had been years since I had seen him and I had grown from boy to man in that time, but still I felt his power, his eyes on my every move. I told no one at work of our relationship. If anything, his name would awaken a vague memory at best, someone who they had read about in a newspaper or seen on some old newsreel footage. He was not a threat to them, but he was to me. I could never shake the feeling that my actions were being monitored, my activities recorded, my every move documented and brought back to his attention. I knew it was probably more paranoia than reality, but I had been raised to be careful. I always took note of who was near me in a restaurant or crowded theater. I checked the sidewalk traffic around me, kept my phone number unlisted and never said anything in public that I wouldn't want heard in private. These were my only concessions to the world I had left behind.

I was twenty-six years old and had brought a secure structure to my life. I read constantly, filling the gaps in my education with books I should have gone through in my younger years. I went to the theater once a month and saw a new movie every week, usually with one of the guys from work. I began to haunt art galleries and openings, buying paintings and hanging them on the walls of my apartment. I had season tickets to the Mets and, on rare occasions, would even venture out to the opera and the ballet. It was a full life and, more important, an honest one.

I did keep up with the business of organized crime, a fascination, I feared, that would never fade. I read as much about the life as I could, always able to separate fact from the gritty sales pitch of a tabloid headline. The rackets had changed in the decades since Angelo and Pudge first shoved a gun in a victim's face. If possible, there was now even more money to be made, more action to cover. The smartest of the young gangsters were busy working on plans to lay down their guns and pick up their computers. They were leaving the murder game to the new ethnic gangs that had invaded their universe, from the Russian hoods to the urban street thugs, neither of whom understood the complexities of modern business. These young crew chiefs knew that a brokerage house could be run in the same manner as a loan-sharking operation. They attempted a quiet takeover, had others front the business for them, while they pulled in all the profits on commissions and investments. It was a much cleaner way to do business without the specter of having to do thirty years behind bars.

The new formula also embraced Angelo's theory that a stretch in prison was not crucial to a gangster's education. "There were people who believed that doing time made you a better criminal," he once told me. "I never bought into that thinking. Me and Pudge were high-profile hoods but we made sure we never rubbed the cops' faces in it, didn't burn them with what we did. We worked under the radar as best we could. In my business, better to be a submarine than a destroyer. Let the other guy make the noise, get the attention, talk to the papers and the TV cameras. That way only leads to indictments. I only cared about profits and growing the business."

There were many days when I wondered how well I would have done, how successful I would have been in taking Angelo's solid criminal foundation and expanding it onto modern turf. But then, I would just as quickly shift my focus back to the ad campaign that needed my attention, knowing that all I had to fear from where I sat was my business losing its edge and failing or a large corporation moving in and attempting a takeover. I found it comforting to know that neither one of those moves would end up costing me my life.

· · ·

JANET WALLACE WAS thirty years old and had been raised in upper-class comfort in a Michigan suburb. She had graduated from Brown University, excelled in every class she took and got her first advertising job in Pittsburgh, with a firm that still farmed work out her way. She had a shy manner that could be perceived as cold by those who didn't know her well and she carried herself with a distant air. She was quick to dismiss any notions of an office fling, making it clear to all parties that she was there only to do a job. I didn't know much about her personal life other than what was in her résumé and cover letter and I didn't care to ask. She mixed in well with my team and was a tenacious worker, clever with words and creative in her concepts. She held her own in the meetings, spoke her mind and demonstrated a sharp sense of humor.

I did get a sense from what she said and, more important, didn't say, that there was a part of her she preferred to keep hidden and out of public view. It helped give her a sense of mystery, one that balanced out the shyness. I hadn't said more than a handful of words to her in the time she worked at my agency, but I felt as if I knew her as well as I did some of the workers who had been with me from the company's first day. The more I saw of her, the more I liked, moving me closer to a place I'd never thought I'd find.

· · ·

I KNOCKED ON her cubicle wall, half-startling her. She looked at me and checked her watch. "The meeting's not for another ten minutes," she said. "I was hoping to finish this design before it started. See what the guys thought of it."

"I like grilled fish," I said to her. "I'm not that big on sushi. How about you?"

"I hate anything that's not cooked," she said.

"Do you know which restaurant makes the best grilled fish in the city?"

"No," she said.

"Good," I said. "Because I do. We'll have lunch there. I'll meet you at one over by the elevator."

"I already packed my lunch," she said. "I was planning to eat at my desk and work straight through."

"Give it to Jeff," I said. "He'll eat it, no matter what it is."

"Do I get a chance to say yes or no?" she asked.

"Is there a chance you might say no?"

"Yes," she said.

"Then no," I said and turned away.

 •   •   •

I SPENT THE next three weeks working alongside Janet, help-ing her and my team bring to life the three campaigns we needed to rush through. We began work while others still slept, sipping coffee and eating buttered rolls under the lights of her desk. We ate our lunch together, the offices cluttered with folders filled with designs and ad copy. We left the office after midnight and stopped for a drink at any open bar we could find, talking strategy and seeking the right words that would help us sell an old product to new customers. The job consumed us both.

We delivered the first draft on our biggest account on a Thursday and I gave the staff a three-day break while we waited for a decision to be handed down. "Do you have plans?" she asked, walking with me on Third Avenue, both of us heading for a small, smoky restaurant that had quickly grown into a regular haunt. "For the three days, I mean."

"Not really. I don't like to make plans too far in advance."

"It might be a good time to catch-up with your girlfriend. Try to explain why you've been spending so much of your time with another woman and a roomful of men."

"That would be a great idea," I told her. "If I had a girl-friend that I needed to explain all of that to."

"I'm sorry to hear that," she said. "I bet you'd make a good boyfriend."

"What about you?" I asked. "Who do you have to explain yourself to?"

"I'm going back to Pittsburgh. I need to finalize my divorce. I've been delaying it until we had the first draft in."

"I didn't even know you were married." I was not able to coat the surprise in my words. "I mean, you never mentioned a husband."

"Technically, I'm not a wife anymore," she said. "And it was never much of a marriage. Lasted less than six months. We both knew soon enough it was a mistake and we looked to get out about as quickly as we got into it."

"That can't be an easy thing to go through," I said, my fingers grasping her elbow, her skin soft and warm.

"I thought like every other woman that it would be perfect," she said, her eyes sad. "But it wasn't. It wasn't even close."

"You'll find somebody again, Janet," I said, trying to ease her obvious pain. "It'd be a cinch to fall in love with somebody like you."

"That's nice to hear. I'm starting to think it's not going to happen. I have a bad habit of picking the wrong guys for all the wrong reasons. It's time I broke myself of that."

"Maybe it's the restaurants you like to eat in." I held the door for her as she walked into the burger shop. "You're not exactly drawn to top of the line cuisine."

"What's wrong with them?" she asked, feigning anger. "You can smoke, the wine comes out of a jug and the cheese-burgers come with a side order of bacon. Besides, the waiters make me laugh."

"You mean like Frank over there?" I followed her down to a corner booth and pointed out a waiter in a stained white shirt. "Did you hear him the other day, talking to a woman at a back table?"

"No, what?"

"He comes to the table and the woman asks him why he has his thumb on her steak. And Frank says, 'So I don't drop it again.' I have to admit. That's something you'd never see at Twenty-one."

Janet snapped her head back and laughed. I found myself staring at her in a way I had never looked at a woman. She caught my look and held it, stretching her fingers across the table and touching my hand. "Thank you," she said in a soft voice. "You've helped make these last few weeks a very special time for me."

"What happens from here?" I fought the urge to wrap my fingers around hers. "After we finish up the other two projects?"

"That's pretty much up to you," Janet said.

I nodded and waited as Frank slid two bacon cheeseburger platters in front of us, winking at me as he did. "I still don't want a full-time job," she announced as soon as he walked away. "And I don't think I can keep working for you."

"Why not? You've been a great addition to the team. As good as my guys are, none of them can do the kind of quality work that you can in a short amount of time."

"I'm not talking about the work. That part was great. But . . . I like you, Gabe. I like you very much. And if we keep working together, seeing each other for as many hours a day as we do, it's not going to be good for either one of us."

"You're too old for me, Janet," I told her.

"And younger men are nothing but trouble," she said, not bothering to hide her smile.

"I have strong feelings for you." I was surprised to hear my own words. "To be totally honest, I don't quite know how to handle them. I've never felt like this about anybody else." At least not anybody who didn't carry a gun, I thought to myself.

Janet wiped her mouth and leaned across the table, holding both my hands. "The time we've spent together has been special to me as well, more than you'll ever know. But there might be too many obstacles in our way."

"Give me a for instance," I said.

"There's the age difference, for one."

"A minor one," I pointed out.

"Well, how about the fact that, even though I'm much better at it than you are, you're still my boss."

"I thought you were quitting."

"Okay, then let's not forget one other small detail. I'm still married. At least in the eyes of the law."

I looked out the window, watching hurried faces rush eagerly back to work or run to catch a distant cab or a moving bus. "I've never been concerned with the eyes of the law," I said.

• • •

OUR TIME TOGETHER was magical. In Janet, I had found someone who made me feel whole, who loved me readily despite all my apparent limitations at grasping life in a world she knew so much better than I did. She loved me without condition, asking little in return and assuming nothing other than I stay with her for as long as our emotional ride lasted. We had grown together as friends before we became lovers and that gave us a solid foundation to build on. I had not known anyone like her before and I felt the same was true from her about me. We trusted each other and knew that neither one would ever do anything to knowingly betray that bond.

We all struggle in our lives trying to find a person somewhere who makes the perfect fit and most of us are never successful in our search. And now, deep into my twenties, I had found that person in Janet, and I was determined not to lose her.

I believed that she would be the final piece of a complicated puzzle that would completely sever the emotional ties I still might have to the gangster life. I had turned my back on a power that I might never know in the civilian world and had adjusted well to it. I did not see what I had done to be any great sacrifice on my part, but rather a breaking of life-restraining bonds which enabled me to feel free and allowed me to fall in love with a woman who had lived only in my dreams. But I also remained cautious; I had spent too many years in the company of hoodlums not to do otherwise. I worried, and had for years, that Angelo had not completely surrendered his quest. That the shadows I suspected of casting their gaze in my direction, alert to my every movement, would soon emerge from their hiding place, ruled by his hand, and lash out at me in a final attempt to weld me to their side.

But for now, I continued my steps toward a real life, with a woman in whose company I felt warm and happy and safe. In those heady early days wrapped in Janet's soft arms and hidden in the womb of her small apartment, I had found the secret to a complete life. I had found my escape in someone with whom I could share my journey.

I had found Janet Wallace.

And I had found love.

20

Fall, 1980

JANET AND I had been together for two months before I told her about Angelo and the early years of my life. We were having coffee at a small table facing a large window that looked out at the New Jersey skyline. She remained silent for several minutes after I had finished and then looked up at me. "Are you in any danger?" she asked.

"If he thought I was a threat to him he would have killed me years ago," I said. "I've never had to worry about that."

"Then maybe you don't have to worry about anything at all," she said. "It's been years since you've seen him. And you said he's never approached or confronted you in all that time. He might just have accepted your decision and left it at that."

I reached for the coffeepot and refilled both our cups. "The only decisions he accepts are his own. No one else's have ever mattered, mine included."

Janet added milk to one and cream to the other and leaned back in her chair. "What are you afraid of?" she asked, her eyes locked into mine.

"I don't think he's ever left me," I admitted. "I feel his hand behind everything I've done since the day I left the bar. It's all gone so well, so quickly, that I just can't lay everything down to hard work and a little luck."

"You're very good at what you do, Gabe. There might not be anything more to it than that."

"About a year ago I was bidding on a job at Nissan," I told her. "It came down to two companies, mine and Tom Hannibal's agency. Two nights before the final bids, I came into work and found a packet on my desk. Inside I found Tom's proposal and projected campaign. It was everything Nissan was looking for and as fresh and clever as anything that was out there. Hands down his was twice as good as mine. He was a lock to land the account."

"And did he?"

"No," I said. "He dropped out the night before the presentations were due. He claimed his agency was overworked and couldn't handle the extra workload."

"Then why go to all the trouble to do the proposal to begin with?" Janet shook her head and finished her coffee.

I reached across the table and held her hand. "I promise I won't ever let him hurt you," I said.

"Me?" she asked. "Why would he want to hurt me?"

"If he's going to make a move, it'll be against you." I was well aware that my words were making her nervous. "You'll be the target to get to me."

"How can you know that for sure?" She took a deep breath as she spoke.

"Because I know Angelo," I said.

"How much longer will he wait?" Now a trace of anger moved in alongside the fear.

"I got a call from one of his men yesterday," I told her. "Angelo wants to see me."

"What did you say?"

"Nothing. I listened, put down the phone and came home to you."

I stood and walked over to the window, staring down at the traffic. Janet stepped up behind me and wrapped her arms around me. "When do you go?" she whispered.

"Tomorrow night," I said.

. . .

THE DRIVER, A burly young associate named Gino, brought
the car to a stop next to a fire hydrant across from the Duane
Reade on Broadway and Seventy-first and watched as I slid
into the passenger seat. He nodded at me, then shifted into
gear and pulled the dark sedan back into the traffic to begin
the slow ride downtown. I was wearing dark slacks and a dark
button-down shirt, clothes I hadn't touched in years, but figured appropriate for this meeting. I leaned my head against
the soft leather and realized what troubled me the most was
the unknown. I was unsure from which direction Angelo's
final attack would come. While I knew it would not be fatal, I
still wondered if, by its end, I would be able to escape from it
intact.

Any gangster can rid himself of an enemy with a bullet. A
great one seeks to conquer the mind of his opponent as well
as his body. In my case, my war with Angelo would not be one
of turf but of control. He was prepared to pit his will against
my love for Janet. It was a match I was sure he looked forward
to as much as I dreaded.

"How long since you've seen the old man?" Gino asked,
weaving his way through street traffic.

"How long have you been working for him?" I asked.

"Five years, going on six now," Gino said.

"And have you ever seen me before?"

"I heard about you from some of the other guys in the
crew," Gino said. "But tonight's the first I laid eyes on you."

"You ever drive Angelo?" I asked.

He shook his head.

"Let me give you some advice then," I said. "Never talk to
people you don't know. And if you really want to go far, it'd
be better not to talk at all. That's especially true if Angelo's
ever sitting in the back. It might let you live a few years
longer."

"I'll try to keep it in mind," Gino said with a shrug.

"You can start practicing now." I turned my head and

stared up at the lights of the empty buildings that lined the streets.

· · ·

ANGELO SAT ON the couch, his feet stretched out on a hand-made stool, the ever-present large glass of milk resting, half empty, on the coffee table. He had aged a great deal in the years since I'd last seen him, his fine facial features beginning their inevitable surrender to the advances of time. His right hand shook slightly and the rasp that rose out of his lungs had grown worse, the scars of birth often forcing him to breath through his mouth and become more dependent on his spray medication.

I stood in the middle of the well-lit den. It was a room where I had spent so many of my younger days reading the books stacked on the shelves while Pudge scanned the day's racing sheet, tracking the bookmaking take. There was a desk near the large window in the corner with yellow folders stacked high on top of it. Next to the desk lamp were two packages, wrapped and tied together with string.

We were both looking at a corner of the den, watching a two-month-old pit bull try to lock jaws around a thick bone-shaped chew. "Did you get yourself another Ida?" I asked, nodding toward the white puppy.

"This one's a Pudge," he said, turning away from the dog to look at me. "And he goes his own way. Just like the guy he's named after."

I stared down at the empty cup of coffee in my hand, thinking of Pudge and how much I missed having him in my life. "He looks like he'll be good company for you," I said.

"It's an interesting business you've chosen," Angelo began, his hands resting flat on his legs. "You come up with the right words and pictures and people go out and buy what it is you tell them to buy."

"Something like that."

"Still, it can be treacherous. A big agency sees a little one doing well, it makes a move to buy it and swallow it up. The little guy ends up with some cash in his hand and his company in somebody else's pocket. That almost happened to you last year. I forget the name of the agency that tried to buy you out?"

"The Dunhill Group," I told him, although I knew it was unnecessary. There was no way he had forgotten the name.

"That's right," he nodded. "They own a couple of construction companies, too. It was the wrong time for them to make a move. Their finances were stretched a little thin."

"I would have handled it," I said.

"Who said you didn't?" Angelo feigned a casual indifference, but I had seen that hard look in his eyes many times and it never reflected a happy mood.

"What did you want to see me about?"

"A woman you know," he said.

"Why?"

"What is she to you?" he asked, ignoring my question.

"Someone I love," I said. "Someone I'd like to marry."

"How much does she know about you? About your life here?"

"I've told her what she needs to know," I explained. "If she's going to marry me, it's only fair."

"And what do *you* know about *her*?"

I looked down and watched the puppy gnaw on the edges of my desert boots, his small teeth sinking into the soft heel. I leaned over and petted the top of his head. "That when she tells me she loves me she means it," I said, looking at Angelo.

"Do you know her well enough to trust her?" he asked.

"More than anyone I know," I said.

Angelo picked up two sheets of paper that were resting on the coffee table. "Her name is Janet Wallace and she's thirty years old," he said. "She comes from a successful, upper-class family in Dearborn, Michigan. Her father was a full partner in a small accounting firm and died when she was in college. Her mother works for the local city council and is active in a variety of civic groups. Janet is an only child and graduated with honors and earns $55,000 in a good year. She smokes a pack of Marlboros a day and drinks wine with lunch and dinner."

"I know all that," I told him, my eyes never straying from his face.

"Now let me tell you what you don't know," Angelo said.

I could feel sweat break out against the back of my neck, my eyes looking at the folders and the two wrapped packages, the room around me suddenly feeling smaller. My mouth was dry and my face felt hot. "I can stop now," he said, walking slowly toward the desk.

I shook my head. "Finish it."

He stood behind the desk, picked up a folder and opened it. "This woman you love and trust so much has had many lovers before you," he said. "These folders will tell you all about them. They're from all over. One's a writer, one an actor, a few lawyers, a plastic surgeon, a cop, even a drug dealer. Three years ago she got pregnant with one of them, only she wasn't sure which one. But she cleared up that problem. She was into drugs pretty heavy, cocaine and grass mostly, and drank a lot more than she does now. This guy she just divorced is an AA dropout who dropped back into cocaine."

He put down the folder and picked up the two wrapped packages. "She's posed for nude photos," he said, looking up at me. "One of her old boyfriends was fond of cameras. He sold the photos to some people in Michigan; that's how I got them. Most are your standard T and A shots. The ones in this package give you a little more. The other package is a video. She went out with an actor for a few weeks, some guy who was in a commercial she was putting together. She spent most of the nights in his place, not knowing he'd hidden cameras all around the rooms. He likes to make films of himself having sex and show them at parties. I bought those, too. You want the full details, you'll find it all in the folders."

I looked at him and took a deep breath. "How?"

"She keeps a diary," he said. "Some of the pictures were even there, up on one of the bookshelves. Once I found that, the rest fell into place."

I glared down at Angelo and walked closer to the desk. "You would never have done this if Pudge were still alive," I said to him.

"Neither would you," he said.

Angelo stood up and walked over to me. "You can stay the night," he said. "Read the folders or throw them away. They belong to you. When morning comes, you can go back to her or stay here, where you belong. She's wrong for you. That world, out there, is wrong for you. This is your place. This is what's right. You can't turn your back to it anymore."

"I'm already where I belong," I said.

"This woman ever say she loves you?" Angelo asked.

I nodded.

"Do you believe her when she says it?" he asked.

Again I nodded.

"Do you think all those other men believed her, too?"

"I believed you when *you* said you loved me," I said. "Was I wrong to do that?"

"Nobody's ever going to love you like I do," Angelo said.

"Was it love or was it just business?"

"We've both thrown away a lot of years if you don't know the answer to that," he said.

"Then why are you doing this?" I asked.

"To save you," he said, lowering his head and walking toward the door.

"What about Nico?" I took a step closer to him. "Was that really a takeover? Or was he another piece of the plan to save me and keep me here with you."

"He was whatever you think he was," Angelo said, glaring at me.

"I have something in my life now that you don't have," I told him. "Something you can't ever have."

"What?" he growled.

"Someone to love," I said. "And someone who loves me."

"I had that." His lips barely moved as he spoke. "You know I had that."

"Then let me have it, too," I pleaded. "Let Janet be my Isabella."

"She can never be that," he whispered.

"You lost her. It was *you*. This life of yours cost you all the years of her love. I won't let that happen to me."

"Does that make you the better man?" he asked.

I shook my head and said, "No, just a lucky one."

He turned to look back at the desk filled with folders. "Luck runs out," he said. "For all of us."

Angelo opened the door and left the room.

$\bullet \quad \bullet \quad \bullet$

I WALKED AROUND the desk and sat down, my hands stretched out across the folders. I picked one up and opened it, resting it on my lap. I tossed aside a head shot of a middle-aged man with dark hair and a thin beard and began to read through the neatly typed, double-spaced information. I sat there well into the morning hours and read through each folder. I then opened one of the wrapped packages and looked at the fifteen 8 x 10 black-and-white photos. Next, I grabbed the video and slid it into the VCR resting under the TV next to the desk. I sat back in the leather chair and stared at the twenty-five-inch screen and watched Janet make love to a thin man with short hair and a wiry body.

I sat in the chair, in a room that held so many warm memories and watched the screen go blank, the photos strewn about the floor around me. I stood up and turned off the television. I picked up an open folder, stared down at it and then tossed it against the farthest wall. I picked up another and did the same. I kept going until I had thrown every folder across the room, all the pages landing on the floor and on top of furniture. I then walked over to one of the bookshelves and picked up a framed photo of Angelo standing in front of the bar with me sitting on a stool next to him, my arms on his shoulders, a big smile on my face. I was twelve in the picture and had been living with him for two years. I wiped at the tears running down my face, lifted the photo and smashed it against the wall.

In that room, hidden behind all those folders and photos and video, Angelo Vestieri had lost his battle.

He had left in his wake a free man.

And even then, even after the brutality of what he had just done, I couldn't help but wonder if all of it had been part of an even bigger plan. That this was his way of opening a final escape path, convinced that I had found a love that was as strong as what he had himself once felt. There was no way for me to ever know the truth.

Such is the mystery and power of Angelo Vestieri.

. . .

I NEVER WANTED Janet to have to defend her life choices to me. After all, the man holding her in judgment had killed and stolen and lived off the blood of others for most of his life. I could not denounce her morally, for I, too, had done much worse than she ever had. She sought out love and romance to quench her lonely desires while, for many years, I looked only to revenge and quick money. She was also a product of the world she knew and in such a place she did not commit a wrong. I was a product of a violent society that held others up to an unforgiving code of honor. We were two different people who met at a point in our lives when each filled a void in the other. From a brief spark of passion a blaze of love had bloomed.

I went back to Janet two nights later and have stayed with her for sixteen years.

I never spoke to her about my night with the folders that were filled with her private history. I didn't have to really; in my silence and in my actions, she was smart enough to know what had happened. Every life has a vulnerable point, a place where the most painful damage can be inflicted. Angelo had found Janet's and exploited it with the full arsenal of his power. His attack had left me weakened, but he had failed in one crucial area. He could not make me stumble from that room hating the woman I loved. Our hearts were strong enough to withstand a gangster's fury.

We were married six months after that night I had spent on the top floor of Angelo's bar. We chose a friend's apartment for the occasion and the short ceremony was presided over by a minister who had driven in from the suburbs and was thirty minutes late. Janet looked happy and beautiful, a bride for the second time in little more than a year. I was still in the midst of climbing out of the large emotional hole Angelo had thrown me into, confident that I no longer needed his care or guidance to find my way.

Janet and I made a life together. We had two children and both managed successful careers. At night, as they were tucked under the warm blankets of sturdy beds, I would tell both my children the stories of the people I knew and the ones I had heard so much about. Their minutes before sleep were filled with the tales of Angus McQueen, Ida the Goose, Pudge Nichols and a string of pit bulls named after each one. Along the way, as they got older, I began to tell them about Angelo Vestieri. They were all an important part of my life. It was my history and now it belonged to them as well.

As with any long marriage, Janet and I faced low periods intermingled with the highs, but the love and passion that had helped forge the union only grew greater with the passage of time. She was all that I hoped and never did I ever regret turning my back on the life that once so clearly seemed to be my destiny. In that way, Janet Wallace proved to be much stronger than Angelo Vestieri.

I now had the life that Paolino Vestieri had envisioned when he landed on these shores so many years ago. I lived and thrived in the America he had hoped to find. I was living his dream, one that he had been unable to pass on to his son. It was a life that Angelo could never have allowed himself to see.

On many occasions, I would think back to that night in the upstairs room with Angelo. I'd been raised in a silent world and knew how important it was to keep such things hidden.

We all need to keep our secrets buried, especially from those we care for the most. To reveal them is neither an act of love nor one of trust. But rather, it is a crime that will wipe away all happiness and bring a chilling freeze to the warmest of hearts.

I would never allow that night to be known to anyone. It is a night that must never see light. A night that was meant to destroy a love and damage a woman. A night that was designed to bring me to my knees and point me toward the life of a criminal.

It was a night that will always be in my memory.

A night that would give birth to a thousand horrible dreams.

A night when I saw the true face of the gangster.

It was the face of evil.

21

Summer, 1996

I WALKED OVER to Mary, sitting by Angelo's shriveled feet, her head buried in her hands, her shoulders shaking with grief. I put my arm gently on her back and held it there as I stared at the man who had given me such joy and caused me such pain. "That's pretty much my story," I said to her, my voice grown hoarse, talking about that night for the first and only time in my life.

"I wish I had known," she said, her head still low, her hands rubbing against her cheeks. "I wish someone had told me. All these years! No one told me, Gabe! I swear to you, no one said a word."

I stared at her for several seconds and then placed a hand on one of her cheeks. "Who are you?" I asked her. "Who are you that anyone would need to tell you?"

"Sit down," she said. "Over there. In my chair. And after you hear what I have to say, what I came here to tell you, I want you to do one favor for me in return."

"What is it?" I asked.

"Try not to hate me," she said.

I stared back at Mary and didn't respond.

"As I told you when I first walked in here, I met Angelo on my father's boat in the summer of 1953," she said. "I wasn't naive about who he was. My father often did business with gangsters and made quite a bit of money doing so. I also didn't think I would ever see him again after that day and dismissed it as a brief flirtation. Then, a few months later, he was at my front door, asking me out to dinner. He didn't bother to call. He just showed up."

"He hated phones," I said, well aware of Angelo's habits and phobias. "In all the time I lived with him, I can't remember seeing him talk on one."

"At any rate, I accepted his invitation," Mary said. "I already had a mild crush on him from that day on the boat. It didn't take long for a mild crush to turn into a romantic affair."

"Was he married when you met him?" I asked, leaning back in the chair and stretching out my legs.

"We both were," Mary said. "Neither Angelo nor I are the types who go and seek out an affair. It's just something that happened between us. I was a lonely young housewife married to a much older man. And he was as sad and equally as lonely. We made a comfortable fit."

"How long did it last?" I asked, a slight tone of cynicism in my voice. "This great love affair?"

"It never ended," Mary said, ignoring the snide remark. "We would get together a few times a year, see each other whenever our other lives allowed. He was always a good friend to me."

I turned to glance at Angelo, his harsh breath coming out in even slower spurts. "Did he love you?" I asked.

"A married woman learns never to ask her married lover such a question," Mary said. "But he treated me as if he did and that mattered as much as saying it."

"What about your husband?" I asked. "Did he ever find out about you and Angelo?"

"He may have suspected," Mary said. "But he didn't know for sure until I told him about it."

"What made you tell him?"

"I got pregnant," Mary said. She took a deep breath and I could see the tremble in her hands. "And he needed to know the child I carried wasn't his."

"Did you have the baby?"

"This all happened a long time ago, Gabe." Mary stood and walked slowly around the bed, facing out the large window. "I was so young, and in those days, if it was known that I was having another man's baby, it would have caused quite a scandal. It needed to be kept quiet. Luckily, my husband was a caring and understanding man."

"You had an abortion?" I asked, losing the harshness, warming once again to her presence.

"No, I had the baby. I was sent away on a long vacation, had the baby and put him up for adoption. Then I came back home and resumed my life, never mentioning it to anyone. That's the way it stayed for the next ten years."

"Were you ever curious?" I asked. "About what happened to the kid?"

"Every single day," Mary said. "It gnawed at me until I could no longer tolerate it. That was when I went to see Angelo and asked for his help. I needed him to find our son."

"You popped this on him after not telling him for ten years?" I shook my head. "I can't imagine he took it all that well."

"He listened and said he would find the boy," Mary said. "And he would make sure that he would be raised the right way. But he insisted that the child never know who his real parents were. He felt we had stripped him of that on the day I gave him up."

"Why would you agree to something like that?" I asked. "Especially after so many years had passed?"

"At least I would know where my son was and who he was with," Mary said. "I didn't have the resources to find him on my own. Angelo was the only one I knew with the power to bring him back. And it was enough for me to know that my boy would be put in safe hands."

"That's a difficult find even for somebody with Angelo's clout."

"I didn't have anything other than the form I filled out when I signed him over to child welfare," Mary said, her voice breaking. "I gave that form to Angelo, kissed him on the cheek and walked out of the bar."

"And he found the boy."

"It took him awhile, but yes, he did." She was now standing directly between Angelo's bed and my chair, a hand on my shoulder. "He had been shuttled from one foster home to another and had spent the years in between in an upstate orphanage. Once he had tracked him, Angelo arranged for the boy to be placed with a family in his own neighborhood."

I stood and stared at Mary, grabbing her arms and gripping them tightly. "Don't stop," I said.

"After a few months, the young boy left his foster family behind and moved into Angelo's bar. And he raised him as if he were his own son. Because he was."

I was short of breath and felt lightheaded, the ground swirling beneath my feet. "How could he have not said anything? How could he keep quiet all these years? And how could you have allowed it to go on for so long and not told me?"

"He raised you as well as any father could have," Mary said. "And he loved you as much as he could love anyone. That was his way of telling you. As for me, I've made quite a few mistakes in my life. Not telling you I was your mother has been, by far, my biggest."

"What do you do now?" I asked. "Disappear again?"

"That's up to you," Mary said. "I've left a card with my address and phone number in his night table. It would be nice if we could get to know each other, even at this late date, but I'll understand if you choose not to contact me."

I nodded.

"There's one final thing you need to know," Mary said.

I did my best to smile, but it didn't come easy. "Please don't tell me I have a brother, too," I said.

Mary shook her head. "Angelo's money is going to be left to his children," she said. "To *all* of his children. But he's leaving you a little something extra. Something he thought you'd want. Something you loved as much as he did."

"What?" I asked.

"The bar you grew up in," Mary said. "It's been a home to your memories. And now it belongs to you."

I stared at her, too choked up to speak.

"I'm glad we finally got a chance to meet," she said. "You've done well with your life. No parents could be as proud of their child."

I walked out into the hall and let the door close gently behind me, allowing my mother a few silent moments with the man she still so very much loved.

EPILOGUE

Summer, 1996

When you really want love you
will find it waiting for you.
—Oscar Wilde, "De Profundis"

THE ROOM WAS dark, the only light the green glow from the machines that were helping to keep him alive. I stood above the bed and looked down at him. I reached out a hand and rested it on top of his. It felt empty of life, the veins pulsing slightly. I had turned my back on him for so many years, allowing his hatred for the choice I made to fuel my anger. Eventually, as he aged and neared his final moments, I came closer, not wanting him to die alone, still feeling a bond and a love that had been established over so many years.

I looked over at his night table, surprised to see rosary beads curled like a snake next to a pitcher of water. I picked up the beads and opened the table's small drawer. Next to a few hospital forms and a box of tissues was an old, tattered wallet. I picked it up and turned on the small overhead light. There was no money or credit cards or any form of identification inside. It was the perfect gangster wallet, no link or trace to any one person or any one place. I snapped open the small plastic photo folder. Inside were three pictures, each one of a woman. The first I knew to be Isabella. The second was of a younger Mary, wearing a black suit and white hat, smiling under the glare of a long-ago summer afternoon. I turned the flap to the final photo. It was a picture of my wife, Janet. As I stared down at it, looking at her sweet, beautiful face smiling back up at me, I remembered something Angelo had said during a dinner we had one week before he was hospitalized. "Every gangster makes a mistake that costs him more than he hoped to lose," he told me. "I made that mistake with you. I made it on that night in that room above the bar. What happened there should never have happened."

I closed the wallet and put it in its place. I turned back to Angelo and leaned across his body and kissed him on the forehead, my lips feeling the cold of his flesh. I held his hands and rested my head against his cheek, his warm breath brushing against my neck.

I had come to watch him die.

His name was Angelo Vestieri.

He was my father.

A gangster.

Read on for an excerpt from the next
thriller by Lorenzo Carcaterra,

STREET BOYS

LUNGOMARE. NAPLES, ITALY.
LATE NIGHT. SEPTEMBER 25, 1943.

TWO HUNDRED BOYS and girls were spread out around a large
fire, the flames licking the thick, crusty wood sending sparks
and smoke into the star-lit sky. Their clothes were dirty and
shredded at the sleeves and cuffs, shoes held together by
cardboard and string. All their memories had been scarred by
the frightful cries of war and the loss that always followed.
The youngest members of the group, between five and seven
years old, stood with their backs to the others, tossing small
pebbles into the oil-soaked Bay of Naples. The rest, their tired
faces filled with hunger and sadness, the glow from the fire illuminating their plight, huddled around Vincenzo and Franco.
They were children without a future, marked for an unknown
destiny.

Vincenzo stepped closer to the fire and glanced up at the
sky, enjoying the rare evening silence. He looked down and
smiled at two small boys, Giancarlo and Antonio, playing quietly by the edge of the pier, their small legs dangling several
feet above the water below. He glanced past them at a girl
slowly making her way toward him, squeezing past a cluster
of boys standing idle and silent. She was tall, about fifteen,
with rich brown hair rolled up and buried under a cap two
sizes too large. Her tan face was marred by streaks of soot
and dirt. She stepped between Vincenzo and the two boys, her
arms by her side, an angry look to her soft eyes.

"Where do we go from here?" she asked.

"The hills," Vincenzo said with a slight shrug. "It seems
the safest place. At least for now."

"And after that?" she asked in a voice younger than her years.

"What's your name?" Vincenzo asked, the flames from the fire warming his face.

"Angela," she said. "I lived in Forcella with my family. Now, I live there alone."

Forcella was the roughest neighborhood in Naples, a tight space of only a few blocks that historically had been the breeding ground for thieves and killers and the prime recruitment territory for the Camorra, the Neapolitan Mafia. "Forcella?" Vincenzo said to her. "Not even a Nazi would be brave enough to set foot on those streets."

"Especially after dark," Franco said, laughing.

"But they did," Angela said, lowering her eyes for a brief moment.

"What do you want me to do?" Vincenzo said. "Where do you think we should go? Look around you. This is all that's left of us."

"So we run," she said, words laced with sarcasm. "Like always."

Vincenzo stepped closer toward her, his face red from both the fire and his rising anger. "There is nothing else to do," he said. "You can help us with some of the little ones. A lot of them are too sick to walk."

Angela glared at Vincenzo for several moments, lowered her head and then turned back into the mouth of the crowd.

• • •

VINCENZO WALKED IN silence around the edges of the fire, the sounds of the crackling wood mixing with the murmurs of the gathered teens. They were all children forced to bear the burden of adults, surviving on the barest essentials, living like cornered animals in need of shelter and a home. They had been scattered throughout the city, gutter rats in soiled clothing, enduring the daily thrashings of a war started by strangers in uniforms who spoke of worlds to conquer.

They were born under the reign of Benito Mussolini and his fascist regime.

For close to two decades, the majority of Italians thrived under the rule of the Black Shirts. From 1922 until 1939, Italy underwent a rebirth of national pride and spirit, as old roads and structures were rebuilt, the train system modernized and the grip of organized crime loosened by the strict rules imposed by Il Duce's followers. While the United States suffered through the pangs of a Great Depression, Italy lived under the warmth of economic prosperity. Its fields were flush with crops and its factories filled to capacity with the products that brought the country head-first into the modern age. But those were the years before the alliance with Adolph Hitler and a World War that never seemed to end. Now, the fields were burnt and barren, the factories bombed and bare. Where there was once hope rested only hunger. Where visions of great victories filled all Italian hearts, there was now nothing more than the somber acceptance of a humiliating defeat. And the people of a country that was once told by a dictator that every one of their dreams would come true, found themselves once again thrust in the middle of a nightmare, a long line of innocent lives left tumbling in thier wake.

"Naples has always been ruled by outsiders," Vincenzo said, stopping alongside Franco and tossing two more planks of old wood onto the fire. "We've always been someone's prisoner. But in all that time, the people have never surrendered the streets without a fight. This war, against this enemy, would be the first time that has ever happened."

"Who are we to stop it?" Franco said, staring into his friend's eyes.

Vincenzo stood in front of the flames, his shirt and arms stained with sweat, light gray smoke filled his lungs. He then turned and walked away, disappearing into the darkness of the Naples night.